PORTUGUESE STUDIES

VOLUME 41 NUMBER 2
2025

MODERN HUMANITIES RESEARCH ASSOCIATION

PORTUGUESE STUDIES

A peer-reviewed biannual multi-disciplinary journal devoted to research on the cultures, literatures, history and societies of the Lusophone world

The **Modern Humanities Research Association** was founded in Cambridge in 1918 and has become an international organization with members in all parts of the world. It is a registered charity number 1064670, and a company limited by guarantee, registered in England number 3446016. Its main object is to encourage advanced study and research in modern and medieval European languages, literatures, and cultures by its publication of journals, book series, and its Style Guide. Further information about the activities of the Association and individual membership may be obtained from the Membership Secretary, email membership@mhra.org.uk, or from the website at: **www.mhra.org.uk**

ISSN 0267–5315 (print) ISSN 2222–4270 (online)
ISBN 978-1-83954-287-9

PORTUGUESE STUDIES VOL. 41 NO. 2
FORTIETH ANNIVERSARY SPECIAL ISSUE
CONTENTS

NOTES FOR CONTRIBUTORS

Articles to be considered for publication may be on any subject within the field but must not exceed 7,500 words, and should be submitted in a form ready for publication in English, sent as an email attachment to the Editorial Assistant at portuguese@mhra.org.uk.

Contributions whose standard of English is inadequate will be returned. Any quotations in Portuguese must be accompanied by an English translation. Submissions in Portuguese may be considered, but full peer review and publication will be conditional on provision of a satisfactory translation by or on behalf of the author.

Text and references should conform precisely to the conventions of the *MHRA Style Guide*, 3rd edn, 2013 (978-1-78188-009-8), £9.50, $19.00, €12.00, obtainable in print or online version from www.style.mhra.org.uk. All articles are subject to independent, anonymous peer review by experts in the field; authors receive written feedback on the editors' decision and guidance on any revisions required. *Portuguese Studies* regrets it must charge contributors for the cost of corrections in proof deemed excessive.

It is a condition of publication in this journal that authors of articles and reviews assign copyright, including electronic copyright, to the MHRA. Inter alia, this allows the General Editor to deal efficiently and consistently with requests from third parties for permission to reproduce material. The journal has been published simultaneously in printed and electronic form since January 2001. Permission, without fee, for authors to use their own material in other publications, after a reasonable period of time has elapsed, is not normally withheld. Authors may make closed-access deposit of accepted manuscripts in their academic institution's digital repository upon acceptance. Full open access to the accepted manuscript is permitted no sooner than 12 months following publication of the Contribution by the MHRA. Contributions may also be republished on authors' personal websites without seeking further permission from the Association, but no earlier than 12 months after publication by the MHRA.

Portuguese Studies aims to publish reviews of recent books within its field of interest in each issue. Publishers wishing to put forward a book for review should contact one or both of the Reviews Editors, Maria Tavares (m.tavares@qub.ac.uk) and Carlos Garrido (carlos.garridocastellano@ucc.ie).

Preface

Jane-Marie Collins

University of Nottingham

This commemorative issue of *Portuguese Studies* marks and celebrates forty years of publication. Fittingly, the issue pays due respect to its origins and founding editor by opening with a reflection piece from Professor Helder Macedo, complemented and supplemented by that of a second long-standing editor, Dr Juliet Perkins. In two more reflection pieces, Professors David Treece and David Brookshaw offer us their wider perspectives on the scholarship of Portuguese and Brazilian studies, especially in the UK. All four contributors have played a pivotal role in the growth, success, and status of the scholarship, as well as the journal, over its four decades of publication. On behalf of the current editorial board, I extend our collective gratitude for their generosity in agreeing to contribute to this anniversary issue. Gratitude is also extended to the now former president of ABIL, Dr Carmen Ramos Villar, and the co-directors of REBRAC, Dr Sara Brandellero, Professor Stephanie Dennison, and Dr Tori Holmes for their contributions. These two academic organizations have been the life blood of Portuguese and Brazilian cultural studies for scholars in the UK, Ireland and — as we saw in Birmingham this year (ABIL) and will see in London (REBRAC) next — from the Europe, the US and beyond. The respective conferences have provided vital spaces for academic engagement and *Portuguese Studies* has regularly featured individual articles and special issues from participants in both as well as from editorial board members. Despite some the challenges modern languages has had to and continues to face in the UK, ABIL, REBRAC and *Portuguese Studies* have managed to not just stand the test of time but thrive.

The seven articles featured in this commemorative issue speak to concerns and themes past and present, some of which are enduring and commented on in the reflection pieces. These articles were selected from a call for papers and represent the journal's breadth of interests and its global relevance. The majority are authors from the Portuguese-speaking world in diaspora, and either PhD, post-doctoral or early career scholars. The journal is proud to support their work in furthering their academic careers.

Finally, while this issue is a celebration of all things accomplished to date, it is with a tinge of sadness that the issue also marks the end of an almost two-decade tenure of our editorial assistant, Richard Correll, who is retiring from

Portuguese Studies vol. 41 no. 2 (2025), doi:10.1353/port.00034, 157–58

his extensive career in academic publishing life. I am one in the long line of lead editors to have had the good fortune of working with him and benefitting not just from his editorial expertise, experience and utter professionalism, but his extensive knowledge of all matters Portuguese — linguistic, historical, geographic, literary, culinary. You will be sorely missed, Richard, and it is fitting that the final words in this introduction are a tribute to you. On behalf of the editorial board, *os meus sinceros agradecimentos.*

Portuguese Studies

HELDER MACEDO

KCL/University of Oxford

In 1982, I was appointed Camoens Professor of Portuguese at King's College, London. At the time, the Department of Portuguese and Brazilian Studies that I would go on to lead was the only one in the United Kingdom exclusively devoted to the study and dissemination Portuguese-language cultures. It was a dubious privilege that came with great responsibilities I sought to fulfil.

The Camoens Chair was founded in 1919, in the aftermath of the First World War. It was created, in part, as amends for the plan to divide up the Portuguese colonies, hatched between Germany and the UK in the run-up to the war. The diplomatic efforts of the fledging Portuguese Republic, established in 1910, and represented in the UK by the remarkable writer and future president, Manuel Teixeira Gomes, gave rise to Portugal's entry into the war on the winning side. As a result, Portugal was able to keep its African territories. At the same time, the presence of Portugal's last king, D. Manuel II, exiled in England, could also have contributed to Britain's guilty good will towards Portugal.

The first occupant of the Camoens Chair (1919–23) was a diplomat who served in the British mission in Lisbon, Sir George Young. He had written an interesting all-encompassing work, titled *Portugal Old and Young: An Historical Study*. His successor, Edgar Prestage (1923–36), a friend of D. Manuel II and a keen supporter of the restoration of the Portuguese monarchy, contributed greatly to the academic spread of Portuguese culture in the UK, through studies and literary translations, as well as multiple entries in the Encyclopedia Britannica. After a considerable hiatus, his successor took up the post in 1947. With an unusual curriculum that was more military than academic, Major C. R. Boxer came to Portuguese Studies via the Orient. He turned out to be one of the greatest historians of the Portuguese Empire in any language. Although he kept the Camoens Chair as primarily research-focused (through publications, conferences and the odd doctoral supervision), it was on his watch that the Chair began to oversee some undergraduate teaching in literature, done by *leitores* subsidized by the Portuguese State. These included the charismatic writer Ruben A (Ruben Andresen Leitão) and particularly Luís de Sousa Rebelo, a scholar of extraordinary erudition, who would eventually become a permanent faculty member at King's College, ending his long career with a personal chair.

Portuguese Studies vol. 41 no. 2 (2025), doi:10.1353/port.00035, 159–61

In 1967, Charles Boxer decided to retire, but not before he had contributed decisively to the expansion of what was by then known as the Department of Portuguese, which now encompassed literary studies. Boxer threw his weight behind the appointment of Stephen Reckert as his successor to the Camoens Chair. An unparalleled practitioner of 'close reading' of poetry in several languages and from different eras, Reckert's studies on the Medieval Galego-Portuguese lyric revolutionized our understanding of these small masterpieces, opening up seminal comparisons with symbolism, and Brazilian and Portuguese poetic modernity. Reckert refashioned the department to include Brazilian Studies, changing its name to the Department of Portuguese and Brazilian Studies. Along with Luís de Sousa Rebelo, he helped to consolidate the autonomous status of Lusophone Studies in the UK. In the department, for example, T. F. Earle, the future King John II Professor of Portuguese at the University of Oxford, would do his doctorate under the supervision of Luís de Sousa Rebelo. I was also a student at King's, with the privilege of having had as my professors both Stephen Reckert and Luís de Sousa Rebelo, as well as J. H. Elliott from the Department of History.

I earned my doctorate from King's and witnessed the establishment of democracy in Portugal in 1974, before serving a brief stint in the Portuguese government as Minister for Culture. I was considering taking up a Chair in Portuguese offered to me at Harvard University when Stephen Reckert decided to retire. I was invited to apply to be his successor and took up the position of Camoens Chair in 1982. In my early years in post, I had the crucial support of colleagues in the Department of Spanish at King's — particularly the Cervantes Professors Patrick Harvey and then Barry Ife — as well as those who at other institutions included in their scholarship on Hispanism a Portuguese component. Examples that come to mind include Frank Pierce at Sheffield (editor of one of the best editions of the Lusiads), Alan Deyermond at Westfield College in London (whose seminal medieval studies included work on Galego-Portuguese lyricism) and Alan Freeland in Southampton (a perceptive analyst of Eça de Queirós's nineteenth-century fiction). We all agreed that a strengthening of the study of Portuguese-language cultures in what was then the only department exclusively dedicated to the task was in the interests of everyone in Hispanic Studies in the UK. It would ideally lead to the creation of new departments of Portuguese at other universities, as came to pass in Oxford.

My initial aims as Camoens Professor were twofold. First, I wanted to consolidate and expand internally the legacy bequeathed by my predecessors. Second, I wanted to create a common academic platform for the study of Portuguese and Portuguese-language cultures in the UK, through the journal *Portuguese Studies*. When I retired in 2004, the department included Lusophone African Studies and a Chair in History, as well as the previously established Portuguese and Brazilian Studies. I had the privilege of proposing that the History Chair be named in honour of Charles Boxer; the chair survives to this day. Likewise, the journal *Portuguese Studies* still thrives, no longer as an annual publication but coming out twice a year, and no longer exclusively attached to King's: it now has diverse editors from several universities across the UK, which is doubtless a welcome symptom of the field's increased academic relevance. When its first issue was published in 1985, Frank Pierce wrote a review that declared that Portuguese Studies in the UK 'had come of age'. In 1987, it was awarded the 'Best New Journal Award' at the *Conference of Editors of Learned Journals* in the USA, where it was described as 'a model scholarly journal'. In fact, the journal counted among its contributors some of the most established names in Portuguese-language cultures, alongside early career researchers who had their first publication in it.

As we celebrate its forty years, we should thank the individuals and institutions that made the journal possible. The project was immediately welcomed by the Modern Humanities Research Association and received invaluable initial financial support from the Fundação Calouste Gulbenkian and the then Instituto de Cultura e Língua Portuguesa (later known as the Instituto Camões). There are also key names associated with those institutions we should remember: Prof. Roy Wisbey at the MHRA; Dr José Blanco at the Fundação Calouste Gulbenkian; and Prof. Fernando Cristóvão and Dr Fernando de Mello Moser at the ICALP.

A final word of praise and gratitude is due to Suzanne Jones, as the Production Editor of the journal in its crucial early years. Without her, *Portuguese Studies* would never have existed.

Portuguese Studies: Some Recollections

JULIET PERKINS

King's College London

Portuguese Studies was a fundamental stage in the development and recognition of Lusophone Studies in the United Kingdom. It was the brainchild of Helder Macedo, who was appointed to the Camoens Chair of Portuguese in 1982 and is so bound up with the Department of Portuguese and Brazilian Studies at King's College London that this memoir will be as much about the academic milieu as about the journal itself. After my retirement in 2011, I remained as an editor for several more years, though admittedly rather a passive one. There are many whose experience of the new series (starting in 2005) is fresher and more current, so I shall hark back mostly to the first series (vols 1–20) and particularly to its early years, which provided a crash course in the editing process for my colleagues and me.

How was it that such a small department (especially when compared to its Spanish counterparts) was able to take on the editing of a pioneering journal? And how was an enterprise like this to be funded?

The answer to the first question lies in the composition of the Department in 1984. It is worth recalling that under the direction of Stephen Reckert (Camoens Professor from 1967 to 1982), the hitherto dominant focus on History in the Department of Portuguese had been modified by the introduction of many more literature courses, and of Brazilian history and literature, which led to the renaming of the Department. He also introduced a final-year Portuguese-African option.[1] His successor, Helder Macedo, immediately set about increasing the academic staff. My appointment was quickly followed by that of Patrick Chabal in Lusophone African history and literature. Then David Treece joined the Department as a Brazilian specialist and went on to the Editorial Committee in 1988, for vol. 4. This meant that from the beginning, the teaching and research of the Department were reflected in the wide range of articles submitted to the journal. The intellectual pillar provided by the Advisory Panel bore witness to the enthusiasm for the project, and its distinguished members ensured the supply of good quality articles right from

---

[1] I believe that I was the first to take this option, in 1975–76. My own teaching responsibilities when I was appointed in January 1983 included Brazilian literature and drama in the nineteenth and twentieth centuries as well as Portuguese drama and contemporary literature.

Portuguese Studies vol. 41 no. 2 (2025), doi:10.1353/port.00036, 162–65

the start. It was, of course, a different academic world in 1985, and a different publishing environment. Long before the days of peer review, the editor and editorial committee had a less circumscribed role; on the other hand, there was no hiding behind anonymity when assessing articles submitted for publication.

Later appointments of the historians AbdoolKarim Vakil, Malyn Newitt and Francisco Bethencourt added greatly to the expertise of the editorial team. However, of the academic staff involved in the first ten years of the journal, only four of us are still living, as happily are the editorial assistants of the first series. Therefore, this memoir, besides being of a personal nature and principally focused on my colleagues, also aims to remind us of the great scholars, Hispanists as well as Lusitanists, Portuguese and Brazilian as well as British, who contributed so much and so readily to the journal.

The answer to the second question lies with Helder Macedo, who secured generous financial support from two leading Portuguese institutions, the Calouste Gulbenkian Foundation and the Instituto de Cultura e Língua Portuguesa. Knowing the value of friendship and contacts, he nurtured them all through his editorship.

Of our colleagues at King's in other departments, they are to be thanked for their support of the venture. In particular, David Hook of the Spanish Department contributed frequently to the journal, in addition to being always available for advice on medieval matters, manuscripts, and palaeography. I remember with fondness Professor Roy Wisbey of the German Department, whose wisdom in matters financial, administrative and academic, was frequently drawn upon. Equal enthusiasm and support were given from the outset by Tom Earle of the University of Oxford. David Brookshaw (University of Bristol), John Gledson (University of Liverpool), and Alan Freeland (University of Southampton) also have their places among our early supporters.

At the beginning then, the Department consisted of four full-time academics and a full-time secretary. Here, I point to the significant part played by two of the latter, who doubled up as Production Editors: Suzanne Jones (1985–92) and Toni Huberman (1993–2004); I shall return to their contribution shortly. To all of us fell the responsibility of editing and preparing copy for publication. The small size of the Department enabled informal and frequent collaboration about the contributions that were submitted. Being an annual volume, it was for several years a blessing in terms of our main academic workload. It also allowed time for reviews to be commissioned and written.[2]

Suzanne Jones was appointed by Helder in 1982. She began as departmental secretary and then divided her time between that role and that of Production Editor. As many of the articles in the early years of the journal were submitted by Portuguese scholars in Portuguese, Suzanne Jones often translated them. A

[2] The decision to expand to two numbers a year in 2006 was a response to new disciplines within Lusophone Studies, and was intended to provide a more frequent outlet for the increasing number of academics working in the field.

Spanish graduate, she could spot when something 'looked odd' and had eyes like a lynx for typos, lapses in grammar and inconsistencies of all kinds. Her meticulous copy editing was undoubtedly a vital factor in the journal's quality of presentation — and to the early award of a prize for best new academic journal.

From vol. 6, the new departmental secretary, Annie Hemingway, became a key part of the team while Suzanne Jones continued as Production Editor for a further year, until her retirement from the Department. Annie held the administrative reins of the Department firmly in her hands while carrying out her editorial role for vol. 7 (1991). When she left the Department during her pregnancy, Suzanne Jones came to the rescue and was joined by Susan Harvey as Production Editor for vol. 8 (1992).

The next year, the Department gained a new Secretary in the person of Toni Huberman, who also took on the role of Production Editor. Toni remained in these two roles till vol. 20 (2004), the last one under the aegis of Helder Macedo. Without Suzanne's Romance languages background, Toni nonetheless was her equal as a stickler for accurate grammar and spelling. Forthright and humorous in the face of the often obscure topics that she prepared for press, in her hands the journal kept up its presentation standards.

Apart from the articles, the journal contained from the outset two very important items: a review section of books published in English; and Bibliographical and Research Information of books and theses in English. That first year, the bibliography was compiled by Pat Odber (University of Birmingham) and subsequently by John Laidlar (John Rylands University Library of Manchester) from vol. 3 to vol. 20. The value of this section in a pre-digital age cannot be emphasised too strongly.[3] Reviews appeared in every volume of the first series. AbdoolKarim Vakil, who joined the Department in 1993, compiled the review section from that year till vol. 20.[4]

With the change, in 2005, to the new series, the role of Production Editor passed to Graham Nelson. For the transitional volume 21, the editorship was shared between David Treece, AbdoolKarim Vakil, and me.[5] Patrick Chabal, Luís de Sousa Rebelo, and Malyn Newitt became members of the Advisory Panel. We editors were joined for 22.1 (2006) by Francisco Bethencourt. The same year saw Rip Cohen join the Department and the editorial team. Issue 22.2 was notable since it marked the recruitment of Richard Correll as Editorial Assistant. A graduate of the BA Hons in Portuguese and Brazilian Studies, Richard was an outstanding student and had displayed great talent as a translator. He became, in effect, the journal's go-to translator, whether editing partially or, increasingly, translating entire articles submitted in Portuguese.

---

[3] These two sections are not included in the 'Index to *Portuguese Studies*, Vols 1–20', published in *Portuguese Studies*, 20 (2004), pp. 229–49, which is why I highlight them here.
[4] There was a hiatus during the first years of bi-annual publication but thankfully reviews reappeared in 33.1 and have occupied an important place ever since.
[5] Those of an ironical bent might have smiled at the new blue-and-white cover, reminiscent of the Portuguese monarchy flag during the years 1830–1910.

An excellent linguist and meticulous proof-reader, he was also copy-editor for Legenda.

For the new series, Emilce Rees took on the task of filling John Laidlar's very big shoes to compile 'Lusophone Studies: A Cumulative Area Bibliography'. This first appeared in 22.2, covering the years 2003–06 and, like its predecessor, has proved a vital research tool ever since. Compiling this section was a truly demanding task and the Editors have reason to be ever grateful to Emilce for her patient and intelligent detective work in tracking down the books and doctoral theses in English.

It was during 2007–08 that the journal moved increasingly towards translating quotations in Portuguese into English. It was also from that time that the first guest-edited volume appeared: 'Pessoa: The Future of the Arcas'. As befitted the sheer size of Fernando Pessoa's output, 24.2 (2008) was a full-length volume.

It is time to look backwards once more, to those contributors who put the journal so firmly on the map. A glance at the early volumes will reveal a 'Who's Who' of distinguished Lusitanists, Portuguese and English, as well as equally distinguished Hispanists. If I mention the following, this is not to create a ranking but to recall scholars of the past: Cleonice Berardinelli, C. R. Boxer, Ronald Cueto, Alan Deyermond, Manuel Ferreira, José-Augusto França, Thomas Hart, L. Patrick Harvey, Eugénio Lisboa, Harold Livermore, Óscar Lopes, Eduardo Lourenço, José V. de Pina Martins, José Guilherme Merquior, Luciana Stegagno Picchio, Giovanni Pontiero, Stephen Reckert, José Augusto Seabra, Roger M. Walker and Clive Willis. From the outset, the journal published original translations, so we should recall Keith Bosley, Alan Freeland, Michael Lowery, Suzette Macedo, John Parker and Michael Wolfers.

This memoir gives me a very good excuse to remember the late Luís de Sousa Rebelo. It was a privilege to have been his student and it was a joy to have him as a colleague. There was no one to match him in erudition. It didn't matter whether it was the Ancient World, the literature and philosophy of Europe through the centuries, the cultural history of Portugal and Brazil, or contemporary literature and drama — nothing could stump him. One's merest request or enquiry about a writer or topic would result the next day in a mine of relevant information, handwritten on filing cards, giving references and quotations. As an editor, he was irreplaceable. Not for the first time, I acknowledge my abiding debt to his scholarship.

As for the moving force behind *Portuguese Studies*, I have on more than one occasion expressed my admiration and gratitude to Helder Macedo who has been, in turn, my tutor, supervisor, and colleague. As an editor, he took the same approach as he did while leading the Department of Portuguese and Brazilian Studies: he appointed those he judged suitable and competent and then left them to get on with their tasks. Thank goodness that micro-management did not feature in his *modus operandi*, for it enabled one to develop and, in this particular case, to take responsibility for one's editorial judgement.

Portuguese as a University Subject over the Course of a Career: A Memoir

DAVID BROOKSHAW

University of Bristol

It is impossible to write about the evolution of Portuguese in UK universities over a period of nearly forty eventful years without delving into personal memory as well as certain landmarks in the academic history of the subject. This essay will therefore extend a little further back from when I was an undergraduate and postgraduate student at one institution between 1968 and 1974, prior to embarking on a career in teaching and research at two UK universities between 1974 and 2011.

In the 1950s, Portuguese was taught at a limited number of British universities, mainly within departments of Spanish. The only exception was at King's College London, where the Camões Chair of Portuguese in the one independent department devoted to the subject had been established in 1919. At this stage, some of the most notable subject leaders in the broad discipline covering the history, literatures and languages of the Iberian Peninsula were of a generation who had served during the Second World War, often in military intelligence, an experience which had brought them into greater contact with the languages they knew. In Portuguese, this period in the growth of the subject will forever be associated with Professor Sir Charles Boxer, who was already an authority on Portuguese colonial history in the Far East when he was interned as a prisoner of war in Japan, following the Japanese occupation of Hong Kong in 1941. It was therefore fitting that Boxer should later be invited to occupy the Camões Chair at King's in 1947, where he remained until his retirement in 1967. At Oxford, Professor Sir Peter Russell had been active in the Spanish Civil War, and in the Caribbean, West Africa and the Far East during the Second World War, before returning to Oxford where he took up the King Alfonso XIII Chair of Spanish in 1953, and also became Director of Portuguese Studies. Even at the University of Bristol, the first Professor of Spanish, Jack Metford, had spent the war years in Brazil, where he had developed an interest in Portuguese; his subsequent commitment to it was confirmed in his appointment in 1963 of its first lecturer in Portuguese, Denis Brass, who had also worked for the British Council in Portugal during the war years.

Early pioneers of Portuguese in British universities preceding my generation included Clive Willis, who was appointed at the University of Manchester in

Portuguese Studies vol. 41 no. 2 (2025), doi:10.1353/port.00037, 166–73
© Modern Humanities Research Association 2025

1956, and Laurence Keates, who developed the subject at the University of Leeds from 1961, both in departments that consistently maintained 'Portuguese' in their titles. In addition, during the 1950s and 60s, Portuguese was offered as a subject in most universities throughout England where Spanish was taught, and delivered by scholars who either had a specialist interest in Portuguese, or had received some exposure to the subject as undergraduates, but were mainly specialists in areas of Spanish literature. The situation in Scotland was similar, Portuguese being offered at both Edinburgh and Glasgow Universities. In Wales, Portuguese flourished at Cardiff University under the stewardship of Alexandre Pinheiro Torres, who took up a post there in the 1960s, after being persecuted by the political police in Portugal for having served on the committee that had awarded the annual literary prize of the Portuguese Society of Writers to the imprisoned Angolan writer and nationalist Luandino Vieira, in 1965.

Many of those who emerged into teaching Iberian languages and cultures in the 1950s were historians, medievalists, or linguisticians, for whom the countries where Spanish and Portuguese were spoken, not to mention regional languages such as Catalan and Galician, formed part of a closely inter-related cultural world. This was why the first professional association for the subject, the Association of Hispanists of Great Britain and Ireland, founded in 1955 by a group of Hispanists whose interests were anchored in medieval and Golden Age Spanish literature, claimed to represent all the languages of the Iberian Peninsula.

The blanket term Hispanism meant Spanish to most members of the educated public rather than a term deriving from the geographical area by which the Iberian Peninsula had been known in the days of the Roman Empire, and in spite of the good intentions of an early generation of 'Hispanists', the term tended to consign Portuguese as a language to invisibility. This was especially so when most departments teaching two or more of the languages of the Iberian Peninsula re-branded themselves departments of Hispanic Studies.

From the 1960s, departments of Spanish or their variants (Hispanic Studies, Spanish and Portuguese) witnessed a growing interest in Latin American Studies. The Cuban Revolution of 1959, and the sudden realization of the economic and political importance of Latin America within Cold War politics, all fed into the government-sponsored Parry Report (1965), which recommended the expansion of Spanish and Portuguese in British universities. In literature, the boom in the Spanish American novel produced a new generation of scholars in Spanish. This dynamic, however, further ensured the invisibility of Portuguese as a language and subject in its own right. The Society for Latin American Studies, founded in 1964, reflected this growing interest among a generation of historians and anthropologists, for whom the details of linguistic differences between Spanish and Portuguese America were a minor irritant of lesser importance. At the same time, the difference between Portugal within

Peninsular Studies and Brazil within Latin America was one of geographic and demographic extension. It was relatively easy to treat the language and literature of a country on the western periphery of Spain with benign absent-mindedness; however, it was far more difficult to forget about a major economy that accounted for more than half of the landmass and human population of South America, and whose coastline dominated the South Atlantic. *The Modern Culture of Latin America* (1967), a pioneering work of its kind by Jean Franco, the foremost Spanish Americanist of her generation in the field of literature and culture, skilfully wove references to some of the most seminal periods of Brazilian literary and cultural history into a more general analysis of the evolution of Latin American literature.

The idea of a Lusophone world with its own set of cultural references circulating internally, even if these reflected responses to and interpretations of pan-European influences emanating from Northern Europe, became lost, except perhaps among early researchers whose interests and teaching commitments spanned both Portugal and Brazil. But within the broader field of Hispanic and Latin American Studies, it was assumed that Portuguese or Luso-Brazilian Studies were destined to march in lockstep with Spanish, or Hispanic Studies. This did not mean that university departments ignored Portugal and Brazil. The first Brazilianists were appointed between 1962, when Giovanni Pontiero took up a lectureship in Latin American Studies at Manchester (even though he is remembered now as a pioneer in literary translation from Portuguese), and 1974, when John Gledson, renowned for his studies on Carlos Drummond de Andrade and Machado de Assis, took up his post at Liverpool. In between, the foremost Brazilian historian of his generation, Leslie Bethell, was appointed by the History Department at University College London in 1966. The first titular lectureship in Portuguese on the island of Ireland was created in 1974, when I took up my first appointment at Queen's University Belfast.

The expansion of Portuguese gathered pace from the mid-1970s onwards, both as an organic development of the subject within departments of Hispanic Studies, and in response to wider social and political changes within the Lusophone world. Firstly, the 25 April Revolution in Portugal in 1974 brought down the forty-eight-year-old dictatorship, and ushered in the independence of the country's colonial possessions in Africa. The anti-colonial struggle in Portugal's African territories had, of course, begun to interest historians in Britain and the United States in the 1960s, but the literatures of the five emerging countries remained relatively unknown and unstudied except for some early pioneers such as Clive Willis at Manchester, and Gerald Moser in Pennsylvania. The emergence of a kind of Afro-Marxist utopianism in these newly independent states in the second half of the 1970s began to interest academics in Portuguese for reasons that were similar to that shown in Cuba among Latin Americanists during the previous decade.

Secondly, the slow demise of the Brazilian military dictatorship between 1974 and 1985 allowed for the re-emergence of cultural expressions which had been stifled for ten years, and certainly during the most repressive years, between 1968 and 1973. These included Afro-Brazilian Studies, along with renewed interest in, for example, the history of slave resistance, black literature, and African and Amerindian cultures. This in turn encouraged a reassessment of the narrative of Brazilian national identity based on the writings of Gilberto Freyre and his theory of Lusotropicalism, which had been co-opted by both the Portuguese and Brazilian dictatorships in the 1960s because of its suggestion of an ability on the part of the Portuguese and their descendants in Brazil and elsewhere to assimilate other ethnicities by means of cultural (and, by extension, physical) *branqueamento*. In Portugal, it justified the country's continuing role in Africa, while in Brazil, it upheld a social order in which race and social class were intertwined. In Brazil, the work of sociologists such as Florestan Fernandes, Otávio Ianni, and Fernando Henrique Cardoso, who had begun to reinterpret the foundations of Brazil's racial democracy myth from a Marxist perspective during the 1960s, and had been persecuted by the military regime, were now discussed much more openly.

This was reflected in British academia from the 1980s through to the early 2000s, with the appointment of new staff in these areas, and a general expansion in Portuguese-related personnel in both teaching and research. At King's College London, the first Lusophone African specialist, Patrick Chabal, was appointed in 1983 to the Department of Portuguese and Brazilian Studies, then under the leadership of Helder Macedo. A few years later, in 1987, King's also appointed its first Brazilianist, David Treece, who apart from expanding the teaching of Brazilian literature, introduced cultural studies in the form of Brazilian popular music. New appointments were made at other UK universities, reflecting interest in long-ignored areas of research: Hilary Owen's appointment at Queen's University Belfast and then at Manchester brought into focus the work of women writers in Portugal and in Lusophone Africa, as did subsequent appointments at Cambridge (Maria Manuel Lisboa) and Oxford (Claudia Pazos Alonso), while the University of Leeds became a focal point for Brazilian film studies thanks first to the research of Lisa Shaw (who later introduced the subject at Liverpool), and then Stephanie Dennison, while protecting Keates's legacy with the appointment of David Frier in Portuguese literary studies. By the early 2000s, this generation of scholars in new disciplinary areas had spawned the next generation to take their spheres of interests forward, with appointments at Nottingham, Bristol, Queen's Belfast, Exeter, and Sheffield. Furthermore, while the subject expanded at King's College London with the creation of a second chair in Portuguese History in 1998, aptly named the Charles Boxer Chair, it lost its monopoly within the loosening federation of the University of London, with Portuguese or Brazilian appointments being made at UCL, Queen Mary, and Birkbeck College.

By this time too, increasing numbers of students entered courses with prior knowledge of Portuguese thanks to gap-year experiences in Brazil, and, in due course, offspring of Portuguese who had migrated to the UK in the 1970s and 80s were sometimes joined by Erasmus students from Portugal, who later returned to do doctoral studies in the UK, and embarked on careers in British academia. All this meant that there was far greater visibility of Portuguese within departments of Hispanic Studies or the now emerging schools of Modern Languages.

The turn of the new century witnessed Portuguese and Brazilian Studies as a brand being increasingly incorporated into the nomenclature of many departments where it had been consigned to invisibility, in many cases since the late 1960s, under the general rubric of Hispanic Studies. The subject is buttressed, as it has been for many years, by support from Portuguese state institutions, nowadays the Instituto Camões, which has teaching agreements with many departments, as well as supporting Portuguese Language Centres at the Universities of Edinburgh, Newcastle, Leeds, London and Oxford, and visiting *cátedras* at the Universities of Birmingham, Manchester and Lancaster. In 2002, the third named chair in the UK, the King John II professorship of Portuguese, was created at Oxford — like the first two, with partial support from the Portuguese State — its first holder being Professor Tom Earle, who had developed Portuguese over many years at that institution. In 2006, the first professional association devoted solely to the histories and cultures of the Portuguese-speaking countries, the Association of British and Irish Lusitanists, held its first biennial conference at the University of Nottingham.

It is probably true to say that most British specialists in Portuguese, whatever their particular zone(s) of interest, are proud of their subject and its linguistic identity within its own rich diversity, but they are also pragmatists, collaborating with their Hispanic colleagues in both teaching and research, given that many of them have also studied Spanish. Moreover, in increasingly challenging times for modern languages as a whole, the blanket title of Iberian and Latin American Studies, while not perfect, offers a sense of common purpose and mutual protection for their subjects.

Most research from the 1960s through to the 1980s was either literary or historical. Literary researchers tended to focus on what were perceived as the canonical writers and texts of their age, and history tended towards traditional historical narratives of nation states as developed by their political elites. During the 1960s, some universities with departments of Spanish/ Hispanic Studies, such as University College London, had introduced a more inter-disciplinary approach to area studies, by including units in its flagship undergraduate course in Modern Iberian and Latin American Regional Studies (MILARS) that were both literature and history based, allowing literary texts to be seen through the prism of history, and history to be seen through that of culture. This was also the case in the postgraduate research centres and institutes for Latin American Studies set up in the wake of Parry at London, Oxford, Cambridge, Liverpool, Glasgow and Essex, which brought together researchers in various disciplines, ranging from literature through to history, sociology and anthropology. Nowadays, of course, these individual scholars would be channelled into wider thematic research clusters.

During the 1980s and 90s, new approaches reflecting emerging theories concerning postcolonial studies (Said, Bhabha, Spivak), and even more crucially gender studies, led to a reappraisal of canonical literary texts, with a greater emphasis on sometimes forgotten women authors, as more women took up academic posts, as well as broadening notions of culture to embrace music, film and the mass media.

For much of the last half century, the research emphasis was in area studies, in which scholars generally learned to consider themselves as either Hispanists (with a special interest in the history and culture of Portugal — in which case they might prefer to call themselves Lusitanists), or as Latin Americanists, with a similar subdivision for those who specialized in the history and culture of Brazil, in which case they referred to themselves as Brazilianists.

In more recent years, the essentially land-based, geographically restricted emphasis on area studies has seen a switch to an emerging interest in the cultural flows that accompanied commerce across oceans, and an appreciation of the importance of the links between what had hitherto been viewed as discrete regions. Regional or area studies have given way to oceanic studies, and an interest in diasporas and the dynamics of the interactions of diasporic communities with their locations of arrival and origin. Clearly, Paul Gilroy's *The Black Atlantic* (1995), which studies the inter-cultural identities of populations of African origin in the Americas, provided a template for re-interpretations of similar links within the Lusophone imperial and postcolonial spaces. Luiz Felipe de Alencastro's *O Trato dos Viventes* (2000) re-evaluates the cultural consequences of the relationship between Brazil and Southern Africa resulting from the Slave Trade, while Miguel Vale de Almeida's *An Earth-Colored Sea* (2004) contributed to the postcolonial debate about race, ethnicity and identity in the Portuguese-speaking world. In this country, Francisco Bethencourt and Adrian Pearce's edited collection of essays, *Racism and Ethnic Relations in the Portuguese-speaking World* (2012), proved a timely reassessment of a subject that had commanded the attention of scholars over the decades, from Freyre through to Boxer.

In part, these and subsequent studies are a rebuttal of a Eurocentric view of the world that had dominated Iberian Studies, and the study of other Western European countries that had once ruled transoceanic empires. Hitherto, the history of empire had tended to be seen from the perspective of the metropolitan centre. Alencastro's analysis of the ebbs and flows of cultural contact emphasized the importance of direct links across the South Atlantic between Brazil and Africa in this process. This reappraisal of the African Atlantic opened out a space for those traditionally viewed as passive participants in the Eurocentric perception of history and culture to gain agency: the study of empire then began to offer an alternative vision in the form of the history and culture of resistance to imperial institutions. In British academia, this was reflected in women's studies in projects such as 'Women of the Brown Atlantic' (based at the University of Exeter), and, in due course, a re-evaluation of the role of Black Africans in resisting the enslavement of Africans in Brazil, in highly original studies such as José Lingna Nafafé's *Lourenço da Silva Mendonça and the Black Atlantic Abolitionist Movement in the Seventeenth Century* (2022).

This new emphasis on transoceanic studies, migration, diasporas, and their literary and cultural representations has also enabled Lusitanists to focus on the contiguities of language within the postcolonial world and contemporary globalization, by studying, among other things, the cultural interactions of Portuguese migrant communities in North America, as well as the Lusophone cultural residues in the literatures and cultures of Asia (Goa, Sri Lanka, Malaysia and Macau). It is as if the centripetal dynamic of area studies were having its borders blurred by the centrifugal counterweight of migratory and diasporic cultural adaptation, emphasizing the notion of cultural identity as being fluid and subject to flux.

Another field which has enabled Portuguese to develop as a subject is that of translation studies. Earlier in this essay, mention was made of one of the pioneers of literary translation in this country, Giovanni Pontiero, whose rendering into English of authors such as Clarice Lispector and José Saramago contributed so much to growing interest in their work in the English-speaking world, as well as heightening the profile of Portuguese as a subject. In those days, although translation was an integral part of teaching modern languages, a practice inherited from the way Latin was taught in schools, it was not considered an area for research outside an exclusively theoretical context. It is probably true to say that the theoretical aspects of translation began to be cultivated in academia in tandem with an emerging interest in comparative literary studies, possibly inspired from the 1970s by George Steiner's *Beyond Babel*, and then Laurence Venuti's *The Translator's Invisibility: A History of Translation* in the 1990s. The last twenty years have witnessed the proliferation of postgraduate degrees in translation, usually involving a study of translation theory along with a practical application of such theory. Portuguese has benefited from this development both within and beyond academia. Forty years ago, it would have been inconceivable for a university press in the UK to sponsor an anthology of short fiction by Afro-Brazilian writers in translation (*Contemporary Afro-Brazilian Short Fiction*, UCL Press, 2024), any more than it would have been possible to assemble enough translators for Portuguese into a professional association (PELTA), and although most of its members are not embedded within universities, many of its younger cohort have attended postgraduate degrees in translation.

It would be inappropriate to reach a firm conclusion about the ongoing development of a subject, but at this point in time it is true that, in the first quarter of the twenty-first century, there are more representatives of Portuguese as a discipline in the general field of modern languages than there were fifty or sixty years ago, and that the subject has broadened considerably, both geographically and culturally. Furthermore, in an environment that has proved particularly challenging for the teaching of modern languages in education over the last decade, Portuguese has continued to attract dedicated cohorts of students, while pushing the boundaries of innovative research in academia and cultural engagement within the wider community.

A Special Case?
Exceptionalism and Interdisciplinarity in Brazilian Cultural Studies

DAVID TREECE

King's College London

The following brief reflections on Brazilian cultural studies in the United Kingdom were originally drafted as a keynote lecture for the occasion of the inaugural conference of the European Network of Brazilianists Working in Cultural Analysis (REBRAC) in 2015.[1] In presenting them here essentially unaltered, I hope they may serve as a modest commentary on the significance of that moment for the history of our discipline, marked as it was by the creation of such an important new scholarly organization. The essay raises more questions than it answers, but if they do resonate with today's reader, then this surely reflects the degree to which the shifts and challenges that faced Brazilianists in 2015 remain just as immediate and urgent a decade on.

Brazilian Cultural Studies and the Changing Higher Education Landscape

Let me begin by remarking on the breadth and scope of the REBRAC conference programme — it includes papers on the culture industries, racism, Indigenous and Afro-Brazilian cultures, digital media, cinema, popular culture and literary figures such as Lima Barreto and João do Rio. This is a dramatic indication of the changes that our field had already undergone since I embarked on my own academic career in the early 1980s. That is, literary studies has by no means been abandoned, but its once nearly exclusive dominance of the field has been relativized by, on the one hand, a radical expansion in the range of media studied and, on the other, a marked shift toward a more contemporary focus and a growing engagement with other disciplinary and geographical areas beyond that of 'Portuguese Studies'.

Is this what is primarily at stake, then, when we consider the cultural 'turn' in Brazilian studies: no more than an extension or diversification of the disciplinary range, and a realignment of the field away from the literary to other media? After all, these are familiar changes to anyone working in what

---

[1] 'Remapping Brazilian Cultural Studies/Remapeando os Estudos Culturais Brasileiros', University of London, 25 September 2015.

Portuguese Studies vol. 41 no. 2 (2025), doi:10.1353/port.00038, 174–79
© Modern Humanities Research Association 2025

has until now been known as 'Modern Languages', or in the Humanities more generally. Perhaps we need to give greater definition to what distinguishes our academic and institutional location as Brazilianists within the higher education landscape, and to what pressures and demands this places on our work.

This paper is self-evidently concerned with the community of academics who are active *outside* of Brazil, more particularly in Europe and the UK. In fact, however, our position as 'outsiders/insiders' is crucial: while living and working 'here', we carry on our teaching, researching and writing about Brazilian topics and, whether in our fieldwork, in conferences and other interventions, we also engage with the Brazilian academic and social worlds and are often involved in them more directly. So how does or should that dual locatedness affect what we do, and how should we act in the light of it? Does it imply an obligation of advocacy or does it require instead (and make uniquely possible) a certain kind of critical independence and distance?

At the same time, we are typically involved in both research *and* teaching, where the demands and expectations can be quite different; not only to be specialist, innovative, original and focused on particular periods or disciplines, but broad-ranging, comprehensive and 'topical', too — especially in taught programmes that are less and less specialized and increasingly combined, panoramic or multi-subject in nature. A further precipitating factor here has been an emerging view within faculty and institutional managements that Portuguese language study might cease to be a compulsory starting point and core disciplinary requirement for the study of culture, including its literary dimension. As a consequence, our institutional and curricular location is increasingly in question, especially as faculty and departmental units become restructured: do we remain within the traditional language-based Portuguese/ Lusophone grouping, as part of a broader Hispanic or Latin American Studies, or are we to figure only sporadically, as an optional specialism delivered exclusively using English-language materials within even larger Modern Languages, Area/Global studies or Liberal Arts programmes?

In considering our possible responses to these tendencies, one useful resource is a group of essays published by Piers Armstrong between 2000 and 2003, which examined the state of Brazilian studies within US university education at the turn of the century; while I do not always agree with Armstrong's analysis, he formulates a number of helpful questions of relevance to us here. One of these concerns the role of political and economic trends in higher education in reshaping the disciplinary field, a decade or so in advance of their appearance on the UK scene; in particular, marketization and the rise of a 'consumerist' model of student-led programme design, which he suggests was probably responsible for the North American growth in Brazilian studies courses and programmes in those years. One outcome of such a model was to place increasing demands on academics to devise ever more topical and diverse materials of study and teaching technologies. But these pressures, warns Armstrong, tend to encourage us Brazilianists to take on the role of cultural 'tour-guides', generalists with a broad and superficial range of expertise, but not necessarily an adequate command of the disciplinary field: 'The teacher has become a sort of a technician of cultural exposure rather than an intellectual "master" of a given art or discipline (thus, it is not surprising to see that technological adaptation by the teacher is more useful on a CV than affirmations about the worth of the intellectual content of a class).'[2]

Brazilian Exceptionalism — All in the Mix?

So much for the institutional pressures faced by Brazilianists, and Armstrong's caveat about taking on the role of 'cultural tour-guides'. But what about the meaning and identity of Brazilian Cultural Studies as a distinct intellectual field? Are we attracted to the idea that certain cultural-historical features that set Brazil apart from, say, the rest of the Latin American continent are enough to warrant attributing to it some sort of exceptional status for the purposes of academic study? For sure, there is the question of the language: the marginalization of Portuguese, despite its demographic significance, no doubt galvanizes our own defensive instincts (such as when a Latin American forum can take for granted the use of Spanish as a *lingua franca*, but not Portuguese). And of course, there is the problem for students of Brazilian literature that internationally, since Brazil missed out on the so-called Latin American Boom of the 1960s and 70s, much of its best writing has struggled for recognition.

Beyond those historical facts, though, it is worth asking whether we 'Brazilianists' or *brasilistas* have a tendency to buy into some of those cultural clichés that are often invoked to justify the exceptionalist idea and, along with it, a kind of academic separatism that resists comparison and assumes that Brazil plays uniquely by its own rules (something Armstrong describes as a 'faith in Brazilian alterity'). While this kind of intellectual nationalism might be the stuff of 'soft' diplomacy, it is not something that, as cultural analysts and critics, we should indulge; for what are typically claimed to be quintessential 'Brazilian' traits do not bear much scrutiny, being little more than cultural stereotypes dressed up in the academic language of social or cultural theory.

A case in point is the cult of 'mixing' as the default explanatory model that is seemingly deployed to describe every cultural interaction and phenomenon in Brazil's social and political life, whether the chosen variant is *antropofagia/*

---

[2]   Piers Armstrong, 'Teaching Brazilian Civilization: Interdisciplinary and Institutional Pragmatics in Cultural Studies', in *Cultural Studies in the Curriculum: Teaching Latin America*, ed. by Danny J. Anderson, Jill S. Kuhnheim (The Modern Language Association of America, 2003). See also Piers Armstrong, 'The Brazilianists' Brazil: Interdisciplinary Portraits of Brazilian Society and Culture', *Latin American Research Review*, 35.1 (2000), pp. 227–42, and Piers Armstrong, 'Pragmatic, Dynamic, Subjective: Mutual Influences between the Social Sciences and the Humanities in the Brazilianist Field', in *Luso-Brazilian Studies in the New Millennium*, special issue of *Luso-Brazilian Review*, 4.2 (2003), pp. 51–71.

cultural cannibalism, hybridity or *mestiçagem*. Virtually a common-sense orthodoxy or 'dominant ideology' within academic Brazilianism, its political corollary is the mythology of mediation, the notion that 'the Brazilian way' is the path of bloodless negotiation rather than confrontation or conflict. Besides mystifying, drastically over-simplifying and reducing a hugely diverse field of social, political and cultural interactions to a set of variations on a single type, this discourse of 'mixing' often obscures the endemic violence of the social process while stifling and inhibiting more complex and nuanced approaches to thinking about inter-cultural contact and change. What is more, in claiming its intrinsic uniqueness and originality as something quintessentially Brazilian, it implicitly minimizes the relevance of such processes to other societies and cultures (aren't we all miscegenated, hybridized cultural cannibals?!), and disables really serious opportunities for comparative work.

For we should certainly be engaged in comparative work that takes account of Brazil's evolving place in a global context; whether comparisons with the post-colonial Southeast Asian experience, with developments in music, cinema and other arts across Europe, Asia and the Americas, or with other racialized societies in Latin America, the United States and the African continent, to cite just some examples. Indeed, in broadening the comparative scope across the Atlantic and Pacific oceans, we should at the same time have no truck with a defensive nationalism that, for example, rejects the validity of comparison with racism and the Black experience in the USA as 'intellectual imperialism'.[3] Above all I believe we should resist the view that argues for Brazil's exceptional status within Latin America and for a corresponding kind of 'academic separatism' in approaches towards its culture.

Let us remind ourselves: Brazil shares with the entire continent a whole number of key formative experiences — the Iberian variant of European colonialism (whatever the distinctions between its Portuguese and Spanish forms) and associated religious, linguistic, legal and cultural impacts; a history of violent, sometimes genocidal assaults on indigenous Amerindian populations, many of which were incorporated into national histories and identities; colonial African slavery and the legacy of modern racism and cultural resistance; large-scale, diverse immigration, ethnic diversity and miscegenation; political traditions of militarism, populism, authoritarianism, peasant and popular revolt and guerrilla warfare, to name a few. Brazil's relationship to the rest of the continent is clearly much more than a matter of geographical proximity, and we will learn much more about its distinctiveness (and there is a huge amount to learn) by embracing comparativist approaches than by rejecting them. Arguably we should be at the forefront of such initiatives, joining the growing number of

---

[3]   See, for example, Pierre Bourdieu and Loïc Wacquant, 'On the Cunning of Imperialist Reason', *Theory, Culture & Society*, 16.1 (1999), pp. 41–58, and John French's brilliant reply, 'Translation, Diasporic Dialogue, and the Errors of Pierre Bourdieu and Loïc Wacquant', *Nepantla*, 4.2 (2003), pp. 375–89.

Brazilian colleagues who are pioneering intra-continental studies across Brazil and Spanish America in the fields of cinema, music, and literature.

Finally, I turn to a rather different kind of exceptionalist argument, not directed at Brazil *per se*, but at Brazilian studies as an academic undertaking: that is to say, the notion that there is something *inherently or inevitably interdisciplinary* about the work that Brazilianists do. Armstrong makes the following assumption in a review essay of 2000:

> Brazilian studies constitute a special case in the current trend towards interdisciplinary studies across the humanities and social sciences [...]. The study of Brazilian literature in ignorance of the country's popular culture (including its music) or of national economic structures without reference to Brazilian social conditions seems inconceivable. Ethnomusicologists must incorporate socioeconomics, history, anthropology, and aesthetics. Moreover, Brazilianists frequently cross the substantial psychological barriers between the social sciences and the humanities.[4]

Many colleagues will recognize this phenomenon (of which the 'cultural turn' in Brazilian studies is a symptom), and it doubtless reflects an ethical commitment to relate our work to the most urgent and compelling problems faced by the majority of Brazilians in their everyday lives, such as poverty, insecurity, violence, and racial, gender and sexual discrimination. I wonder, though, whether the same tendency also corresponds to a particular aspect of academic and artistic life in Brazil itself: the 'Pestana complex', defined by José Miguel Wisnik as 'a porosidade e a reversibilidade entre o popular e o erudito' [the porosity and the reversibility between the popular and the erudite], and exemplified by that Machadian character, Pestana, who aspires to artistic celebrity as a classical composer but finds himself helplessly penning popular dance hits.

Arguably, however, our interest in popular culture and mass media should reflect more than a democratic impulse to broaden and diversify the field of study so as to do fuller justice to the totality of the cultural and social landscape, laudable though that aim is in itself. We should ask ourselves how well we manage to cross those disciplinary frontiers, how ready are we for this, and what we do to prepare our students for interdisciplinary work. Let us embrace the expanded field, but let us be wary of being overly pragmatic and reactive to topical trends and fashions, and wary, too, of the lures of cultural advocacy and celebration. Above all, let us take seriously our role as *interpreters*, *critics* and *revisionists*. In this we have a lot to learn from Brazil's own original thinkers, with whom we should be debating and arguing, while being confident in bringing other sources of critical reflection to bear on those debates and in devising new methodological and theoretical approaches.

Challenges such as these are not posed in a political vacuum. It is worth recalling that the cultural studies project that emerged out of the New Left

---

[4] Armstrong, 'The Brazilianists' Brazil', p. 227.

during the 1950s, 60s and 70s, associated especially with the Birmingham Centre for Contemporary Cultural Studies (CCCS), its founder Richard Hoggart and his successor Stuart Hall, was a political as well as a scholarly intervention. Paying serious attention to previously unstudied aspects of mass media, youth subcultures and popular culture also implied a radical identification with marginalized subaltern subjects and a commitment to the task of deconstructing, critiquing and challenging the structures of power that oppress them. Sadly, in 2002 the direct successor to the CCCS, the University of Birmingham's Department of Cultural Studies, was closed down in the wake of the results of the 2001 Research Assessment Exercise. It was therefore one of the casualties of the conditions that we confront today: the marketization of higher education, a growing climate of hostility toward the humanities and an assault on the principle of the public university. As our colleagues in Brazil face not only the same challenges but a wholesale onslaught on the fragile, painfully won democratic rights and social gains of the last three decades from a resurgent far-right movement, we could do well to remember the vision and radicalism of the Birmingham cultural studies project and its ethos of political critique and social justice.

A Short History of the Association of British and Irish Lusitanists (ABIL)

Carmen Ramos Villar

University of Sheffield

ABIL started as a conversation between friends during a sunny break in the AIL conference in Santiago de Compostela (2005). A couple of us, who were then at the start of our career, watched as the plan solidified into what quickly became ABIL. In 2005, there was a growth in numbers learning, teaching and researching Portuguese across British and Irish universities, and we had a very good academic journal, *Portuguese Studies* (celebrating its fortieth year in this issue). It was time to create a space of our own, where people interested in research and teaching within the Portuguese-speaking world could share what we were all doing, and where we could continue to raise the profile of Portuguese Studies.

We are an academic association that is recognized as the prime representative of those working within the Portuguese Studies field in the UK. We have links to TROPO (Association of Teachers and Researchers of Portuguese), APSA (American Portuguese Studies Association), the Instituto Camões, AIL (Associação Internacional de Lusitanistas), REBRAC (Rede Europeia de Brasilianistas de Análise Cultural), and the Anglo-Portuguese Society. We also have links to the AHGBI (Association of Hispanists of Great Britain and Ireland), and the UCFL (University Council for Languages, previously known as the UCML — University Council for Modern Languages).

ABIL has always sought to be a space to discuss our research and teaching, and a way to connect to a support network. ABIL was, and is, very specifically, a way for us all to come together and find support and advice. Our membership is open to persons who study, research and/or teach the languages, cultures and literatures of the Portuguese-speaking world, no matter the stage in their career. Our membership currently stands at around 120, representing institutions not only in Britain and Ireland, but also the United States, Brazil, Portugal, and various other European countries.

The main activity of ABIL is the biennial conference. Very soon after the first conference in Nottingham, in 2006, the pattern of when to hold the conferences was quickly established to being every two years, in September, in a British or Irish university. Our executive committee also acts as a small support network that offers practical advice on how to organize the conference. So far, we have

Portuguese Studies vol. 41 no. 2 (2025), doi:10.1353/port.00039, 180–82
© Modern Humanities Research Association 2025

held ten conferences, eight of which have been in the UK, and two in Ireland. A special mention goes to Fernando Beleza and his team at the University of Newcastle, who hosted the first, and very successful, ABIL hybrid conference after COVID in 2021.

Looking back at the conference programmes, there have been impressive keynote speakers. Lúcia Nagib was the first keynote of what has been an all-star cast. Naming a few, without wanting to discriminate, we have had John Gledson, Paulo de Medeiros, Vanda Anastácio, Antonio Feijóo, Anna Klobucka, Cláudia Pazos Alonso, and Cristiana Bastos, as well as various past presidents of the Association. We have also had writers giving the keynote speech (Luís Bernardo Honwana; Pedro Rosa Mendes), and film directors (Henrique Goldman; Tata Amaral). The conference programmes also show that, since the beginning, PhD students and ECRs have not only been encouraged to attend and participate, but we hope that they have also been made fully welcome. The aim has always been to make our conferences affordable and inclusive to all members, both in terms of the registration and conference fees, and also in terms of providing bursaries to our PGR/ECR members. In addition to papers based on research by individual members, our conferences now regularly feature three dedicated sessions: one on topics suggested by our postgrad reps (such as experiences and tips on publishing, or life after the PhD); one by TROPO; and one where our UCFL representative opens the discussion by reporting back on discussions at the UCFL, which usually leads to us sharing experiences and information.

The programmes of past conferences map out the evolution of Portuguese Studies over the twenty years since that conversation in Santiago de Compostela led to the formation of ABIL. In recognition of this, in 2021, with support from the Anglo-Portuguese Society, we introduced the Fallow Year Bursary. This bursary aims to support Early Career researchers and Postgraduate students, and the promotion of Portuguese Studies, by providing some funding towards events that take place in the non-conference year. The first call was extremely successful, supporting five very impressive events during the academic year of 2022–23. By the time this text is published, the events supported by the second call will also have taken place.

ABIL also acts in support of colleagues facing difficulties in their own institutions, both in the UK and abroad, as they navigate the changing landscape of Higher Education. This often comes in the form of advice, but it also involves writing letters to institutions within and beyond the UK and Ireland to help make the case for maintaining and promoting the place of Portuguese Studies in the curriculum.

There are also numerous stories about ABIL that could enter into its history as an association over the last twenty years that cannot be included for reasons of space. Some of them are very funny. As a former treasurer and now president, I could tell a few, mostly involving how to get any new treasurer added to the bank account, an experience akin to a rite of passage in creatively navigating not being in the same geographical place.

I want to finish by offering ABIL's congratulations to *Portuguese Studies* on its fortieth anniversary. As this special anniversary edition of *Portuguese Studies* shows, we have a lot to be proud of, and to celebrate.

Carmen Ramos Villar is current past president of ABIL. This text was written with the help and input of former presidents of ABIL Tom Earle (2005–09), David Frier (2009–13), Phillip Rothwell (2013–17), and Stephanie Dennison (2017–21), and also of Hilary Owen and Cláudia Pazos Alonso, who have been there from the beginning.

Building a Brazilian Cultural Analysis Network in Europe and Beyond: Reflections on a Ten-year Milestone and Future Plans for REBRAC

Sara Brandellero,
Stephanie Dennison, and Tori Holmes

Leiden University, University of Leeds, and Queen's University Belfast

As *Portuguese Studies* marks its fortieth anniversary of dissemination of scholarship on and from the Portuguese-speaking world, the landmark provides us with a fortuitous opportunity to reflect on the work of REBRAC (Rede Europeia de Brasilianistas de Análise Cultural/European Network of Brazilianists Working in Cultural Analysis), a fellow initiative that marks an anniversary of its own in this same year.

REBRAC was launched in 2015 by Sara Brandellero (Leiden University), Stephanie Dennison (University of Leeds), and Tori Holmes (Queen's University Belfast) to provide a networking space for both established and postgraduate or early career scholars working in Brazilian cultural studies/cultural analysis in the UK and mainland Europe. Its aim is to provide scholars with a forum to exchange ideas and raise their profiles online and in person, in an atmosphere of conviviality and mutual support. REBRAC also seeks to share information on developments in Brazilian cultural affairs, as well as on academic activities in Europe, Brazil and elsewhere linked to cultural studies, and to forge and develop potential links and collaborations between Brazilianists based in Europe and beyond.

Since 2019, membership of REBRAC (which is free of charge) has been open to scholars of Brazilian cultural studies anywhere in the world. There are two categories of membership: full (for members based in Europe) and associate (for members based outside Europe). The categories allow members to quickly identify where researchers are based for ease of networking. Lists of members in both categories are freely available on our website, <www.rebrac.net>. As of April 2025, we have just over 150 members, of whom around two thirds are full members and the remainder are associate members. Our full members are based in fourteen different European countries, while our associate members are predominantly based in Brazil, with others in the USA, elsewhere in

Portuguese Studies vol. 41 no. 2 (2025), doi:10.1353/port.00040, 183–87

Latin America, and Asia/Australia. Thus, while we highlight our European credentials in our network name, we acknowledge the importance of reaching beyond Europe (and Brazil) to other communities of 'Brazilianists'.

To date REBRAC has organized six conferences, and these have been a particularly rich and central part of the network's activities. The first conference, which marked the network's founding, took place in London in 2015, under the title 'Remapping Brazilian Cultural Studies'. We recognized that a taking stock of the state, the significance and the academic limits of Brazilian cultural studies was overdue: not since 2000 and the King's College London conference entitled 'Brazil — Representing the Nation: Alternative Voices and Identities in the Year 2000', and the University of Manchester's 'The New Latin Americanism: Cultural Studies Beyond Borders' (2002) had Brazilian cultural studies been laid open to scrutiny in UK academia in the context of a conference open to all. One key development in the intervening ten-plus years had been the impressive growth of access to the internet and digital technologies in Brazil, which had not just generated new objects of study, but also stimulated a rethinking of established objects of study and the methodologies used to analyse them.

The 2015 inaugural conference was followed by 'Brazil in the Spotlight' hosted at Queen's University Belfast in 2016. In a year in which Brazil was experiencing a period of political instability and Rio de Janeiro hosted the Olympic Games, the conference provided an opportunity to reflect critically, from the perspective of cultural studies/cultural analysis, on the international visibility of Brazil (in political, economic and cultural terms) at the time, as well as on the impact on cultural studies of the recent changes that had occurred in the Brazilian socio-political panorama. In 2018 the University of Copenhagen hosted our third conference, with the theme of 'Living Il/legalities', which took place just over a week before the second round of presidential elections that would bring Jair Bolsonaro to power. It was clear to us at that time that the phenomenon of 'il/legalities' would go on to have even greater weight in Brazil, where the demolition of the rule of law was happening at pace.

Our next conference, 'The Country of the Future/The Future of the Country' (Oxford, 2020 — postponed to 2021 due to the Coronavirus pandemic), cited the well-worn adage of Stefan Zweig. Presentations sought to analyse how Brazilians looked ahead to the future in past eras, as well as to consider how Brazilians see the future today: the narratives that were/are constructed, and what moral or ethical values were and are at stake. 'The 22s: Brazilian Cultural Entanglements, Then and Now', held in Leeds in 2022, reflected on commemorations around the bicentenary of Brazil's independence and the centenary of the São Paulo Week of Modern Art and how discussions around cultural legitimacy and inclusion inform current debates on decolonization and what is understood by 'Brazilian culture' itself. Our most recent conference was held at the University of Leiden in 2024 on '(Re)Democratisation of Culture and Through Culture in Brazil' and took its cue from present-day threats to democratic governance that have affected Brazil and that resonate in other contexts worldwide, thinking through the important connections between politics and culture in times of crisis. In January 2026 we will return to London, where the network was conceived, and will celebrate our tenth anniversary, which coincides with the UK/Brazil Season of Culture (2025–26) promoted as a joint diplomatic and cultural venture by the UK and Brazilian governments. In this way, REBRAC again positions itself as a forum for academic debate keenly attuned to current socio-political and historical contexts.

A key principle of REBRAC conferences has been to run a single unified programme, with no parallel sessions, to maintain focus and engagement and to build a shared conversation amongst participants across the sessions. Although this has meant that we have not been able to accept all abstracts submitted for consideration for each event (REBRAC conferences normally run over two to three days), it has undoubtedly resulted in coherent and intimate events, with ample opportunities for conversation, exchange, and networking both in the sessions and in the breaks and social events. A key shift since the Covid-19 pandemic has been running REBRAC conferences as hybrid events. In March 2020, we were about to hold our IV International Conference in Oxford, when — like so many academic networks and associations — we were forced to cancel. We eventually ran the conference as a fully online event in March 2021, ably hosted by colleagues at the University of Oxford. Both our 2022 Leeds and 2024 Leiden conferences were fully hybrid, with the majority of participants attending in person, but some presentations given remotely via video platform and some audience members listening and watching at a distance. Although this definitely brought technical challenges it also enabled a wider group of participants to join us.

Our approach has been to develop an inclusive, trans-disciplinary network, which has provided opportunities for exchange and collaboration between established academic scholars as well as interventions from non-academics in diverse arts and cultural spheres. This is reflected in the keynotes that we have been honoured to welcome and which, over the years, have included, in chronological order, David Treece (Emeritus, King's College London), John Gledson (Emeritus, University of Liverpool), Leonardo Tonus (Université Paris–Sorbonne), Friedrich Frosch (University of Vienna), Daniel Hirata (Universidade Federal Fluminense), Adriana Jacobsen (filmmaker), Gabriel Mascaro (filmmaker), Peter W. Schulze (Universität zu Köln), Florencia Garramuño (Universidad de San Andrés/CONICET), Adilson Moreira (Fundação Getúlio Vargas), Flávio Cerqueira (sculptor), Sérgio Vaz (poet and cultural activist) and Ellen Lima Wassu (writer and indigenous activist). We look forward to welcoming Lilia Moritz Schwarcz (Universidade de São Paulo/Princeton/Academia Brasileira de Letras) and Nuno Ramos (artist and writer) as keynotes at our 2026 conference.

REBRAC's conferences and thematic panels have resulted in a series of publications, both edited volumes and special issues of journals. Most recently, December 2024 saw the publication of a special issue of *Brasiliana: Journal for Brazilian Studies* (vol. 13, no. 2) on 'Ruptures and Continuities in Brazilian Cultural Production', edited by Stephanie Dennison, Tori Holmes, and Sara Brandellero, inspired by the V International REBRAC Conference held in Leeds in October 2022. In 2020, the volume *Living (Il)legalities in Brazil: Practices, Narratives and Institutions in a Country on the Edge* was published by Routledge. Drawing on the III International REBRAC Conference held in Copenhagen in October 2018, it was edited by the event's organizers, Sara Brandellero, Derek Pardue, and Georg Wink. In 2018, Stephanie Dennison edited a special issue of the *Journal of Iberian and Latin American Studies* (vol. 24, no. 3) on 'Cordiality and Intimacy in Contemporary Brazilian Culture', which was based on the REBRAC panels at the Association of British and Irish Lusitanists (ABIL) conference held in Sheffield in September 2017. (As well as its own conferences, REBRAC has also organized panels at the annual conferences of related subject associations.) Also in 2018, Sara Brandellero and Derek Pardue edited a special issue of *Veredas: Revista Internacional da Associação de Lusitanistas* (no. 27) on 'Cultura e poder no Brasil hoje', which developed out of the REBRAC panel at the first conference of the Associação de Brasilianistas na Europa (ABRE), held in Leiden in May 2017. Finally, in 2017 Stephanie Dennison edited a special issue of *Trama Interdisciplinar* (vol. 8, no. 3) on 'O Brasil dentro e fora do cenário internacional', inspired by the II International REBRAC Conference held in Belfast in November 2016. One of the most rewarding aspects of REBRAC for Sara, Stephanie and Tori, who still run the network, is the opportunity to publish the work of a very wide range of contributors, from postgraduates and early career researchers to high-profile cultural commentators such as Marcia Tiburi and Jean Wyllys.

REBRAC has also sought to keep in touch with its members and fulfil its aim of sharing information relating to Brazilian cultural studies/cultural analysis via email bulletins, its blog, and a presence on social media platforms. The 'BOLETIM REBRAC', which now normally goes out two to three times a year, combines news from REBRAC itself (e.g. about its own conferences and publications) with information about upcoming seminars, conferences, and events, calls for papers and announcements of new publications, details of job and funding opportunities, and information about resources such as online databases and archives. Our website/blog, which is followed by a larger audience going beyond our own members, has become a repository for full information about REBRAC conferences and panels (including calls for papers, programmes, conference reports, along with photos and minutes of REBRAC network meetings held as part of those events), publications, members, and other ad hoc initiatives such as 'Brazilian film in the time of Coronavirus', a curated list of online resources and platforms relating to Brazilian film, as well as individual films freely available to view online, prepared in the midst of the Covid-19 pandemic.

Our main social media presence was for many years on Twitter (now X), where we surpassed 1000 followers, and regularly shared details of events, publications, resources, opportunities, and news relating to Brazilian cultural studies/cultural analysis, with good levels of engagement from our followers. As with the blog, our Twitter profile allowed us to reach an audience and build a network going far beyond our own members. The platform served both as an invaluable source of information that would later go on to be included in the BOLETIM REBRAC, via the accounts we followed, and as a means of sharing time-sensitive news that would go out of date before the next edition of the BOLETIM, such as calls for papers, as well as more varied content. Sadly, the dynamic has changed on X and we are now focusing on Bluesky. We warmly invite you to follow us there: <https://bsky.app/profile/rebracweb.bsky.social>. We also have a presence on Facebook and use it to post occasional updates about the network's activities, similar to what we post on our blog.

As we mark our own ten-year anniversary, we look forward to fostering many more opportunities for mutual learning and collaboration. The growth of the REBRAC network as a truly international community, also inviting us to rethink the label of 'Brazilianist' — traditionally understood as a non-Brazilian, based at an academic institution outside of Brazil — is an indication of its ambition and aim of providing a forum for a clear focus on Brazil's culture and society through a democratic understanding of what culture is, and harnessing connections with the broader Lusophone scholarship. Within the paradigm of Brazilian Studies/Latin American Studies, cultural studies scholarship, while often overlooked, can make an incisive contribution to the field, as ably demonstrated by the interdisciplinary work of REBRAC, with its focus on culture, power and democracy.

We congratulate *Portuguese Studies* on reaching its fortieth anniversary and warmly invite any contributors and readers who are active in the field of Brazilian cultural studies/cultural analysis and are not yet members of REBRAC to join the network at <www.rebrac.net/cadastro-membership>.

Translating India:
Latin Accounts of Vasco da Gama's
Encounter with the Zamorin

SHRUTI RAJGOPAL[1]

University College Cork

In this article I examine Latin descriptions of the very first interaction between Vasco da Gama and the King of Calicut, the Zamorin, which took place in India in 1498. The same event appears in four accounts, namely by Jeronimo Osorio (1571), Giovanni Pietro Maffei (1588), Thomas Faria (1622) and Andreas Baianus (1625). Vernacular accounts frequently included this interaction and circulated widely prior to the completion of Latin accounts.[2] Nevertheless, my study explores Latin translations of this interaction and India's representation as part of the humanistic tradition.

Although India's appearance in this neoclassical garb has been explored less frequently, classicists and historians have examined India's connection to the Roman Empire. Because of frequent voyages Latin translations included details of India, which illustrate how it was part of the Roman world and its descriptions with additional comments and corrections. Moreover, observations of culturally characteristic details led to the need of and contribution to the Latin lexicon.[3] My study offers one of the first attempts to situate Latin's role in representing and translating India and its characteristic features to its European audience. Following the stylistic features of classical authors, humanists described details known and unknown to the Romans.[4] Latin continued to be the language of the scholarly crowd who were trained through the curriculum of the *studia humanitatis*. This gave rise to intellectual circles such as the republic of letters.[5] Circulation of texts through this republic ensured wider dissemination of

---

[1] My research is funded by the National University of Ireland Travelling Doctoral Studentships in the Humanities and Social Sciences and the School of History, UCC. All translations into English are my own, unless otherwise indicated.

[2] Note, throughout the article, I use the term 'vernacular' to suggest accounts written in European languages, unless otherwise specified.

[3] Donald Lach, *Asia in the Making of Europe, vol. II: A Century of Wonder. Book 3: The Scholarly Disciplines* (University of Chicago Press, 2010), pp. 525–26, doi:10.7208/chicago/9780226467139.001.0001.

[4] Apuleius, *Florida*, Book 15; Pliny, *Historia Naturalis*, Book VI; Cicero, *Tusculan Disputations*, Book V.

[5] Christopher Celenza, *The Intellectual World of the Italian Renaissance: Language, Philosophy, and the Search for Meaning* (Cambridge University Press, 2018), p. 2, doi:10.1017/9781139051613.

Portuguese Studies vol. 41 no. 2 (2025), doi:10.1353/port.00041, 188–206
© Modern Humanities Research Association 2025

materials; simultaneously, it offers a chance to examine humanists' stylistic and linguistic preferences through their descriptions. It is these preferences that I examine as part of this article through a comparative study of the interaction as seen in the four translations. Before examining the interaction, it is worth exploring the nature of Latin accounts of India.

Latin gained its cosmopolitan role because of its use across political and geographical boundaries.[6] However, its role and inclusion in the descriptions of India is more frequently seen in the form of translations. These translations can be divided into two categories, namely: 1) close translation of one specific account, e.g. Camões's poem (1622, 1625); and 2) translations carried out through examination of a range of vernacular sources and integrating information from them, for instance, Maffei's and Osorio's texts. There were also original compositions in Latin of India, two of which in particular are worth mentioning, Antoni de Montserrat's *Commentarius* (1590) and Francesco Benci's *Quinque Martyres* (1594). These original compositions, although significant contributions to this field, need to be studied in the light of previously executed Latin works — available in the form of translations. This helps in evaluating the options of classical and more recent works available to Neo-Latin authors. Moreover, descriptions of the same event make comparisons between these texts possible and allow me to examine their options. The four translations focus on the Portuguese expeditions and explore the first encounter between Vasco da Gama and the Zamorin, the prose translations focusing on Portuguese historiography, whereas the verse translations are based on the use of epic formulae. The inclusion of the interaction brings the four translations together. Their choices and methods of translation reveal classical echoes and translations of vernacular sources. These Latin accounts help in evaluating Portugal's status as the 'New Rome', although this needs to be examined as a separate study. Here, I examine the prose texts first, followed by translations in poetry.

Descriptions of Portuguese voyages to the east in the vernacular were popular through histories and chronicles by João de Barros (1496–1570), Fernão Lopes de Castanheda (1500–1559) and Gaspar Correia (1492–1563). Barros's and Castanheda's accounts are particularly important since Osorio and Maffei used them as their sources. Barros's account was a significant contribution for two reasons: 1) for offering complete details of the Portuguese voyages; and 2) for following the Roman author, Livy.[7] Livy's *Ab urbe condita* offered Barros the framework to compose his work which outlined Portuguese historiography. Osorio and Maffei's translations, although not translated verbatim from these sources, offer a variety of such classical models as will become clear from this analysis. These translations illustrate European descriptions of early modern India — its wealth, opulence and hierarchical society.

---

[6]   Peter Heather, *The Fall of the Roman Empire* (Pan Books, 2005).
[7]   Christina Shuttleworth Kraus (ed.), *Cambridge Greek and Latin Classics: Livy Ab Urbe Condita Book VI* (Cambridge University Press, 1998), pp. 19–23.

The Zamorin became a renowned figure in European literature from the fifteenth century. Barros, like the Neo-Latin authors, gives a complete description of Gama's visit to the Zamorin's court to establish trade relations. In fact, Barros offers an etymological explanation for the use of the title 'Zamorin',[8] saying that 'he is called the Samory, which among them is equivalent to the title of Emperor among us'.[9] Considering the vernacular term, *Samuthri raja*, Barros offers an example of culturally translating the term 'Zamorin' for a European reader. He explains the location of Calicut and the king's power over this region. The Latin translations instead compensate by describing details echoing Greco-Roman traditions to enlighten their European readers of the riches of the Zamorin. Variations in the method of descriptions show Latin's flexibility to align with prose and poetic choices made by writers, further emphasizing their references and faithfulness to the original text. As stated earlier, these approaches can be seen as a reflection of the myriad vernacular sources authors used as part of the process of translation. Multilingual approaches were on the rise towards the end of the sixteenth century, as can be seen from the increasing number of travel narratives in the vernacular. Hence, comparisons of the same detail in these Latin translations reveal humanists' choices from the range of sources they used. These stylistic choices illustrate the circulation of both vernacular and classical Latin texts that these authors used.

The interaction between the Zamorin and Gama is one of the most celebrated examples of courtly encounters incorporated in various early modern texts.[10] This comparative study examines: 1) how authors translate this scene for their European audience; 2) the similarities and differences between the translations of this scene; 3) the choice of classical references they adhere to; and 4) whether they were inspired by each other's work and if we can measure this influence. For instance, in what ways can we analyse whether Baianus (1625) was inspired by Faria's (1622) style? Nineteenth-century biographies enumerate Faria's and Baianus's attempts at translation, but there has been no study comparing their works, revealing classical intertextual references.[11] Hence, each translation is unique and indicative of India's connection to neoclassical Latinity.

Key features of this interaction include Gama's encounter with Catual, the administrative governor at this king's court, the use of the palanquin to travel to the court, Gama's observation of a place of idol worship, and details of the court's portrayal of luxury.[12] Although the four texts narrate this detail and are

[8] Barros, *Décadas da Ásia* (Impressa per Iorge Rodriquez, 1628), fol. 74; Krishna Ayyar, 'The Importance of the Zamorins of Calicut', *Proceedings of the Indian History Congress*, 37 (1976), pp. 252–59 (p. 252).
[9] Barros, *Décadas da Ásia* (1628), fol. 74.
[10] Meera Juncu, *India in the Italian Renaissance: Visions of a Contemporary Pagan World, 1300–1600* (Routledge, 2019), pp. 141–64, doi:10.4324/9781315696737.
[11] John Adamson, *Memoirs of the Life and Writings of Luis de Camoens* (Longam, Hurst, Rees, Orme, and Brown, 1820), p. 79.
[12] Sanjay Subrahmanyam, *The Career and Legend of Vasco da Gama* (Cambridge University Press, 1997), p. 131.

analogous, their classical echoes tell a different story. Following a chronological sequence, the next section examines Osorio's attempt.

Jeronimo Osorio (1506–80), a Portuguese humanist, contributed extensively to the field of Neo-Latin literature through his writings. Among these, his *De rebus Emmanuelis Regis Lusitaniae Invictissimi virtute et auspicio gestis* (1571) illustrates India's representation through this stylistic tradition. Osorio's narration is gradual, clear and follows an indicative and direct method of description. The *De rebus Emmanuelis* focuses on Manuel's reign (1495–1521), and includes outline narratives of the geography, the political struggles and the ethnography encountered through these voyages.[13] He yields to the reader's fascination by giving a factual account and narrating ancillary information, aiding the reader's understanding of the topic.

Osorio begins with Gama and his retinue's arrival along the Malabar coast, followed by Gama's interaction with Monçaide, the Tunisian interpreter.[14] He indicates the location where the king resided (Ponnani) and its distance from Calicut — a detail which may have facilitated voyagers in the sixteenth century for commercial and colonial purposes.[15] He explains Gama's meeting with the Catual, described as the 'magistratum'.[16] Then, he outlines how Paulo Gama and Nicolo Coelho remained behind, and of Gama's procession with the Catual to the court, using a palanquin. Carmen Nocentelli, in *Empire of Love*, has explored how palanquins caught Europeans' attention through travel literature.[17] Following Nocentelli's research, Osorio explains the palanquin as being 'lectica sublatus [carried in a litter]', whereas the Roman author, Cicero, informs his readers of this lavish method of travel as 'lectica octaphoro ferebatur' [carried by eight [men]].[18] Humanists favoured Cicero's works because of multitude of texts that he wrote. Osorio's description aligns with Cicero's vocabulary but not in the detail of the number of men who carried this bed. It is worth mentioning that even Castanheda follows Cicero's style and explains that each 'lectica' was carried by four people; however, Osorio does not translate this detail verbatim.[19] Instead, he emphasizes this luxurious vehicle by suggesting how it carried Gama and Catual in separate 'lecticas', whereas the rest of the group walked to the king's residence.[20] This description informs readers of how palanquins represented luxury, emphasizing the subaltern position of those carrying the carriage. This use of palanquins showcases the

---

[13] Osorio, *De rebus Emmanuelis Regis Lusitaniae Invictissimi virtute et auspicio gestis* (1586).
[14] Osorio (1586), 31ʳ. Note, I have referred to the 1586 edition for Osorio's text and will cite it as Osorio, followed by the folio number.
[15] Osorio, 31ʳ.
[16] Osorio, 31ᵛ.
[17] Nocentelli, *Empires of Love: Europe, Asia, and the Making of Early Modern Identity* (University of Pennsylvania Press, 2013), pp. 71–72, doi:10.9783/9780812207774.
[18] Osorio, 31ᵛ, Cicero, *In Verrem* 2.5.27.6 (the bed is carried by eight [men]) (Loeb Classical Library, Harvard University Press, 1928).
[19] Castanheda, *História do descobrimento e conquista da Índia pelos Portugueses*, Book I (1833), p. 55.
[20] Osorio, 31ᵛ.

hierarchical society in India. Osorio's description is clear but also indicates that he follows neither Castanheda nor Cicero entirely but selects details from each text and creates a unique stylistic choice. This is also one of the rare instances where his text lacks details to give a clearer picture of this carriage.

This detail is followed by his description of the place of idol worship. Here, Osorio's description reveals his reference to Castanheda's *História*. Castanheda explains this place of idol worship as 'igreja' and alludes to the presence of Christians in this region. This information can be traced back to the *Roteiro*, the journal written by one of the voyagers on this expedition, explaining and mistranslating this place of idol worshippers as that of Christian believers.[21] Contrarily, Osorio's use of Latin allows him to emend the description of this place of worship as being different from a church.

The walls of the temple ('templi') were adorned with many painted images. In the centre of the temple was a raised chapel, round in shape, to which one ascended by many steps. The door was made of bronze and was very narrow. Inside the chapel ('sacellum') was a statue placed on the opposite wall, the form of which our people were unable to see due to the darkness of the place ('obscuritatem aspicere'), for the place was completely shielded from every ray of the sun ('solis radio seclusus').[22]

His use of 'templum' indicates classical vocabulary for a place of worship — an option that he decided was closer in this case as opposed to the terms 'fanum' [shrine], 'delubrum' [temple/shrine], or 'pagoda' [idol/temple] which were frequently used by Jesuits in the later years.[23] His vocabulary indicates how early modern readers were directed by classical references despite the lack of an intertextual reference. Osorio describes the presence of a chapel in the middle and the walls embellished with images. Here, he seems to be referring to the 'Sanctum sanctorum', or the 'garbhagriha' in Sanskrit, which indicates the altar where the idol is placed. He further notes that this space was circular in form, which indicates the custom of circumambulation, practised by worshippers visiting a temple. He explains the darkness associated with this inner sanctum, due to the lack of windows — also explained as 'lack of light' in his text.[24] Osorio's account lacks any direct comparison with Roman or Greek temple architecture. Instead, he allows the readers to differentiate Greco-Roman temples from those in India. Contrary to his details of the interiors, he

---

[21] Castanheda, *História do descobrimento e conquista da Índia pelos Portugueses*, Book I (1833), pp. 56–59; *Em Nome de Deus: The Journal of the First Voyage of Vasco da Gama to India, 1497–1499*, trans. by Glenn J. Ames (Brill, 2009), pp. 22–23, 75.

[22] Osorio, 31ᵛ–32ʳ.

[23] Maffei, *Historiarum Indicarum Libri XVI* (1589), p. 24. Also refer to Ananya Chakravarthi, *The Empire of Apostles: Religion, Accommodation, and the Imagination of Empire in Early Modern Brazil and India* (Oxford University Press, 2018), p. 100.

[24] In a similar vein, even Francesco Benci explains the darkness associated with temples in India, *Quinque martyres: Introduction, Translation, and Commentary*, trans. by Paul Gwynne (Brill, 2018), p. 176, doi:10.1163/9789004356610. References to this work will be cited as Benci, followed by the page number.

avoids descriptions of the exterior form, shape or materials used in this form of architecture — again, this can be seen as a reflection of the sources that he used, which do not outline these details. Following this detailed description, Osorio continues to create a much-needed framework before giving an account of the interaction between the Zamorin and Gama. He outlines the groups of men who form the king's council — the Naires (who are compared to the militia in Europe), the Caimales identified as the 'dynasty' in this kingdom, and the Brahmins.[25] Osorio clearly identifies the groups according to their ranks in the royal court, which allows him to select from his vocabulary in Latin ('rex', 'dynasta') accordingly. This technique allows him to allude to the Zamorin's power and Portugal's newfound status as the 'New Rome' through Gama's visit.

Entering the king's residence, Osorio explains the room that Gama visited. He compares the layout of the room to a theatre — a feature associated with Roman and Greek architecture.[26] Like the seating arrangement in the Colosseum, an early modern reader is reminded how hierarchy determined one's position in the Zamorin's court. Following this, he skips the detail of the king chewing betel leaf — the second instance, like the case of palanquins, where he does not elaborate. He outlines how the king commands his position through his attire, embellished with jewels, and reclining on the bed. He portrays his authority by suggesting that 'the king commanded Gama to come closer and take a seat near him'.[27] By emphasizing such details, Osorio develops the importance of courtly encounters to suggest Portugal's status as the 'New Rome'. He continues to build on this status through details of King Manuel's message for the Zamorin. The chapter ends by explaining the prolonged delay by the Zamorin in delivering a response to Gama's request. Readers gasp at the representation of the wealth of this oriental king and sympathize with the experience Gama endured to prove his mettle against the eastern kingdoms. Hence, his descriptions allow readers to gather a factual image of what happened in this first interaction. Furthermore, he neither uses the term 'Zamorin' nor, like Barros, alludes to its cultural interpretation. He inserts information of the misdeeds of Arabs and Saracens — a common feature among early modern Latin writers. Switching between direct and indirect voice, his text ensures clarity of the information provided, simultaneously showing the flexibility of Latin through classical intertextual references. In some ways, his choices outline what his audience knew, and what he thought they needed to know about India.

Nearly two decades after Osorio's publication, an Italian Jesuit, Giovanni Pietro Maffei, echoed this detail in his *Historiarum Indicarum Libri XVI* (1588). The text is divided into sixteen parts, each of which explores Portuguese voyages to establish political and religious control in these regions, covering a longer timespan (1415–1557). Maffei considered the administrative letters

[25]   Osorio, 32[r].
[26]   Osorio, 32[v].
[27]   Osorio, 32[r].

written by Jesuits and vernacular histories and chronicles such as those by
Barros and Castanheda. Contrary to Osorio, Maffei offers a succinct version of
these details. Moreover, unlike Osorio, who subtly weaves classical references
into his text, Maffei makes sure to name some of his authors such as Ptolemy
and Strabo, in addition to his citations of Barros and Osorio in his work.[28]
These references reveal how Maffei draws inspiration from contemporaries
such as Osorio.

Maffei begins with Gama's arrival, followed by introducing the king as the
Zamorin and outlines his skin tone, a feature absent in Osorio.[29] Maffei focuses
on details of the temple and its resemblance to Greco-Roman architecture,
the hierarchy observed in this court, a description of the palanquin and the
betel leaf that the Zamorin consumed as part of this interaction. Details of
Coelho and Paulo remaining behind or of Monçaide are either absent or only
briefly explained.[30] Maffei begins by explaining the hierarchy (Catual and the
council in the court).[31] Expanding on this detail, he notes Gama's visit to a
place of worship and the trinity that locals worshipped. He reveals the name
of the god ('Parabrahman'), his three sons (who form the trinity), and the
grandeur of this place, and he compares its spatial layout with Roman temples.
The magnitude, arrangement and scale remind Maffei of the Pantheon ('they
rival the columns of Agrippa, that can be seen in the Pantheon, once the most
renowned temple in Rome').[32] This comparison connects India to the Greco-
Roman world and identifies the glories and riches embedded in these places.
He then elaborates on local attire before engaging with details of the much-
awaited interaction between Gama and the Malabar king.[33] Once he sets this
scene, he then engages with Gama's journey to the Zamorin's court. Analysing
this description further, readers are drawn to details of the 'palanquin' —
identified as 'tetraphoro' ('dein Gammam tetraphoro impositum' — then Gama
is positioned on a carriage borne by four people).[34] Echoing Cicero's 'octaphoro',
Maffei's 'tetraphoro', clearly reveals the number of people involved in this
act.[35] Using classical methods, Maffei identifies the extravagance employed by
the eastern kings to represent their hierarchy in the society. His description
of the 'tetraphoro' is a justification of the opulence and alterity seen in the
Malabar society. Elaborating on this extravagance, Maffei explores the visual
representation of this court:

> Stratum erat pauimentum serico eteromallo viridi: parietes vero bombycine
> peristromata intertexto auro magnifice vestiebant: ligneis gradibus affabre

---

[28] Maffei, p. 137, 43.
[29] Maffei, p. 27.
[30] Maffei, p. 27.
[31] Maffei, p. 24.
[32] Maffei, p. 24.
[33] Maffei, p. 25.
[34] Maffei, p. 26.
[35] Cicero, *In Verrem* 2.5.27.6 (Loeb Classical Library, Harvard University Press, 1928).

factis in theatri formam circumque eminentibus: ea procerum subsellia sunt.[36]

[The floor was covered with silk and green brocade; the walls were magnificently adorned with silk hangings interwoven with gold. The wooden steps were skilfully crafted, forming a theatre-like shape, with elevated benches around them: these were the seats for the nobles.]

Maffei echoes Strabo with his use of 'eteromallo' to explain the layout of the king's chamber.[37] Strabo had used 'eteromallo' to outline the rich variety of wool found in various parts of Italy. Maffei borrows this context of opulence to describe the Malabar court. Following this, he describes the bejewelled king and his habit of chewing betel leaves. Unlike Osorio, Maffei names the species as 'Tambul Arabicum', which was known among locals as 'Malabaricum betel'.[38] He skilfully switches between sub obliquity and the indicative to determine the visual aspects that the Portuguese observed.[39] He continues to develop Greco-Roman comparisons as he outlines the layout of the king's chamber through the Roman lens. His representation of hierarchy — inspired from Osorio — outlines the 'theatre'-like layout, where nobles are allocated along the higher benches. While Maffei leaves his readers spell-bound with representations of the extravagance of the Malabar king, he does not shy away from identifying the 'empty superstitions' or the 'blind faith' of the Zamorin.[40] As the reader continues to grasp the essence of this region, the description of the actual encounter is brief and the focus immediately switches to the misdeeds of the council, with the involvement of the Arabs and Saracens.[41] Maffei, who covered a longer span (1415–1557) in his history, is forced to narrate details at a quicker pace than Osorio. Although this has resulted in succinct translations of key moments, such as this interaction, it reveals his stylistic choices. His precision with intertextual references such as 'tetraphoro' or 'eteromallo' and accuracy with comparisons of Greco-Roman traditions gives a more comprehensive insight into India. Reasons for this could have been correspondence with Jesuits like Alessandro Valignano (1539–1606), who consulted with Maffei and stressed the accuracy of details as part of his work.[42] Moreover, Maffei's translation offers a glimpse of how those Europeans who did not travel to India were still able to compare it with Greco-Roman traditions based on factual accounts received through their training in the *studia humanitatis*. Evidently, his description is rich in classical intertextual references, in addition to creating a visual framework for his readers.

---

[36] Maffei, pp. 26–27.
[37] Strabo, 'Book V', *Geography* (Loeb's Classics, Harvard University Press, 1917), pp. 332–33.
[38] Maffei, p. 27.
[39] Maffei, p. 27.
[40] Maffei, p. 26.
[41] Maffei, p. 27.
[42] Josef Wicki (ed.), *Documenta Indica*, vol. XIII, letter 55 (Monumenta Historica Societatis Iesu, 1975), p. 818.

Both Osorio and Maffei illustrate classical echoes and offer unique neoclassical representations of India. Their descriptions are not identical because of the myriad range of sources they used. Contrary to the prose texts, Faria and Baianus translated Camões's epic, *Os Lusiadas*. Camões spent a major portion of his life travelling through the perilous Indian Ocean, while crafting his poem in the classical style. Throughout the poem, he echoes Vergil's *Aeneid*.[43] Like Cicero for prose literature, Vergil enjoyed a similar fame for poetry among humanists. Vergil describes the tumultuous journey taken by Aeneas to found Rome; consequently, Camões's poem can be seen in the light of his own struggles as a Portuguese resident in the east, thus illustrating the journey of the Portuguese through Aeneas's analogy. Hence, I examine whether the Latin translations insert Vergilian echoes or if are they faithful translations from the Portuguese epic. Canto VII outlines Gama's successful expedition to Calicut.

Thomas Faria, a resident of Lisbon, dedicated his translation to Philip III (r. 1598–1621), without directly acknowledging Camões.[44] He states that his translation was from a work 'written over fifty years ago'.[45] As Faria's work was published in 1622, his comment of 'fifty years' is an indication of Camões's poem, which was published in 1572. Like Camões, he frequently imitates classical verses from the *Aeneid*. His translation begins with 'arma virosque cano' [I sing of arms and men] imitating Vergil's famous introduction to Aeneas's turbulent journey. Examining the interaction in Canto VII, I analyse the extent to which it is faithful to the original poem and where in particular Faria has inserted classical references. Camões wrote each stanza with eight lines, whereas Faria varies between eight and ten lines, though sometimes he uses fewer, especially after a stanza of more than eight lines. Canto VII in the translation has 669 lines, whereas the Portuguese has 696 lines. There is no fixed, recognizable pattern that allows us to determine his technique of translation; nevertheless, there are a few features worth noting.

Camões introduces Calicut in Stanza 16.[46] Comparing this stanza briefly, Faria writes:

> Clara Calecutii fessi pertingere nauta.
> Ista Malabareas vrbs vincit maenibus vrbes,
> Diues opum, locuples auri, et lux vnica terrae[47]

[The weary sailors reached their destination, Calecut. This city in Malabar surpasses all others in riches; it is wealthy in resources, rich in gold, and the sole light of the Indian land.]

[43] Camões, *Os Lusíadas*, Leitura, Prefacio, e notas de Álvaro Júlio da Costa Pimpão (Instituto Camões, Ministério dos Negócios Estrangeiros, 2000), p. 1. References to this work will be cited as Camões and followed by the page number. English translations are taken from Camoens, *The Lusiads*, trans. by William C. Atkinson (Penguin, 1952), cited as Atkinson followed by the page number.

[44] Adamson, *Memoirs of the Life and Writings of Luis de Camoens*, p. 79; Thomas Faria, *Lvsiadvm Libri Decem* (Ex officina Genardi de Vinea, 1622). References to the latter will be cited as Faria, followed by the folio number.

[45] Faria, Preface.

[46] Camões, p. 304; Atkinson, p. 167.

[47] Faria, fol. 94^r.

Faria adds a few more details to describe Calicut, whereas Camões focuses on how the Portuguese proceeded to this city. His 'Ista Malabares urbs vincit maenibus vrbes', seems like an elaborate translation of 'Porque esta era a cidade, das milhores' [for this had been [one of] the best cities]. Furthermore, Faria echoes Vergil by identifying Calicut as 'diues opum'. Vergil used this descriptor to recognize Carthage — Rome's most significant enemy. Faria further describes this 'diues opum' with a few more details, seen only through Camões's use of 'milhores'. Faria's 'diues opum' is a stylistic choice for translating 'milhores' and needs further attention.

Vergil's use of this phrase illustrated the strained connection between Carthage and Rome. Through its classical use, 'diues opum' alludes to the difficulties Portugal would encounter with Calicut. The translation was published in 1622, by which time Europeans would have been aware of Portugal's political dealings with Calicut. Faria's use of this phrase at the beginning may seem pre-emptive but illustrates the history of the connections Portugal had established with India since 1498. Faria also inserts 'diues opum' for Mombaça and Malacca, suggesting the riches observed in these locations, but also seems to remind readers of the struggles the Portuguese encountered in these regions.[48] Consequential to these turbulent connections with these locations, Faria was conscious about his use of 'diues opum' to outline the wealth of this region and to emphasize the turbulent relations that were yet to cross their paths. This can be proven by how differently he describes regions where the Portuguese succeeded in their tumults such as Goa ('beautiful Goa'), or Diu ('courageous Diu').[49] Hence, like the prose versions, even Faria explains the riches of Calicut, but also gives a hint of how Portugal, like Rome, would have to defeat this opulent city.

Expanding on the theme of opulence, Faria continues to explore the wealth Gama observed on this expedition. Indeed, his translation helps in identifying the wealth amassed by locals, and the years of turmoil which the Portuguese embark upon following this interaction. In this case, Faria enumerates details of Gama's use of the palanquin. Like the prose versions, Camões explains the 'palanquin' as 'a portable (portátil leito), a rich bed, they offered to him (as is customarily used)', Faria says, 'and he is carried on the shoulder of men on a litter (lecticam) to the royal palace, as is used by the Malabaris since antiquity'.[50] Evidently Faria follows Camões's description, using Cicero's vocabulary, but lacks the latter's clarity in outlining the number of men involved. Faria's choice of vocabulary showcases his intertextual reference, although his choice may also have been for metrical purposes.[51]

---

48   Faria, Canto I, fol. 9^r, Canto II, fol. 23^v.
49   Faria, Canto II, fol. 23^r.
50   Camões, p. 311; Atkinson, p. 169.
51   See notes 44 and 45.

Elaborating upon this extravagance, Faria describes the king's physical appearance. To capture the significance of this encounter, he explains how the king is embellished as follows:

> His dictis Aulam ingreditur Dux gama potentis
> Induperatoris, lecto lucent smaragdis
> Accubat ille, grauem gestu se ostendit et auro
> Antextum cingit pannum, diadema supremam
> Ornabat frontem gemmis, auroque coruscans.
> Assistitque senex, regi quandoque virentis
> Huic folium genibus flexis qui porrigit herbae.[52]

[Having said these things, the noble Gama enters the hall of the mighty emperor, whose couch gleams with emeralds. He lies there, displaying his grave demeanour, wrapped in a cloth interwoven with gold, a diadem adorning his lofty brow, glittering with jewels and sparkling with gold. An old man stands next to the king, occasionally offering him, on bended knees, a leaf of a green herb.]

Unlike Osorio and Maffei's descriptions, Faria is specific in recognizing the jewels ('smaragdis' — a green stone) and the crown ('diadema supremam frontem'). Portugal had been an ally of Spain since the Iberian Union of 1580. Faria seems to indicate Portugal's discovery of this region and possible access to its wealth through this detail. Nevertheless, this is also one of Faria's patterns to add to details already included by Camões. Description of the king's wealth is then intertwined with his habit of consuming betel leaf. Here, Faria foregoes providing any further detail of the species of this leaf. Since this translation circulated in the seventeenth century, readers would have been aware of this species through previous descriptions made available in Latin and other vernacular languages. Dedicating a stanza to the representation of the Zamorin and his customs helps in establishing the importance given to both this region and its kingdom. Early modern commentators such as Manuel de Faria Sousa have explored how Gama can be seen as a portrayal of Aeneas, aiding in building Portugal's image as the 'New Rome'.[53] In this context, Faria's attempt at using details such as 'diues opum' or exploring the king's wealth extensively helps in measuring his stylistic choices. Translating it into Latin showcases India's appearance in this garb, and the Portuguese attempt to develop and maintain its position as the 'New Rome'.

Faria meticulously continues to build India's image in Latin by providing details of the king's council. Like Camões, he explains the groups of Naires, Poleas (not mentioned in the prose texts) and the Brahmins. He translates the Naires as

---

[52]   Faria, fol. 99[r].
[53]   This a recurring theme in his commentary. Manuel de Faria Sousa, *Lvsiadas de Lvuis de Camoens* (Ivan Sanchez, A costa de Pedro Coello, 1639).

Nayribus est vitium, sunt magna piacula, tangent
Si fortasse illos Poleae, nam ritus vtrinque
Nullus abest, turpes qua purificantur, et vndis
Sese iterum, atque iterum, pollutaque corpora purgant.[54]

[For the Naires it is a sin, a great offence, if any of the Poleas should
happen to touch them, for they spare no ritual by which they may cleanse
themselves of this filth, washing themselves and their polluted bodies over
and over again in water.]

Here, Faria Sousa, Camões's commentator, outlines how Camões echoes Vergil's
description included as 'Pera os Naires é, certo, grande vício' [For the Naires
it is, certainly, a great offence].[55] Faria comes close to Camões's expression
and therefore seems to imitate Vergil as well. Hence, Faria inserts classical
references through faithful translations of the Portuguese and by inserting
intertextual references. This can also be seen in his description of Brahmins,

Antiquum nomen, sublimique ordine summum
Religionis opus sortitur Bragmana semper
Namque Deis ornat falsas, ac praeparat aras,
Pythagorae praecepta colit, qui Palladis arti
Imposuit primus nomen...[56]

[The work of religion always falls to the lot of the Brahmin, an ancient
name exalted in its lofty rank. For it is he who prepares and decorates altars
for the gods and who follows the teachings of Pythagoras who first gave a
name to the art of Pallas [i.e. philosophy].]

Here, Faria offers additional details for Brahmins as 'Pythagorae praecepta'.
There was a long tradition among humanists to describe and compare
Brahminic practices with Pythagoreanism.[57] Faria's comparison enables
Europeans to identify Brahmins through their philosophical training. The
extract outlines the king's administrative council and their religious practices,
which were distinctly different from Christians'. His translation of 'Bramenes
são os seus religiosos, Nome antigo e de grande proeminência' [Their priests
are called Brahmins, a name ancient and of great pre-eminence] as 'Religionis
opus sortitur Bragmana semper Namque Deis ornat falsas' clearly outlines
what differentiated this group from the Portuguese. Faria's 'falsas aras' is an
additional comment to their sacred practices, outlined through 'religiosos' in
the Portuguese. Furthermore, in Stanza 17, Camões gives a broad explanation
of the various faiths observed among locals in this region. Here, he examines
idol worshippers as 'alguns os Ídolos adoram, Alguns os animais que entre eles
moram' [some worship idols, some the animal-like figures that live among
them], which is translated as 'hic mandata colunt, alii simulacra deorum Falsa,

---

[54]   Faria, fol. 96ᵛ.
[55]   Faria Sousa, p. 269.
[56]   Faria, fol. 97ʳ.
[57]   Faria Sousa, p. 272.

alii brutis tribuunt animantibus aras' [in this place, some worship false idols of gods, a few pay tribute to the altars with brutish creatures].[58] Evidently, Faria is not translating verbatim. His 'brutis animantibus' clearly captures the essence of Camões's 'os animais'. Álvaro Júlio da Costa identifies Camões's tendency of using 'bruto' to represent customs and traditions unfamiliar to Europeans as yet another example of how Europeans viewed the world beyond their borders.[59] Additionally, as part of this encounter, Faria inserts an admonition against idol worship:

> O superi funestum auertite crimen,
> Decepti falsum ante Deum sua flectere Lusi
> Genua parant, prohibit diuinum lumine flamen.
> Numina falsa aris, foedisque insculpta figuris
> Aere, ac argento, lignis, et marmore duro,
> Aspiceres varios gestus, deformia vultu
> Corpora. Sic hominum daemon fera corda premebat.[60]

> [O gods above, avert this dreadful crime! The Lusians, deceived, prepare to bend their knees before a false god. The divine spirit of light forbids you to behold false gods, inscribed on altars with vile figures of bronze, silver, wood, and hard marble, various gestures and bodies deformed in appearance. This is how the demon oppresses savage hearts.]

In this case, Faria's use of 'foedis figuris' is comparable to Vergil's 'terribiles uisu formae'.[61] Both poets outline the abhorrence observed in the exhibition of the idols worshipped by their protagonist's enemy. Additionally, Faria's repetitive use of 'falsa' reiterates the fallacies of this practice to his readers. Indeed, Faria follows a similar trend for descriptions of Islamic believers in this region.

In the same stanza, Camões describes the Muslims in this region as 'vicioso' [vicious], translated in a less harsh tone in this instance [mahometica quidam]. However, in Stanza 33, Faria translates 'o culto Mahomético trouxessem' [they embraced the Islamic belief], as 'tunc dogmata vatis infandi sumpsit, Mahomet...' [then he [the king Pyrimalius] accepted the decrees of the unspeakable prophet, Mahomet].[62] His use of 'infandi' here translates as 'unspeakable' which encompasses the Portuguese method of expressing their vehemence against this group. Hence, through the comparison of this section Faria clearly adds to the novelty of translating India, simultaneously showing traces of how neoclassical Latinity facilitates the representation of Portugal as the 'New Rome'. His endeavours illustrate his attempts at translating and adhering to classical tradition making features of India commensurable to a seventeenth-century European reader. In some cases, his erudition in the

---

[58] Faria, fol. 94ʳ.
[59] Camões, Os Lusíadas, Leitura, Prefacio, e notas de Álvaro Júlio da Costa Pimpão (Instituto Camões, Ministério dos Negócios Estrangeiros, 2000).
[60] Faria, fols 97ᵛ–98ʳ.
[61] Faria Sousa, p. 286.
[62] Camões, pp. 304, 308; Atkinson, pp. 167, 169, 170; Faria, fols 94ʳ, 96ʳ.

classical tradition is embedded in Camões's method of imitating ancient Latin poetry, whereas in cases like 'diues opum' he alludes to how classical texts continued to influence the execution of translations. Therefore, like the prose Latin texts, Faria's translation offers the same details with classical echoes, composed in a dactylic hexameter. He provides a comprehensive translation of Camões's epic poem, frequently by imitating classical Latin poetry.

Andreas Baianus, a contemporary of Faria, translated this poem in 1625. Baianus provides a succinct, concise version of this epic. We are not informed whether or not Baianus had access to Faria's translation. Massimiliano Malavasi describes his Portuguese nationality and explains his residence in Goa prior to moving to Europe.[63] Not much is known about his early years, except the mention of his training in Latin at a school in Goa.[64] His translation is a key feature to measuring his early training in Latin and residence in Goa.

Justino Mendes de Almeida, in the introduction to the facsimile reproduction of this 1625 work, emphasizes Baianus's method of concision. He compares the length for Stanza 54 of Canto I and illustrates Baianus's brevity in translating this epic.[65] Examining Canto VI, Baianus explores Gama's visit to Calicut,

> Ventum erat ad littus, quod Evoo clauditur Indo
> Gangeque terreno ducente exordia caelo
> Nunc age gens Invicta nevo, qui in Marte triumphos
> Quaeris: iam tandem venisti: en aurea tellus.[66]

[They had now arrived on land that was enclosed in the east by the Indus and the Ganges, which flows forth from the earthly paradise. Now come, O invincible people, who seek triumphs in war: at last, you have arrived. Behold, the golden land.]

There are a few features that need attention when compared to the Portuguese. For instance, Baianus translates 'aurea' to suggest the Portuguese 'riquezas abundante!'. In this case, Faria used 'ditissima' which is closer to the Portuguese; however, Baianus's choice aligns to the notion of poetry more closely in this case. Furthermore, Baianus's use of 'en' encompasses Faria's 'ante oculos vobis astat ditissima'.[67] Evidently, Baianus employs brevity to narrate the Portuguese voyages, instead of adding details or following a literal translation. A few more examples from this section will further showcase this method.

Baianus introduces Calicut closer to the Portuguese version, 'Visa quae Calecut'. Note, even for metrical purposes Baianus does not spell Calicut as

---

[63] Massimiliano Malavasi, 'Accademico di trope accademie: Andrea Baiano e la vita culturale romana di inizio Seicento', *Le accademie a Roma nel Seicento* (Edizioni di Storia e Letteratura, 2020), p. 71, Rossi, *Pinacotheca* (1643), pp. 258–59.

[64] Adamson, p. 88.

[65] Mendes de Almeida, *Os Lusíadas de Luís de Camões traduzidos em versos Latinos por Frei André Baião Natural da India Portuguesa* (Junta de Investigacões do Ultramar, 1972), pp. VIII–IX. References to this work will be cited as Baianus followed by the page number.

[66] Baianus, p. 243.

[67] Faria, fol. 91ᵛ.

'Calecutt', prior to the elision observed in his construction of 'quae ad' followed by 'antigua ubi'. If his choice of spelling were based on his local knowledge/ pronunciation of this place, then it gives an insight to how Latin may have been colloquially used in these parts.[68] Scholarship by Joan-Pau Rubiés offers essential signposting to explore Baianus's approach. In 'Outsiders and Insiders', Rubiés explores François Bernier's description of Mughal India. He argues that Bernier's description switches between an insider and an outsider's view, based on the details he offers in his account.[69] Baianus's choice of spelling Calicut needs to be explored in a similar way. Analysing Baianus's description further, he does not add any descriptors like Faria to identify Calicut as 'diues opum'. In fact, any use of adjectives is a clear indication of their presence in the Portuguese version of this poem.[70] Instead of expanding the stanza with details of Calicut's opulence, he enumerates this as 'in regno Malabaris erat quippe optimas...' [in the kingdom of Malabar, which had been great].[71] Hence, he accomplishes his translation in a brief manner, imitating Camões in his descriptions.

Following Camões's footsteps in translating the wealth of this kingdom, Baianus's translation of how Gama was led to the court is fascinating.

> Dein hominum gestata humeris rheda excipit,
> Rheda cubilis erat, procerum gestamen instar eoum.[72]

[Then he is received on a chariot borne on the shoulders of men — a carriage similar to a litter used for the conveyance of eastern nobles.]

There are two things worth noting in this extract. First, he translates 'portátil leito ũa rica cama' as 'rheda cubilis'. His is the only translation that uses the term 'rheda' for a 'palanquin'. This is not a choice based on metrical purpose, as we have seen in Faria's use of 'lectica'. Lack of any details of interaction of Baianus's early life in India make it much harder to trace his vocabulary choices. Indeed, this is another example where we may see him as an 'insider', using 'rheda' either through his connection with locals or his knowledge of local languages. What this choice indicates is an attempt to describe the litter as a method of transport in its own right, as opposed to a 'bed, which was used to transport'. Indeed, there are numerous examples in classical Latin works that use 'raeda', but Baianus's use of this term explains his stylistic choice and possibly emphasizes his connection to India. Additionally, like Maffei, his use of 'rheda' clearly indicates four people carrying the carriage, which has not been

---

[68] In this regard, Paul Gwynne has noted such details in Benci's *Quinque Martyres*. In particular, Gwynne examines Benci's way of pronouncing Salcete throughout his work and explains how Benci follows the Greek method of declining this place name in his epic poem, Benci, p. 9; however, there is no such explanation for Baianus's choice of spelling.

[69] Rubiés, 'Outsiders and Insiders: European Perceptions of India and the Problem of Cultural Distance', in *India and the Traveller: Aspects of Travelling Identity* (Bloomsbury, 2022), pp. 23–44, doi:10.5040/9789354359408.ch-001.

[70] See note 78.

[71] Baianus, p. 250.

[72] Baianus, p. 258.

outlined by Camões or Faria.[73] Hence, while Camões's vocabulary portrays the portable nature of this bed, Baianus gives a more vivid image of a culturally characteristic object used for travel by locals. He emphasizes the number of people carrying the bed, thus alluding to the hierarchical society of India, prior to the period of Portuguese colonization.

Elaborating on the wealth of Calicut, he engages with the description of the king's council. Following Camões's sequence, Baianus introduces groups of people as 'pars dicta Polea Naira pars' [some are called Polea, some as Naires].[74] In the same canto, he uses this construction to explain details of Islamic believers and idol worshippers as well.[75] Here, Baianus's choice is not necessarily done for metrical purposes, as Faria demonstrates a different approach for this group. Hence, Baianus's stylistic choice is telling of his observations of how groups of people are distinguished between each other in India. Yet again, this is one of the ways in which we can reconstruct his observations of his life in Goa, or any other region in the country.

Like Camões and Faria, Baianus focuses on the Naires' participation in warfare.[76] Furthermore, all three versions of this poem explain how the Naires did not form alliances or mix with the Poleas in any way. Even though the mention of 'tetraphoro/lectica/rheda' helps in measuring subaltern positions in this region, this detail needs further attention. European accounts frequently indicate the encounters between the 'self' and the 'other'; through this detail they emphasize societal taboos clearly observed in the Malabar region. While Baianus explains this as 'nequeunt miscari sanguine Naires' [the Naires cannot mix [their] blood] Faria says, 'Nayres est vitium, sunt magna piacular, tangent... Si fortasse illos Poleae, nam ritus utrinque... Nullus abest, turpas qua purificantur, et undis sese iterum, atque iterum, pollutaque corpora purgant' [It is vice for the Naires, they are extremely pious, for if they touch the men of Polea, for there is no ceremony absent from both sides, how they are cleansed from the defiled, they [Naires] wash [their] polluted bodies again and again with water].[77] Clearly, Camões observed this through his journey and comments on it. However, the translations explore this detail either by suggesting the absence of inter-caste unions (Baianus) or by explaining the need for a self-cleansing ritual (Faria). Hence, analysing these Latin translations evidently aids in measuring characteristic practices which formulated the complex social fabric of India.

Like his use of the *pars...pars* construction to introduce Naires and Poleas, his description of Brahmins is equally fascinating. Baianus indicates them through the term *sophis*, instead of the Pythagorean precepts like Faria. Translating

---

[73]   Perseus online dictionary.
[74]   Baianus, p. 256.
[75]   Baianus, p. 250.
[76]   Baianus, p. 256.
[77]   Faria, fol. 96ᵛ. Even Osorio explains how unions are formed between people belonging to the same class or group, fol. 35ᵛ.

as 'wise, sage, shrewd', Baianus's 'sophis' encompasses all these meanings as
has been explored by various other European writers.[78] Baianus's choice of
vocabulary showcases a conscious effort to recognize these groups based on
his sources and his awareness of both European and local understandings
of these details. This helps in reconstructing the sources he may have read.
Comparing Faria's method of spelling Brahmins as 'bragmana', Baianus gives
us 'Brachmannas'. Certainly, there are examples where the 'g' is interchanged
with the 'ch'. Baianus's use of 'nn' is telling of the way the term may have been
pronounced by locals, another example, like his description of Calicut, where
we may see him as an 'insider'.[79] Exploring this section further, Brahmins
formed an integral part of the Zamorin's court and performed priestly duties.
Before attending the king, as has been noted, Gama's entourage visited a place
of worship, which Baianus has also described.

To depict idol worship, Baianus uses various methods and vocabulary to fully
encapsulate Camões's comprehension. Baianus translates Camões's 'animais',
as 'pecus indignis (infandum) altaribus' [some worship the abominable beast in
the unworthy altars]. Not word-for-word, but Baianus's use of 'pecus indignis'
gauges the essence of what Camões states as 'animais'. Note, here again we see
two different stylistic choices to describe idols. Faria uses 'brutis animanitibus',
whereas Baianus focuses on the 'animais' and offers 'pecus indignis' followed by
his 'infandum' in parentheses. Mention of this practice as 'infandum' explains
European perceptions of worship, whereas the 'pecus' gives a clearer visual
representation of how the idols were designed. Like instances where we see
Baianus as an 'insider', this is one of the examples where his role as an 'outsider'
is clear. The range of vocabulary also illustrates the wide array of imagery
available to Europeans to depict this scene with such clarity.

Baianus's description of the temple in this translation needs further attention.

> Apparet templum. Inuisunt, portisque subintrant
> Prodigiosa deum hic stygio dictata tyranno
> Numina...[80]

[A temple appears. They approach and enter beneath the gates. Here
monstrous gods, decreed by the Stygian tyrant, are worshipped.]

Camões clearly indicates the use of images that resemble demons, and his
insertion of 'abomináveis esculturas' adds emphasis to visual exhibitions of
the idols worshipped in the temple. In similar vein, Baianus indicates the same
idol through his use of 'stygio tyranno', thus drawing an infernal comparison.

---

[78]   Henry James Coleridge, *The Life and Letters of St. Francis Xavier* (1874), p. 157.
[79]   Benci also illustrates this trend when he uses the term 'religio,' where Gwynne notes that 'spellings
common in the sixteenth century, but alien to classical usage, can be found: relligio (religion, *religio*),
'Vt fera relligio, quae duro ut robore quercus', p. 156. Comparing this example with Baianus, the
interchangeable use of 'ch' and 'g' was common in early modern literature; however, the use 'nn' seems
to be Baianus's stylistic choice, possibly based on his own experience and residence in India.
[80]   Baianus, p. 259.

Note, even Camões draws this comparison in various other sections of the poem; however, Baianus's inclusion of this comparison here is significant, yet again allowing us to consider whether his descriptions are a window on to his own visual experience of such temples or if he is drawing on other European travel literature. Thirdly, his comparison here may also reflect his training in classical literature and poetry, thus drawing on intertextual references as well. Therefore, Baianus's method of translation raises many aspects of how he carefully translated Camões's sections on idol worship.

Faria feels the need to add details to make his composition more relatable to his readers. Contrarily, Baianus seems to offer a visual representation rather than just a monolithic translation of this epic poem. Indeed, this can be seen through his narration of the 'rheda' and idol worship. This can further be proven through his description of the Zamorin's encounter with Gama. Faria focuses on the jewels — their colours, and various forms used to adorn the Zamorin. Instead, Baianus focuses on his honour and dignity ('fulget honos, dignusque' [he gleams with honour and dignity]), characteristically employing stylistic brevity to suggest a parallel between the lustre of his jewels and his illustrious character. While Faria indicates the king reclining on his bed ('accubat lecto'), Baianus instead choses to depict him reclining on an 'aureo thalamo' [golden bed]. Indeed, this detail describes the furniture upon which the Zamorin was first seen by Europeans; however, the multiple ways of translating this object showcases their *copia verborum* and the rhythm that dictates their choices in this instance. Both Faria and Baianus showcase the king's opulence through this furniture, but one defines the colour of jewels while the other simply iterates the wealth fixed on it. Both contribute to improving the visual representation of this king through this epic poem. The reader is enthralled with the extravagances seen in this court. This opulence allows them to understand the reasons the Portuguese may have wanted to establish friendly agreements with this court — its propitious location which would enable control over a longer stretch along the western coast.

* * * * *

The aim of this article has been to examine how India is represented in Latin translations — characteristic objects, customs, and its peoples. By analysing the same passage in different texts, it is evident how Neo-Latin authors use their training in the *studia* to explore novel techniques to outline features of India — unfamiliar and unexplored by Romans.

The four examples discussed facilitate the examination of India's appearance in neoclassical Latinity. The nature of the chosen examples also reveals how some of them also contribute towards representing Portugal as the 'New Rome'. Although this has not been the focus of this article, it offers a glimpse of how Neo-Latin literature of Portuguese voyages to the east, and of India specifically, need further attention to explore this field. Furthermore, the nature of the chosen texts (historiography for prose and epic poetry), the patrons commissioning these works, and the period in which it was published have influenced some of their linguistic and stylistic choices. These choices further illustrate the circulation and use of classical Latin literature and contemporary vernacular sources they used, with the exception of Baianus. We are not informed of his sources, nor his early background, which makes his translation an important one — especially, considering his years spent in India. By tracing the details enumerated as part of this journey, we are informed how each author has meticulously engaged with varied choices of classical traditions in order to portray the exact same details of early modern India. These choices reveal the contours and limitations of Neo-Latin in representing early modern India.

War and the Walls within: A Study of *A General Theory of Oblivion* by José Eduardo Agualusa

ALEXANDRA LOURENÇO DIAS

King's College London

The epigraph to Jorge Luis Borges's *El Aleph*, drawn from Francis Bacon's *Essays LVIII* — 'Solomon saith: there is no new thing upon the earth [...] all novelty is but oblivion'[1] — frames a philosophical meditation on memory and the illusion of innovation. Echoing Plato's theory of anamnesis, Bacon suggests that what seems new is merely knowledge forgotten and then recovered. Borges develops this idea by imagining a mystical point in space that contains all other points, destabilizing linear conceptions of time and originality. In *El Aleph*, all things coexist — past, present, and future — collapsing the boundary between remembering and inventing. Borges further explores the limits of cognition in 'Funes, el Memorioso',[2] a short story in which Ireneo Funes, after a traumatic accident, acquires a perfect, inescapable memory. This 'gift' renders him incapable of abstraction or generalization; every moment is experienced as unique and unrepeatable: 'Pensar es olvidar diferencias, es generalizar, abstraer' [To think is to forget differences, it is to generalize, to abstract], Borges writes.[3] The story functions as an allegory for epistemological excess: without forgetting, memory turns into a kind of imprisonment. Borges thus anticipates a central question for modern literature and philosophy alike — what role does oblivion play in the creation of meaning?

This deliberate act of forgetting is especially resonant within the context of the present study, which focuses on José Eduardo Agualusa's novel *A General Theory of Oblivion*,[4] particularly on the protagonist, whose seclusion is reconfigured through the interplay between memory and forgetting, both as existential conditions and as responses to trauma and historical violence.

Across the novel, oblivion is framed as both a personal refuge and a broader political condition, intricately linked to memory and survival — a dynamic embodied in the protagonist, Ludo, short for Ludovica Fernandes Mano. She is a Portuguese woman who isolates herself in an apartment in Luanda,

---

[1]   Jorge Luis Borges, *El Aleph* (1957) (Emecé, 1982), p. 3; my translation.
[2]   Idem, 'Funes, el Memorioso', in *Artificios* (1944), repr. in *Obras completas* (Emecé, 1974), p. 485.
[3]   Ibidem, p. 490; my translation.
[4]   For the purposes of this study, we have used the English edition of the novel translated by Daniel Hahn: *A General Theory of Oblivion* (Harvill Secker, 2015).

Portuguese Studies vol. 41 no. 2 (2025), doi:10.1353/port.00042, 207–29
© Modern Humanities Research Association 2025

Angola, bricking herself into the flat just before the country's independence in 1975. Her seclusion is preceded by what she calls '*the accident*' — an event from her youth kept deliberately vague until the closing pages, when the reader finally learns of the episode that drove her to cut herself off entirely from the world.[5] Ludo arrives in Angola as an adult, with her sister and brother-in-law, but when both die, she becomes increasingly fearful of the violence and upheaval associated with the end of Portuguese colonial rule. After an attempted robbery, she walls herself into the apartment, cutting off all contact with the outside world. Over the course of nearly thirty years, she survives by rationing food, collecting rainwater, and reading her brother-in-law's books in a library that proves vital not only to her intellectual resilience but also to her physical survival. Ludo keeps track of her thoughts and memories by writing on the walls of the apartment — sometimes poetry, sometimes diary entries — forming a fragmented chronicle of both her internal experience and the changing world beyond the walls. These inscriptions do more than merely record; they become acts of meaning-making, attempts to impose coherence on the disintegration of both personal and historical time. In this sense, oblivion gradually transforms into a creative and interpretive space. Through her writing and attentive observation, Ludo sustains a fragile, self-fashioned link to the world she has renounced. Through these solitary acts, she resists erasure and affirms the endurance of memory within isolation. Read through her experience, the novel reframes forgetting not as a passive absence but as a dynamic, if precarious, strategy of endurance — a means of reassembling a fractured self in the face of loss. Read as a national allegory, *A General Theory of Oblivion* portrays post-independence Angola as marked by collective amnesia, where the aftermath of violence compels individuals to assume new identities, retreat into madness, or pursue acts of self-reinvention. Ludo's prolonged isolation thus becomes a metaphor for the historical amnesia and psychological toll engendered by decolonization. Although the novel gradually broadens its scope to incorporate a network of interwoven characters and narratives — as will be discussed later in this article — Ludo remains its anchoring presence: a figure of silence, erasure, and reluctant witness to Angola's transition from colony to postcolonial nationhood.

In doing so, Agualusa's novel extends Borges's philosophical tensions — between total recall and the necessity of forgetting, between presence and erasure — into the realm of lived political experience. These questions are not confined to metaphysical speculation but emerge within contexts marked by upheaval, silence, and rupture. In this light, *A General Theory of Oblivion* becomes more than a story of isolation; it is a meditation on the ethics of memory and survival.

---

[5]   In time, it becomes clear that she was the victim of sexual violence, the assault leaving her pregnant with a child she later gave away. Her father's response to what had happened was one of rage rather than protection, his violence fuelled by the belief that the incident had brought shame upon the family.

The novel's very title invites a dual reading, as both a theoretical construct and a narrative of personal endurance. The author complicates the Angolan war narrative by shifting the emphasis away from collective struggle and militarized resistance that are so often foregrounded in Lusophone African literature from the mid-twentieth century onwards, especially when dealing with the period encompassing both wars. Instead, he offers an alternative form of witnessing — one that values partial knowledge, silence, and the protective power of forgetting. This reorientation challenges conventional frameworks of historical visibility, asking what it means to remember — and what it costs to forget — in the aftermath of colonial collapse. This reading resonates with Paul Ricoeur's reflections in *Memory, History, Forgetting*, particularly his notion that forgetting is not simply a failure of memory but a condition that makes remembering possible. Ricoeur's idea of 'happy forgetting'[6] finds a subtle analogue in Ludo's self-imposed isolation: through selective withdrawal, she reclaims a measure of agency and constructs meaning in the face of historical violence. Her retreat, while extreme, reveals forgetting not as erasure but as a strategy of survival.

Building on this perspective, this article examines the dual themes at the heart of Agualusa's novel: external conflict and internal retreat. Ludo's isolation becomes a metaphor for the psychic scars, the boundaries that history and trauma inscribe upon the self. Her apartment is both sanctuary and tomb, echoing Borges's Funes in its claustrophobic abundance of memory and Agualusa's Angola in its suspended transition. The article also argues that Agualusa reconfigures the Angolan war narrative by shifting focus away from external conflict. The analysis unfolds in three parts. Part I lays out the philosophical foundations of memory and oblivion, drawing on the works of Ricoeur and on Genette's theory of the paratext, with particular attention to the role of the title. Part II situates *A General Theory of Oblivion* within the historical context of post-independence Angola and the broader field of Lusophone war literature, examining how Agualusa repositions the genre and employs digital humanities tools to map the novel's structure and thematic constellations. Part III explores the spatial and poetic dimensions of oblivion as embodied by Ludo, drawing on intertextual and philosophical frameworks — including Borges, Eco, Rilke, and Rowlands.

A General Theory of Oblivion has attracted substantial scholarly attention for its probing of the relationship between literature and history. Critical discourse has emphasized its sustained engagement with narrative consciousness, the act of writing, and the capacity of literature to serve as a site of critical reflection.[7]

---

[6] Paul Ricoeur, *Memory, History, Forgetting*, trans. by Kathleen Blamey and David Pellauer (University of Chicago Press, 2004), pp. 501–05.

[7] Among the many critical contributions, the work of Anna Wolny, Sakiru Adebayo, Dorothée Boulanger, and Emanuelle Santos is particularly noteworthy for the precision with which each articulates a distinct interpretative framework. Wolny reads Ludo's confinement as a metaphor for Angola's suspended political transition, charting her gradual movement toward a relational sense of

Extending these perspectives, this study introduces a new methodological dimension by integrating digital humanities tools to visualize the novel's structure and thematic dispersion. Through this interdisciplinary approach — merging close reading with narrative theory, text mining, and philosophical reflection — the article argues that Agualusa reconceptualizes forgetting not as erasure, but as a productive form of historical reconfiguration and imaginative survival.

I.

Is it possible that history 'overly remembers' some events at the expense of others? Paul Ricoeur's *Memory, History, Forgetting* addresses this reciprocal relationship between remembering and forgetting, revealing how it affects both the perception of historical experience and the construction of historical narrative. Ricoeur does not treat forgetting merely as the negation of memory but explores its complex roles, distinguishing between forgetting as the effacement of traces, the persistence of latent traces, and the forgetting of recollection — each with implications for the reliability and ethical dimensions of historical representation.[8] He shows that forgetting is not simply a loss but also a *condition* for memory, enabling selectivity and intelligibility in how the past is recalled. This dialectic culminates in his exploration of the possibility of an *ars oblivionis*, or 'art of forgetting', particularly in relation to forgiveness and reconciliation.[9] Here, forgetting is no longer a deficiency but becomes a moral and political necessity — an active element in healing historical wounds and shaping narrative identities. Through this hermeneutical approach, Ricoeur demonstrates that memory and forgetting are not opposites but interdependent forces that shape both individual and collective understandings of the past. In the chapter titled 'Forgetting', Paul Ricoeur explores the paradoxical nature of forgetting, arguing that it is not simply a cognitive failure or passive loss, but an active and necessary condition that enables memory to function meaningfully. He proposes the notion of 'happy forgetting', a conceptual counterpart to 'happy

identity; Adebayo interprets her withdrawal as a counter-archive that challenges and resists official historiography; Boulanger foregrounds the novel's metafictional structure as a critique of historical representation, viewing Ludo's self-imposed isolation as emblematic of both individual and collective psychic retreat; Santos, meanwhile, analyses how the narrative unsettles nationalist mythologies, exposing the performative and fragmented character of state power. Anna Wolny, 'Memórias de um cárcere voluntário: José Eduardo Agualusa, *Teoria geral do esquecimento*', *Romanica Cracoviensia*, 21.2 (2021), pp. 115–24, doi:10.4467/20843917RC.21.012.14067 [accessed 5 August 2025]; Sakiru Adebayo, 'The Anatomy of Oblivion in José Eduardo Agualusa's *A General Theory of Oblivion*', *Journal of the African Literature Association*, 12.2 (2018), pp. 218–33, doi:10.1080/21674736.2018.1528282 [accessed 5 August 2025]; Dorothée Boulanger, 'Writing History; Writing War', in *Fiction as History: Resistance and Complicities in Angolan Postcolonial Literature* (Legenda, 2022) <https://www.jstor.org/stable/j.ctv33b9px6.11> [accessed 5 August 2025]; Emanuelle Santos, 'Late Postcoloniality: State, Violence and Wealth in the Literatures of Early 21st Century Portuguese-speaking Africa' (unpublished doctoral thesis, University of Warwick, 2016), pp. 120–31.

8   Paul Ricoeur, idem, pp. 412–57.
9   Idem, p. 68; p. 412.

memory', suggesting that forgetting can be essential for well-being and mental clarity. This framework challenges our assumptions about history's authority and completeness, suggesting that memory must be selective in order to be coherent, and that oblivion can serve a protective, even generative, role. Ricoeur questions whether it is possible to speak of happy forgetting in the same way we speak of happy memory, ultimately arguing that forgetting lacks the event-like quality that characterizes memory, particularly its moment of recognition. Whereas a memory returns with a certain clarity and affective force — what he terms 'the small miracle of memory'[10] — forgetting is a more passive, untraceable process. Forgetting, he notes, is not an event but a condition that is only noticed retrospectively through the operations of memory itself. This asymmetry leads Ricoeur to conclude that forgetting cannot mirror memory in terms of fulfilment or achievement. Instead, he explores the possibility of an *ars oblivionis*, a counterpart to the *ars memoriae*, which might consist not of active erasure but of subtle, ethical practices of letting go — particularly in the context of forgiveness and historical reconciliation.[11]

This reflection opens a space for examining how memory and forgetting are shaped within literary form, particularly in *A General Theory of Oblivion*. Gérard Genette's concept of the paratext — those thresholds and framing devices that mediate a reader's encounter with a text — offers a complementary lens through which this work can be read as both staging and unsettling acts of memory. The novel exemplifies this interplay beginning with its title, which mimics the form of a scholarly treatise and thus frames it as a conceptual inquiry into forgetting. In doing so, it challenges the reader's *horizon of expectations*[12] and creates a productive tension between philosophical discourse and fictional narrative. As Genette observes, the paratext serves as 'the privileged site of a pragmatics and of a strategy, of an influence on the public [...] at the service of a better reception of the text'.[13] The narrative's strategic framing invites the reader to consider memory and oblivion as central concerns, while simultaneously complicating them through the fragmented and poetic form of the narrative itself. While *A General Theory of Oblivion* is not a philosophical treatise, its title works paratextually to pose questions that remain central throughout the novel: What is forgotten? What must be remembered? What role does forgetting play in survival?

As the reader soon learns, the novel was first conceived as a screenplay, with Ludo at its centre. Her radical withdrawal operates as a dual metaphor: on one level, it reflects the historical retreat of colonial power; on another, it embodies a psychological strategy of defence, resonating with Paul Ricoeur's

[10]   Idem, p. 495.
[11]   Ibidem.
[12]   Hans Robert Jauss, *Toward an Aesthetic of Reception* (1982), trans. by Timothy Bahti, 7th impression (University of Minnesota Press, 2005), pp. 22–23.
[13]   Gérard Genette, *The Architext: An Introduction*, trans. by Jane E. Lewin (University of California Press, 1992), p. 2.

notion of forgetting as a mechanism of self-preservation. Yet Ludo's experience of forgetting is not merely symbolic. As a Portuguese woman stranded in Angola at the end of empire, her retreat is also a deeply personal response to trauma — including the sexual violence she endured as a youth — and to her liminal, often precarious status in a transforming political landscape. Her agoraphobia, far from signalling simple psychological fragility, becomes a formal device through which the novel probes the limits and textures of historical remembrance. By emphasizing her confined vantage point and the poetic, fragmentary record she leaves behind, the novel foregrounds how memory and forgetting function as philosophical or political categories and as lived, gendered, and historically embedded practices. Ludo's eventual re-entry into the world at the novel's close reframes forgetting as a provisional, adaptive gesture — not erasure, but a means of survival, ethical transformation, and the possibility of renewed belonging.

This reimagining of oblivion as a creative and ethically charged act finds a structural echo in the novel's paratextual architecture. The title, revisited again through the lens of Genette, becomes an undecidable zone — a site of interpretive ambiguity where philosophical resonance meets narrative strategy. In this context, oblivion unfolds across political, historical, and deeply intimate registers, embedded within Ludo's subjective world. This interpretive framework sets the stage for a new set of questions: how is war, a dominant theme in post-1975 Angolan fiction, represented here? What is the significance of depicting war through the fragmentary, peripheral experiences of a vulnerable, reclusive woman — a character conceived by Agualusa as a metaphor for colonialism itself? And how do the spatial constraints of Ludo's self-imposed confinement shape both her character and the novel's broader meditation on history, trauma, and the ethics of remembrance?

II.

The shaping force of war in Angolan literature predates independence. As early as the seventeenth century, António de Oliveira de Cadornega's *História Geral das Guerras Angolanas* offered a literary-historiographical account of colonial conflict.[14] This long-standing entanglement of war and narrative carries through to contemporary fiction, particularly during and after the armed struggle for independence (1961–75) and the civil war that followed (1975–2002). Initiated in 1961, these conflicts ushered in a decades-long period of violence, political instability, and ideological realignment. The novel, more than poetry,

---

[14] António Filipe Soares situates Cadornega's *História Geral das Guerras Angolanas* within a 'period of creolization' in colonial literature (sixteenth to mid-nineteenth century), underscoring its significance as both a historical document and a work of literary expression; *Literatura angolana de expressão portuguesa* (Instituto Cultural Português / Edições Caravela, 1983), p. 27. The view is also shared by Ana Mafalda Leite, 'Angola', in *The Post-Colonial Literature of Lusophone Africa*, ed. by Patrick Chabal with Moema Parente Augel, David Brookshaw, Ana Mafalda Leite, and Caroline Shaw (Northwestern University Press, 1996), pp. 103–64 (p. 104).

offered a site for exploring the cultural, psychological, and ideological legacies of war, working through these experiences in both scope and narrative strategy.[15] While war has at times emerged as an explicit or dominant theme, it more often resurfaces in later narratives as a background condition, a residual trauma, or a symbolic structure that informs character, space, and memory.[16]

The Angolan novel of the mid-twentieth century, once anchored in representations of the colonial past, has been reconfigured as a literary project in which historical experience is aesthetically transfigured and a critical, patriotic consciousness engages with the complexities of nation-building.[17] In this reimagining of the novelistic form — particularly in the immediate fictional responses to the war — the term *war* not only recurs with notable frequency but has also become a central literary trope.[18] Its presence reflects both the material conditions of conflict and the symbolic weight it carries in shaping post-independence identity and memory.

In Angolan literature, the trope of war registers the history of the liberation struggle and opens imaginative space for utopian possibilities of freedom. In her seminal essay 'Utopian Eyes and Dystopian Writings in Angolan Literature', Ana Maria Martinho traces a trajectory from the revolutionary optimism of the independence era to the heterotopian and often dystopian visions of the post-independence period. In the 1960s and 1970s, guerrilla movements and writers such as Pepetela and Luandino Vieira invested literature with pan-African ideals, ancestral narratives, and anti-colonial resistance, producing works like *Mayombe* (1971), *As Aventuras de Ngunga* (1972), and *Luuanda* (1963) that celebrated ethnic diversity, linguistic hybridity, and the *musseques* [shanty towns] as sites of popular mobilization. From the 1980s, the utopian promise recedes, replaced by narratives of disillusionment — Pepetela's *A Geração da Utopia* (1992), Uanhenga Xitu's *O Ministro* (1993), and Manuel Rui's *Quem Me Dera Ser Onda* (1982) — while later heterotopian works, such as Ruy Duarte de Carvalho's *Vou Lá Visitar Pastores* (1999), explore plural, often conflicting, visions of national identity. For Martinho, the work of these authors remains both a witness to the wars that have indelibly shaped the nation and a critical arena for interrogating and reimagining its political and cultural trajectories.[19]

Within this literary space, war emerges as a constitutive element of the

---

[15]   Fernando Arenas, 'Angolan Literature: After Independence and under the Shadow of War', in *Lusophone Africa: Beyond Independence* (University of Minnesota Press, 2011), pp. 159–200 (pp. 159–60).

[16]   Carmen Lúcia Tindó Ribeiro Secco, in her article 'Por entre memórias e silêncios: representações literárias das guerras em Angola e Moçambique', examines how literature reworks the traumatic legacies of post-independence wars in Angola and Mozambique, framing them not simply as civil wars but as conflicts shaped by foreign intervention. Focusing on poetic responses, she highlights the power of literary imagination as a space for mourning, resistance, and memory (*Scripta*, 12.23 (2008), pp. 13–25).

[17]   Fernando Arenas, 'Angolan Literature'.

[18]   In the sense attributed to it by Lausberg in *Elements of Literary Rhetoric* [paragraph 176.2], p. 144.

[19]   Ana Maria Mão-de-Ferro Martinho, 'Utopian Eyes and Dystopian Writings in Angolan Literature', *Research in African Literatures*, 38.1 (2007), pp. 46–53.

narrative lexicon, recounting the conflicts that accompanied decolonization. It functions simultaneously as testimony to the political violence endured and as a vehicle for affirming the resilience of a people intent on reclaiming dignity amid the devastation of struggle, the trauma of massacre, and the precarious negotiation between death and survival. To a lesser extent, *war* also emerges in the Angolan literary field as a genre in its own right. Some of the most significant artistic responses to the conflict come from Pepetela, Sousa Jamba and Luandino Vieira, whose works consolidate key conventions of the war novel. These include a focus on battlefield settings, realistic depictions of combat and atrocity, and the portrayal of characters as politically and socially engaged individuals shaped by the microcosm of guerrilla warfare. Recurring themes include the internal contradictions of the ideological movements for which these characters fight, revealing the complexities and tensions of revolutionary struggle. Through such representations, both authors have contributed to the formation of the Angolan novel as a voice of dissent — occupying the space between historical reality and literary imagination. As Carmen Lúcia Tindó Secco argues, war occupies a central place in the Angolan postcolonial literary imagination, functioning not only as a historical reality but also as a symbolic and narrative engine. It serves as both a thematic axis and a structuring metaphor, shaping representations of national identity. In the context of the colonial war and the liberation struggle, literature frequently frames armed conflict as a necessary path to independence, with narratives celebrating heroism, sacrifice, and revolutionary ideals. Works from this period display a strong didactic and mobilizing impulse, aligning literary production with political and military objectives. The protracted civil war, however, adds a second and darker narrative layer, challenging earlier utopian visions; its violence, destruction, and moral fragmentation shift the tone from celebratory to critical, often exposing contradictions in postcolonial governance. This evolution is reflected in stylistic and thematic shifts: early works tend toward collectivist perspectives and a linear teleology aimed at liberation, whereas later works fragment this vision, incorporating personal trauma, localized perspectives, and morally ambiguous landscapes. Among the key contributors to this body of literature, Pepetela's *Mayombe* stands as an emblem of the liberation struggle, while his later novels register disillusionment; Manuel Rui and Arnaldo Santos similarly depict the everyday realities of war, blending political commentary with social observation. In this way, Angolan literature operates as an archive of conflict, preserving and reinterpreting collective memories while negotiating between the imperative to honour the past and the need to interrogate its legacies.[20]

José Eduardo Agualusa is part of a generation of Angolan writers who turn to the novel as a space for negotiating national identity in preference to overt political militancy. Unlike their predecessors, whose work was often shaped by revolutionary discourse and ideological commitment, this generation

[20]   Carmen Lúcia Secco, 'Por entre memórias e silêncios', pp. 13–25.

approaches fiction as a space for articulating subjectivity and reimagining belonging. Their writing interrogates the enduring ties between Angolan literature and Portuguese cultural frameworks, seeking instead to disrupt and decentre this legacy. In doing so, they contribute to the emergence of a renewed Lusophone literary field — one grounded in a distinctly African sensibility. It is, in essence, a literary gesture that asserts: *'I am here, in this country, and I am Angolan in this way'.*[21] This literary attitude resonates with Luís Kandjimbo's definition of *Angolanity* as a cultural expression of the imaginary construction of the world in time and space — a dimension that emerges through processes of categorization and the formation of social identity. It is through this lens of belonging to Angolan culture that the narrative strategies of contemporary writers take shape.[22] In this context, fiction and history maintain a dynamic and interdependent relationship. The texts produced by these authors construct *fictional memories*, employing protagonists and multiple narrative voices to articulate collective aspirations and unresolved longings. The reader, in turn, is invited to enter into a *fictional pact* with the text — to accept the narrative's internal logic and verisimilitude, thereby participating in the imaginative reconfiguration of Angola's cultural memory.[23]

This literary expression of Angolanity is articulated in the novel under study, particularly in the reference to the Mucubals' territory, which we shall examine further on, where the nation's past appears as an imaginary construction — a narrative devised to legitimize the post-independence regime that has remained in power. Yet the plot disrupts this official history by recovering silenced and marginalized voices, opening space for alternative discourses and counter-memories.

War surfaces as a recurring trope, both as a historical event and as an enduring presence woven into the fabric of daily life — a backdrop against which the narrative unfolds and a lived reality with which characters continually grapple. Luanda becomes the principal stage for these stories, depicted as a capital 'full of mysteries', in the words of one former guerrilla fighter: 'I've seen things in this city that would be too much even in a dream'.[24] Agualusa's portrayal of Angola reflects its dramatic historical transitions — from a Cold War frontline, where a Soviet- and Cuban-backed government fought against the US and South African-supported insurgents, to a Marxist-Leninist regime, and eventually to one of the world's fastest-growing economies. In *A General Theory of Oblivion*, war is represented not as a central narrative event but as a persistent background condition — the substratum upon which the characters' actions gain fictional origin, purpose, and legitimation. It forms the structural framework within which the lives of individuals unfold. The characters function, in accordance with Greimas's actantial model, as elements

---

[21] José Eduardo Agualusa interviewed by Anabela Mota Ribeiro in 2014.
[22] Luís Kandjimbo, 'A disciplinarização da literatura Angolana: história, cânones, discursos legitimadores e estatuto disciplinar', *Revista de Estudos Literários*, 5 (April 2020), pp. 181–96.
[23] Umberto Eco, *Six Walks in the Fictional Woods* (Harvard University Press, 1994).
[24] Agualusa, *A General Theory of Oblivion*, p. 206.

within a broader narrative constellation, each fulfilling a specific role in the progression of the story.[25] They include former soldiers, mercenaries, nurses, performers, journalists, detectives, anonymous victims of persecution, and ordinary citizens. Rather than heroes or prominent political figures, they are everyday individuals whose paths intersect, often involuntarily, in a conflict that exceeds their control or understanding. Collectively, they enact all six actantial roles defined by Greimas's semiotic theory, contributing to the unfolding of improbable events. Their actions reverberate through the narrative like toppling dominoes — each impacting another in a chain of consequences that cannot be halted.

While fragmented storytelling is a well-established literary device, particularly in postmodern fiction, Agualusa's narrative invites a distinctly cinematic reading. The book's chapters are structured around two main narrative axes that alternate — Ludo's axis[26] and Monte's axis — progressing in parallel, and, at times, in reverse chronological order. As in many films, it is only at the end of the book that we are able to piece together the cast of characters and episodes that remained unconnected. From the viewer's perspective — the reader is transformed into a spectator with a heightened sense of visuality, as if the text were unfolding on screen — this narrative strategy adopts a cinematic idiom, shaped by the novel's original conception as a screenplay. This form of expression creates a clear difference between the one who narrates and the one who sees. The narrative voice, which alternates between the first person, Ludo, and a depersonalized third person, seems to hold a camera, showing events to the reader either from Ludo's perspective, or externally, and establishing a synthesis between literary narrator and filmic narrator, as if asking literature to play a role exclusive to the language of cinema: *monstration*.[27] This cinematic strategy is most evident in the scene in which Little Chief is chased. First we have Ludo's testimony, from her terrace, on the 27 May, 'zooming-in' on this scene, and we then 'cut-to' a flashback of Little Chief's episode in jail, which shows the reader/viewer why he was arrested, freed, and later chased by a soldier.[28]

The predominance of both 'see' and 'eyes' in the text — 'to see' occurs 138 times, making it the fifth most frequent verb, while 'eye' appears 36 times —

[25] Greimas's actantial model distinguishes characters and action elements according to their function within the plot. The model considers an action as divided into six facets: Subject / Object / Helper / Opponent / Sender / Receiver.

[26] Ludo's axis also includes the pages of her diary, which appear in isolated chapters, written in italics.

[27] 'Monstration' (showing) is the fundamental mode of a film's storytelling function, as defined by André Gaudreault in *Du littéraire au filmique: système du récit* (1988), distinguishing cinematic narration from verbal narration through the direct presentation of images and actions rather than their description.

[28] The resort to cinematic vocabulary is not to suggest that such techniques are exclusive to film, but to highlight how the novel draws on filmic syntax — particularly montage, zooming, and cross-cutting — to structure perception and narrative temporality. Given that *A General Theory of Oblivion* was originally conceived as a screenplay, the visual grammar of the novel — its sharp transitions, perspective shifts, and emphasis on visuality — demands a vocabulary capable of capturing this cross-media sensibility. In this context, the cinematic idiom offers a productive lens for understanding how Agualusa modulates between internal consciousness and external event.

places sight at the top of the sensory hierarchy (see Fig. 8). Ludo, with whom the verb 'see' is most frequently associated, becomes the 'great eye'.[29] She experiences the war from a strategic vantage point, one from which she can see without being seen. The war reaches her only in fragments: at times through the sound of voices, at other times via the radio. Ludo is an orphan of the empire,[30] brought by force to Luanda and left there to grapple with her own inner conflicts in isolation. As a metaphor for colonialism, Ludo embodies the reactionary backlash to national liberation discourse. She bristles at the anti-colonial speeches broadcast on the radio; she wakes in panic, gripped by the fear that her apartment will be invaded; she despises everything she sees — the people, their behaviour, and the language she cannot understand. From her high terrace, she imagines herself a queen, much as Portugal once saw itself as the sovereign head of an empire. But, like Portugal, she lacks a court — a submissive populace to affirm and legitimize her illusory royalty. Echoing Portugal's self-image under Salazar, who in his 1965 speech described the nation as 'proudly alone' while Portuguese troops fought in Africa without international support, Ludo remains isolated: not so proud, one might infer, but quietly confident in her capacity for self-preservation. She retreats behind closed doors, protecting her fragility and vulnerability. Yet in the end, it is Angola that saves her — the very Angola she once feared. It is under the Angolan sky, once a source of dread, that she finally finds peace and a sense of belonging.

To gain a deeper understanding of the novel's narrative architecture and to visualize the function of each character within the broader plot, it is analytically valuable to represent the web of relationships through a networked structural model. This approach reveals how seemingly disparate or unpredictable elements converge into a cohesive whole, forming a narrative mosaic in which each connection contributes to the text's structural integrity. What initially appears fragmented or incidental gradually emerges as part of a tightly inter-woven system, highlighting the relational logic that underpins Agualusa's novel.

The network visualization in the drawing (Fig. 1) clearly demonstrates that Ludo occupies a central position within the narrative, serving as the primary node through which all other characters are connected. She functions as the structural and emotional core of the text. To produce the diagram, we employed *InfraNodus*,[31] a tool designed to visualize texts as conceptual networks based on co-occurrence of terms within a defined proximity window (typically 5–10 words). In this case, we imported the entire novel's text and tagged character names as semantic nodes, generating links between them based on their co-appearance within narrative proximity — either through direct dialogue, shared scenes, or thematic juxtaposition. Thus, the arrows in the network

[29] 'The Great Eye is ever watchful', words of Boromir in *Lord of the Rings: The Fellowship of the Ring*, dir. by Peter Jackson (USA, 2001).
[30] José Eduardo Agualusa, interview for 'Mar de Letras' (RTP África and RTP2) <https://www. youtube.com/watch?v=3J2zbbux8mY>.
[31] Dmitry Paranyushkin, InfraNodus: Network Thinking Tool (2020), <https://infranodus.com>.

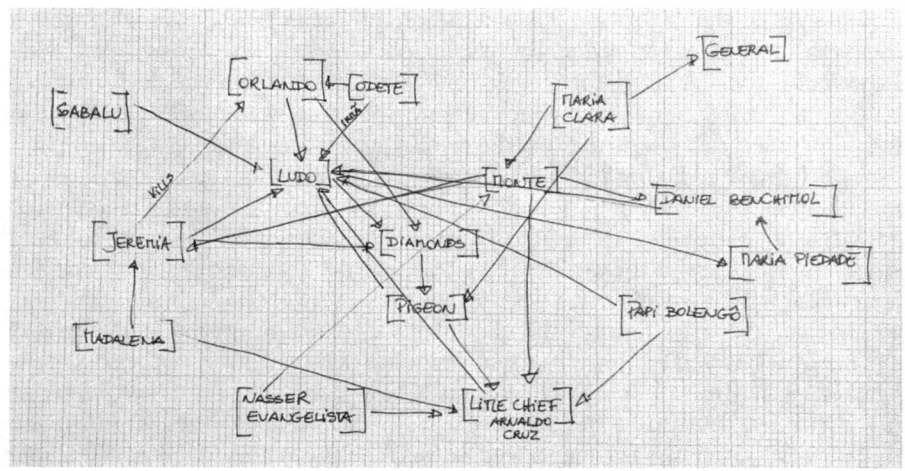

FIG. 1. Hand-drawn network of character relationships in Agualusa's *A General Theory of Oblivion*, showing Ludo at the structural centre of the narrative (created by the author).

do not necessarily reflect direct speech but rather the narrative co-function of characters: who appears when, in relation to whom, and how often. This creates a non-hierarchical, yet tightly knit, narrative mesh, revealing that the removal of even minor characters alters the overall cohesion. This approach highlights key clusters, their interrelations, and the structural gaps between them, offering insight into how meaning is distributed across the novel and reinforcing the argument that Ludo's presence is not merely symbolic but narratively indispensable.

For this analysis, we applied the 'Statements to Link' filter with a proximity window of 5 words, which allowed us to detect conceptual links based on narrative adjacency. This setting was selected to preserve local coherence while revealing broader relational patterns across the text. Character names were treated as anchor nodes, and the graph was modularized using the built-in community detection algorithm (modularity 0.33), helping to identify clusters of meaning that correspond to narrative subplots and thematic threads.

In this graph (Fig. 2), we can see Ludo as the most prominent and complex node, covering the entire network. The flight node, isolated from the rest of the network, is important but inconsequential; it represents the flight that left Ludo in Angola (the word 'left' also comes up as an important node). She is connected to 'men', 'time' and 'people', who appear here as the most influential elements in this novel. Sabalu,[32] this visualization suggests, is the character that has the most relevance to Ludo. At a deeper level of visualization (in Fig. 3), the

---

[32]   Sabalu is a young boy who befriends Ludo after years of her isolation. He becomes her link to the outside world, bringing her food and supplies and gradually earning her trust. Through Sabalu's visits and stories, Ludo learns about the events unfolding in Luanda, which reintroduces her — albeit cautiously — to human connection and the changing reality beyond her bricked-up apartment.

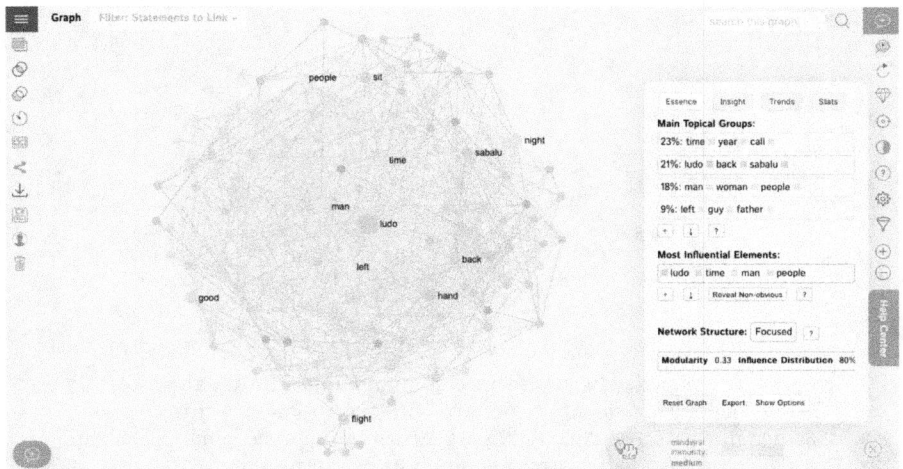

FIG. 2. Digital network of Ludo's narrative environment in Agualusa's *A General Theory of Oblivion*, generated with InfraNodus <https://infranodus.com>. Analysis by the author.

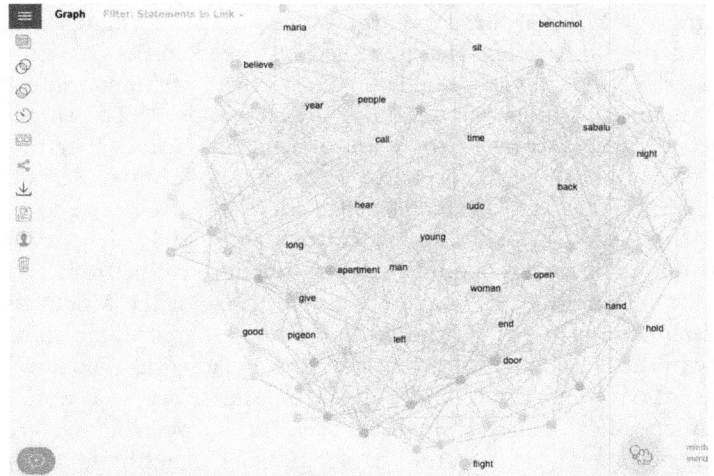

FIG. 3. Expanded digital network of key terms and characters, highlighting shifts in prominence and connectivity across nodes at a deeper level of analysis. Analysis by the author.

characters that are shown as the most influential in Ludo's life are Maria da Piedade, her daughter, and Daniel Benchimol, the journalist who reunites them.

The frequency patterns identified in InfraNodus are corroborated by lexical statistics generated using Sketch Engine, a tool designed for large-scale text mining and corpus analysis.[33]

---

[33]   Adam Kilgarriff and others, 'The Sketch Engine: Ten Years On', *Lexicography*, 1.1 (2014), pp. 7–36 <https://www.sketchengine.eu>.

Lemma	Frequency	Lemma	Frequency	Lemma	Frequency	Lemma	Frequency	Lemma	Frequency
man	144	sabalu	56	hand	38	voice	30	maria	27
ludo	105	wall	52	orlando	37	word	30	guy	26
time	84	door	50	floor	37	city	30	water	26
woman	76	night	47	house	37	head	30	tree	26
people	75	boy	46	eye	36	daniel	30	moment	26
day	71	jeremias	46	way	36	angola	30	life	26
monte	66	pigeon	39	building	34	light	28	face	26
year	59	luanda	39	baiacu	34	sky	27	terrace	26
chief	58	morning	39	friend	33	car	27	money	26
little	57	apartment	39	month	32	window	27	thing	25

WORDLIST — General Theory of Oblivion — noun

Rows per page: 50 · 1–50 of 2,457

FIG. 4. Frequency list of the most common nouns in Agualusa's *A General Theory of Oblivion*, generated with Sketch Engine <https://www. sketchengine.eu>. The data highlights recurrent themes of time, space and character presence. Analysis by the author.

Fig. 4 presents the most frequent nouns in the novel. A close reading of the list reveals that the majority of these terms relate to the narrative categories of time (e.g. *time, day, year, night*) and space (e.g. *wall, door, Luanda, apartment*). As Mikhail Bakhtin argues, these two formally constitutive elements of the literary text are inextricably linked, reflecting the ways in which historical time and geographic space intersect in fiction — a relationship he conceptualizes through the notion of the *chronotope*.[34] The chronotope of this novel is structured by thirty years of Angolan history, beginning with the War of National Liberation, and by a single building in Luanda — the setting in which the main character isolates herself in response to the threat posed by that very war. The literary cartography[35] of *A General Theory of Oblivion* unfolds across geopolitical and symbolic terrain: from Portugal to Angola, and internally from Luanda to the territory of the Mucubals. Yet its narrative remains primarily anchored in Luanda — a city that ranks 18th in frequency in the lexical table above — and in Angola (36th). The novel reflects what Edward Said, in *Culture and Imperialism*, describes as a 'world picture' shaped by specific historical circumstances in the postcolonial era, where '[s]patiality becomes, ironically, the characteristic of an aesthetic rather than of political domination, as more and more regions — from India to Africa to the Caribbean — challenge the classical empires and their cultures'.[36] In *A General*

---

[34] Literally translated as 'time-space', the term *chronotope* is developed by Mikhail Bakhtin in *The Dialogic Imagination*, where he defines it as the intrinsic connectedness of temporal and spatial relationships in literature; Mikhail Bakhtin, *The Dialogic Imagination*, trans. by Caryl Emerson and Michael Holquist (University of Texas Press, 1981), p. 84.

[35] A term coined by Robert T. Tally Jr. to describe the novel; he writes: 'I discuss the space of the novel in terms of both its formal characteristics and its variegated content, and I argue in particular that the novel is a form of literary cartography'; 'The Space of the Novel', in *The Cambridge Companion to the Novel*, ed. by Eric Bulson (Cambridge University Press, 2018), pp. 152–67 (p. 153).

[36] Edward Said, *Culture and Imperialism* (Vintage, 1993), pp. 189–90.

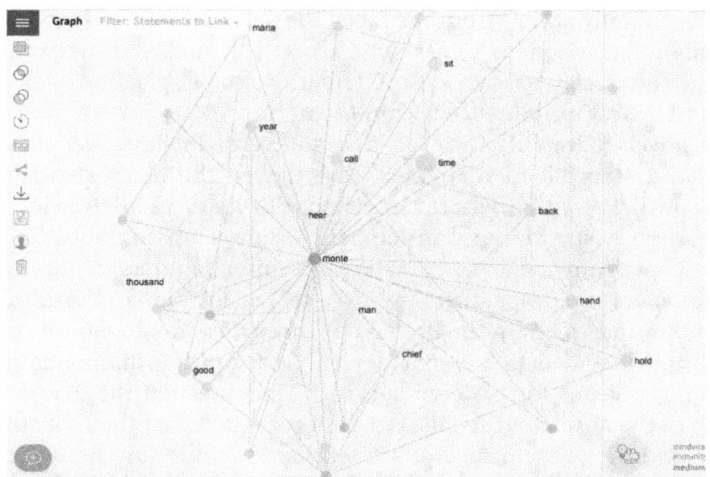

FIG. 5. Digital network highlighting Monte's area of influence in
Agualusa's *A General Theory of Oblivion*, generated with InfraNodus
<https://infranodus.com>. Analysis by the author.

Theory of Oblivion, the Mucubals' territory is evoked as the essence of Angola
— a symbolic landscape that reaches back to a pre-colonial past. It represents a
primordial space that embodies cultural identity, purity, and richness; a place to
be preserved and protected. Within the narrative, it is also imagined as fertile
ground for renewal, where the seeds of a new social order might be planted.
Symbolically, the Mucubals' territory becomes the site of redemption, where
even the novel's most morally compromised character, Jeremias Carrasco, is
granted a second chance, finding the possibility of transformation through
contact with its people and traditions.

Fig. 4 also indicates that the most frequently mentioned characters are
Ludo and Monte — thus supporting the formulation of the two narrative
axes discussed earlier — followed by Little Chief and Sabalu. Fig. 5 shows
the centrality of Monte within the social-relational network, even though his
presence is more distributed and less focal in the plot.

By comparing the initial network generated from close reading (Fig. 1) with
the graphs and tables produced through text mining using InfraNodus and
Sketch Engine, it becomes evident that 'diamonds' and 'pigeon' are not only
closely linked but also function as key structural elements within the narrative.
In terms of Greimas's actantial model, *diamonds* occupy the position of the
object, while the *pigeon* assumes the role of the subject, thereby reinforcing
their narrative centrality through both semantic and structural analysis.

If we exclude all terms associated with the narrative categories of *characters*
and *time* from Fig. 4 (most frequent nouns, as generated by Sketch Engine), the
next most frequent noun is *pigeon*, which appears 39 times. Although the word

diamond is initially absent from the table, the narrator refers to it both directly and through the synonym *stones*, which occur 21 and 22 times respectively. Combined, these references yield a total frequency of 43, placing *diamond* ahead of *pigeon* in lexical prominence within the narrative.

In the novel, diamonds function as a source of intrigue, yet they are not represented as the 'blood diamonds' that fuelled the macrostructure of the Angolan conflict. Rather, they are associated with characters driven by a corrupt, though human, desire for rapid enrichment — not as villains, but as individuals seeking escape from their harsh realities. Diamonds intersect the lives of all major characters and propel them toward a central location in the narrative (see Fig. 6): Ludo's apartment in the Prédio dos Invejados.[37] Ludo, however, remains uniquely indifferent to their monetary value, using the diamonds merely as tools to hunt pigeons for her own survival. Unaware that the diamonds lie at the origin of the novel's events, she does not recognize that they constitute both the cause and the consequence of the tensions surrounding her. They are, in effect, the narrative's organizing principle — the axis around which its thematic structure is woven. Paradoxically, by the novel's end, diamonds impact the characters' lives positively, even those who have committed murder to obtain them. Little Chief becomes a successful entrepreneur and, in turn, provides Ludo with a comfortable life in her old age. Jeremias Carrasco, once an agent of violence, ultimately finds forgiveness. Notably, both *diamond* and *pigeon* are linked to the term *good* in the InfraNodus network graphs, reinforcing their unexpected association with care, survival, and moral transformation.

Data mining enabled the formulation of significant insights and opened new avenues of analysis that had not previously emerged through traditional close reading alone.[38] The combined use of both tools allows the text to be examined as a system, revealing patterns of connectivity and structural dependencies. By selectively removing key nodes from the narrative network (see Fig. 7), it becomes possible to observe the reorganization of the system and to formulate new interpretative hypotheses. This digital reading not only illustrated and reinforced prior inferences but also uncovered previously unnoticed data and relationships whose relevance became more apparent through computational analysis.

The reading experience of this novel is largely defined by the prominence of Ludo, whose presence shapes both the emotional tone and structural focus of the narrative. Her actions — at times marked by deep fragility, at others by bursts of desperate violence — along with the introspective conflict articulated

[37] The name *Prédio dos Invejados* translates as 'Building of the Envied'; it likely suggests that those outside the building envy the people who live there — perhaps for their comfort, safety, and status compared to the surrounding conditions in Luanda.

[38] For instance, close reading did not fully account for the structural centrality of Sabalu, whose name appears less frequently than Ludo's but whose high betweenness centrality indicates a pivotal role in linking narrative threads. The network analysis also revealed overlooked thematic bridges — such as the cluster linking 'flight', 'left', and 'back' — which helped reframe the novel's logic of movement and exile.

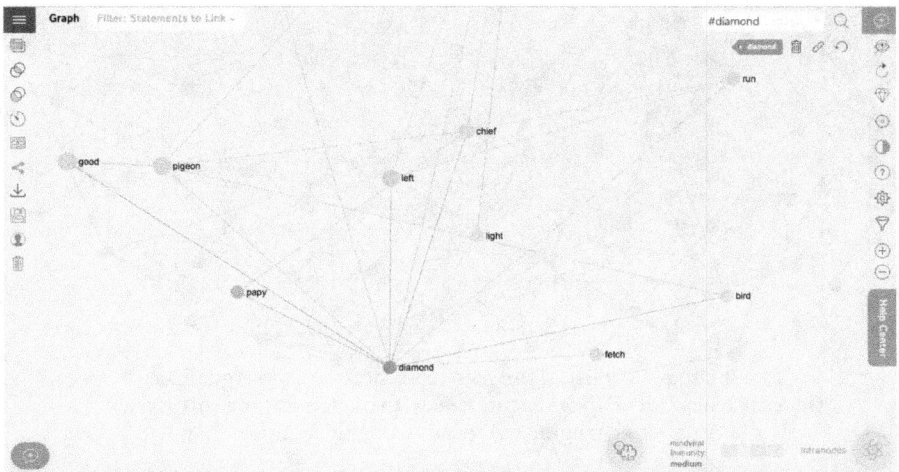

FIG. 6. Digital network focusing on 'diamond' and its associated nodes in Agualusa's *A General Theory of Oblivion*, generated with InfraNodus <https://infranodus.com>. Analysis by the author.

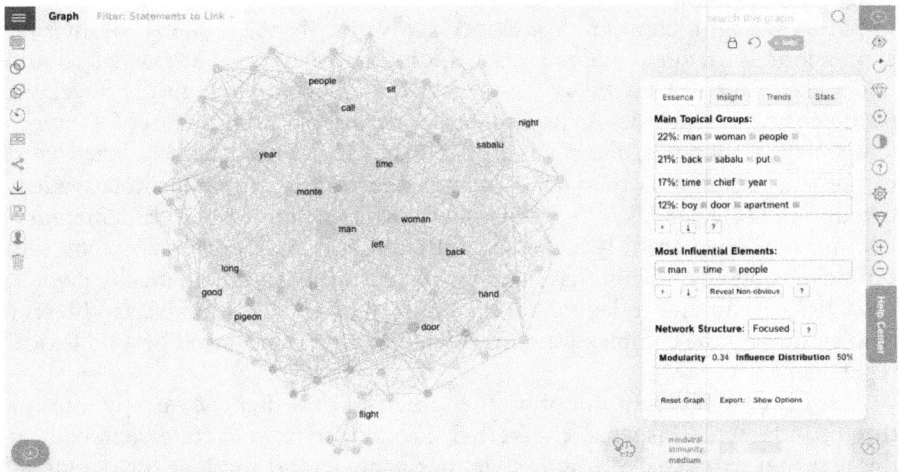

FIG. 7. Digital network showing the reorganization of Agualusa's *A General Theory of Oblivion* without the 'Ludo' node, generated with InfraNodus (https://infranodus.com). Analysis by the author.

in her diaries and later inscribed on the walls of her apartment, convey a raw and lyrical humanity. Her poems, scattered across the narrative, intensify this lyricism and tend to overshadow the experiences of other characters. The language of war, prominent in the early chapters, gradually recedes as Angola — in line with historical developments — enters a period of relative calm. The novel's internal structure foregrounds the role of books, libraries, writing,

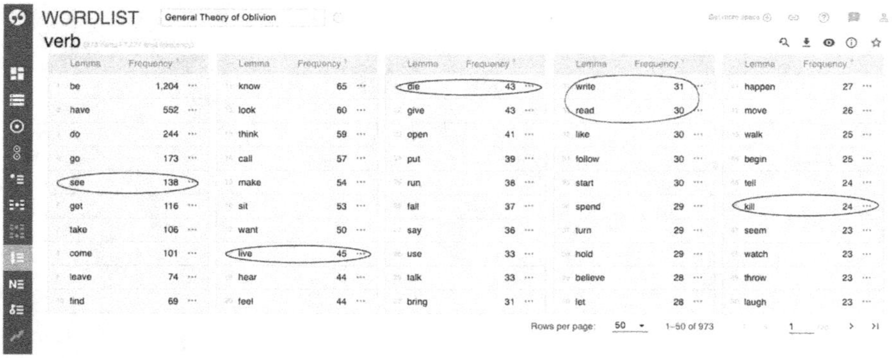
WORDLIST General Theory of Oblivion

verb

Lemma	Frequency	Lemma	Frequency	Lemma	Frequency	Lemma	Frequency	Lemma	Frequency
be	1,204	know	65	die	43	write	31	happen	27
have	552	look	60	give	43	read	30	move	26
do	244	think	59	open	41	like	30	walk	25
go	173	call	57	put	39	follow	30	begin	25
see	138	make	54	run	38	start	30	tell	24
get	116	sit	53	fall	37	spend	29	kill	24
take	106	want	50	say	36	turn	29	seem	23
come	101	live	45	use	33	hold	29	watch	23
leave	74	hear	44	talk	33	believe	28	throw	23
find	69	feel	44	bring	31	let	28	laugh	23

Rows per page: 50 1–50 of 973

FIG. 8. Frequency list of the most common verbs in Agualusa's *A General Theory of Oblivion*, generated with Sketch Engine (https://www.sketchengine.eu). Analysis by the author.

and reading as thematically central. In this regard, the data visualizations and frequency tables proved particularly revealing: while the semantics of book are richly represented, the lexical field of war holds surprisingly little statistical weight in the overall narrative (see Fig. 9).

But how significant are statistical measures in the context of literary expression? If frequency alone were the metric of importance, what should one make of the word *oblivion*[39] — a term that appears rarely in the novel, yet occupies a central position in its semantic and symbolic architecture? Despite its low statistical presence, *oblivion* is arguably the most conceptually charged word in the text, shaping its thematic concerns and framing the interpretative lens through the title itself. While words such as 'forget', 'remember', and 'memory' appear more frequently, it is the semantic intensity, narrative placement, and symbolic value of oblivion that mark it as structurally and thematically pivotal. This disparity invites reflection on the limits of quantitative analysis in literary studies, and on the complex ways in which meaning is produced beyond lexical repetition.

According to Tzvetan Todorov, the structure of a literary work comprises three fundamental aspects: the verbal, located in the concrete sentences of the text and expressed through style, perspective, and diction; the syntactic, which accounts for the logical, temporal, and spatial relations between the text's parts; and the semantic, which concerns the text's themes and conceptual organization.[40] Within this framework, the statistical presence of the word *oblivion* acquires significance not only in terms of its frequency, but also through its strategic scarcity. The fact that the word appears only twice in the novel confers upon it a kind of 'rarity value', intensifying its expressive force and foregrounding its thematic centrality. Its placement within the text further

39 Here, the focus is on the word *oblivion* as it appears in the text, rather than on *oblivion* as a sememe (the abstract concept of forgetting). For this reason, occurrences of *forget* and allusions to *remember* in negative contexts are not counted.

40 Tzvetan Todorov, *Introduction à la littérature fantastique* (Seuil, 1970), p. 56.

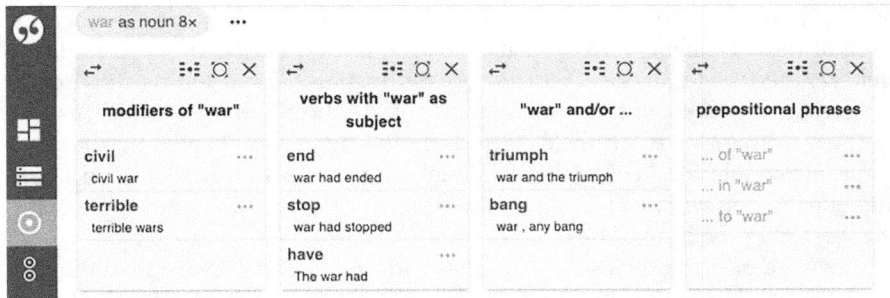

FIG. 9. Concordance patterns for the noun 'war' in Agualusa's *A General Theory of Oblivion*, generated with Sketch Engine (https://www. sketchengine.eu). Analysis by the author.

reinforces this function: it appears first in the title, then midway through the narrative (on page 100), and finally at its conclusion (page 229). This spatial arrangement contributes to the novel's structural cohesion, anchoring *oblivion* as both a semantic thread and a narrative pivot — a *leitmotiv*.

III.

If I still had **the space**, the charcoal, and available walls,
I could compose a great work about forgetting:
a general theory of **oblivion**.

I realise I have transformed the entire apartment into
a huge book. After burning the library, after I have died,
all that remains will be my voice.

In this house all the walls have my mouth.[41]

Oblivion is a word attributed to Ludo and used by her only twice throughout the novel. Its first appearance occurs in one of her diary entries, embedded within a verse that also gives the novel its title. At this point, the title sheds its peripheral or paratextual role and emerges as a central organizing principle within the narrative. In this moment of heightened lyricism, *oblivion* is invoked as the defining purpose of Ludo's existence — the imagined writing of a treatise. Notably, the clause in which it appears is introduced by a conditional conjunction, signalling an unrealized hypothetical:[42] an aspiration that remains suspended, never fully materialized.

The term *oblivion* is never deployed within the conventional binary of memory–forgetting. Nowhere does Ludo, as a first-person narrator, express a desire to erase a specific memory. However, the narrative provides indirect clues that gesture towards a traumatic past: reference is made to an unspecified incident known only as 'the accident'; it is revealed that she has committed manslaughter in self-defence; and her identity as a white Portuguese woman

---

[41]   Agualusa, *A General Theory of Oblivion*, p. 100.
[42]   Relation defined in grammar as a 'counter-factual condition'.

positions her as particularly vulnerable within a war she explicitly condemns. Each of these elements offers a plausible rationale for her desire to formulate a 'general theory of oblivion'. Yet the true motivation behind Ludo's fixation on forgetting — as well as the explanation for her self-effacement and status as a 'faceless' woman — is withheld until near the end of the novel, only six pages before its conclusion. This delayed disclosure sustains narrative suspense and aligns with a cinematic logic of withholding, akin to the technique of 'keeping the viewer on the edge of their seat'.

The word *oblivion* is closely associated with the spatial dimension of the *wall* — the tangible surface upon which writing becomes possible once Ludo has exhausted all conventional means. As she states: 'I have no more notebooks to write in. I have no more pens either. I write on the walls, with pieces of charcoal'.[43] The wall thus becomes both a physical boundary and a site of inscription, where the act of writing persists in the face of material scarcity and isolation.

In literary studies, space — or place — has often been marginalized, traditionally regarded as a static and secondary dimension in comparison to time. Temporality, with its associations with historical development and personal experience, has attracted far more critical attention. However, in recent years, scholars have increasingly emphasized the importance of spatiality in narrative theory, particularly within the study of the novel.[44] In *A General Theory of Oblivion*, the significance of space extends beyond geography or *chronotopic* framing — aspects already addressed above — to encompass a dynamic force that actively shapes character development,[45] especially in the case of Ludo.

Were one to create a stop-motion film capturing only the physical space of the apartment from the beginning to the end of the narrative, the viewer would witness its gradual metamorphosis: from a richly furnished bourgeois-colonial interior to a hollowed-out, deteriorated shell — and eventually, to a refurbished Luandan-style apartment. This physical transformation mirrors Ludo's internal evolution. The space degrades as she tears up the floor, burns furniture, and writes on the soot-blackened walls with charcoal, only to be later reconstituted as a site of care, renewal, and belonging. The apartment thus operates as an autophagic organism: consuming itself for survival and later reconstituting its form. This spatial metamorphosis parallels Ludo's ideological and emotional journey — from a reclusive, anti-decolonization figure shaped by racial prejudice to a caregiver and surrogate grandmother to a young Black boy who teaches her to love Luanda. In embracing forgetfulness, Ludo releases herself from pain and severs ties with a traumatic past. Her ultimate gesture — prescribing oblivion to Jeremias Carrasco — affirms her belief in forgetting as a form of ethical repair and emotional survival.

---

[43]   Agualusa, *A General Theory of Oblivion*, p. 81.
[44]   Robert T. Tally Jr., 'The Space of the Novel'.
[45]   As previously noted, the Mucubal territory serves as a catalyst for significant transformation in the character of Jeremias Carrasco; similar instances of narrative and ethical reconfiguration could be identified elsewhere in the text.

Ludo exhibits clear signs of agoraphobia, though the narrative does not specify whether 'the accident' was its cause or a contributing factor. What is evident, however, is her perception of external space as inherently threatening. She ventures outside only under the protective cover of an umbrella, suggesting a heightened sensitivity to the exposure of open environments. Her relocation to another country — from Portugal to Angola — is neither voluntary nor without resistance. Indeed, she must be sedated with tranquillizers in order to board the plane to Luanda. Once in the city, her movement remains severely restricted, confined to Orlando's apartment. There, she encounters a new enclosed microcosm: the library. This space, unlike the threatening exterior world, provides a sense of freedom and security, functioning as a sanctuary in which intellectual exploration replaces physical mobility:

> Often, as she looked out over the crowds that clashed violently against the sides of the building, that vast uproar of car horns and whistles, cries and entreaties and curses, she experienced a profound terror, a feeling of siege and threat. Whenever she wanted to go out she would look for a book in the library. She felt, as she went on burning those books, after having burned all the furniture, the doors, the wooden floor tiles, that she was losing her freedom. It was as though she was incinerating the whole planet. When she burned Jorge Amado she stopped being able to visit Ilhéus and São Salvador. Burning *Ulysses*, by Joyce, she had lost Dublin. Getting rid of *Three Trapped Tigers*, she incinerated old Havana. There were fewer than a hundred books left.[46]

The depiction of the library borders on the fantastical, evoking a space that resists realistic representation. Whether coincidental or intentional, the intertextual parallels with Jorge Luis Borges's *The Library of Babel* are numerous and striking:[47]

A General Theory of Oblivion José Eduardo Agualusa	*The Library of Babel* Jorge Luis Borges
a valuable library — thousands of titles (pp. 4–5)	The universe (which others call the Library) is composed of an indefinite, perhaps infinite number of hexagonal galleries. (p. 65)
An elegant, anachronistic wrought-iron staircase climbed in a tight spiral (pp. 4–5)	Through this space, too, there passes a spiral staircase (p. 65)
I've been losing my eyesight [...] I can only see shadows now [...] one might perhaps call this dying. (pp. 99–100)	Now that my eyes can hardly make out what I myself have written, I am preparing to die (p. 66)
I could compose a great work about forgetting: a general theory of oblivion. (p. 100)	That discovery enabled mankind [...] to formulate a general theory of the Library (p. 67)

---

[46] Agualusa, *A General Theory of Oblivion*, pp. 138–39.
[47] Jorge Luis Borges, 'The Library of Babel', in *Fictions*, trans. by Andrew Hurley (Penguin, 2000), pp. 65–74 (page numbers given are from this translation).

As a character, Ludo appears to be subtly modelled on Borges's Librarian. Like him, she eventually loses her sight — a symbolic indication that the end is near. Borges's Librarian reflects that 'for every rational line or forthright statement there are leagues of senseless cacophony, verbal nonsense, and incoherency',[48] whereas Ludo, inversely, asserts that she is able to discover truth within error: 'I get things wrong as I read, and in those mistakes, sometimes, I find incredible things that are right'.[49] While for Borges's Librarian, the universe is composed entirely of bookshelves and 'enigmatic books',[50] for Ludo, the universe becomes Orlando's library — a space where, through reading, everything is rendered 'suddenly congruent'. The affinity between the two figures lies not only in their physical and symbolic circumstances, but also in their metaphysical orientation toward language, meaning, and the interpretive act.

In his short essay *Library*, Umberto Eco proposes that if a library is, as Borges suggests, a model of the universe, then it ought to be transformed into a universe adapted to human needs.[51] Although caught in a logic of survival, Ludo enacts this proposition quite literally. Books sustain her intellectually, but they also become a fortress of survival. Once the furniture has been consumed as fuel, she is compelled to burn her beloved volumes — echoing the fate of other great libraries throughout human history. On another level, beyond the realm of reception and into that of production, books become a metonymic extension of Ludo herself: 'I realize I have transformed the entire apartment into a huge book. After burning the library, after I have died all that remains will be my voice [...] In this house all the walls have my mouth'.[52] It is in this sphere of poetic creation that another dimension of oblivion emerges, what philosopher Mark Rowlands, following Rainer Maria Rilke, terms Rilkean memory — 'a certain kind of transformation that memory undergoes for artistic creation',[53] a process which depends on the capacity to forget in order to write.

Rainer Maria Rilke famously observes in *The Notebooks of Malte Laurids Brigge*: 'To write a single line of verse...'

> one must see many cities, people, things, one must know animals, one must feel birds flying and know the movements flowers make as they open up in the morning. One must be able to think back to roads in unfamiliar regions, unexpected encounters, and partings which one saw coming long before; one must be able to think back to those days in one's childhood that are still unexplained [...]. One must have memories of many nights of love [...] one must also have been with the dying [...] And having memories is still not enough. If there are a great many, one must be able to forget them, and one must have the patience to wait until they return. For the memories are not what's essential. It's only when they become blood within us, become our

---

[48]   Ibid., p. 67.
[49]   Agualusa, *A General Theory of Oblivion*, p. 99.
[50]   Borges, 'The Library of Babel', p. 67.
[51]   Umberto Eco, *A Biblioteca* (Difel, 1994).
[52]   José Eduardo Agualusa, *A General Theory of Oblivion*, op. cit., p. 100.
[53]   Mark Rowlands, 'Rilkean Memories', *Southern Journal of Philosophy*, 53.S1 (2015), p. 6.

nameless looks and signs that are no longer distinguishable from ourselves — not until then does it happen that, in a very rare moment, the first word of a verse rises in their midst and goes forth from among them.[54]

Ludo undergoes a process analogous to the one described by Rilke, and it is this process that underpins the writing she produces. She is a shy and fragile woman, shaped both by experiences she has already forgotten and those she forgets continually — as well as by the observations she makes daily. These, as Rilke notes, are not sufficient on their own to yield 'a rare verse'. Inspiration, for Rilke, arises only when lived experience is transformed — when memory becomes 'blood' and 'body', internalized and unnamed. In *A General Theory of Oblivion*, words emerge in Ludo's writing only at this point of embodiment and metamorphosis, taking the form of fragmented poems or narrative sketches.

As Guido Mazzoni argues in *Theory of the Novel*, the modern novel is shaped by two principal modes of narrating individual lives. The first privileges a subjective register, centred on particularity, confession, and idiosyncrasy — a mode that seeks to express the inner life and uniqueness of a character. The second emphasizes the objective multiplicity of the external world, situating individuals within broader social, historical, and structural contexts.[55] *A General Theory of Oblivion* offers a synthesis of both, oscillating between inner retreat and outward observation, between private lyricism and collective memory.

[54] Rainer Maria Rilke, *The Notebooks of Malte Laurids Brigge*, trans. by William Needham <https://ia800907.us.archive.org/32/items/TheNotebooksOfMalteLauridsBrigge/TheNotebooksOfMalteLauridsBrigge.pdf> [accessed 30 March 2025].
[55] Guido Mazzoni, *Theory of the Novel* (Harvard University Press, 2017).

Representations of Austerity Urbanism in Contemporary Portuguese Film: The Case of *São Jorge*

MARIA INÊS CASTRO E SILVA

University of Warwick / University of Birmingham

The precarization of work brings in its wake the precarization of life and citizenship, and has a profound impact on the social organization of urban space. Subject to the dynamics of precarity and social exclusion, the Portuguese financial crisis (2008–14) reshaped urban space, forming what we could term geographies of precarity.

This article focuses on the consequences of the politics of austerity implemented in Portugal and how subsequent precarity and entrapment is expressed through cinematic space in the film *São Jorge* [*Saint George*] (2016), directed by Marco Martins. Here I consider the concept of precarity in the context of the financial crisis in Portugal and the intervention of the Troika. The impact of austerity and precarity manifests materially and spatially, often most notably in urban spaces, but also in the workspace and within domestic spaces. My analysis of the film argues that the divisions traditionally maintained between the space of home and the space of work are less distinct in *São Jorge*. As my study will show, the difficult decisions taken in the workspace impact on domestic space and vice-versa, contributing to a cross-contamination of both spaces. Furthermore, the analysis of space in the film also points to the ways in which gender roles and race are associated with particular types of space. In *São Jorge*, the reproduction of certain stereotypes of women, but also of foreign and marginalized communities living in Portugal (Brazilian, Eastern European, Roma, Asian), includes the association of foreign communities and women with specific types of jobs and particular spaces (peripheral neighbourhoods and informal settlements).

The consequences of the politics of austerity implemented in Portugal are demonstrated through cinematic space in Portuguese film. I focus on the concept of *austerity urbanism*, disseminated specifically in studies by geographers such as Jamie Peck, Fran Tonkiss, Neil Brenner and Nik Theodore, and assess its relevance to the film. This concept deals specifically with the repercussions of austerity policies on urban space, namely harsh cuts in urban modernization projects and the subsequent social segregation that this brings about.

Portuguese Studies vol. 41 no. 2 (2025), doi:10.1353/port.00043, 230–47

My work argues that social segregation and precarity are direct consequences of austerity urbanism. In order to analyse the landscapes of precarity in Portuguese film, I draw on the works of Judith Butler and Zygmunt Bauman. *São Jorge* depicts empty spaces, abandoned factories and building works that have been interrupted, sites that represent a country that stagnated and decayed during the intervention of the Troika in Portugal. As my analysis will argue, the choice of these abandoned spaces, as well as confined film settings, handheld cameras, naturalistic sound, and frame-within-a-frame techniques will demonstrate the entrapment of characters.

São Jorge is part of the 'Portuguese Cinema of Austerity'. This expression is borrowed from Iván Villarmea Álvarez and it encompasses a group of films that, according to the author, are the harbingers of a crisis and a country in ruin. According to Villarmea Álvarez, the cinema of precarity 'has evolved into "the cinema of austerity", a new film cycle that reflects and responds to the effects of the Great Recession at a thematic, formal or allegorical level.'[1] Villarmea Álvarez goes even further to claim that Iberian austerity cinema 'is characterized by a "politics of pain and suffering" in which "political and physical vulnerability" go hand in hand.'[2] In sum, the Portuguese Cinema of Austerity, including *São Jorge*, focuses on characters who, living in precarious circumstances, are victims of the economic crisis and who face issues such as unemployment and poverty. Portuguese cinema's relationship with the cinema of austerity not only opens the discussion with regards to the place of Portuguese film in the European film circuit, but it also allows us to examine the financial means available to filmmakers to produce films in Portugal. Following harsh financial cuts to the Portuguese film industry, filmmakers have seen their aesthetic and technical choices and possibilities reduced. Hence the need to film on location in peripheral areas of cities, as well as the use of non-professional actors, and intimate film settings like small apartments; these are among the strategies adopted in order to compensate for the lack of funding within the Portuguese film industry.

This article is divided into four parts. It starts with the historical context of the Portuguese financial crisis, focusing on the consequences of the politics of austerity implemented in Portugal. Following the economic effects, the article shows how the concept of austerity urbanism can be framed as a consequence of austerity measures put in place with the intervention of the Troika in Portugal. The second part places the film *São Jorge* in its cinematic context in Portuguese film and its physical setting in the neighbourhoods of Lisbon, the nation's capital. The third part considers how austerity urbanism is at the origin of

---

[1] Iván Villarmea Álvarez, 'Crisis-spaces in Portuguese Austerity Cinema', in *Reframing Portuguese Cinema in the 21st Century*, vol. 1, ed. by Daniel Ribas and Paulo Cunha (Agência da Curta Metragem, Vila do Conde, 2020), pp. 29–42 (p. 30).

[2] Iván Villarmea Álvarez, 'It could happen to you: Empathy and Empowerment in Iberian Austerity Cinema', in *Cinema of Crisis: Film and Contemporary Europe*, ed. by Thomas Austin and Angelos Koutsourakis (Edinburgh University Press, 2020), pp. 150–63 (p. 151).

spaces of precarity and social segregation, and finally the article moves on to argue that austerity and precarity have their correspondence in terms of urban space, but also at the level of domestic space and the workplace. My analysis argues that the entrapment of characters is observable through the uses of specific film techniques, but also through the choice of constrained spaces.

Financial Crisis and Austerity

After integration into the former EEC (European Economic Community, 1958–93) in 1986, as well as the signature of the Stability and Growth Pact (1997),[3] and following accession to the Eurozone common currency (1999),[4] Portugal underwent a financial crisis (2008–14) which in turn had its origins in the wider context of the so-called *subprime* crisis (2007), leading to the bankruptcy of the bank Lehman Brothers, in the United States of America, in September 2008. Indeed, this bankruptcy gave rise to the beginning of the biggest international economic crisis since the Great Depression of the 1930s, and it contaminated the rest of the world. Europe was not untouched by this global scenario. Following Zygmunt Bauman's and Carlo Bordoni's view of Europe as 'a dumping ground for globally generated problems and challenges',[5] European countries, in particular the so-called 'PIIGS' (an implicitly derogatory term used to refer to Portugal, Italy, Ireland, Greece and Spain),[6] were dramatically affected by this international crisis. In 2007, Greece, Spain and Portugal became 'problematic cases' in the European Union due to their high levels of external debt.[7] In the Portuguese context, the increase in debt started in the first half of the 1990s thanks to the increasing privatization and deregulation of the financial sector and the liberalization of capital. It is important to note that at the time Portugal's economic growth was very poor, unlike other affected PIIGS, such as Ireland. In fact, it can be argued that the structural issues in Portugal's economy go beyond the international crisis of 2007. The funds coming from the European Union in the 1990s, following the country's accession to the EEC (1986), facilitated the development of a culture of consumerism in the Portuguese context. Moreover, the years between 1986 and 1992 consolidated

---

[3]   The Stability and Growth Pact was an agreement signed in 1997 by the 27 member states of the European Union with the focus on the stability of the Economic and Monetary Union.
[4]   See Paulo Trigo Pereira, *Portugal: dívida pública e défice democrático* (Fundação Francisco Manuel dos Santos, 2012), p. 34.
[5]   Zygmunt Bauman and Carlo Bordoni, *State of Crisis* (Polity, 2014), p. 25.
[6]   The use of the term PIIGS also contributes to what Elsa Peralta and Lars Jensen refer as 'domestic orientalism' in relation to the views towards Southern and Northern European countries. 'The South […] is characterized by lacks — of responsibility, productivity and rationality. The North, through the verbalizing of the shortcomings of the South, comes to operate as an invisible and hence uncontested model of the perceived ideal characteristics'; Elsa Peralta and Lars Jensen, 'From Austerity to Postcolonial Nostalgia', in *Austere Histories in European Societies: Social Exclusion and the Contest of Colonial Memories*, ed. by Stefan Jonsson and Julia Willén (Routledge, 2017), pp. 74–91 (p. 74).
[7]   See Alexandre Abreu, and others, eds, *A crise, a Troika e as alternativas urgentes* (Tinta-da-china, 2013), p. 22.

neoliberal politics in the country, stressing the abolition of financial control on the way to the introduction of the Euro currency.[8]

During the crisis, Portugal faced many economic challenges, such as 'paying for large past debts, controlling future public spending, restarting economic growth and lowering unemployment, improving competitiveness and capital allocation'.[9] In 2011, facing financial difficulties, the Portuguese government led by Pedro Passos Coelho of the *Partido Social Democrata* (PSD) sought international help and signed a Memorandum with the Troika (a group formed by the European Central Bank, the European Commission and the International Monetary Fund) on 17 May 2011. This Memorandum between the Troika and Portugal, which was frequently reviewed, established a new programme of governance until June 2014. On the one hand, the Troika gave Portugal a 78€ billion loan, but on the other hand, repayments led to huge social pain.[10] Putting this project forward, their plan was based on three main points of action: austerity, liberalization, and privatization. The intervention of the Troika entailed a long period of recession, unemployment, social inequality, erosion of social rights, and a general mood of fear towards an economic system that was already unproductive and uncompetitive.[11] The social pain lived in the context of austerity has been satirized in recent Portuguese film; for instance, volume 1 of the trilogy *As Mil e Uma Noites/Arabian Nights* (2015), directed by Miguel Gomes, ironically portrays this situation by representing the government riding camels, arguably referring to the subservient position of Portuguese society — the camels — in the context of the austerity measures.

The project to restructure Portugal's debt, and its rigidity, led the country to severe economic austerity with a particular impact on employment (youth unemployment, long-term unemployment, precarious job conditions with part-time workers discouraged from looking for full-time jobs, and highly qualified workers leaving the country to seek job opportunities abroad). In Portugal the group of precarious workers became known as the *Geração à*

---

[8]   As expressed by João Rodrigues: 'O essencial da economia política neoliberal foi fixado entre 1986 e 1992, entre a entrada na CEE e a adesão ao Sistema Monetário Europeu, com a abolição definitiva dos controlos de capitais, no caminho para o Euro' [The basis of the neoliberal political economy was fixed between 1986 and 1992, between the entry into the EEC and joining the European Monetary System, with the definitive abolition of capital controls, in the move to the Euro]; João Rodrigues, *O neoliberalismo não é um slogan* (Tinta-da-china, 2022), p. 203.

[9]   Ricardo Reis, 'Looking for a Success in the Eurocrisis Adjustment Programs: The Case of Portugal', *Brookings Papers on Economic Activity* (2015), pp. 433–47 (p. 435).

[10]   David Birmingham, *A Concise History of Portugal* (Cambridge University Press, 2018), p. 209.

[11]   'A intervenção externa da chamada troika confronta hoje o país com um quadro prolongado de recessão, com o aumento do desemprego e das desigualdades, acentuando-se a erosão de direitos sociais e laborais e instituindo-se uma liberticida economia do medo' [The external intervention of the so-called Troika today confronts the country with a prolonged period of recession, with an increase in unemployment and inequalities, accentuating the erosion of social and labour rights and instituting a paralysing economy of fear]; José Reis and José Rodrigues, 'A crise como oportunidade?', in *Portugal e a Europa em crise: para acabar com a economia de austeridade*, ed. by José Reis and José Rodrigues (Actual Editora, 2011), pp. 11–15 (p. 12).

Rasca [Desperate Generation].[12] This group has its equivalent in the context of Spain through the *Indignadx*. The expression *Geração à Rasca* was coined on the 12 March 2011, following a street protest organized through Facebook and it became a turning point in Portuguese national politics. In the 2000s statistics showed that around 30% of the employees in the context of the total number of employments were precarious workers (including here fixed-term contracts, temporary workers, self-employed workers and zero-hours contract workers).[13] From 2011, the words precarity and austerity became central and critical in Portuguese everyday life, particularly because the rule of austerity placed the financial recovery upon the citizens' shoulders, thereby exacerbating their already declining living standards. Along with that, austerity and precarity not only affected the population's pockets, but also their self-image and self-representation, and this is also transferred to the means used by the filmmakers in the struggle to produce their films. The intervention of the Troika also brought hard times to the audio-visual industry, and this became clear when, in 2012, the government suspended all funds to the audio-visual sector, the so-called 'year zero' of Portuguese film, as shown by Olga Kourelou, Mariana Liz, and Belén Vidal:

> The new government, elected in June 2011, just two months after the bailout was agreed, dismantled the ministry of culture and suspended all public funding for the audio-visual sector. Previous governments in Portugal had dismissed the ministry of culture. However, the blanket suspension of funding was an unprecedented measure in a sector that had received large sums of state support since 1971. This was the 'year zero' since, for the very first time, no funding was made available. 2012 thus became a new watershed in the history of Portuguese film.[14]

This difficult environment for film production created a space for Portuguese filmmakers to explore new ways of producing films. It is clear that the means of production are now very different, considering a director's visibility and gender. For instance, Marco Martins's films show a larger investment and financial support whereas Pedro Pinho's films are clearly produced with less financial support. Film directors such as Miguel Gomes, Marco Martins, João Canijo and Pedro Costa are examples of acclaimed filmmakers that clearly benefit from financial support, contrasting with other directors such as Leonor Teles, Pedro Pinho, João Salaviza, Raquel Freire and Luísa Sequeira. Measures of austerity in the film sector led many filmmakers to produce their films in small settings,

---

[12]   Between 2011 and 2014, it was possible to observe the formation of many groups protesting against austerity, such as: Geração à Rasca, Movimento 15M, Que se Lixe a Troika, Indignados, Precariações, APRe!, Acampada Lisboa — Democracia Verdadeira Já, Portugal Uncut, ATTAC Portugal, Plataforma 15-O. See Renato Miguel do Carmo, and others, eds, *O trabalho aqui e agora: crises, percursos e vulnerabilidades* (Tinta-da-china, 2021), p. 242.
[13]   See Elísio Estanque, *A classe média: ascensão e declínio* (Fundação Francisco Manuel dos Santos, 2012), p. 69.
[14]   Olga Kourelou, Mariana Liz, and Belén Vidal, 'Crisis and Creativity: The New Cinemas of Portugal, Greece and Spain', *New Cinemas*, 12.1+2 (2014), pp. 133–51 (p. 135).

restricted apartments, using naturalistic sound and handheld cameras, as well as bringing non-professional actors to the films.

Precarity and Austerity Urbanism

Austerity measures implemented at the time also had an impact in terms of space. In the field of geography, austerity urbanism has been a critical concept in the study of the effects of financial crisis in urban spaces. Austerity urbanism, as a mutation of neoliberal urbanism, is often discussed by geographers such as Jamie Peck, Fran Tonkiss, Neil Brenner and Nik Theodore as a key consequence of the politics of austerity, particularly during or in the aftermath of moments of financial crisis.[15] This concept gained popularity specifically in moments of crisis, but also as a single way to rule countries, particularly in the context of the United States. If, in the United States, austerity urbanism seems to be a normalized attitude towards the population, this is quite a new phenomenon for Southern European countries in the wake of the financial crisis of 2008. Public austerity became the government response to the financial scenario, and those targeted were unavoidably the most vulnerable.[16] Government policies take cities as 'key targets for a punitive politics of austerity'.[17] The huge cuts promoted by austerity have a serious impact, above all in peripheral areas of cities: these urban spaces suffer from financial cuts to the modernization of neighbourhoods and the people in greatest need of support lose access to government housing. This has resulted in the decline of urban space where many city sites become spaces of abandonment and ruin. The neoliberalization of space during the recession in southern European countries 'has created highly uneven and differentiated geographies of enclaves of wealth and new regions of deprivation, dispossession and marginalization'.[18] In cinematic terms, my analysis considers austerity urbanism firstly through the importance attributed to empty spaces.

Precarity and spatial segregation have been clearly identified as ineluctable consequences of austerity urbanism. There are different approaches to the concept of precarity, but there are also common patterns around the term, including words such as insecurity, vulnerability, and uncertainty. In his theorization of precariousness, Zygmunt Bauman articulates the combination of three key features as part of this experience — insecurity, uncertainty and

---

[15]   See Jamie Peck and Adam Tickell, 'Neoliberalizing Space', *Antipode*, 34.3 (2002), pp. 380–404; Jamie Peck, Nik Theodore, and Neil Brenner, 'Neoliberal Urbanism: Models, Moments, Mutations', *The SAIS Review of International Affairs*, 29.1 (2009), pp. 49–66; Jamie Peck, 'Austerity Urbanism: American Cities under Extreme Economy', *City*, 16.6 (2012), pp. 626–55.
[16]   See Jamie Peck, 'Austerity Urbanism: American Cities under Extreme Economy', *City*, 16.6 (2012), pp. 626–55 (p. 626).
[17]   Fran Tonkiss, 'Austerity Urbanism and the Makeshift City', *City*, 17.3 (2013), pp. 312–24 (p. 312).
[18]   Margit Mayer, 'First World Urban Activism: Beyond Austerity Urbanism and Creative City Politics', *City*, 17.1 (2013), pp. 5–19 (p. 10).

'unsafety':

> The phenomenon [precariousness] which all these concepts try to grasp
> and articulate is the combined experience of *insecurity* (of position, entitle-
> ments and livelihood), of *uncertainty* (as to their continuation and future
> stability) and of *unsafety* (of one's body, one's self and their extensions:
> possessions neighbourhood, community).[19]

My analysis suggests that uncertainty and instability in the context of
precarity are expressed through the use of handheld cameras. Furthermore,
we see the back of the characters' heads, emphasizing the sense of characters'
entrapment.

Precariousness and precarity are historically interconnected, but authors
such as Judith Butler, although recognizing the links, distinguish between the
two terms by attributing a more politicized effect to the term precarity, while
precariousness has a more existential conception.[20] In this sense, according to
this author, lives would be by definition precarious, and precarity would be a
consequence of the failure of social and economic networks of support, exposing
people to violence, injury and death.[21] Considering the twenty-first-century US
context, Butler suggests dependency as a way of living, which becomes very
important during times of crisis. The author notes: 'To say that life is precarious
is to say that the possibility of being sustained relies fundamentally on social
and political conditions, and not only on a postulated internal drive to live.'[22] In
this dependency, the characters of *São Jorge* live in constrained circumstances,
begging for help from the state, but failing to be heard. To some extent,
geographers respond to precarity by offering a spatial organization of precarity.
Geographies of capitalism, geographies of vulnerability or geographies of
precarity are essential concepts when analysing the shape of precarity observed
in urban areas. The experience of precarity, particularly as experienced by
migrant communities, and the forcing of precarious workers to the peripheral
areas of big cities creates stereotyped perceptions of specific communities,
generating social segregation and exclusion — a demonizing belief that
particular social groups are not expected to be hardworking people. The crisis
aggravated this idea, also by pushing certain communities to the outskirts
of cities with very loose access to the city centres. As the article will show,
the perpetuation of common stereotypes around Roma, Asian and Brazilian
communities is a key point in *São Jorge*. These stereotypes cover the type
of jobs or the absence of them associated with these communities but also
the space they inhabit in the urban periphery. Immigrant communities are

---

[19] Zygmunt Bauman, *Liquid Modernity* (Polity 2000), p. 161.
[20] See Judith Butler: 'The more or less existential conception of "precariousness" is thus linked with a
more specifically political notion of "precarity".' Judith Butler, *Frames of War: When is Life Grievable?*
(Verso, 2016), p. 3.
[21] Judith Butler, *Frames of War*, p. 25.
[22] Judith Butler, *Frames of War*, p. 21.

particularly affected by this, seen then as non-productive social groups.[23] In terms of geography, social groups denote their vulnerability through the space they inhabit in the city. The harsh policies hitting urban space in times of crisis push many dwellers to the peripheral space of the city, and in this sense austerity urbanism not only brings consequences in terms of class, but also in an intersectional dimension with race.

Precarity has been also analysed through the lens of film studies and it has consequences not only for film settings as well as the dynamics of the film industry. Filmmakers in Portugal hit by measures of austerity in their work have been approaching the theme of crisis in film in such a constant manner that it is possible to observe the trend of a so-called 'Cinema of Precarity'. Alice Bardan, working on the concept of the European cinema of precarity, brings important points to bear on the definition of precarity. On the one hand, Bardan suggests that precarity refers to a multiplication of unstable forms of living, and on the other hand, this concept also brings new forms of political struggle and solidarity.[24] This is clear in this film: it is possible to observe the struggle to survive the crisis with clear oppositions between the government and the population, but a strong sense of community exists among characters too. Both scenarios have also their counterpart in the Portuguese film industry. Although there were harsh cuts in the film sector, filmmakers remained together through national strikes against the precarity of the film industry.

Cinematic Context of *São Jorge*

After *Alice* (2005) and *Como Desenhar um Círculo Perfeito* [*How to Draw a Perfect Circle*] (2009), Marco Martins released *São Jorge* (2016). The protagonist, Jorge, moves between the *Bairro da Jamaica* (in Seixal) and the *Bairro da Bela Vista* (in Setúbal) in order to perform his job. These two areas in Portugal have been largely stigmatized due to their inhabitants and the economic crisis only accentuated this trend. Immigrant communities mainly from the former colonies live in these areas, and the inhabitants have been targets of successive relocations that exacerbate the stigma towards them. As far as Jamaica is concerned, the history of the neighbourhood started in the 1980s with an increased number of construction projects in the area. The aim was to construct tower blocks, but the project never came to fruition. In the 1990s these unfinished constructions started to attract migrants coming from Portuguese-speaking African countries (PALOPs), especially São Tomé and Príncipe.[25] In

[23] See Isabel Pato and Margarida Pereira, 'Austerity and (New) Limits of Segregation in Housing Policies: The Portuguese Case', *International Journal of Housing Policy*, 16.4 (2016), pp. 524–42 (p. 531).
[24] See Alice Bardan, 'The New European Cinema of Precarity: A Transnational Perspective', in *Work in Cinema: Labor and The Human Condition*, ed. by Ewa Mazierska (Palgrave Macmillan, 2013), pp. 69–187 (p. 71).
[25] Cristina Faria Ferreira and Daniel Rocha, '"Saiam do bairro, mas não o levem convosco." Começou o realojamento do bairro da Jamaica', *Público*, 17 December 2018 <https://www.publico.pt/2018/12/17/

2018, there was a project to relocate the inhabitants of Jamaica and the government aimed to conclude the relocation by the end of 2023, but the process only finished in February 2024. The notion of austerity urbanism becomes fundamental to the analysis of *São Jorge*, particularly in light of the layout of urban space and the levels of segregation promoted by austerity measures. Austerity urbanism creates spaces of precarity where segregated communities are targets of racism and sexism. My analysis of *São Jorge* reveals that austerity urbanism is depicted through the settings of abandoned landscapes, as well as the links between public space and domestic space.

São Jorge is filmed in the *Bairro da Jamaica* and the *Bairro da Bela Vista*, and it depicts Jorge (Nuno Lopes), an unemployed boxer, who becomes a debt collector with a debt-collection agency during the Troika intervention in Portugal. Following his dismissal from a factory, Jorge sees in this agency an opportunity to gain money and to pay his own debts. This agency uses violent methods to collect money from people. Hired to coerce people to pay their debts, Jorge feels unable to act violently towards debtors who have difficulties in paying, because he is himself struggling to pay his own debts.

In *São Jorge*, the viewer is confronted with a mobile camera and, very importantly, the workspace of the protagonist is the street, the flats of strangers, restaurants, and factories that Jorge visits to collect debts; importantly, we realize that he himself is no different to the other people in debt. This explains Jorge's inability to be violent towards other people: the problems experienced by Jorge in his household are similar to the ones experienced by the community. The blurred boundary between Jorge's domestic space and his workspace (as his workspace is other people's domestic space) contributes to a sense of disorientation, but also calls attention to the survival mode of characters in times of austerity.

The urban film settings of *São Jorge* very frequently portray empty spaces, arguably because austerity measures affect urban planning and imply the displacement of populations to different areas of cities due to financial issues. This is a pattern in *São Jorge*, but it also seems to be a *topos* in the Portuguese cinema of the crisis. Manuel Mozos with his film *Ruínas [Ruins]* (2009) has previously drawn attention to an image of Portugal as a country made of abandoned spaces. *Ruínas* opens the discussion of spatial abandonment, almost as a premonition, that suggests a Portugal in crisis. The first volume of *As Mil e Uma Noites* (volume 1: *O Inquieto*), directed by Miguel Gomes, also starts with the setting of the shipyard of Viana do Castelo, framing the landscape of the workplace and its workers with no work to carry out. The *estaleiros* [shipyards] of Viana do Castelo are very well-known for playing an important role in the

local/noticia/saiam-bairro-nao-levem-convosco-comecou-realojamento-bairro-jamaica-1855077> [accessed 17 September 2025]. See also Joana Gorjão Henriques, 'Realojamento do Jamaica: "Promessas há muitas mas não vejo nada feito"', *Público*, 20 September 2018 <https://www.publico.pt/2018/09/20/local/noticia/realojamento-do-jamaica-promessas-ha-muitas-mas-nao-vejo-nada-feito-1844562> [accessed 17 September 2025].

identity of the people of that region in the north of Portugal. These shipyards are responsible for the construction of many ships spread worldwide and, in fact, this company suffered considerably from the consequences of the crisis in Portugal and in Europe.

When it comes to empty and abandoned spaces, *São Jorge* seems to follow the same pattern, and here I flag up the constant scenes of factories that have closed down or building work that has been halted, representing a country that stagnated and decayed during the intervention of the Troika in Portugal. In the case of *São Jorge*, the beginning of the film portrays a series of empty spaces or ruined places. To denote ruined spaces, the director offers viewers a series of shots portraying an old outdoor hoarding without advertisements or announcements, but with the traces and marks of past advertisements, an empty apartment with broken windows while it is possible to hear a telephone, observe empty buildings, a road that has become a dead end, and a completely embargoed port. The settings are gloomy, with the use of natural lighting, illustrating the depressive mood of the critical context.

São Jorge arguably recalls one of the first films of the Portuguese *Cinema Novo* of the 1960s — *Belarmino* (1964) — directed by Fernando Lopes. In an interview with the Portuguese journalist Baptista-Bastos, the ex-boxer Belarmino Fragoso talks about his professional experience as a boxer during the dictatorship in Lisbon which opens up a discussion of the poverty lived amongst working-class groups and the financial difficulties experienced under the Portuguese dictatorial regime.[26] In *Belarmino* there is the expression of a bourgeois society, where characters like Belarmino are deliberately excluded. This is the cinematic space of a busy downtown Lisbon and modern neighbourhoods of the Avenida de Roma and the Avenida dos Estados Unidos da América, where exclusion is seen at a local level, but it can also be considered in a global scale.[27] Belarmino and Jorge are not so distant in relation to the construction of their characters — they both represent the image of the giant body perpetuated by boxing films, and both of them are victims of poverty. The metaphor of Belarmino's position taken to mean the position of Portugal

[26] *Belarmino* and *Os Verdes Anos* (Paulo Rocha, 1963) were the inaugural films of the Portuguese *Cinema Novo* and they both were looking at a new representation of the city and to marginal characters, in clear opposition to the films produced during the *Estado Novo* Regime. As expressed by Tiago Baptista: 'Os Verdes Anos (Paulo Rocha, 1963) e Belarmino (Fernando Lopes, 1964), os dois filmes que inauguraram o movimento [Cinema Novo], ancoraram estas mudanças numa nova representação da cidade. Ao contrário das "comédias de Lisboa" dos anos 30 e 40, onde todas as personagens estavam integradas numa qualquer comunidade solidária, os protagonistas dos filmes de Paulo Rocha e Fernando Lopes são indivíduos que a cidade marginalizou' [Os Verdes Anos (Paulo Rocha, 1963) and Belarmino (Fernando Lopes, 1964), the two films that inaugurated the Cinema Nova movement, anchored these changes in a new representation of the city. Contrary to the 'Lisbon comedies' of the 30s and 40s, where all the characters were integrated into some binding community, the protagonists of the films of Paulo Rocha and Fernando Lopes are individuals that the city has marginalized]; Tiago Baptista, 'Nacionalmente correcto: a invenção do cinema português', *Estudos do Século XX*, 9 (2009), pp. 307–23 (p. 313).
[27] See Tiago Baptista, p. 313.

as a poor country in relation to the rest of Europe could be also drawn in the context of *São Jorge*. Along with *Belarmino*, it is possible to name other boxing films, such as *Documento Boxe* (2005), a documentary directed by Miguel Clara Vasconcelos, and *Gabriel* (2018), directed by Nuno Bernardo. Much inspired by the Hollywood film tradition, Portuguese boxing dramas always revolve around class struggle and, importantly, bring racism into the discussion.

The *Bairro da Jamaica* is a target of racism as a place of precarity and one where most of the population belong to minority groups. In *São Jorge* there is an intersectional dimension that shows not only discrimination through race, but also with regards to gender. The boxing film tradition generally portrays women as a diversion, often with the purpose of reinforcing the male's hero's heterosexuality.[28] In this sense, female characters as the loved ones or the family are seen as distractions to the boxer's focus on the fight. *São Jorge*, arguably following this trend, portrays a central female figure — Susana — who is the protagonist's loved one. A victim of social prejudice and patriarchy, Susana lives in the *Bairro da Jamaica*, and she is also black and Brazilian.[29] She is potentially the strongest character of the film, but portrayed by the director as a diversion. It can be argued that Susana thus occupies multiple and intersectional spaces of segregation. Jorge's father constantly refers to her as '*preta*' and '*puta*', clearly expressing his racism and sexism towards the female figure. In this film, like a common stereotype within Portuguese society, Brazilians are frequently seen as outsiders who eventually marry a Portuguese person to get a residence visa. They are often stereotyped by the Portuguese as 'kind', 'happy', 'smart', or 'chilled',[30] accentuating their subalternity. The stigma is precisely a consequence of the continuity between lusotropicalism and the concept of lusophony, as well as the influence of Brazilian soap operas in Portuguese television.[31] Through these

[28] Kath Woodward points to the key role of women in boxing films as a way of glorifying the male's role. Women frequently appear in contrast to men to underscore their strength and virility; Kath Woodward, *Boxing, Masculinity and Identity: The 'I' of the Tiger* (Routledge, 2017), p. 134.

[29] Note that when referring to the presence of Brazilian communities in Portugal (and specifically in Lisbon) they are to be found particularly in Arroios, but also in areas on the periphery of the city, such as Costa da Caparica, Cacém, Rio de Mouro, Cascais, Alcabideche, and Odivelas. See Simone Frangella, 'Fomos conhecer um tal de Arroios: construção de um lugar na imigração brasileira em Lisboa', in *Cidade e império: dinâmicas coloniais e reconfigurações pós-coloniais*, ed. by Nuno Domingos and Elsa Peralta (Edições 70, 2013), pp. 463–502 (pp. 463–64).

[30] See Igor José de Renó Machado, 'a de que ele [Brazilian] é naturalmente alegre, simpático, malemolente e esperto. As representações sobre o Brasil oferecem um lugar subalterno, que é constantemente reafirmado pela submissão de muitos brasileiros aos estereótipos' [the Brazilian is naturally cheerful, kind, easy-going and smart. Representations of Brazil create a subaltern role that is constantly reaffirmed by the submission of many Brazilians to the stereotypes]; Igor José de Renó Machado, 'Imigrantes brasileiros no Porto: aproximação à perenidade de ordens raciais e coloniais portuguesas', *Lusotopie*, 11 (2004), pp. 121–40 (p. 130).

[31] Simone Frangella, exploring common views of Portuguese people in relation to Brazilians, observes: 'do ponto de vista de um saber comum português, as imagens sobre o Brasil, sejam as reificadas por um discurso "luso-tropicalista", ou promovidas por uma coleção de imagens brasileiras "de exportação", ou veiculadas com grande influência pelas telenovelas, são uma amálgama de estereótipos, os quais acabam por marcar de forma quase banal as interações sociais entre brasileiros e portugueses' [from the point of view of Portuguese common knowledge, images of Brazil, whether

vehicles the old colonialist fantasies are perpetuated through stereotypes. Based on this, it is not unusual to hear Jorge's father accusing Jorge of having a child with a Brazilian woman, the one who 'sacou os papéis' [got the visa sorted], and also the one who is taking advantage of Jorge's money ('Ando aqui eu montado nuns ténis de cinco euros e tu a dares o arame [slang term for money] todo à preta' [Here I am in five-euro sneakers and you give all the dough to the black girl]), asking at the same time if Jorge is intending to give a 'subsídio de putice' [bitch allowance] to Susana. The evidence of racism towards Brazilian women is also ventriloquized by Susana when towards the end of the film she shouts against prejudice. Susana herself repeats ironically Jorge's father words: 'não casa com ela' [don't marry her], 'a puta da preta' [the black whore], 'a puta da brasileira' [the Brazilian whore], 'ela só engravidou para te foder' [she only got pregnant to screw you over], 'não vê que ela só quer casar, Jorginho, para ter o passaporte' [don't you see, Jorginho, she only wants to get married to get the passport]. Susana is a victim of the intersection between race, gender, and class exclusion. Racism is not only articulated by Jorge's father, but it is a common claim within the whole community in the film.

Along with Brazilians, Eastern European migrants, and Roma communities,[32] the Chinese are also targets of the racism depicted in *São Jorge*, and stereotypes are generally fostered in conversations that take place at dinner tables. In times of crisis, immigrants as well as Portuguese minority groups become the favourite target to be blamed for the lack of opportunities in terms of employment, issues of social services or housing shortages. In the Portuguese context, as demonstrated in the film, the Chinese are frequently perceived as the ones who build empires of chain stores. João Pedro Rodrigues and João Rui Guerra da Mata have been making short films about this theme, with films such as *Mahjong* (2013), directing the viewer to Varziela in Vila do Conde, the biggest Chinatown in Portugal. The directors reflect on the portrait of the Chinese population living in Portugal as the 'maus da fita' [bad guys]. Eastern European migrants have been extensively present in films directed by Sérgio Tréfaut, such as *Lisboetas* (2004) and *Viagem a Portugal* (2011); Tréfaut's films show the persistent stigmatization of Eastern European communities, seen mainly as job-stealers. Although scarcely problematized in Portuguese cinema, Roma communities are also targets of racism in the Portuguese context. Leonor Teles is one of the youngest Portuguese filmmakers and one of the main names working on Roma communities. Born in 1992, she has roots in the local Roma community of Vila Franca de Xira (a municipality located to the north of Lisbon) and her films *Rhoma Acans* (2012) and *Balada de um Batráquio*

they are reified by a 'Lusotropicalist' discourse, or promoted by a collection of images of Brazil 'for export', or transmitted by the great influence of soap operas, are an amalgam of stereotypes, which end up characterizing in an almost banal way the social interactions between Brazilians and Portuguese]; Simone Frangella, p. 468.

[32] In *São Jorge*, these communities are referred as *ciganos*, a dismissive term in Portuguese to refer to Roma communities.

[*Batrachian's Ballad*] (2016) redirect the viewer to the stigma against Roma communities. This is not exclusive to Portugal; within a white and privileged Europe, Roma people are interpreted as 'problematic', mythically seen as 'uncivilized', a 'real danger' and a 'threat'.[33] The tension between white people and Roma communities is not new, and is expressed through one character's voice: 'temos que meter os ciganos na nossa sociedade, não me metam a mim na sociedade deles' [we have to integrate the gypsies into our society, don't integrate me into their society].

Blurred Boundaries between Domestic Space and the Workplace

In the context of *São Jorge*, austerity urbanism can be seen in the abandoned landscapes as mentioned above, but it is also related to the director's choice of small settings and constrained mise-en-scène. Furthermore, it can be posited that the blurred boundaries between domestic space and workspace suggest disorientation arising from measures of austerity. The entrapment of the characters can be observed through a dynamic of circularity between the chasers and the chased. Constrained spaces, both in the domestic space and the workplace are essential markers of characters' entrapment.

In this film, domestic space consists of very small rooms, impairing the characters' movement in the house. At the dining tables of *São Jorge*, the viewer is introduced to conversations about precarious employment, unemployment, and job opportunities; minimum wages and job centres; state benefits and racism. Constrained domestic spaces equate with austerity urbanism. Small houses and apartments, different obstacles that hinder characters' movements, and the use of frame-within-a-frame techniques are all examples of common trends in the Portuguese cinema of austerity. My approach questions the traditional view of observing private space and workspace as independent spaces. Indeed, Marco Martins's film suggests the blurred boundaries between domestic space and workspace. Decisions taken at work affect the living conditions in the domestic space and vice-versa. The boundaries often applied to distinguish the private sphere from public space have been prolifically discussed by geographers such as Krishan Kumar and Ekaterina Makarova who suggest the 'domestication of public space' as key to a consideration of contemporary urban space.[34] In their perspective, this concept points to the fact that 'many things once done privately, in the confined domestic space of the home — eating, talking intimately, expressing emotions, entertaining oneself — are now increasingly being done outside the home, in what were formerly thought of as public spaces.'[35] Although their work focuses particularly on the

---

[33]   See Sebijan Fejzula, 'A Europa civilizada e sua violência política contra o povo roma', in *O estado do racismo em Portugal: racismo antinegro e anticiganismo no direito e nas políticas públicas*, ed. by Silvia Rodríguez Maeso (Tinta-da-china, 2021), pp. 289–98.
[34]   See Krishan Kumar and Ekaterina Makarova, 'The Portable Home: The Domestication of Public Space', *Sociological Theory*, 26.4 (2008), pp. 324–43.
[35]   Krishan Kumar and Ekaterina Makarova, p. 325.

dynamics played out in the domestic space and the public sphere (spaces such as the shopping mall, the church), this theoretical work can be framed in the context of *São Jorge*, whose protagonist projects onto the street the vulnerability he experiences at home. Jorge's job can also be seen as an invasion of others' domestic and private space as he chases debtors in their own houses to recover their debts, so that the boundaries between domestic space and workspace are blurred. Workspaces, as well as domestic spaces of the film are always confined, and it can be argued that this feature exacerbates characters' entrapment.

In *São Jorge*, constrained spaces also enable us to think about characters' vulnerability, and the use of a frame-within-a-frame technique contributes to the sense of entrapment of characters. Jorge's bedroom is very small and it is there where we can see the character frequently framed within a frame with a lot of obstacles between the viewer and him. Towards the end of the film, Jorge forces Susana to stay with him, and an argument also happens between two lockers of a changing room. Furthermore, blurred characters are created using long-focal-length lenses, as well as long shots, while stark contrasts of light accentuate the dimension of shame experienced by characters. In *São Jorge*, along with stereotypes, tables become communitarian spaces where people discuss the crisis. They are central in Jorge's house. The few different moments at the table always involve different characters, so this is not about a particular family, but about of a community which enters and leaves the house. This becomes clear with the frontal framing of characters talking about their own houses and buildings. Moreover, in Jorge's house it is common to see his father receiving guests and helping them to resolve bureaucratic matters related to jobs and State benefits; Jorge asks a woman to take care of his son for a night. However, none of these characters are part of the household — they come and go without a single bedroom to stay in. The subjects of the conversations that take place in the dining room reveal the effects of the crisis on Portuguese working-class groups: minimum wages, the issues with bureaucracy encountered at job centres, and the choices of either working or living on State benefits. The complaint about the politicians is constant, and the theme of racism is again brought to the table as well. The conversations at the table become important because they will then have their visual correspondence in urban space. In fact, the segregation that becomes the theme of a lot of conversations between characters shows forms of segregation at a geographical level in the city.

This perspective of entrapment is also supported by the repeated presence of bars throughout the film, an effect that symbolically emphasizes characters' cramped living conditions. The bars are frequently shown through the use of rack focus shots, and the rapid shifts in perspective create ambiguity between the chasers and the chased. For instance, in Jorge's last chase, when pursuing the restaurant owner, both characters run, and it is possible to see bars of a fence in a fast travelling of the camera. In the end, I argue that we can judge all characters as victims — all of them are survivors, all of them are facing debt. Circularity can also be observable when using the frame-within-a-frame technique. Jorge is frequently framed in frame-within-a-frame, as are anonymous people and even children too, as a pessimistic prediction for future generations. Jorge is frequently caught observing people and landscapes through bars and many times in the moments after is caught by the viewer behind bars. This proves once again that Jorge is not different from the other characters in the film — he is a chaser and chased. Jorge first hears stories of debts behind a wall of bars. He can see people struggling as if they were in jail, and immediately afterwards the viewer is able to see Jorge framed on the side of the debtors, as if he was in jail too. This is a constant feature in *São Jorge*, and it soon becomes a pattern: Jorge observes people as if he were contemplating a picture in a museum, to then take part in the scene. Jorge looks through a glass window and listens to agency employees attempting to collect money from debtors, and he sees his image reflected in the glass, as if it was a mirror. At the restaurant, while chasing the owner to put pressure on him to pay his debts, Jorge also observes the restaurant from the outside before going inside. The restaurant shot is an important one, showing the aquarium with big fish and small fish. Every time Jorge goes to the restaurant he stares at the fish, he feeds them, and at the end of the film he even argues that the restaurant owner's fish get better food than he does. In this sense, the aquarium and Jorge's obsession with it become a very important nuance to this analysis. The presence of the aquarium may suggest the claustrophobia lived by the most vulnerable. The aquarium, as a small square, also carries the sense of suffocation of the fish. In my analysis, claustrophobia works in two different contexts — it may be a space of suffocation, but it also may work as a bubble for moments of love, arguably recalling the unity in moments of precarity as suggested by Alice Bardan. If on the one hand, the use of the frame-within-a-frame technique, as well as small spaces such as the aquarium, refer to suffocation, on the other hand, the space of the car enables one of the rare opportunities for love, when, as for instance, Jorge has sex with Susana. The rare moments of affection between Jorge and his son also happen in Jorge's small bedroom.

In an early scene in the film, the viewer is presented with the image of anonymous people, all asking for help to pay their debts in a chorus of voices. Their anonymity is emphasized through the use of long-focal-length lenses, which blurs the image of these characters. This is further conveyed through the stark contrast between light and shadow. These techniques may imply what I call *pobreza envergonhada* [shameful poverty], the dimension of shame lived particularly by middle-class groups. Shame here is also fostered by the uses of long-shots. When Jorge is returning from the supermarket with his son, he waits for people to leave a shopping cart, so he can collect the cart and get the coin from strangers. This is presented through a long shot, so we cannot see clearly that it is Jorge and his son. Distance in this context is crucial for reinforcing the shame associated with poor living conditions. The viewer is confronted with a middle class that progressively loses its purchasing power or old privileges and status, and *São Jorge*'s characters also illustrate this theme.

In the film, the mobile camera may suggest instability, and it often follows the characters closely, almost as if it attached to the body of the protagonist. This is a common technique used in the cinema of the crisis and it goes beyond Portuguese film — directors such as Ken Loach and the Dardenne brothers have used this technique too. In the case of *São Jorge*, the framing of Jorge with his back to the camera while walking may work as a counter-discourse in relation to the politics of austerity. In fact, the repetition of this type of camerawork stresses a political statement, working as a form of resistance towards the state and the intervention of the Troika. Jennifer M. Barker and Adam Cottrel refer to this type of camerawork as the 'follow-shot' in the context of recent American cinema, 'in which the camera seems to float behind a male character, his head neatly centred in the frame'.[36] Both authors consider the link between this type of shot and masculinity and how this camerawork represents the need to act in relation to the immediate present, leaving emotions behind.[37] Along with the need to act quickly and survive, the critical portrait of austerity is also given by Jorge's eye, and from the start of the film this seems to be a strategy for showing the crisis through the eyes of the victims as a protest. Jean-Pierre Dardenne and Luc Dardenne frequently use the same filmic approach when framing their characters. Focused on the violent reality of unemployment or immigration of the *sans-papiers* (immigrants without papers) in the context of the Belgian periphery, films like *La Promesse* [*The Promise*] (1996) or *Deux Jours, Une Nuit* [*Two Days, One Night*] (2014) make use of handheld camerawork, direct sound, and very importantly, the frame of the back of the characters. These techniques are also used extensively by Marco Martins in *São Jorge*. Sarah Cooper has reflected on the Dardennes' work, and discussed the point of view of the viewer. More than just putting the viewer in the place of the character, there is an expression used by Luc Dardenne that Cooper reminds us about: 'the space of the secret'.[38] The space of the secret is precisely the distance that the Dardenne brothers want to make very clear and it stresses the characters' possibility of having an existence of their own.[39] This important distance can also be identified when Martins frames Jorge, particularly because we are in not in front of point of view shots, but watching the backs or the back of characters' head, imposing a distance that makes the viewer unable to take the place of the character. Referring to the distance between the viewer and the

---

[36]   Jennifer M. Barker and Adam Cottrel, 'Eyes at the Back of His Head: Precarious Masculinity and the Modern Tracking Shot', *Paragraph*, 38.1 (2015), pp. 86–100 (p. 87).
[37]   See Jennifer M. Barker and Adam Cottrel, 'Masculinity as presented by the follow-shot, then, seems to be something entirely of the body. Leaving emotion and intellect behind in favour of the immediately physically present', p. 95.
[38]   Sarah Cooper, 'Mortal Ethics: Reading Levinas with the Dardenne Brothers', *Film-Philosophy*, 11.2 (2007), pp. 66–87 (p. 84).
[39]   Sarah Cooper, p. 84.

characters, Sarah Cooper claims:

> The possibility of seeing or feeling for the characters is replaced by a
> closeness, which serves paradoxically to register both the other characters'
> and our own distance from those filmed. It is the ability *not* to take
> the place of the characters by identifying with an image that facilitates
> recognition of responsibility.[40]

In the context of *São Jorge*, I argue that the use of this distance also emphasizes
the entrapment of Jorge. Jorge is alone in his fight and even the viewer is unable
to 'get inside' the character. Mobility in the context of this article denotes the
power to chase, but also the weakness to be chased. The uses of the mobile
camera denote the powerlessness of characters to overcome the consequences
of austerity, but they also establish a distance between the viewer and the
character. Jorge depends on his feet and strength, and the instability of a mobile
camera accompanying him gives the viewer access to the characters' lack of
power.

Jorge's wandering of streets goes beyond the simple chasing of other people
because walking around for this character is a crucial way to chase himself —
when he runs after people, he is really running after himself, implying a sense
of circularity that demonstrates how cramped this character is. This means that
chasing other people works as a mirror of his own experience of precarity and
explains Jorge's inability to attack a debtor in a factory. The street wanderer has
frequently been associated with the *flâneur*. Walter Benjamin wrote prolifically
about the figure of the *flâneur*, created by the poet Charles Baudelaire in the
nineteenth century. The *flâneur*, a street wanderer of the French arcades, is
linked to a privileged and bohemian Parisian lifestyle. The character-wanderer
of this film contrasts with the Baudelairean idea of the *flâneur* precisely because
Jorge is not privileged. Furthermore, his walks express intentions different to
those of Baudelaire's wanderer. Away from privileged *flânerie*, considering a
person wandering within the modern arcades, Jorge's movement attempts to
figure out his own condition. As demonstrated by Dimitris Eleftheriotis when
referring to the studies of Benjamin and Crary in relation to *flânerie*: 'the
flâneur is not a glorious outsider who opposes and antagonizes capitalism and
the power of the market but he is part of it.'[41] Jorge fits this description — he is
indeed the victim and the pursuer. Jorge is pursuing other people as an agent
of capitalism and chasing himself at the same time as a victim of capitalism.
Another example of this pursuit has its crucial moment at the bridge. The
owner of the restaurant is chased by Jorge and ends up committing suicide at
the bridge. Although it does not represent his own physical death, Jorge 'dies'
with the other character. With no possibility of escaping and without money to
pay his debt, the owner of the restaurant desperately jumps from the bridge and

---

[40]   Sarah Cooper, p. 85.
[41]   Dimitris Eleftheriotis, *Cinematic Journeys: Film and Movement* (Edinburgh University Press,
2010), p. 17.

is hit by a train. Bridges have been frequently studied as spaces of transition,[42] enabling the mobility of people from one point to another, and in the context of *São Jorge*, more than taking the characters from one point to the other in geographical terms, the bridge imposes the transition from life to death — it is the chosen place to commit suicide (the suicide of the character chased by Jorge, but also Jorge's metaphorical suicide). His frustration at facing the suicide of the other character illustrates once again his double facet of chaser and chased.

Conclusion

My analysis of *São Jorge* has reflected on the consequences of measures of austerity at the time of the economic crisis and subsequent intervention of the Troika in Portugal. This article has taken the concepts of austerity urbanism and precarity to show how entrapment of characters can be seen in the film *São Jorge*. Struggling to survive crisis, particular foreign communities, as well as certain social classes, are pushed to the outskirts of cities. Factories and stores, once dynamic and productive, become inactive in times of crisis. I have shown how the Portuguese cinema of austerity enables us to think about precarity at a local level, but also to consider precarity in Portugal in a European context.

This article has also examined the social pain created by harsh economic obligations imposed by the state and its correspondence in space, namely domestic space and workspace. A correlation was suggested between domestic space and workspace: decisions taken at work interfere with the dynamics of the household. Thus, the boundaries between the two types of space are eroded and broken down. It can be argued that this fluidity of borders suggests the disorientation that is characteristic of precarity. Confined film settings, handheld cameras, naturalistic sound, and frame-within-a-frame techniques demonstrate the entrapment of characters. The uses of non-professional actors as well as restricted film settings show the struggle of filmmakers to deal with low budgets to produce their films. In this sense, it can be argued that Portuguese cinema of austerity not only portrays the living conditions of certain fringes of society, but it also marks a generation of filmmakers who struggle to produce their films due to the lack of financial support.

---

[42] See Ulf Strohmayer, 'Bridges: Different Conditions of Mobile Possibilities', in *Geographies of Mobilities: Practices, Spaces, Subjects*, ed. by Tim Cresswell and Peter Merriman (Ashgate, 2013), pp. 119–35 (p. 127).

Geospatial Analysis of *O Quinze*
by Rachel de Queiroz:
Mapping Literary Spaces with ArcGIS Pro

MARIA VITÓRIA DE REZENDE GRISI

Ohio State University

Studies at the intersection of geography and literature demonstrate that literary spaces influence not only how we interpret the real world but also how it is materially experienced. Scholars such as Victoria Saramago,[1] Aarti Smith Madan,[2] Robert Tally,[3] and Sally Bushell,[4] among others, have examined the interconnectedness of fiction and reality. In this article, I shift the perspective: by engaging with real spaces, I demonstrate how mapping can generate new insights into those elements of a novel that have received little critical attention, and whose significance becomes clearer when visualized cartographically. Rachel de Queiroz's *O Quinze* (1930) provides a compelling case for this approach. The novel is deeply tied to themes of space, place, and displacement, and mapping technologies open new avenues for interpretation. Debates in literary geography, literary cartography, and geocriticism are longstanding, offering multiple perspectives on the relationship between two well-established disciplines: literature and geography. This article contributes to that dialogue by testing the boundaries between them. The maps presented here mediate between fictional and real spaces, proposing new ways of reading the novel and understanding the characters' experiences. They also expose the stark inequalities between the *retirantes* and the landowners in the backlands of Ceará.

By working with ArcGIS Pro, a GIS software package for mapping and spatial analysis, I was able to examine how geographical elements not only inform the characters' experiences but also support the *O Quinze*'s broader social critique. Mapping the topography of the region exposes the physical hardships faced by the *retirantes*, the name given to the poor migrants escaping

[1] Victoria Saramago, *Fictional Environments: Mimesis and Deforestation in Latin America* (Northwestern University Press, 2020).
[2] Aarti Smith Madan, *Lines of Geography in Latin American Narrative: National Territory, National Literature*, Geocriticism and Spatial Literary Studies (Palgrave Macmillan, 2017).
[3] Robert Tally, *Spatiality* (Routledge, 2013).
[4] Sally Bushell, *Reading and Mapping Fiction: Spatialising the Literary Text* (Cambridge University Press, 2020).

Portuguese Studies vol. 41 no. 2 (2025), doi:10.1353/port.00044, 248–68
© Modern Humanities Research Association 2025

the drought, and deepens the reading of the characters' suffering. While keeping in mind the tension between fictional and real spaces, I argue that there is value in layering fiction and reality if that means providing a visualization of what was originally only textual. Furthermore, the layered maps revealed a parallel pattern in the displacement of characters, with some undertaking their journeys on foot, facing famine and death along the way, while others travel the same distance by train, in relative comfort. As the analysis will make clear, this parallelism is not evident while reading the novel, since readers may not be familiar with the landscape and infrastructure that inspired the author. By exploring these elements through maps, the study demonstrates not only the interpretive potential of GIS (Geographic Information Systems) for literary analysis but also the growing importance of digital tools as resources available to us as humanities scholars.

Mapping in Literary Analysis

The use of cartography for literary analysis is not particularly new. In *Graphs, Maps, Trees: Abstract Models for Literary History* (2005), Franco Moretti asked a fundamental question about literary maps: 'What exactly do they do? What do they do that cannot be done with words, that is; because, if it can be done with words, then maps are superfluous'.[5] What Moretti is saying is that when creating maps from literary texts it is important to consider the possibility of redundancy, since it is possible to spend valuable time creating a map that simply repeats information already available in the text. For Moretti, the value of maps lies in their role as tools to prepare a text for analysis. By isolating elements of the literary text and organizing them in maps, together 'with a little luck', these visual representations can reveal 'emerging' qualities that were not previously visible through the words of the text alone.[6] At the same time, scholars have noted that Moretti's own experiments often fell short, reducing literary works to cartographic data without necessarily yielding richer readings of the texts themselves.[7] My approach acknowledges this critique but insists on a constant negotiation between fictional and real spaces. Rather than treating maps as ends in themselves, I use them as tools that can, at times, open up new interpretive possibilities. Whether they do so can only be tested in practice, by attempting to map the literary text and evaluating the insights that emerge.

Indeed, mapping, topography, and spatiality have become critical cross-disciplinary tools of analysis within and beyond social sciences. Sally Bushell extends this discussion by reminding us that mapping fiction entails a constant

---

[5]   Franco Moretti, *Graphs, Maps, Trees: Abstract Models for Literary History* (Verso, 2005), p. 35.
[6]   Ibid., p. 53.
[7]   Sally Bushell, 'Mapping Fiction: Spatialising the Literary Work', in *Literary Mapping in the Digital Age*, ed. by David Cooper, Christopher Donaldson, and Patricia Murrieta-Flores (Routledge, 2016), pp. 130–42; Madan, *Lines of Geography*.

negotiation between fictional and real space, and she cautions against the trap of mistaking one for the other.[8] While the base layers of the maps presented in this study draw on the real world, the thematic maps emerge from interpretations of the fictional text itself. In this way, the map becomes a dual construct: rooted in geographic reality but activated through acts of reading and analysis.

The dialogue between fictional and real spaces resonates with studies that explore how literature both reflects and shapes environmental perception. Victoria Saramago, in *Fictional Environments: Mimesis and Deforestation in Latin America* (2020), presents a powerful way of rethinking the relationship between fictional places and the real world. She argues that 'in particular circumstances, literary works not only represent specific environments but also help forge and negotiate public perception of these environments'.[9] By highlighting these entanglements, Saramago shows how fiction can exert environmental agency, shaping public perception and, at times, even material outcomes. This perspective showcases the importance of research that examines the reciprocal dynamics between fiction and reality — how texts both reflect and transform the environments they depict, while those same environments influence the forms and meanings of literary works.

Grounded in these perspectives, these explorations of spatial relationships also require us to consider how human experiences shape our connection to places over time. It is therefore important to examine closely the idea of spatial experience. The connection between humans and their space, what the geographer Yi-Fu Tuan called the sentiment of *topophilia*, can be observed in settlement or mobility.[10] This relationship is not necessarily confined to specific locations. Put another way, experiences are dynamic and the significance we attach to certain spaces can evolve. And, in some cases, continuous movement becomes our place — or non-place — especially when dislocation becomes a permanent condition. What we see here is the profound interrelation between time and space. Experiences, whether literary or lived, are a result of both vectors, and scholars should consider them when analysing a literary text. According to David J. Bodenhamer:

> Narrative space, however, is not a simple construct, a mere representation of the world (fictional or real) that acts as a container for events; instead, it encompasses several types of spaces, all of which have implications for spatial narratives. It is the setting or the physically existing environment in which actions occur and through which people move, but even this concept involves more than we might assume intuitively.[11]

---

[8] Bushell, 'Mapping Fiction'.
[9] Saramago, *Fictional Environments*, p. 8.
[10] Yi-Fu Tuan, *Topophilia: A Study of Environmental Perception, Attitudes, and Values* (Columbia University Press, 1974).
[11] David J. Bodenhamer, 'Narrating Space and Place', in *Deep Maps and Spatial Narratives*, ed. by David J. Bodenhamer, John Corrigan, and Trevor M. Harris (Indiana University Press, 2015), pp. 7–27 (p. 13).

Building on Bakhtin's concept of the *chronotope* — the intrinsic link between time and space — Bodenhamer suggests that both dimensions must be considered together in the study of spatial narratives. This framework helps reveal how physical environments are imagined, organized, and experienced, showing that space is never only material but also symbolic and interpretive. In this sense, it suggests a way in which scholars could analyse not just the settings of a narrative but also the temporal and imaginative dimensions that give meaning to those settings for both characters and readers. This argument opens new paths to the potential of the mapping process.

The ideas discussed above indicate that mapping literature can be a critical approach to gaining new perspectives on literary texts. In order to achieve this goal, the analytical process needs to include both temporal and spatial dimensions. As such, the research methodology of this study centres on Geographic Information Systems (GIS), chosen because of its ability to capture both spatial and temporal data. According to Trevor M. Harris, John Corrigan, and David J. Bodenhamer, editors of *The Spatial Humanities* (2010), GIS uses location data to reveal patterns and connections that remain obscured in conventional text and tables.[12]

This is made possible because of its advanced computing power and its ability to combine and integrate disparate datasets from different formats based on their shared geography.[13] The significance of using GIS in literature was presented in an article by Patricia Murrieta-Flores, Christopher Donaldson, and Ian Gregory, where the authors highlighted the differences between point-based and a GIS-based approach to maps in the study of the journeys documented by three canonical eighteenth-century British travellers.[14] According to the scholars, point-based maps are suitable for 'structuring the analysis of quantitative geographical phenomena, such as proximity and scale', but are limited when it comes to qualitative data such as human experience or even movement from one place to the other. On the other hand, GIS-based approaches allow scholars to 'analyse the geographical experiences and spatial relationships represented in literary works and, even more specifically, in works of travel writing and topographical literature'.[15] GIS technology enables literary scholars to combine quantitative geographical information (distances, elevations, coordinates) with qualitative experiential data (character perceptions, emotional responses, landscape descriptions) through a database structure where each spatial element can be associated with multiple attributes.

Furthermore, GIS-based maps visualize spatial-temporal relationships

---

[12]   Trevor M. Harris, John Corrigan, and David J. Bodenhamer, eds, *The Spatial Humanities: GIS and the Future of Humanities Scholarship* (Indiana University Press, 2010).
[13]   Ibid., p. vii.
[14]   Patricia Murrieta-Flores, Christopher Donaldson, and Ian Gregory, 'GIS and Literary History: Advancing Digital Humanities Research through the Spatial Analysis of Historical Travel Writing and Topographical Literature', *Digital Humanities Quarterly*, 11.1 (2017).
[15]   Ibid., p. 2.

through dynamic mapping, tracking not just where characters move but also how their experiences evolve across time and space. These capabilities are invaluable for analysing works like Queiroz's novel, where movement through space is central to both the narrative and the author's intended social critique. By representing multiple dimensions and layers simultaneously, GIS-based maps can provide a visual framework for understanding complex interplay between geography and human experiences that traditional textual analysis could struggle to capture.

The GIS-based methodological framework is particularly well-suited for analysing works from Brazil's Northeastern regionalism movement, which emphasized the relationship between people and their environment. Among the key figures of this literary movement, Rachel de Queiroz stands out for her detailed geographical representations and her focus on human mobility in response to environmental challenges. Her work provides an ideal case study for demonstrating how spatial analysis can enhance our understanding of literature that is deeply rooted in specific geographical contexts.

Born in Fortaleza, Ceará, in 1910, Rachel de Queiroz was a Brazilian author linked to the Northeastern regionalist movement and later classified within the *Romance de 30*, a literary current that united depictions of the social realities of Brazil's Northeast with the broader traditions of realism and naturalism. Her first novel, *O Quinze*, was published before she turned twenty. Her body of work later focused on exploring social issues and portraying the harsh realities of life in Northeastern Brazil by depicting not only the physical landscapes but also the symbolic ones, providing detailed insights into the environment, culture, traditions, and communities of the Northeast.

O Quinze stands out as a particularly fascinating work because it intertwines fiction with history, alluding directly to the devastating drought that afflicted Ceará in 1915 (the title itself, 'The Fifteen', points to this year of crisis). The novel follows the lives of characters from different socio-economic classes. Conceição is a single twenty-two-year-old teacher who spends her vacations with her grandmother on the family farm in the backlands of Ceará. Vicente is the son of rich farmers who dedicates himself to manual labour to keep the farm going. Chico Bento is a poor farmer who has worked on Dona Maroca's farm with his wife, sister-in-law, and three sons. Due to drought, the landowners are forced to release their livestock, leaving Chico Bento without work, forcing him to migrate to the capital and become a *retirante* — the name given to those escaping drought. Hunger and malnourishment become constant issues for Chico Bento's family during their journey through the parched land. One of their children dies from poisoning after eating raw cassava, and another one of their sons goes missing after following a different group of migrants. Desperate, the family seeks help from the village delegate and godfather of their missing child. He provides them with food and puts them on a train towards Fortaleza. As the drought worsens, Conceição persuades her grandmother to go with her to Fortaleza. Meanwhile, Chico Bento's family arrives in Fortaleza and is forced to live in government internment camps, where the conditions are terrible. By chance, Conceição volunteers at the camp and recognizes them. She offers to help the family move to São Paulo to find better jobs and to become the godmother to their last remaining son, Manuel, raising him for them. Although hesitant, the parents agree, knowing their child will have a better life with her. In December, when the rains finally come, Conceição's grandmother returns to the farm while Conceição stays in the city to raise her godson.

The literary narrative of *O Quinze* is premised on a historical understanding of the impact of the 1915 and 1919 droughts that affected the Northeast of Brazil. The first one had profound socioeconomic consequences for the state of Ceará, where the narrative takes place, as described by historian Marco Antonio Villa: 'Tal qual em outras secas, começaram a chegar os primeiros retirantes à capital: logo já eram 20 mil' [as in other droughts, the first *retirantes* began to arrive in the capital: soon there were already 20,000].[16] In 1914, the local government of Fortaleza created the 'campo de concentração do Alagadiço', an internment camp, to confine the *retirantes* fleeing drought in the backlands.[17] This measure aimed to prevent the devastating consequences experienced during the *Grande Seca* [Big Drought] of 1877–79, when Fortaleza and other Northeastern state capitals suffered from smallpox epidemics and widespread violence. The cities had lacked adequate planning and infrastructure to handle the massive influx of *retirantes*, resulting in severe poverty and social unrest. Frederico de Castro argues that the Alagadiço internment camp can be understood based on the social knowledge that led to its creation, which primarily involved isolating that particular population.[18] Castro outlines the primary objectives of the camp:

> Evitar o contato dos *retirantes* com a cidade, cercá-los num único local onde possam ser fiscalizados, dirigir para este local toda a assistência pública e privada, gerências a mão-de-obra disponível para obras de utilidade do governo, organizar centralizadamente a imigração para a Amazônia diretamente do campo.[19]

> [To avoid contact of the *retirantes* with the city, enclose them in a single space where they could be inspected, direct all public and private assistance to this location, manage the workforce available for government utility works, centrally organize immigration to the Amazon directly from the camp.]

---

[16] Marco Antonio Villa, *Vida e morte no sertão: história das secas no nordeste nos séculos XIX e XX*, 1st edn (Editora Ática, 2001), p. 109.

[17] While the literal translation of the government plan is 'concentration camp', I find it more appropriate to refer to it as 'internment camp', as it has no relation to the concentration camps of the Holocaust. The Alagadiço internment camp was constructed as the only one that year. However, during the drought of 1931–32, the project was expanded, and at least six camps were created, holding up to 105,000 people, according to Castro.

[18] Frederico de Castro, 'Curral dos bárbaros: os campos de concentração no Ceará (1915 e 1932)', *Revista Brasileira de História*, 15.29 (1995), 93–122.

[19] Ibid., p. 105.

Despite these official objectives, the actual conditions within the Alagadiço internment camp diverged significantly from what was being promoted by the government. Rachel de Queiroz's description of the camp reveals a much harsher and darker reality: it was disorganized and overcrowded, leading to higher mortality rates than officially acknowledged. As depicted in Queiroz's novel, child mortality was particularly devastating, with children dying from diseases and starvation both inside and outside the camp.[20] This contrast between official purpose and lived reality is a central tension of the novel that spatial analysis can help illuminate.

The geographical and spatial dimensions of O Quinze make it particularly suitable for a map-based analytical approach. I identified two primary rationales that justify this methodology. The first stems from the environmental context in which the story unfolds: a period of severe drought in the state of Ceará, Brazil. Drought is a recurring climatic phenomenon that affects millions of lives in Brazil's Northeast region, even today, and is deeply embedded in the nation's history. Brazilian scholars who study the Northeast consistently show that drought became a more severe problem due to political inefficacy, and its recurrence has made it a defining feature that influences the people living there. The second rationale for applying spatial analysis to O Quinze relates to how drought shapes human movement and identity. The novel centres on people directly affected by this climate phenomenon, with forced migration becoming a central theme. The need to depart from one's home to find better conditions to survive is a vital characteristic that has shaped both the narrative and the Northeast region itself. This is exemplified by the creation of the term retirantes which refers to those who migrated from the sertões [backlands] of the Northeast in pursuit of better living conditions. The term emerged directly from the reality of drought, which forced large numbers of people into migration, so that displacement became their primary social identity.

Given the novel's deep engagement with questions of space, place, and displacement, mapping tools offer unique analytical possibilities. As Bushell cautions, though, this kind of work requires negotiating between fictional and real spaces, and as Saramago argues, fiction itself can shape public understandings of environments. By visualizing the spaces traversed by characters like Chico Bento's family, we can layer factual topographical data (such as elevation profiles) with the narrative's emotional content (the desperation experienced during their journey), creating a more comprehensive understanding of how geography shapes human experience. This approach also allows us to see how the novel's representation of space intersects with historical realities of drought management and the socio-political responses to climate crisis in early twentieth-century Brazil. In my analysis, I use maps not merely as illustrations but as interpretive tools that reveal new dimensions of meaning in Queiroz's canonical text.

[20] Villa, Vida e morte no sertão, p. 111.

Mapping the Journeys:
Interpreting the Geographic Movements in O Quinze

The contrast between how characters from different social classes experience the same environmental crisis is striking and unmistakable in O Qunize. This disparity reveals how drought functions not merely as a natural phenomenon but as a mechanism that amplifies existing social inequalities. The political implications of the drought arise when the government fails to invest in solutions to the problem. At first, it might seem as if there is a lack of technology to tackle the issue. However, as Marco Antonio Villa argues, this is not the case in the Brazilian context. The phenomenon of drought has been extensively studied, and numerous institutions have been created to address it. Currently, the area that is frequently impacted by droughts has been officially designated as the 'Drought Polygon' (Map 1). Not only Villa, but many other scholars who study the Northeastern droughts, recognize the political implications of inefficient and inadequate public policies.[21] Albeit from different disciplines, these scholars have examined the historical impacts of the drought in depth, and all reach the same conclusion, that more could have been done to combat the effects of the many periods of drought the region has faced. According to the report Seca: o homem como ponto de partida, published by the Northeast Federal Caucus in 1999, this phenomenon is, above all, a physical and natural occurrence in the Northeast, recurring eight to ten times per century and sometimes lasting three to five years.[22] Droughts have been recorded in Brazil at least since 1583, when a Portuguese Jesuit named Fernão Cardim wrote 'houve tão grande seca e esterilidade nesta província (cousa rara e desacostumada, porque é terra de contínuas chuvas) que os engenhos d'água não moeram muito tempo' [there was such a great drought and barrenness in this province (a rare and unusual thing, since it is a land of continual rains) that the water-powered sugar mills did not grind for a long time].[23] However, it was only in 1877 that the drought would become a defining aspect of the region. Known as the Great Drought (1877–79), this period became a symbolic landmark. Beyond its devastating impact in terms of mortality, this drought forged an imaginary about the affected regions that endures to this day and is present in works such as Os Sertões by Euclides da Cunha (published in 1902). Hunger, disease, and violence became factors exploited by the media creating challenges for governments. Waves of migrants headed toward the capitals, leaving behind a trail of deaths and looting. Mass emigration became both a reality and a problem for local governments. The geographic isolation of some of the regions affected by the drought hindered not only the flow of news to population centres but also the arrival of scarce relief. The drought seemed to

---

[21]   Durval Muniz de Albuquerque Jr., A invenção do Nordeste e outras artes, 5th edn (Cortez, 2011)
[22]   Seca: o homem como ponto de partida, Ação Parlamentar, 92 (Coordenação de Publicações, 1999), p. 15.
[23]   Cited in Villa, Vida e morte no sertão, p. 18.

attract greater attention as the migrants, finding that life was unsustainable in the small towns and inland cities, moved on to the capitals.[24] The images we encounter in Rachel de Queiroz's novel trace back to the Great Drought, while the large-scale migration she depicts had been a reality since the nineteenth century.

Moreover, the full impact of this climate event on the socio-cultural landscape is complex, as it involves the entanglement of biopolitics and biopower, as formulated by Michel Foucault.[25] The asymmetrical suffering portrayed in Queiroz's novel — where wealthy landowners like Vicente's family face economic hardship but survive, while Chico Bento's family endures displacement, starvation, and death — illustrates how, in real life, environmental disasters become integrated into systems of power that determine which populations receive protection and which are left vulnerable to suffering and mortality.

In Queiroz's novel, we can see how the authorities exploit the surplus population created by the drought, allocating them to the Alagadiço internment camp. Once there, the only choice for these people is to work on government projects, often for inadequate pay, as demonstrated by Chico Bento's experience. At the same time, due to the limited number of job opportunities, many of them remain unemployed.

> Agora, felizmente, estavam menos mal. O de que carecia era arranjar trabalho; porque a comadre Conceição bem via que o que davam no Campo mal chegava para os meninos.[26]

> [Now, fortunately, things were a little better. What they really needed was steady work, because Conceição could see that the aid given out at the Campo was hardly enough to feed the children.]

This situation exemplifies Zygmunt Bauman's concept of 'wasted humans' — individuals rendered redundant and disposable.[27] The *retirantes* occupied precisely this position: not treated as citizens with rights, but as exploitable labour. The authorities recognized their usefulness as a cheap workforce, employing them not only in the Northeast but also in the Amazon rubber industry and in the construction of southern cities like São Paulo and Rio de Janeiro.[28] Bauman's framework clarifies how Queiroz's novel depicts drought victims transformed by crisis and state neglect from citizens in need into commodified, disposable labour.

---

[24] Ibid., p. 44.

[25] Michel Foucault, *The History of Sexuality, Volume I: An Introduction*, trans. by Robert Hurley (Pantheon Books, 1978); Michel Foucault, *The Birth of Biopolitics: Lectures at the Collège de France, 1978–1979*, ed. by Michel Senellart, trans. by Graham Burchell (Palgrave Macmillan, 2008).

[26] Queiroz, *O Quinze*, 82nd edn (José Olympio, 2006), p. 103. Translations into English are my own.

[27] Zygmunt Bauman, *Wasted Lives: Modernity and Its Outcasts* (Polity, 2003).

[28] For more studies on this, see Paulo Cesar Gonçalves, *Migração e mão-de-obra: retirantes cearenses na economia cafeeira do centro-sul (1877–1901)*, Série Teses (Editora Humanitas, 2006); and Adnilson de Almeida Silva and others, 'O processo de des (re) territorialização dos trabalhadores nordestinos no território amazônico durante os ciclos da borracha', *Revista Geografar* (Curitiba), 5.1 (2010), pp. 61–82.

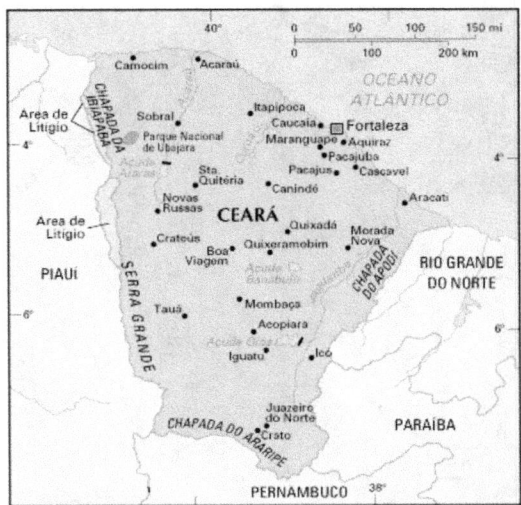

MAP 1. Reference map of the state of Ceará
(source: *V-Brazil.com* <http://www.v-brazil.com/tourism/ceara/map-ceara.html>)

Even if readers are not familiar with the history of drought in Brazil, the novel *O Quinze* creates a feeling of discomfort through its vivid descriptions of the characters' struggles and the impact of the drought on the environment (fauna and flora). The narratives of the characters, who are all dealing with the same problem, can seem disjointed despite their interconnectedness:

> Recebendo o dinheiro do Zacarias da Feira, se desfazendo da burra e matando as criaçõezinhas que restavam, para comerem em caminho, que é que faltava? Nem trem, nem comida, nem dinheiro...[29]

> [After receiving the money from Zacarias da Feira, selling the mule, and killing the little animals that were left to eat along the way — what else was there? No train, no food, no money...]

Chico Bento and his family have no resources, not even enough money to buy train tickets. They are left with two choices: starve where they are or risk a journey in search of better conditions elsewhere.

The story begins in the Quixadá municipality, located in the backlands of Ceará and far from the coastal capital city of Fortaleza. Many drought victims seek refuge in Fortaleza specifically to escape the harsh conditions and devastating impacts of the climate in the backlands, but in 1915, there are few transportation options available to travel from Quixadá to Fortaleza. Conceição takes the first option, which is the train.[30] Chico Bento's family has no such

[29]   Queiroz, *O Quinze*, p. 32.
[30]   According to Igor Carlos Feitosa Alencar, the Baturité Railway was the first in Ceará and was built in 1872 with the goal of connecting Fortaleza to the backlands, promoting 'modernization' and

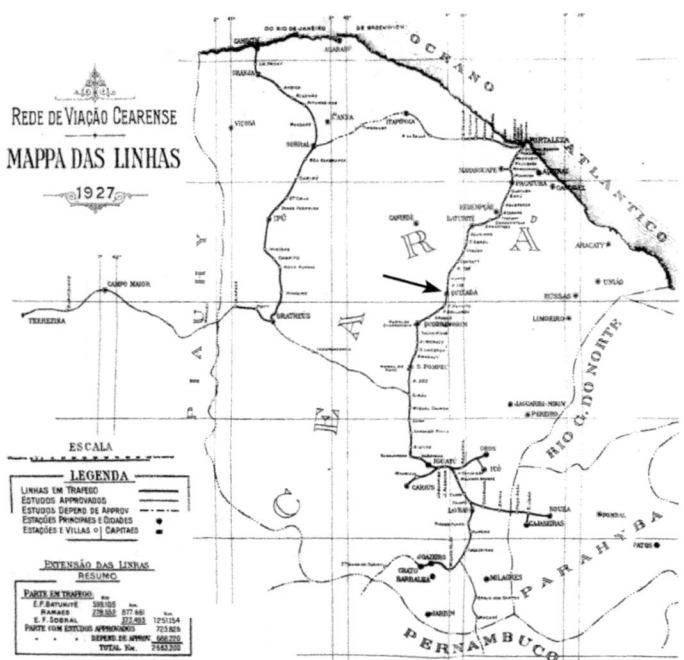

MAP 2. Railway map from 1927. The arrow (added here) shows the location
of Quixadá, whose railway is represented in the novel.

privilege as Conceição has, and the only option for them is to walk along the
roads, enduring the difficulties of a long-distance journey. Chico Bento and his
family embody the social class of the *retirantes*.

Having heard that the government is distributing free train tickets to the
capital, he decides to try his luck. The scale of the crisis is captured in the
following passage, where the clerk refers to the Great Drought and explains that
no tickets remain:

> Mas foi em vão que Chico Bento contou ao homem das passagens a sua
> necessidade de se transportar a Fortaleza com a família. Só ele, a mulher, a
> cunhada e cinco filhos pequenos. O homem não atendia.
> — Não é possível. Só se você esperar um mês. Todas as passagens que eu
> tenho ordem de dar, já estão cedidas. Por que não vai por terra?
> — Mas meu senhor, veja que ir por terra, com esse magote de meninos,
> é uma morte!
> O homem sacudiu os ombros:
> — Que morte! Agora é que *retirante* tem esses luxos... No 77 não teve
> trem para nenhum. É você dar um jeito, que, passagens, não pode ser...[31]

'progress' in those regions. Igor Carlos Feitosa Alencar, *À espera do progresso: a estrada de ferro de
Baturité rumo a cidade do Crato no século XIX* (XVI Simpósio de Geografia Urbana, 2019), p. 2131.
[31]   Queiroz, *O Quinze*, p. 34 (emphasis mine).

[But it was in vain that Chico Bento explained to the ticket clerk his need to travel with his family to Fortaleza. Just him, his wife, his sister-in-law, and five small children. The man would not listen.

— Impossible. Only if you wait a month. All the tickets I've been authorized to give have already been handed out. Why don't you walk?

— But, sir, look, going by land with this bunch of kids would be a death sentence!

The man shrugged his shoulders:

— Death! Now these *retirantes* want such luxuries... Back in '77 there wasn't a train for anyone. You'll have to find a way, because tickets — those are out of the question...]

They are aware of the deadly consequences of the drought. They believe that if the rain does not arrive by the 'dia de São José' (Saint Joseph's day),[32] they will have a dry winter. The signs of the impending drought are evident, and Rachel de Queiroz paints a bleak and melancholic picture of the landscape:

> Chico Bento parou. Alongou os olhos pelo horizonte cinzento. O pasto, as várzeas, a caatinga, o marmeleiral esquelético, era tudo de um cinzento borralho.
>
> O próprio leito das lagoas vidrara-se em torrões de lama ressequida, cortada aqui e além por alguma pacavira defunta que retorcia as folhas empapeladas.[33]

> [Chico Bento stopped. He stretched his eyes across the grey horizon. The pasture, the meadows, the caatinga, the skeletal quince grove, it was all a grey cinder.
>
> The very bed of the lakes was glazed in clods of dried mud, cut here and there by some defunct wild plantain with its twisted dried leaves.]

Chico Bento's precarious social position makes him particularly vulnerable to the dangers of a dry season. Unlike landowners who can weather periods of scarcity through accumulated resources, he works as a hired hand on Dona Maroca's farm with no property of his own. This arrangement leaves Chico Bento and his family entirely dependent on employment for survival. When he receives a letter from Dona Maroca's nephew warning that if rain does not arrive by Saint Joseph's Day, the cattle will be released and work will cease, Chico Bento faces an existential choice. Though Dona Maroca offers him the possibility of remaining on the property, this gesture carries little practical benefit — without work and wages, his family will inevitably face starvation. Even his connection to Vicente, son of wealthy landowners, proves futile as drought conditions threaten Vicente's family farm as well and eliminate any possibility of alternative employment.

The warnings of drought eventually became reality; the characters have to make the hard decision to leave their lands. Conceição persuades her

---

[32] Saint Joseph's Day is traditionally recognized as the day that reveals predictions for the upcoming winter season: if it rains before this day, the winter will not be dry.

[33] Queiroz, *O Quinze*, p. 20.

grandmother, Dona Inácia, to join her on a train to Fortaleza. Although the old woman is deeply attached to the land and devastated to have to leave it, she agrees. The instances of departure are described with deep images of grief. And, although all the characters are impacted by the drought, we are exposed to the unbalanced reality of this impact. Everyone feels deep sorrow at leaving home: for Chico Bento, it means losing the little he has managed to achieve through hard work, while for Dona Inácia it means parting from her land and her place of comfort. Yet only the one group of characters faces true uncertainty. Dona Inácia knows her departure is temporary — just until the rains return — and so it is:

> Desde as primeiras chuvas, dona Inácia iniciou seus preparativos de viagem. Desejava ir embora o mais depressa possível. Enfim! Voltava ao Logradouro, ao seu alpendre, à sua almofada, à queijaria![34]

> [From the first rains on, Dona Inácia began preparing for her trip. She wanted to leave as quickly as possible. At last! She was returning to Logradouro, to her porch, to her cushion, to the cheese-making room!]

This disparity illustrates how the drought intensified existing power imbalances, pushing those already living at the margins into impossible situations while the propertied classes enjoy a greater capacity to endure them.

To fully comprehend the depth of Queiroz's social critique and the uneven impact of the drought she portrays, we must engage with the novel's spatial dimensions. While the narrative unfolds in fictional space, it is anchored in geographical realism — a hallmark of Brazil's regionalist literary movement. Queiroz does not merely create abstract settings but reconstructs the physical and social geography of 1915 Ceará with remarkable precision, including accurate references to specific streets, villages, and regional landmarks. This commitment to geographical authenticity transforms her novel from pure fiction into a form of literary documentation of the drought's impact.

Therefore, to better grasp the physical intensity of the characters' journey and how it affected their bodies, I chose to examine the possible experience of the journey by mapping what these spaces might have looked like. This approach allows us to visualize not just the distances covered, but also the topographical challenges faced by the *retirantes* in real life, those who inspired Rachel de Queiroz: the steep inclines, rough terrain, and harsh exposure that compounded their suffering. By using the state of Ceará as a base layer, I was able to create maps that aim to offer a reading of the fictional space. Map 3 illustrates the correlation between geographical data provided in the novel and the actual landscape with which it corresponds, focusing only on Chico Bento's journey to Fortaleza. As mentioned above, the mapping of routes was facilitated through georeferencing techniques, made possible by the author's inclusion of the names of real places throughout the narrative. By plotting these locations

---

[34]   Ibid., p. 144.

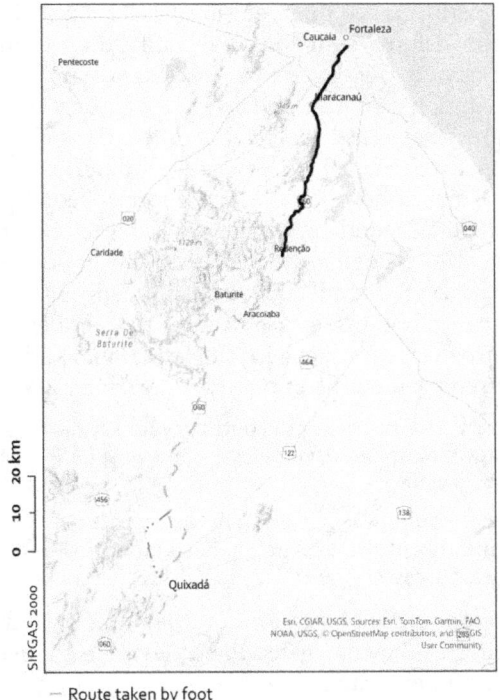

— Route taken by foot
— Final train route taken by all characters
··· Alternative to the route taken by foot

MAP 3. Map created using ArcGIS Pro and
geographical locations presented in the novel.

precisely and connecting them according to the narrative sequence, we can
reconstruct the likely paths taken by characters like Chico Bento's family. Such
visualization transforms abstract descriptions of suffering into measurable
physical challenges, providing empirical support for Queiroz's critique of how
the drought's impacts were unevenly distributed across social classes. This does
not mean that the fictional space in the novel is identical to the real world, but
it does provide enough evidence to map the narrative onto base maps, offering
insights into the experiences that inspired the author.

Despite the precision afforded by the names of real places in the narrative,
some interpretive decisions were necessary when mapping the characters'
routes. The exact path taken at the beginning of Chico Bento's journey could
not be represented with certainty. This uncertainty arose because the family
had two viable options to reach their first stop after the starting point (the farm
in Quixadá). Map 3 illustrates this situation by presenting an alternative initial
route in blue (dash-dot line). Since both viable routes covered nearly identical

distances, I kept the path marked in green (long dashes) as being the one taken by the family. This decision was made to simplify the examination without compromising accuracy, as the differences in distance and elevation between the two initial route options are minimal.

As the story progresses, we seem to be able to feel the suffering experienced by the *retirantes*, mostly because of the narrator's description of the desolate landscapes. The base map used reflects contemporary geography, but it is fair to assume that the fundamental topography has remained stable over time. Moreover, it is critical to recognize that during the period of the narrative, these routes would have presented far greater challenges than today, lacking the infrastructure, shelter options, and assistance that modern travellers might find. Rachel de Queiroz was familiar with the landscape, and had seen it when she was a child. She represented the precarity in her narrative:

> Em toda a extensão da vista, nem uma outra árvore surgia. Só aquele velho juazeiro, devastado e espinhento, verdejava a copa hospitaleira na desolação cor de cinza da paisagem.[35]

> [As far as the eye could see, not another tree appeared. Only that old juazeiro, worn and thorny, kept its green, hospitable crown amid the grey desolation of the landscape.]

The physical demands imposed by the natural features would have increased the *retirantes*' suffering, as they navigated these elevation changes while already weakened by hunger and exposure. In one of the most tragic moments of the narrative, the family faces the loss of one of their children, Josias:

> De tarde, quando caminhavam com muita fome, tinham passado por uma roça abandonada, com um pau de maniva aqui, outro além, ainda enterrados no chão. Josias, que vinha atrás, distanciou-se. Viu o pai descuidado dele, pensando em encontrar um rancho; a mãe, com o menino no quadril, marchava lá mais na frente. Ele então foi ficando para trás, entrou na roça, escavacou com um pauzinho o chão, numa cova, onde um tronco de manipeba apontava; dificultosamente, ferindo-se, conseguiu topar com uma raiz, cortada ao meio pela enxada. Batendo de encontro a uma pedra, trabalhosamente, arrancou-lhe mais ou menos a casca; e enterrou os dentes na polpa amarela, fibrosa, que já ia virando pau num dos extremos. Avidamente roeu todo o pedaço amargo e seco, até que os dentes rangeram na fibra dura.[36]

> [That afternoon, as they walked on, very hungry, they passed an abandoned field, with a few cassava stalks still stuck in the ground. Josias, who was lagging behind, fell even further back. He saw his father paying no attention to him, thinking only of finding shelter; his mother, with the baby on her hip, marched on ahead. So he slipped into the field and, using a small stick, dug at the ground where a cassava stump jutted out. Struggling and hurting himself, he managed to find a root that had been cut in half by a mattock.

---

[35]   Ibid., p. 39.
[36]   Ibid., p. 58.

Banging it against a stone, he slowly peeled off some of the bark and sank his teeth into the yellow, fibrous pulp, already turning to wood at one end. Hungrily, he chewed the whole bitter, dry piece until his teeth scraped against the tough fibres.]

Josias has eaten raw cassava, which is poisonous. The description of his condition brings the reader closer to the horror that the family is going through: 'A criança era só osso e pele: o relevo do ventre inchado formava quase um aleijão naquela magreza, esticando o couro seco de defunto, empretecido e malcheiroso' [The child was nothing but skin and bones: the bulge of the swollen belly looked almost like a deformity in such thinness, stretching the dry, corpse-like skin, darkened and foul-smelling].[37] After he dies, the whole family falls into despair, and faces the brutal task of having to bury him by the side of the road and continue their journey.

Hidden behind tragic moments in the narrative, such as the death of Josias, the descriptions of the journey's path might seem like mere contextual detail. Yet the recurring droughts that afflict Brazil's Northeast remind the reader that real people endured the hardships Rachel de Queiroz depicts through the story of Chico Bento's family. The *retirantes* walked long stretches of road without knowing when the next incline would appear or when they might find the next patch of shade. This struggle, suggested by the novel's descriptions of the landscapes, becomes even clearer when we look at the terrain of Ceará. To bring reality closer to the fictional space, I used the ArcGIS Pro Elevation Profile tool. As shown in Map 4, the route from Quixadá to Acarape — where the characters finally board a train — presents a total elevation gain of 1400 metres (almost 4600 feet). The narrator tells us that, as they are nearing Acarape, their older son runs away. Having already lost one of their sons to food poisoning, this second loss is a devastating blow. The breakdown of the family confirms the level of suffering endured and the sense of hopelessness this induced. Thus, the topography sheds light on their journey in ways that are not explicit in the narrative. Although the elevation difference is not described in the novel, the topography of the landscape and length of the journey provide insights into the hardships encountered in the quest to escape the drought and seek out a better way of life. If Chico Bento's family represents the real-life *retirantes*, then the real world can help us empathize with the struggles of the fictional characters.

Other elements of the narrative also seemed to offer insights into the characters' experiences and bring out the author's critique. I wanted to explore Queiroz's choice to contrast the tragic reality of Chico Bento's family with the subplot of Vicente's unfulfilled love for Conceição. While Vicente longs for her, Conceição does not appear to place romantic love at the centre of her life; her concerns lie elsewhere, making this storyline seem almost futile when set against the novel's harsher realities. Many scholars have approached this part of the book through a feminist lens. While that is certainly a valid

[37]   Ibid., p. 60.

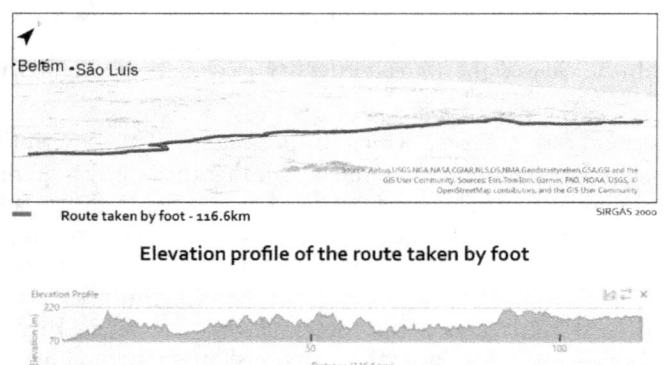

Route taken by foot - 116.6km   SIRGAS 2000

Elevation profile of the route taken by foot

MAP 4. Topography corresponding to the route represented on Map 3.

interpretation, I argue that this subplot also serves to add depth to Conceição's character and to illustrate how, during the drought, members of the upper classes could still be preoccupied with concerns beyond the basic struggle for survival.[38] The narrator also insists on mentioning the train throughout the novel, and, although it remains only a distant possibility for the *retirantes*, its persistent presence in the narrative suggests that it carries a deeper significance. To explore this meaning in spatial terms, I created Map 5 by combining two elements: Map 3, which shows the route of Chico Bento's family journey, and the railway route, which depicts Conceição's train journey. This allowed me to compare the travel experiences of both groups of characters by first establishing their geographical connections. To verify the accuracy of their journeys, I georeferenced the historical railway map (Map 2) against a modern map created with ArcGIS Pro. This confirmed two important points: first, that the historical railway routes still exist on contemporary maps, and second, that the locations mentioned in the novel were indeed connected by this railway network. With the confirmation, I traced the train route in blue and kept in red the route taken by Chico Bento and his family. The final route in black still represents the train route but has its own colour because Chico Bento's family also boarded the train.

What Map 5 confirms is one of the novel's most powerful implicit criticisms and something that scholars seem to have overlooked when analysing the novel: the role of the railway as a social marker and active agent in the fate of

---

[38]   For more on the feminist readings see: Yls Rabelo Câmara, Yzy Maria Rabelo Câmara and Melina Raja Soutullo, 'O Quinze: revisitando a importância de Rachel de Queiroz para a cultura cearense, a literatura brasileira e o feminismo no Brasil do século XX', *Revista Entrelaces*, 5.6 (2015), pp. 116–30; Thifane Oliveira de Alencar, 'A ruptura do padrão feminino nas personagens das obras *O Quinze* de Rachel de Queiroz e *São Bernardo* de Graciliano Ramos' (unpublished undergraduate dissertation, Universidade Federal do Pampa, 2022); and Elisângela Campos Damasceno Sarmento and Geraldo Jorge Barbosa de Moura, 'Conceição em O Quinze: uma abordagem feminista e decolonial', *Revista Estudos Feministas*, 31 (2023).

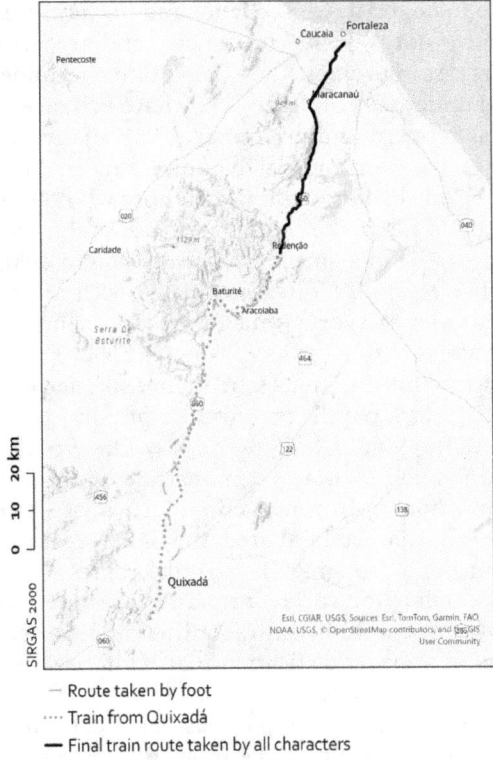

— Route taken by foot
···· Train from Quixadá
— Final train route taken by all characters

MAP 5. Overlapped maps showing the different journeys.

those who fled the drought. Unlike the elevation analysis, this map provides a broader perspective by comparing the different journeys to Fortaleza. What Map 5 strikingly demonstrates is that while the physical distances travelled by different characters are remarkably similar, and while their routes are parallel, their experiences diverge dramatically due to socioeconomic factors. The wealthy characters and the impoverished *retirantes* travel nearly identical distances, yet their journeys represent entirely different realities.

Conceição typifies a (female) member of the *nordestino* landowning class in the First Republic through her embodiment of European standards of civilization, progress, and modernity. She is educated; she reads novels by Coulevain and Sienkiewicz. The railway, to which Conceição had privileged access, was a symbol of Brazilian modernization and progress. It connected the backlands to the state capital, Fortaleza, and bridged the cultural gap between two worlds which were otherwise isolated. Conceição's association with the railway elevates her from the supposed ignorance and isolation of backlands life, connecting her to the urban values of the capital as a site of

Brazilian modernity. In contrast, Chico Bento and his family are the antithesis of modernity. They are not welcome in the city and are instead regarded as uncivilized intruders. As *retirantes*, they constitute the underdeveloped and so-called uncivilized underbelly of Brazil. They have no place in the republican elite view of Brazil as modern and progressive. This distinction mirrors what Foucault identifies as the workings of biopower. In his analysis of capital punishment, he notes: 'one had the right to kill those who represented a kind of biological danger to others'.[39] In the context of the drought, the railway and the internment camps operated in a similar way, exposing to death those deemed a threat to society. The *retirantes*, often associated with diseases, hunger, and disorder, fell into this latter category, while figures like Conceição moved freely along the lines of progress.

While I expected to find differences in their experiences, I did not anticipate discovering such stark parallelism in their physical routes. This finding significantly enhances our understanding of how Queiroz deliberately juxtaposed these contrasting realities. Map 5 demonstrates with clarity how Queiroz captured the drought's uneven impact across social classes. The visualization confirms that while all characters shared the same destination (Fortaleza) and objective (escaping the drought), the parallel routes on the map serve as a powerful visual metaphor for social inequality. Despite their geographical proximity, these journeys unfold in entirely different experiential worlds — a spatial representation of social stratification that reinforces the novel's critique more powerfully than words alone.

One group of characters was able to purchase the tickets to the modern and fast way of transportation, the train. The other group was left with the only other possible option, which was to walk almost the same route and distance, around 120 km, to get to the same place. These different experiences take us back to the concepts of Lefebvre and Tuan, since the characters experienced the same places, creating different spaces from them. As Murrieta-Flores, Donaldson, and Gregory write:

> Although we are accustomed to thinking about places as being 'static', or as being defined by fixed boundaries, their cultural significance is in fact defined by other factors, such as the interconnected flow of experiences that converge in them and the roles they play as nodes in larger spatial networks.[40]

The way Queiroz narrates the journeys shows us how brutal the walk was for the *retirantes* and how easy it was for those with financial means to travel from one point to another. The author portrays Conceição and her grandmother as lamenting their departure from their land while she demonstrates how convenient the trip was for them. At the other end of the social spectrum is Chico Bento's family, who not only had to leave the place they thought of as

---

[39] Foucault, *History of Sexuality*, p. 138.
[40] Murrieta-Flores, Donaldson and Gregory, *GIS and Literary History*, p. 4.

home, but also experienced every single challenge of the route, losing two children along the way.

Therefore, Map 5 provides a visual representation of the criticism Rachel de Queiroz was building against the inefficiency of the political project to combat the drought and its consequences. This criticism is embedded in the painful parallelism between the journeys because of how close they were geographically, but how far apart they were in reality. The combination of the poignant narrative, emotive descriptions, and the visual representation of the maps presented here offers a comprehensive understanding of Rachel de Queiroz's critique of the negligence of public authorities.

Final Considerations

Advanced maps that incorporate various datasets can enable the exploration of the many layers of a narrative, allowing for comparison between fictional and real-life spaces or even the understanding of entirely fictional spaces. While it is impossible to fully experience the reality of literary texts, utilizing digital tools can illuminate the complex, intimate relationships between characters and their environment. Although these experiences are not easily translatable through traditional textual analysis alone, leveraging innovative digital tools demonstrably enriches our comprehension of literary narratives, revealing dimensions of meaning that might otherwise remain unexplored.

The topographical analysis uncover physical challenges and the striking parallel between the routes of rich and poor characters were interpretive insights made possible through the use of GIS-based methods. ArcGIS Pro provided quantitative elevation data and spatial visualization capabilities that illuminated these parallel journeys, enabling a deeper and more nuanced reading of the novel than conventional analysis alone offered. This methodological approach uncovered spatial dimensions of Queiroz's social critique that were implicit, demonstrating how digital humanities tools can enhance our understanding of literary texts, inviting us to revisit canonical works.

Comparing the railway's role in Queiroz's novel to that of digital mapping tools in literary analysis reveals a compelling reflection on technology's dual nature. In *O Quinze*, the railway represents both modernity's promise and its exclusionary nature — it provides easy transportation for those with means while remaining visible yet inaccessible to the *retirantes*. Similarly, as we embrace digital technologies like GIS for literary analysis, we must remain mindful of this duality. These tools expand our analytical capabilities and reveal previously hidden dimensions of texts, much as the railway connected distant regions of Brazil. Yet without critical human interpretation, such technologies risk becoming merely technical exercises that fail to capture the full humanity of literary experiences. Just as Rachel de Queiroz critiqued the uneven implementation of technological progress in the Brazil of 1915, we must approach digital humanities methodologies with awareness of both their revelatory potential and their limitations. The most valuable insights emerge not from technology alone, but from the interaction between technological capabilities and the human critic's sensitivity to nuance, context, and the emotional dimensions of literary works. This study demonstrates that digital tools such as the ones available on ArcGIS Pro can illuminate spatial relationships in literature. But it is, as always, the critic who ultimately connects these visualizations to the human experiences they represent.

'Orphans of water. Orphans of land': Capitalism's Life of Violence in *Maria Altamira* and *The Need for Roots*

Pedro Daher

Maine College of Art & Design

Early in *The Need for Roots* (1987), Simone Weil asserts that progress can only be measured in relation to the fulfilment of our one and only obligation: 'duty towards the human being *as such* — that alone is eternal'.[1] Maria José Silveira's novel *Maria Altamira* (2020) tackles capitalism as the life-system that runs *against* the obligation Weil insists on and sits at the core of their analyses of modern violence. Centring the displacement, dispossession, extraction, and death that the Belo Monte hydropower dam generated in the city of Altamira (Pará, Brazil) and upon the populations of the Xingu River, *Maria Altamira* furthers Weil's analysis of uprootedness as the fundamental mark of modern capitalist life and its construction of the meaning of progress. Not only does Silveira bring into sharp relief the ontoepistemological-cosmophilosophical mode of uprootedness that Weil attends to, she also ties it clearly to the uprootedness capitalism creates — of land, of labour, of place, of life. Taken together their works provide a window into the systems of thought, being, and material structures under global capitalism that simultaneously critique its philosophical underpinnings and its worldly consequences. Although Weil was more concerned with the European context of uprootedness during the Second World War and built since the seventeenth century,[2] her analysis of modern violence largely applies to all contexts dominated by capitalist progress and to a greater degree to colonial and postcolonial societies.[3] Weil initially explores the issue of (up)rootedness by linking how material-concrete uprootedness becomes possible because uprootedness becomes the dominant structure of life since it conquers being itself:

> to be rooted is perhaps the most important and least recognized need of the human soul. It is one of the hardest to define [...] Every human being needs to have multiple roots. It is necessary for him to draw wellnigh the

---

[1] Simone Weil, *The Need for Roots: Prelude to a Declaration of Duties towards Mankind* (Ark Paperbacks, 1987), p. 5, my emphasis.
[2] Weil, *The Need for Roots*, p. 235.
[3] Weil often analyses and criticizes European colonialism, racism, and imperialism (*The Need for Roots*, pp. 47–48, 134, 234–35).

Portuguese Studies vol. 41 no. 2 (2025), doi:10.1353/port.00045, 269–84

whole of his moral, intellectual and spiritual life by way of the environment
of which he forms a natural part [...] whoever is uprooted himself uproots
others. Whoever is rooted himself doesn't uproot others.[4]

Rootedness, therefore, is not simply about place in its border-literal meaning.
Rather, it can only take hold when 'moral, intellectual and spiritual life' are
in tune with the 'environment' that surrounds one — that is, rootedness only
takes place if all dimensions of being itself are promoted simultaneously,
precisely what capitalism as totality-oriented system attacks. The issue of
what constitutes rootedness and its social-collective definition is targeted by
Eduardo Viveiros de Castro with his famous polemical sentence: 'in Brazil,
everyone is indigenous except who isn't'.[5] Briefly, he argues that 'defining'
who is an indigenous person belongs to affinity, kinship, and neighbouring
relations determined by the indigenous communities themselves since the
concept indigenous is already a colonial-state invention. That is, Viveiros de
Castro highlights a mode of being, or rootedness, as a 'mode of becoming' as an
'incessant infinitesimal movement of differentiation', which refuses the capital-
state nationhood formation of roots since the latter is rooted in uprootedness
itself because of its overdeterminations and reifications ('the massive state of
an anteriorized and stabilized "difference", that is, an identity').[6] These all-
encompassing senses of roots — Weil's 'needs of the soul' enmeshed within their
surroundings and Viveiros de Castro's spotlighting of Amazonian indigenous
nations' general refusal of resolved concepts by living with endlessness as
the non-reducible reality of identity — are what *Maria Altamira* reveals to
the reader as the main sites of capitalist structural violence. That is, through
Belo Monte the novel shows the multipronged nature of the capitalist mode of
assault by narrating how it targets every dimension of existence — social bonds,
political-economic structures, land and environment sovereignty, human and
nonhuman bodies, ontoepistemologies and cosmophilosophies — since its goal
is a total annihilation of any mode of rootedness that do not entail capitalist
roots. Whilst Weil tackles the violences and lack of roots constituted throughout
capitalist modernity with a philosophical excavation of uprootedness, Silveira
highlights uprootedness as the structure which itself structures the conditions
under which structural material uprootedness becomes the expected and the
norm. That is, uprootedness is capitalism as a system of thought and being
actualized in the world via forced displacement-expropriation which feeds itself
by controlling the proper juridical and moral terms and conditions of perfected
free social relations through the ever-expanding frontier of global capitalist
market integration throughout the history of modernity.[7] Starting from this

---

[4]   Weil, *The Need for Roots*, pp. 40, 45.
[5]   Eduardo Viveiros de Castro, *Encontros: Eduardo Viveiros de Castro*, ed. by Renato Sztutman,
Coleção Encontros (Beco do Azougue Editorial, 2007), pp. 130–61, chapter title, 'No Brasil todo mundo
é índio, exceto quem não é'.
[6]   Ibid., pp. 135–37.
[7]   For historical and philosophical accounts of this process refer to, for example, Rosa Congost, '¿Qué

structure, I argue that because the novel functions as a historical document grounded in Latin America's never-ending cycles of death, dispossession, and extraction, it furthers Weil's philosophical and ontoepistemological account of modern violence and thus creates a more comprehensive framework to critique ongoing forms of structural violence created by the capitalist world system and its institutions.[8]

Maria Altamira and Belo Monte

Maria Altamira opens with a natural tragedy (an earthquake at Yungay, Peru) which forever uproots the life of Alelí, one of the novel's protagonists (the other is Maria Altamira, her second daughter and the titular character). After the earthquake destroys her home and kills her family and most of her town's population, Alelí, entirely uprooted, starts in(di)stinctively walking/travelling from country to country in South America (from Peru to Bolivia, Chile, Argentina, Paraguay, and finally Brazil).[9] During these constant dislocations, Alelí is faced with multiple instances of uprootedness such as the violence of South America's dictatorships[10] and the forced displacements born out of poverty and necessity.[11] In Bolivia, for example, where she starts to (re)grow some sense of rootedness with Don Rodrigo and Doña Anita, the couple that welcomes her, Alelí witnesses the first of the novel's *uprootings* in the name of capital-progress: a new highway is announced, and local expulsions ensue. Don

es la propiedad en la Época Moderna?', in *Mesa-Redonda 'Proprietas': um debate sobre o domínio territorial em contextos coloniais* (presented at the IV Encontro Internacional de História Colonial, Belém, PA, Brasil, 2012), Paolo Grossi, *História da propriedade e outros ensaios*, trans. by Luiz Fritori Ernani and Ricardo Marcelo Fonseca (Editora Renovar, 2006), Manoela Pedroza, *Por trás dos senhorios: senhores e camponeses em disputa por terras, corpos e almas na América portuguesa (1500–1759)* (Paco Editorial, 2021), John C. Weaver, *The Great Land Rush and the Making of the Modern World, 1650–1900*, 1st paperback edn (McGill-Queen's University Press, 2006), and Laleh Khalili, *Sinews of War and Trade: Shipping and Capitalism in the Arabian Peninsula* (Verso, 2020).

[8]   Although Silveira's novel isn't a historical novel per se, it is helpful to read it as such given that the genre is concerned with and, most importantly, helps to elucidate and critically examine the 'transition to the capitalist mode of production', as Ashwin Bajaj argues. Whilst Silveira is not necessarily working on the moment of transition — even if, arguably, the novel could be read as such since it covers the transition from the time before the hydropower dam to the arrival of its capitalist ruins — her main focus is the totality of the 'capitalist mode of production' having Belo Monte as its representation. Ashwin Bajaj, 'Amitav Ghosh's Ibis Trilogy and the So-Called Secret of the Historical Novel', *Novel*, 57.2 (2024), pp. 180–203, doi:10.1215/00295132-11186497.

[9]   The earthquake took place in 1970 and destroyed Yungay entirely. Only 92 people survived out of 25,000 between the towns of Ranrahirca and Yungay. One of the aspects of the uprootedness Alelí experiences is an almost total lack of structural support. She becomes a displaced migrant also because there is no institutional or social structure in place to help her recover from the tragedy. Whereas earthquakes of this magnitude cannot be prevented, mitigating some of its impacts and having structures in place for the aftermath are feasible. Although the uprootedness of the earthquake would always remain perhaps the re-establishing of roots would be possible. *Correio Braziliense*, 'Peru lembra 70 mil mortos do maior desastre natural das Américas', *Acervo*, 31 May 2008, section Mundo <https://www.correiobraziliense.com.br/app/noticia/mundo/2008/05/31/interna_mundo,10043/peru-lembra-70-mil-mortos-do-maior-desastre-natural-das-americas.shtml>.

[10] Maria José Silveira, *Maria Altamira* (Instante, 2020), pp. 40, 51. All the translations from the novel and other Portuguese sources are mine.

[11] Silveira, *Maria Altamira*, pp. 48, 155.

Rodrigo narrates the commonplaceness of forced removals[12] when he explains that the population has 'spoken to the authorities but it is useless, they do not want to listen [...] they said they are going to indemnify. But what has the value of the place where a person has built their home?'[13] Eventually, Alelí arrives in Altamira and meets Manuel Juruna, a warrior and leader of the Yudjá (Juruna) people. There, she starts to build a new life with Manuel amongst the Yudjá until he is assassinated by the region's loggers. Pregnant and convinced she is cursed, Alelí leaves her new-born daughter, Maria Altamira, with her friend Chica. After leaving, Alelí continues her life as rootless walker-migrant until, at the novel's end, she sees Maria once more to save her from Manuel Juruna's murderer.

Maria Altamira witnesses the long-term impacts of Belo Monte and the changes and destruction the hydropower plant brings to Altamira. Through her, Silveira tells the story of capitalist uprootedness, that is, the abuse, dispossession, racism, and neglect the local indigenous, poor, and *ribeirinho*[14] populations of the city (and surrounding communities) suffer in the name of economic development. From communities that were rooted to the Xingu river and to the land-place more generally, who had a strong sense of belonging and shared reality,[15] to the death of the river itself and all its life-giving qualities — water, trees, animals, and humans slowly and suddenly lose their lives. Slowly, because for most it is a death of despondency, of destitution, of a loss that cannot be grieved, while for others it is the immediate death caused by (political-economic) assassinations. Silveira exposes the 'unpayable debt'[16] created and attached to the populations of Altamira, a concept that philosopher Denise Ferreira da Silva develops in her essay 'Unpayable Debt'. There, she deploys capital-colonial-racial violence as a method to expose total violence as that which established the world and continues to rule it in the Post-Enlightenment era: 'the image of the other that racial knowledge manufactures is an effect of a double violence, namely the juridical total violence that ensures

[12]   For recent accounts of forced removal processes and environmental destruction projects in the name of development in Peru and Brazil, refer to, for example, Ana Aranha and Jessica Mota, 'Ninguém os ouviu', *Agência Pública*, 9 February 2015 <https://apublica.org/2015/02/ninguem-os-ouviu/> and Ben Hallamn and Roxana Oliveira, 'Corrida do ouro', *Agência Pública*, 23 April 2015 <https://apublica.org/2015/04/corrida-do-ouro/>.

[13]   Silveira, *Maria Altamira*, p. 28.

[14]   In broad terms, these are peoples who usually live alongside the river margins and build their lives in relation to the environment around them. Generally, they live in the North and Northeast regions of Brazil.

[15]   The novel does not romanticize or idealize their living conditions for, even before *Belo Monte*, it also highlights the material and social difficulties of the city and region more broadly (pp. 95, 106, 194).

[16]   Antônia Melo da Silva, a leader in the struggle for justice in the region, unambiguously states: 'the government and *Norte Energia* have an immense and *unpayable debt* with Xingu's and Altamira's population'. Melo da Silva defines the unpayable debt by denouncing the forced removals, the loss of traditional ways of life, housing, food sources, and security, and the invasion of diseases such as pneumonia, diabetes, hypertension, and malnutrition — especially among children (Lola Hierro, '"O Governo e Belo Monte têm uma dívida impagável com a população do Xingu e de Altamira"', *El País Brasil*, 23 October 2017, section Brasil <https://brasil.elpais.com/brasil/2017/10/09/politica/1507550012_733072.html> [accessed 24 April 2024]).

colonial expropriation and the scientific productive violence of the tools of modern knowledge that transubstantiate colonial expropriation into a natural, that is, racial, deficit'.[17] Ferreira da Silva argues that modern life imbues debts to the others of the capital, colonial, racial trio that are not theirs to pay — and yet, they own/owe it. The holding together of the three modes of power which represent total violence — racial, colonial, capital as an 'entanglement' that 'retain[s] their difference' and exposes them as 'deeply implicated in/as/with each other'[18] — without turning them into signifiers for justification permits an encounter with domination which refuses to explain away violence by isolating it or turning it into a mistaken gear of capitalism as mode of being. Violence *is* the system. Because it highlights how structural uprootedness is the mark of capitalist violence, *Maria Altamira* articulates the simultaneity of the apparent modes of violence of capitalist life (accumulation put broadly and its structural effects such as land theft, genocide, class domination) while also showing the deeper ontoepistemological underpinnings that articulate the system itself (individual-possession philosophical ordering put broadly and its daily effects, that is, the establishment of the proper juridical and moral mode of being which articulate domination as the logic of life — or violence as norm). Enter Belo Monte and its devastation.

In 'Belo Monte: a anatomia de um etnocídio' [the anatomy of a ethnocide], federal prosecutor Thais Santi gives a long interview to journalist Eliane Brum and details how the dam's project, the biggest investment of the first era of the Workers' Party in power (the left-wing Lula–Dilma 2003–16 cycle), is built through a 'suspension of the law'. This suspension creates, according to Santi, a 'terrifying world in which, at the margins of legality, Belo Monte slowly becomes consolidated fact'.[19] With Belo Monte, one witnesses how the institutionalized stability of capitalism and modern liberal democracies relies upon constant violence, that is, how the political-justice system establishes itself *as* justice through decisions which defend and promote capitalist interests put broadly.[20] Santi describes in detail how the dam is solely sustained through political 'legitimacy' and is alien to 'legality', which turns Altamira and the Xingu into the 'world in which all is possible' ('o mundo do tudo possível').[21] And

---

[17] Denise Ferreira da Silva, 'Unpayable Debt: Reading Scenes of Value Against the Arrow of Time', in *The Documenta 14 Reader*, ed. by Quinn Latimer and Adam Szymczyk (Prestel Verlag, 2017), pp. 81–112 (p. 99).

[18] Ibid., p. 92.

[19] Eliane Brum, 'Belo Monte: a anatomia de um etnocídio', *El País Brasil*, 1 December 2014 <https://brasil.elpais.com/brasil/2014/12/01/opinion/1417437633_930086.html> [accessed 2 October 2024].

[20] For a literary-philosophical tracing of how the law establishes fact from its own fiction and its never-ending deadly consequences through the farce of institutional predictability from a Latin American perspective, see Alexandre Nodari, 'A Única Lei do Mundo', in *Antropofagia hoje? Oswald de Andrade em cena*, ed. by João Cezar Castro Rocha and Jorge Ruffinelli (É Realizações, 2011), pp. 455–83.

[21] Santi is articulating a world in which all and anything is *made* possible, that is, the creation and sustaining of a world-life where nothing is outside of the permissible: dislocation, removal, dispossession, and assassinations are more than allowed. They are expected and repeated as established *reality*.

the possible is the destruction of the Xingu and the ethnocide of indigenous populations.[22] In this world, built by the Brazilian federal government and its private partner Norte Energia, the company that wins the public contract (the ever-so-modern state–capital twin relationship), Santi describes the 'rupture of social bonds'; the contempt for traditional modes of being; how Norte Energia attracted the indigenous populations to the urban centres and threw them into the consumer life of the worst kind (especially cheap, processed foods, which leads to a crisis of diabetes and hypertension); and the fragmentation inside indigenous communities and the increase in racism against them in the cities — both of these because of the company's 'emergency plan' that distributed consumer goods to indigenous populations, which on the one hand tended to lead to internal confusion and on the other to anger from poor, local individuals who were also being forcefully removed but who mostly did not receive any type of 'compensation' for their losses. Santi highlights the conditions of the Arara indigenous nation:

> It looked like a post-war scenario, a *holocaust*. The indigenous individuals ('os índios') didn't move. They would stand still, waiting, wanting crackers, asking for food, asking for the housing to be built. Traditional medicine was gone. They kept begging. They stopped talking amongst themselves. Didn't get together anymore. The only moment they gathered was during the night to watch the soap opera on a plasma TV. It was brutal. And the garbage around their land ('aldeia'), the amount of garbage was astounding [...] the company's action was ruinous ('avassaladora'). Thus, again, what's Belo Monte's impact? *Indigenous ethnocide.*[23]

In *Maria Altamira*, a deeply detailed and researched novel, given Silveira's background in journalism, anthropology, and political science,[24] the realism of the incident comes both through the macrolens of national structures, economic and land dispossession, and the microlens of the individual lives of the people affected — the characters might be fictional but they are the result of extensive visits to the region.[25] Silveira traces the beginnings of the project in the 1980s and how it was received as a declaration of war by the local populations. When Belo Monte's construction is almost completed, Silveira narrates the 'profound desperation' in the eyes of the displaced families and persons: '[they] would gaze at the water [of the Xingu] and did not recognize it. It wasn't the same. Neither did they recognize themselves. They weren't the

[22] Brum, 'Belo Monte'. An in-depth discussion about legal-juridical regimes and capital is beyond the scope of this article. For examples of these, refer to Brenna Bhandar's *Colonial Lives of Property*, Ana Sabau's manuscript in progress 'Race, Land and Property in Mexico from Pimentel to Molina Enríquez', and Lígia Osório Silva's *Terras Devolutas e Latifúndio*.
[23] Brum, 'Belo Monte', my emphasis.
[24] Amora Livros, 'Escritoras brasileiras: entrevista com Maria José Silveira', Amora Livros, n.d. <https://www.amoralivros.com.br/post/literatura-brasileira-maria-jose-silveira-maria-altamira> [accessed 10 July 2025].
[25] *MARIA ALTAMIRA, Com Maria José Silveira e Humberto Conzo Jr. | LiteraTamy*, dir. by LiteraTamy (2020) <https://www.youtube.com/watch?v=yWH7LIErmxk> [accessed 10 July 2025].

same. The water had also swallowed their identity, their world, their history, and their lives. Who would they be from now on?'[26] The foundation that constituted self- and collective-recognition processes, the sense of roots-identity, wanes dramatically. That is, not identity as in reduction to self-granted or modern-attached identity. Rather, identity as the sharedness of ontoepistemological and material conditions which allow a population to not be uprooted.[27] Here, one witnesses the deadness introduced by economic development. Ailton Krenak argues this is the result of humanity's long historical process of creating an exclusive club for itself that, in the name of the idea of progress, leaves behind everything that is not in its interest. This path of progress engulfs everyone that belongs to 'sub-humanity': human and nonhuman beings and the natural world.[28] The ever-growing assault on nature is tackled by Maristella Svampa's work on the global capitalist mode of consensus that crosses over ideologies and political parties in the name of infinite growth through the never-ending commodification of Nature.[29] It is the totality of sickness and death produced by capitalism which Davi Kopenawa's and Bruce Albert's *A Queda do Céu* tackles:

> the whites are also contaminated and, in the end, it ends up eating them as much as us because the xawara epidemic, in its hostility, does not have a preference! [...] they are reached, like us, by the smoke of the minerals and of the oil [...] they make them spread everywhere by extracting and manipulating these heinous things [...] with the smoke from minerals, oil, bombs and atomic things, the whites will make the earth and sky sick.[30]

Kopenawa analyses capitalism as a site of total war that contaminates all life which aims at any and all foundations that appear on its way, resulting in the sickness of all being(s). What becomes clear when one reads about Belo Monte, Norte Energia, the Xingu, Altamira and its populations, is how capitalism as metonym for life[31] articulates its permanence by having uprootedness as

---

[26] Silveira, *Maria Altamira*, p. 181.

[27] This is illustrated by Leanne Simpson's 'grounded normativities' as a practice that guides how the Anishinaabe peoples and nations conceive of all life's relations, or what could be called a practice of rooted recognition: '[grounded normativities] are ethical frameworks generated by [...] place-based practices and associated knowledges [...] that aren't based on enclosure, authoritarian power, and hierarchy [...] that place includes land and waters, plants and animals, and the spiritual world — a peopled cosmos of influencing powers'. Leanne Betasamosake Simpson, *As We Have Always Done: Indigenous Freedom through Radical Resistance*, 3rd edn (University of Minnesota Press, 2017), p. 22.

[28] Ailton Krenak, *A vida não é útil*, ed. by Rita Carelli (Companhia das Letras, 2020), p. 7.

[29] Maristella Svampa, 'Commodities Consensus: Neoextractivism and Enclosure of the Commons in Latin America', *South Atlantic Quarterly*, 114.1 (2015), pp. 65–82, doi:10.1215/00382876-2831290; Maristella Svampa, *Neo-Extractivism in Latin America: Socio-Environmental Conflicts, the Territorial Turn, and New Political Narratives*, Cambridge Elements: Politics and Society in Latin America, 2515–5253 (Cambridge University Press, 2019); Breno Bringel and Maristella Svampa, 'Energy Transition and the New Shape of Green Colonialism: The Emergence of the Decarbonisation Consensus', in *Dependency Theories in Latin America* (Routledge, 2024).

[30] Davi Kopenawa and Bruce Albert, with Beatriz Perrone-Moisés, *A Queda do Céu* (Companhia das Letras, 2021), pp. 365, 370.

[31] I derive this from Marx's analysis of the reality of private property as metonym for being. Karl

the 'invisible', fundamental structure which allows total uprootedness to manifest itself as the architecture which organizes life for all beings — that is, uprootedness organizes the level of being itself as it manifests as unrestricted violence. In a very real way, the characters in the novel represent the impossibility that Weil describes below:

> Uprootedness is by far the most dangerous malady to which human societies are exposed, for it is a self-propagating one. For people who are really uprooted there remain only two possible sorts of behaviour: either to fall into a spiritual lethargy resembling death [...] or to hurl themselves into some form of activity necessarily designed to uproot, often by the most violent methods, those who are not yet uprooted, or only partly so.[32]

This impossibility is not meant to exclusively witness capitalist ruins in the era of inescapable precarity marked by the dominance of global supply chains which have ended the possibility of the illusory even if very real global-teleological narratives of (capital-economic) progress, as Anna Tsing argues.[33] After all, as Silveira often notes, *Maria Altamira* emphasizes the lives formed within and outside capitalist ruins through the resistance to the attempt at totality wrought by uprooting's two unescapable options depicted above.[34] Akin to Tsing's 'latent commons' which argues for accentuating difference to articulate political projects 'here and now' to promote 'not-yet-articulated common agendas', Silveira points to the coalescing of multiple desires around the commonality of justice against capitalist uprooting through Maria Altamira's engagement with social struggles in urban spaces and in the Xingu region.[35] Nevertheless, to illuminate the simultaneity of uprooting as a structure of being and as a material structure, this essay aims at the generalized condition of life under late capitalism which sits at the novel's core and directly details Weil's all-enveloping claim.

Around the novel's midpoint, the choiceless-like life of capital is spotlighted. As Belo Monte nears inauguration, Maria Altamira and her friends' (Nice, Lino, Saião, Biu, and Curau) debates start to 'change in tone'. As the discussions amongst the local population intensify, Maria and Curau continue to be adamantly against the project while Nice and Lino begin to argue that at least

---

Marx, *Economic and Philosophic Manuscripts of 1844*, trans. by Martin Milligan, Great Books in Philosophy Series (Prometheus Books, 1988), pp. 93–94, 97.

[32]   Weil, *The Need for Roots*, p. 44.

[33]   Anna Lowenhaupt Tsing, *The Mushroom at the End of the World: On the Possibility of Life in Capitalist Ruins* (Princeton University Press, 2015).

[34]   Silveira writes: 'It is true I met a people who suffered all types of impacts in their life and culture but whose most emphasized characteristic was its struggle and the self-esteem that their resistance generated. An extraordinaty people. They cultivate their culture and know their strength'. Amora Livros, 'Escritoras Brasileiras', 21 Nov. 2022, no pagination.

[35]   In São Paulo, Maria draws uprooting as the structure that links urban struggles and indigenous fights for sovereignty by observing 'the shared and simultaneously unique suffering of each person, the daily struggle and [...] the thread knitting it all together, the right to be happy and affirm oneself: we are here. Her people, the Yudjá, also fought in this way, that is, for their rights to live, to dwell, to be happy and, in the same manner, to affirm: we have the right to be here' (p. 149).

more jobs will be available, that it could be a way to 'make money to survive', and ask others to 'see the good side' of the project.[36] Since the dam will be built regardless, Lino argues, one should stop 'denying everything' and take what one can from the situation. That is, uprootedness as the mode of life that capitalism institutes starts to infiltrate the horizon of possibility for the city's inhabitants.[37] Although characters such as Nice, Lino, and Jurandir are not involved in the more direct mode of uprootedness as violence (since they are workers whose larger function ends up serving uprootedness and, without the work, would be among the mass of jobless who cannot sustain themselves and thus would be doubly uprooted themselves — a choiceless choice), *Maria Altamira* constantly depicts individuals that more fully represent this reality: raw material and sex traffickers increasingly appear;[38] patriarchal and gender violence increases;[39] politicians, doctors, and engineers openly despise indigenous and local populations in the name of development.[40] The 'self-propagating' nature of uprootedness Weil accentuates is forcefully shown by Silveira as the construction of Belo Monte slowly but surely changes the shared reality of the populations of the region: food sources disappear,[41] substituted by processed diets,[42] and modes of being are replaced by consumer goods;[43] ways to make a living are gutted and replaced by a handful of jobs at Belo Monte, Belo Sun, and similar extractive-based industries;[44] the possibility of having a simple, dignified life, is destroyed;[45] drug trafficking and conflict start to dominate the city;[46] urban-male violence becomes commonplace.[47] The examples are almost endless. They help to discern the underlying structure of uprootedness that manifests through uprooting as structural violence — that

---

[36] Silveira, *Maria Altamira*, pp. 112–13.

[37] Silveira narrates common arguments around the project: 'In the city, there were people who would say: "it will be the biggest infrastructure project of the country in several decades and the third biggest dam in the world", "the city will become a part of Brazil's map", "progress will arrive in the region". And there were the ones who said, indignant: "they will kill our river", "they will kill our people", "cause havoc in our city", "flood our beaches", "*steal what is ours*"' (Silveira, *Maria Altamira*, p. 104, emphasis added).

[38] Silveira, *Maria Altamira*, pp. 51, 59, 99, 190, 193, 228, 254.

[39] Silveira, *Maria Altamira*, pp. 23, 73, 110, 111, 198, 245, 267.

[40] Silveira, *Maria Altamira*, pp. 62, 89–90, 145, 158–60.

[41] In the episode 'Peixe, farinha e miojo', the podcast *Prato Cheio*, which focuses on food issues, painfully details this process through Brazil's most successful program to combat poverty, the *Bolsa Família*. They highlight the total infiltration and domination of industrialized food for *ribeirinho* populations in the Amazon — one of the biggest impacts of economic projects and an (perhaps) unintended consequence of *Bolsa Família* (a largely successful project in its basic mission of taking people out of misery — the program warrants a larger discussion beyond the scope of this article).

[42] Silveira, *Maria Altamira*, pp. 158, 203.

[43] Silveira, *Maria Altamira*, p. 157.

[44] Silveira, *Maria Altamira*, pp. 219, 249.

[45] Silveira, *Maria Altamira*, p. 63.

[46] Silveira, *Maria Altamira*, pp. 125, 192.

[47] Silveira, *Maria Altamira*, pp. 132, 210. The novel also deals with patriarchal violence more generally (especially, but not limited to, domestic abuse). However, as Belo Monte gets built, the overgeneralization of male violence takes root: trafficking of women and girls increases, and sexual violence becomes more frequent. Maria herself is attacked.

which articulates modern life and sustains the mode of progress antithetical to the one Weil insists on.

Uprootedness and the Growth Imperative under Capitalist Life

Simone Weil and Maria José Silveira aim at capitalist devastation across time and continents to excavate what allows the never-ending cycle of modern violence to stay in place by targeting the creation of the conditions under which these processes become the sole possible. Weil is unambiguous in identifying capitalist uprootedness as disease:

> there are two poisons at work spreading this disease [uprootedness]. One of them is money. Money destroys human roots wherever it is able to penetrate, by turning desire for gain into the sole motive. It easily manages to outweigh all other motives, because the effort it demands of the mind is so very much less. Nothing is so clear and so simple as a row of figures [...] For the second factor making for uprootedness is education as it is understood nowadays [...] a culture very strongly directed towards and influenced by technical science, very strongly tinged with pragmatism, extremely broken up by specialization, entirely deprived both of contact with this world and, at the same time, of any window opening on to the world beyond.[48]

Here, the words money and education in themselves matter less than what they represent in their dominant modern forms: techniques of extraction, of exploitation and expropriation of any place's ecology. Money as private property, [dis]possession, accumulation, and education as isolation, language, discipline; they function as a combination of separation and domination to subdue life to the whims and desires of capitalist progress through the total 'deprivation of contact with this world and the world beyond'. Or, as Marx would put it, private property (capitalism) can dominate humans and become a world historical power by corrupting belonging: 'the more powerful the alien objective world becomes which he creates over-against himself, the poorer he himself — his inner world — becomes, the less belongs to him as his own'. While this is very much concerned with owning the means of production to recover the lost sense of self that has turned the 'life of the species into a means of individual life', Marx is also pointing to belonging more universally (outer belonging) and particularly (inner belonging). That is, the 'objective world' is not simply the world 'out there'. It is, more importantly, the emphasizing of a world which becomes impossible to be within, to be grasped, to belong *to* because everything can only be *outside* of the human; nothing belongs to us; everything belongs to capital (private property).[49] Emphasizing capitalism's total attack on all dimensions of being which targets everything from thought(s) to all kinds of

---

[48] Weil, *The Need for Roots*, pp. 41–42.
[49] Marx, *Economic and Philosophic Manuscripts of 1844*, pp. 72, 76, 97.

bodies, Davi Kopenawa deploys 'paper money' ('papel de dinheiro') as a concept widening Weil's and Marx's argument concerning its spread and domination:

> In the beginning, the lands of the ancient whites looked like ours [...] but their thinking steadily lost itself on a dark and entangled trail. Their wisest ancestors, who were created and given their words by *Omama*, died [...] their children and grandchildren had numerous offspring. They began to reject the sayings of their elders as if they were lies and slowly forgot them. They felled their entire forest to build ever larger farms [...] they began to viciously rip out the minerals from the soil. They built factories to melt them and manufacture commodities on a large scale. Then, their thinking was embedded in the commodities, and they fell in love with these objects [...] that made them forget the beauty of the forest [...] Then they made paper money ('papel de dinheiro') proliferate [...] they visited each other in their respective cities and all the whites ended up living the same way. And thence the words of the commodities and of money spread throughout their ancestors' lands. That's how I think it. Because they want to possess every single commodity, they were overcome by an unmeasured desire. Their thinking [...] became closed to all other things. It was through the words of the commodity that the whites began cutting all the trees, mistreating the earth, and spoiling the rivers.[50]

These diseases ('money' and 'education' that create an 'unmeasured desire' which closes 'thinking to all other things') are emphasized by *Maria Altamira*. Many of those who work at the construction site and later end up working at the plant itself have received an education *designed* to make them fit in there.[51] Even those who get an education not conspicuously geared towards violence, like Jurandir who is an airline pilot,[52] end up using their skills to bolster the accumulation-dispossession-extraction process. These simultaneous and multifaceted *uprootings* are spotlighted when Maria listens to the testimonies of the city's population:

> the men became like living dead, dear [...] they didn't know where to go. Before, they used to go to the river and bring back fish for their children. Now, they leave [the house] to avoid seeing their children begging for food [...] Do you know what fear is like, dear? It overtakes your body and paralyses you [...] They took us from our ground and hanged us upside down [...] Before we fished, farmed, reaped. Now we need to buy. Where's the river? Where's the forest? Where are the animals? All our references are gone. [...] What they did to us is a psychosocial crime. [...] I don't know how to deal with money, I told them, I only know how to deal with dignity. After that, they disappeared. So far, they haven't come back yet.[53]

Here, uprootedness is total. Individual, collective, and shared identities are disrupted; purpose is substituted by living-deadness; every single reference

---

50 Kopenawa and Albert, *A Queda do Céu*, p. 407.
51 Silveira, *Maria Altamira*, pp. 196, 249.
52 Silveira, *Maria Altamira*, pp. 215–17.
53 Silveira, *Maria Altamira*, pp. 208–09.

point is displaced; fear becomes a constant presence; dignity is replaced by money. The destruction caused by economic progress narrated above is centred on the limitlessness and specialness granted to 'growth' as all-encompassing ideology, argues Weil:

> Everything is done to make children feel — not that they don't feel it naturally — that things concerning the country, the nation, the nation's growth have a degree of importance which sets them apart from other things. And it is precisely in regard to those things that justice, consideration for others, strict obligations assigning limits to ambitions and appetites — all that moral teaching one is trying to instil into the lives of little boys — never get mentioned.[54]

Economic development as metonym for reality becomes the rule through which all is reckoned with and replaces every other measure of human progress and justice. Whilst Weil might be read as making a moralistic argument since one could follow her with a theological or categorical imperative-like commandment, I am highlighting that institutionalized justice procedures in the era of capitalism, imposed to maintain the ruse of measurable just outcomes, refer solely to justice as that which furthers the logic of dispossession.[55] Justice, in this social configuration, is not even an after-thought.[56] That is, justice in liberal democracies in the era of capitalism might be deployed as an absolute necessity for the system to impose itself as stable, predictable, and rightful. Nevertheless, this era is fundamentally marked by the wheels of justice being driven exclusively by and towards private property and its needs — manifesting as ongoing capital, colonial, gender, and racial violence. Revisiting Brazil's

---

[54] Weil, *The Need for Roots*, pp. 134–35.

[55] For accounts that deal with the history of capitalist constitutionally and justice-institutional articulated violence, refer to, among others, Glen Sean Coulthard, *Red Skin, White Masks: Rejecting the Colonial Politics of Recognition*, Indigenous Americas (University of Minnesota Press, 2014), Aileen Moreton-Robinson, *The White Possessive: Property, Power, and Indigenous Sovereignty*, Indigenous Americas (University of Minnesota Press, 2015), Nick Estes, *Our History Is the Future: Standing Rock versus the Dakota Access Pipeline, and the Long Tradition of Indigenous Resistance* (Verso, 2019), and, Jodi A. Byrd, *The Transit of Empire: Indigenous Critiques of Colonialism* (University of Minnesota Press, 2011).

[56] Weil discusses the limits of rights in constructing a society based on actual justice when exploring the difference between rights (conditioned by facts and socially constructed) and obligations (independent of conditions). I reinforce that this very much can be read in a theological/categorical imperative-like fashion and, thus, can be placed in the moralistic arena — something this essay is attempting to avoid. However, it can also be seen as a sharp critique of how *legality* and *institutions* are what guarantee the front that is justice under capitalism. Not because justice systems don't exist but precisely because their role is to guarantee capitalist, or property's (in oneself, out in the world) justice. Hence, right and the human for Weil are not totalizing or abstractly universalizing categories but rather attempts to displace the pursuit of totality and universality that capitalism seeks through its claim to being the perfect representation of human freedom (Weil, *The Need for Roots*, pp. 2, 3, 5, 49–50, 273). Akin to Weil, whilst Glen Coulthard's *Red Skin, White Masks* argues that one cannot vacate the institutional struggle since some placation to capitalism's destructive desire can take place in that realm, when it comes to indigenous self-determination specifically and anti-capitalist based justice put broadly, it is not solely through the courts and liberal legality that the oppressed (working class, racialized and gendered populations, the global south, etc.) and the oppressive regimes of capitalism can, or will be, displaced.

nineteenth century, Yuko Miki argues that the country's constitutional formation (liberal justice system) has inclusive models of nationhood and citizenship while simultaneously maintaining and reinforcing racial violence (e.g., slavery and land theft) and the cultural, economic, social, and political privileges of its ruling capitalist class.[57] Ariovaldo Oliveira and others argue that this parasitic relation between legal-juridical propriety and state-capitalist progress is the fundamental mark of Brazilian territorial formation through theft.[58] In other words, it is infinite growth-extraction that becomes inculcated through all dimensions of social life as the default mode one must abide by in the name of the supposed improvement brought by the naturality attached to the dominant narrative around (economic) development. In Silveira's novel, one witnesses Altamira at the mercy of the never-ending cycle of capital-uprootedness, or 'the plague' as Manuel Juruna names it:

> I fought the cronies of the guy [a farmer-logger] who wants to invade the land of our [indigenous] relatives down the river. Our warriors, like myself, gathered and we went after them. They fled. But they'll come back. They always do. Seems like a plague. It doesn't seem like one. It is one [...] [the damned cycle of] rubber, bringing the rubber tappers; *Tranzamazônica*, opening the road through lands they said were empty, as if indigenous peoples and *ribeirinhos* hadn't always lived there; the arrival of the loggers, stealing wood from the indigenous [populations] [...] the *grileiros*[59] in the region, expelling families.[60]

These ever-expanding cycles are the aim of Jason Moore's Capitalocene. Tracing the unquenchable thirst of capitalism from the fifteenth century till today, Moore argues that the capitologenic era impedes us from seeing and *being* with(in) the web of life — not because we *are not* but because it tells us that we are not, which leads to the ever-growing uprooting of life for capitalist existence. That is, uprooting as ontoepistemological system *and* as material consequence. Moore depicts the world market as the direct result of the Human/Nature dualism[61] by highlighting the devastating transformations of early capitalism, the initial ecological crises created by the production of the four Cheap Natures that sustain it (labour, food, raw materials, and energy), and all the death it has incurred (e.g., destruction of continent-sized forests and rivers, enslavement and genocide).[62] By tracing the creation of 'Cheap Nature' as the 'world praxis'

[57]   Yuko Miki, *Frontiers of Citizenship: A Black and Indigenous History of Postcolonial Brazil*, Afro-Latin America (Cambridge University Press, 2018).
[58]   *A grilagem de terras na formação territorial brasileira*, ed. by Ariovaldo Umbelino de Oliveira (FFLCH, Faculdade de Filosofia, Letras e Ciências Humanas, Universidade de São Paulo, 2020).
[59]   Individuals who fake official documents and submit them to the government in order to steal land.
[60]   Silveira, *Maria Altamira*, pp. 59, 107.
[61]   Jason W. Moore, 'The Capitalocene Part II: Accumulation by Appropriation and the Centrality of Unpaid Work/Energy', *The Journal of Peasant Studies*, 45.2 (2018), pp. 237–79 (p. 244), doi:10.1080/030 66150.2016.1272587.
[62]   Jason W. Moore, 'The Capitalocene, Part I: On the Nature and Origins of Our Ecological Crisis', *The Journal of Peasant Studies*, 44.3 (2017), pp. 594–630 (pp. 609–10, 601, 606, 604, 612), doi:10.1080/0 3066150.2016.1235036.

for boundless accumulation, Moore highlights the philosophical-historical conditions that came to organize the ontoepistemological and material wars taking place in Altamira and the world over. In a similar vein, Enrique Leff argues that the 'valuation-devaluation-revaluation' circuit of the accumulation process is fundamentally structured by the overexploitation of cheap labour in the Third World and the capitalizing of Nature.[63] Belo Monte represents a culmination of this cycle. Through and around its monstrosity, it consolidates a particular actualization of a global-universal modern-capitalist historical pattern of all the violences that the Xingu and akin populations the world over had had, and continue to, live with. Everyone and everything is uprooted:

> The Indigenous Territory wouldn't be touched, but its river would [...] The water of the Xingu [...] became dirty and murky. Filled with poisonous residues [...] And the fish, ah!, how did they die [...] their tails fell from rot. They were rotting alive [...] with so much [artificial] light [because of the construction], the birds lost their way. Flying aimlessly, not knowing where they came from or where they were going to. Died. Even the bees suffered with the turning of night into day. The *castanheiras* stopped producing, lost their pollinators. The trees that surround the river also stopped giving fruit...[64]

The total uprooting and destruction reported by *Maria Altamira* is at the centre of Kopenawa's tackling of life under capitalism. He critiques the commodity life-cycle by centralizing the simultaneity of uprootedness as both fundamental ontoepistemological and philosophical articulations and daily-material existence:

> We saw the whites spread their epidemics and kill us with their shotguns. We saw them destroy the forest and the rivers. We know they can be avaricious and nefarious and that their thought is usually filled with obscurity. They have forgotten that *Omama* created them. They have lost the words of their ancestors ('maiores'). They have forgotten who they were in the first time, when they also had culture [...] Maybe the whites think that we would stop defending our forest if they gave us a mountain of commodities. They are mistaken. Desiring their things as much as they do would only tangle our thought. We would lose our own words and that would kill us [...] I don't know how to calculate like they do. I only know that the land is more solid than our lives and that it does not die. [...] The value of everything that grows and walks in the forest or underneath the waters and also all of the *xapiri* and humans is too important when compared to all of the whites' commodities and money [...] The breath of our life is worth infinitely more![65]

Uprooted from the words of their ancestors ('maiores') and living under the dictates of the unquenchable desire brought by the form of value developed

[63] Enrique Leff, *Political Ecology: Deconstructing Capital and Territorializing Life* (Springer International Publishing AG, 2021), pp. 103–40.
[64] Silveira, *Maria Altamira*, pp. 145–47.
[65] Kopenawa and Albert, *A Queda do Céu*, pp. 250–51, 354–55.

by the capitalist commodity life-cycle, Kopenawa helps to articulate a critique of capitalism that goes beyond its manifestation (capital, colonial, and racial violence) to aim also at that which makes said manifestation, in its specificity, feasible. As Maria Altamira learns when listening to the Yudjá people, the only possible horizon of uprooting as ontoepistemological ground is violence as that which organizes human existence through total bodily uprooting (of humans, nonhumans, and land): 'they turn our Xingu into a river of death. To make us give up. Forcing us to live our ethnocide every day. A little bit every day.'[66] Perhaps the most brutal example the novel brings concerning the value form articulated by global capitalism, and how it does not accept Kopenawa's description of worthiness-value, is through the murder of Maria Altamira's father. Lenzenil Machado, Manuel Juruna's killer, actualizes the life of uprootedness/capitalist violence. Through him, Silveira gives prominence to the ultimate representation of one of Weil's central claims: 'whoever is uprooted himself uproots others'. After the novel introduces Lenzenil as a past hired assassin for businessmen of all types (farmers, loggers, etc.) involved in land theft and his Christianized male-centred organizing principles, he states:

> He who is innocent can say what I have done wrong. I have only killed who needed to be killed. Those who didn't let others earn their living in peace. Those who were impairing the man who knows what is best for the world. Have I killed someone who was sitting on their own, quiet? No, I did not kill. Have I killed to steal? No, I have not killed. I have only killed people who were getting in the way.[67]

The life of Lenzenil, who proudly displays the teeth of his victims in a necklace, is solely dedicated to uprooting.[68] His existence is thoroughly protected by the justice system of (Brazilian) capitalism. Maria attempts to investigate her father's assassination but is constantly prevented from doing so by various police stations that always reaffirm the impossibility of looking into the case not only because it is 'old' but also because, while the justice system knows who ordered the murder (Rei Mogno, a logger who represents the extractive landgrabbers of today's Brazil), it will not touch him precisely because of his connections and importance. In addition, Lenzenil's grandson is a police officer and tips off his grandfather to kill Maria and Jurandir before they can find out anything about Lenzenil's identity.[69] Protected by the state-capital twins, at the last pages of the novel Lenzenil attempts to kill Maria and Jurandir. Yet again travelling with a

---

[66] Silveira, *Maria Altamira*, p. 204.
[67] Silveira, *Maria Altamira*, p. 268.
[68] Entirely rooted to uprootedness as the structure of being itself, that which shapes the material structures of capitalist (modern) violence, he chooses who is righteous ('he who is innocent can say what I have done wrong'); closes being and overdetermines it towards *one* actualization of the *proper* mode of being ('I kill those who impair those who know what's best for the world'); severs himself from any sense of shared ground ('I have only killed people who were getting in the way'); overgeneralizes private property as being ('earn their living', that is, earning property in all its co-founding meanings via distinction-possession-domination).
[69] Silveira, *Maria Altamira*, pp. 233–38, 262, 264–65.

group of itinerant uprooted migrants, Alelí, who sees Maria for the first time since leaving her in the care of Chica, ends up saving her daughter and Jurandir by throwing herself in front of the shots fired by Lenzenil and his grandson. What *Maria Altamira* forcefully demonstrates is that in the face of capitalism's never-ending genocides, Weil's progress, the 'duty towards the human being *as such*', cannot exist.

The 1890 British Ultimatum in the International Satirical Press

Mário Sequeira

Faculdade de Ciências Sociais e Humanas —
Universidade NOVA de Lisboa (NOVA FCSH)

On 11 January 1890, a political earthquake shook Portugal and the House of Braganza. A short memorandum by Lord Salisbury, Prime Minister of Portugal's oldest ally, Great Britain, informed the government of the *Partido Progressista* that if Portugal did not immediately withdraw from disputed zones in Africa, the small Iberian country would suffer the consequences. It was the highpoint of mounting British–Portuguese tensions during the second half of the nineteenth century. In Portugal, the memorandum triggered nationalist protests, led to the fall of José Luciano de Castro's government, tarnished the image and prestige of the Portuguese royal family, and exacerbated the rising anti-British sentiment of recent years.

This article demonstrates how the international satirical press reacted to this event, the reception and consequences of which amounted to a political catastrophe for Portugal and especially for the monarchist regime. The chronological markers for the selection of newspapers encompasses the years of 1889, 1890 and 1891. Those years correspond to the period that we can point to as the conjuncture of the British Ultimatum, from June 1889, when the Portuguese expropriated the Delagoa Bay railway line from the British, until the final treaty that would resolve the issue on 11 June 1891.[1] Indeed, while the British Ultimatum is a major event in Portuguese historiography, it was a rather minor concern in the foreign satirical press of the time, with interest limited to this narrow time frame. Thus, this study compares evidence about the British Ultimatum of 1890 and respective Anglo-Portuguese relations as depicted in the satirical press of Portugal, Great Britain, Austria, France, Germany, Spain, and Switzerland.

While the evidence is uneven, confirming that the Ultimatum was a minor concern to most European nations other than the British, a comparative

---

[1] Ana Simões, Maria Paula Diogo, and Paula Urze, 'Cartoon Diplomacy: Visual Strategies, Imperial Rivalries and the 1890 British Ultimatum to Portugal', *The British Journal for the History of Science*, 56.2 (2023), pp. 1–20 (p. 11), doi:10.1017/S0007087423000067; José Miguel Sardica, 'Ultimato Britânico', in *Dicionário de História da I República e do Republicanismo*, ed. by Maria Fernanda Rollo, 3 vols (Assembleia da República, 2013–14), III (2014), pp. 1023–33 (p. 1032). All translations are responsibility of the author.

Portuguese Studies vol. 41 no. 2 (2025), doi:10.1353/port.00046, 285–306
© Modern Humanities Research Association 2025

analysis of the visual and textual evidence in the contemporary European satirical press provides critical insights into how the rest of Europe regarded Portugal and expands the current, and especially Portuguese, historiographical understanding of the Ultimatum. Moreover, bearing in mind that the satirical press is by definition more daring and distanced from political power, this study takes a novel and critical lens on wider attitudes towards Portugal and goes beyond the official discourses of the political elite of the respective European nations. The opinions on the Ultimatum from some of the countries that we will examine, such as Germany or Italy, have never been addressed in historiography, aside from the reactions of their respective governments. This is precisely the gap that this research seeks to fill.

As indicated, the British Ultimatum is a major theme in Portuguese historiography. Most relevant to this study are those historians who have considered the event from the point of view of public opinion and the press, most notably Amadeu Carvalho Homem and Maria Teresa Pinto Coelho. The former has examined Portuguese public opinion on the Ultimatum and press reactions to it, while the latter has considered how the British viewed the incident. Taken together, the two scholars provide the opportunity for some indirect comparative analysis of the British Ultimatum. Indeed, while Teresa Pinto Coelho does use the satirical press (mainly Rafael Bordalo Pinheiro for the Portuguese side and *Punch* for the British side), it does not constitute the focus of her analysis. For works where the satirical press is the focus of the investigation we can point to the article 'Cartoon Diplomacy: Visual Strategies, Imperial Rivalries and the 1890 British Ultimatum to Portugal' by Ana Simões, Maria Paula Diogo and Paula Urze and the article 'John Bull and Zé Povinho: The Clash between Two National Stereotypes' by João Medina; while the Ultimatum is not the focal point of this latter article, it does appear multiple times. The most studied foreign press for this event is, indeed, the British press.

Beyond the Anglo-Portuguese world, there has been considerably less academic interest in the topic but the studies are nonetheless noteworthy, such as 'Le Conflit anglo-portugais de 1890 dans la correspondance diplomatique et la presse françaises', Victor Lopes's PhD thesis. Another relevant work is 'Espanha ante o "Ultimatum"', by Pilar Vasquez Cuesta, which covers the general reaction of Spain to the British Ultimatum, including responses from student organizations, republicans, the press, and the Spanish government. The present article intends to insert itself in this theme of the international reaction to the Ultimatum, focusing only on the satirical press and establishing a comparative view between the different European countries from where we selected material.

Before we analyse the satire associated with the Ultimatum, it is imperative to contextualize those years of intense diplomatic activity and Anglo-Portuguese tensions. The Ultimatum happened in the context of a crucial phase in European imperialism, with the reinforcement and consolidation of a European presence on the African continent, predicated on the demand for imports of raw materials to sustain the industrialized economies of Europe. The Berlin Conference of 1884–85 was central to this context and pivotal to this process as it established that rights to African territories depended on effective occupation of those regions (noting that this principle applied only to coastal areas) rather than historical rights (as Portugal defended).[2] In fact, such historical rights were already in danger in 1876 with the Brussels conference. With the Franco-Belgian advances in the region, Portuguese diplomacy rushed negotiations with the British, resulting in the Zaire Treaty of 1882, by which Great Britain recognized the sovereignty of Portugal over the disputed territories along the West African coast.[3] However, this treaty was never enforced, mostly because of pressure from the British public opinion and diplomatic protests from France and Germany, which prompted the Portuguese government of the time to request an international conference to solve the problem.[4]

Following the Berlin Conference, Portugal was forced to enter bilateral treaties, signing accords with France and Germany in 1886.[5] The strategy used to occupy Africa often involved creating spheres of influence and dividing them between European nations. This system, being the basis of the Anglo-Portuguese conflict, would eventually culminate in the British Ultimatum.[6] Despite this, it is worth recalling that tensions between Great Britain and Portugal had been constant during the nineteenth century at least from the 1830s and, particularly, since 1879 with the Delagoa Bay affair in Mozambique.[7] Tensions peaked with the colonial project of Barros Gomes, Minister of Foreign Affairs in José Luciano de Castro's government (1886–90), envisaging the occupation of land east to west between the two biggest Portuguese colonies, Angola and Mozambique, illustrated on the famous 'Pink Map'. This directly clashed with Cecil Rhodes's project to connect the Cape to Cairo by railway, north to south, with British pressure against Portugal's plan starting in 1887.[8] To accomplish this plan, Portugal began sending colonial expeditions from 1887 onwards. One such campaign, Serpa Pinto's expedition to the Makololo region, heightened tensions between the British and the Portuguese. When Serpa Pinto reached the Shiré Valley in November 1889, he found not only the Makololo tribe hostile to him, but also a hoisted British flag. This did not prevent the conquest of the region during the last two months of the year, which was seen by Great Britain as an act of war, prompting a series of responses from

---

[2]   Nuno Severiano Teixeira, 'Política externa e política interna no Portugal de 1890: o Ultimatum inglês' *Análise Social*, 23.98 (1987), pp. 687–719 (pp. 688–90), <http://hdl.handle.net/10362/39568> [accessed 7 March 2024].

[3]   Ibid., p. 690.

[4]   Ibid., pp. 691–92.

[5]   Ibid., p. 692.

[6]   Ibid.

[7]   João Medina, 'John Bull and Zé Povinho: The Clash between Two National Stereotypes', *Revista Islenha*, 10 (1992), pp. 19–34 (p. 20).

[8]   Teixeira, 'Política externa e política interna no Portugal de 1890', pp. 692–93.

the British — a refusal of any kind of negotiations that did not result in the immediate withdrawal of Portugal, the concentration of British naval forces on the African coast and, last but not least, Lord Salisbury's Memorandum of 11 January 1890, threatening to send warships to Lisbon itself.[9]

The Portuguese Council of State met urgently on the night of 11 January and quickly decided to cede to every British demand, which opened a cycle of anti-British, patriotic and even republican protests.[10] The conjuncture of the Ultimatum did not end with the memorandum and the backdown of the Portuguese, but was prolonged until the summer of 1891. Until the Treaty of August 1890, Great Britain assumed an aggressively inflexible position, convinced of the possibility of the total capitulation by Portugal. However, in the face of the political instability in Portugal, the danger posed by Portuguese diplomacy successfully involving a world power in the conflict, and because the main British objectives were already accomplished, Great Britain adopted a more moderate position of dialogue after the collapse of the Treaty of 1890; notably, the acceptance of the *Modus Vivendi* of 14 November. The Treaty of 1891, despite being less generous for Portugal, was well received, concluding this conjuncture.[11]

In summary, the political consequences of the British Ultimatum were the fall of two Portuguese governments (of José Luciano de Castro and António Serpa), the discrediting of the two monarchist parties (*Partido Progressista* and *Partido Regenerador*) and of the Crown itself, and the considerable growth in popularity of the Republican movement in Portugal.[12]

The British Satirical Press

Naturally, among the non-Portuguese press it was the British that covered the Ultimatum the most and, if in the non-satirical press there were newspapers clearly against the foreign policy of Lord Salisbury,[13] in the satirical press such a thing was impossible to find. On the whole, the British satirical press fully supported both the British cause and the attacks against the Portuguese, portraying the country and its people as inferior to the British.

In 1889, the British press covered the Anglo-Portuguese tensions arising from the Portuguese military expeditions in Africa, such as those commanded by Serpa Pinto. In contrast to the international press, which only covered the British Ultimatum after the event, British satire had turned its attention to these issues in the year prior to the Ultimatum. In the context of the revitalized Delagoa Bay affair, *Punch* published a cartoon on 13 June 1889 presenting what

[9]   Ibid., p. 693.
[10] Ibid., p. 694.
[11] Ibid., p. 696
[12] Ibid., pp. 699–704.
[13] Robert Howes, 'The British Press and Opposition to Lord Salisbury's Ultimatum of January 1890', *Portuguese Studies*, 23.2 (2007), pp. 153–66 (p. 157), doi:10.2307/41057959.

would be a recurring image of Portugal in the British press — cheeky, but a small and fragile being.[14] In this caricature, Portugal has been caught by Great Britain (represented by John Bull) confiscating part of the Delagoa Bay railway, which had actually happened one month before. When caught, Portugal had pleaded for a mediator to resolve the issue — which, as we saw before, was something that Britain always refused, due to her position of power in relation to Portugal. *Punch* subsequently published a poem together with the cartoon where, among other things, it warns Barros Gomes that he would regret it if anything happened to a British convoy or train.[15]

On this same day, *Moonshine* published a satirical text that discusses 'Portuguese Gratitude', intending to show the readers how the Portuguese are ungrateful, now backstabbing the ally that helped them so much, and reminding them of the commercial, financial, and military support given by Great Britain to Portugal.[16] In return, the periodical argued, Portugal showed its thanks to Britain by ruining British capitalists, stealing from her, and allying itself with Great Britain's enemies (in this case, the Boers).[17] The themes of Portuguese ingratitude and the indignation of the British press due to the 'cheekiness' of Portugal for daring to confront its oldest ally are recurring topics, as we will see.

In December 1889, *Punch* directly attacked Portuguese colonial policy, representing the Iberian country as a 'mischievous monkey' and the Pink Map as a simple result of a 'great mess', illustrating the illegitimacy of Portuguese claims (see Fig. 1).[18] In this way, the British periodical reduced the plan of Barros Gomes, and the Portuguese hopes for a grand Empire in Africa, to mere mistakes on the part of an inferior nation and an incompetent government. According to *Punch*, the moral of the story was a warning to Portugal of the power of Great Britain; namely, that the Portuguese should behave unless they want to face the might of John Bull.[19] The *Moonshine* published a cartoon on 4 January 1890 mocking the audacity of Portugal, depicted as such a small and inoffensive man that Lord Salisbury asks his Commander-in-Chief, Viscount Wolseley, to put him on a chair so they can see him better.[20] The intent of this illustration is clear — paint the imbalance of forces between Portugal and Britain, and represent the Portuguese as arrogant but without the power to legitimize their claims.

---

[14] *Punch*, 13 July 1889, p. 19.
[15] *Punch*, 13 July 1889, p. 18.
[16] *Moonshine*, 13 July 1889, p. 15.
[17] Fernando Costa and Pedro Lains, 'Portugal e a Guerra Anglo-Boer', *Ler História*, 42 (2002), pp. 153–74 (pp. 155–61), <https://journals.openedition.org/lerhistoria/1794> [accessed 5 May 2024]. This article refers to the utilization of the Portuguese railway lines by the Boers to import products and the general proximity of Boer and Portuguese commercial relations.
[18] *Punch*, 14 December 1889, p. 278.
[19] *Punch*, 14 December 1889, pp. 278–79.
[20] *Moonshine*, 4 January 1890, retrieved from Maria Teresa Pinto Coelho, *Apocalipse e Regeneração: o Ultimatum e a mitologia da pátria na literatura finissecular* (Edições Cosmos, 1996).

FIG. 1. 'The Mischievous Monkey', Linley Sambourne, *Punch*, 14 December 1889, p. 278. Available at <https://doi.org/10.11588/diglit.17688#0283>.

After the delivery of Lord Salisbury's memorandum, the hostility towards the Portuguese remained unchanged. On 15 January 1890, *Fun* depicted the conflict between the 'cheeky' Portuguese and the Makololos. In this illustration an African man is seen with a British flag raised on his head, symbolizing how his tribe belongs to the British Empire.[21] The periodical devalues this campaign, affirming that the 'Portu-geese' (mocking term for Portuguese, combining the words 'Portuguese' and 'geese') were simply arrogant men. *Punch* returned to the topic on 18 January 1890, explaining to the Portuguese what they must do, in a cartoon.[22] Portugal, represented by Serpa Pinto, and shown stepping

---

[21] *Fun*, 15 January 1890, p. 21.
[22] *Punch*, 18 January 1890, p. 31.

on the Union flag, must immediately get off the British flag, meaning the only thing the Portuguese can do, in the eyes of *Punch*, is leave the territories claimed by Britain. Notable is the use of expressions like 'little friend' and 'little feelings', a good example of the condescending attitude towards Portugal and the somewhat paternalistic sentiment expressed by the British. Moreover, this periodical describes a possible open conflict between these two countries as a 'Pigmy versus Titan' fight, leaving no doubts what *Punch* thinks of the balance of powers. Developing the story of the caricature, *Punch* reminds Portugal how they were saved by the Duke of Wellington in the era of the Napoleonic Wars and that the Portuguese no longer live in the times of Camões, Vasco da Gama or Pedro Álvares Cabral.[23]

On 22 January 1890, *Fun* presented a triumphant Lord Salisbury drinking a cup of wine named 'Africa', placed on a table covered by the British flag, possibly symbolizing the hegemony of Great Britain over Africa, and a table reservation sheet called 'Ultimatum' sitting on top of the table.[24] In addition, Salisbury holds a bottle of wine labelled 'Portugal'. The cartoon's intention is to show how a mixture of these two wines, Africa and Portugal, symbolizing the Anglo-Portuguese conflict, resulted in a satisfactory win for the British, since Portugal easily yielded to the British demands. However, at the time of the publication of this illustration, the conclusion of the Ultimatum conjecture was yet to be reached.

After the collapse of the Treaty of August 1890, the topic kept appearing in the British satirical press. In October 1890 *Punch* covered the issue again, this time with a caricature, the title of which was a play of words between the expressions 'L'onion' and 'L'union'.[25] The illustration seems to be in step with a moderation of British diplomacy, since it compliments Portugal, with John Bull saying that the Portuguese are strong and also wise, so they should use those attributes to stay out of trouble. If we further analyse the caricature, we see a fence dividing the scenario between the Portuguese and the British. On the British side, *Punch* put Mashonaland, while the Portuguese try to destroy the fence, labelled as 'convention', therefore most likely referring to how the Portuguese parliament blocked the signing of the Treaty of August 1890, as well as the penetration of the Portuguese into lands claimed by Great Britain. We also have a mention of the South Africa Company, founded by Cecil Rhodes in 1889,[26] representing the role of Rhodes in this conjuncture. The company in question had been expanding at Mozambique's expense since its creation, as the undefined borders allowed it to enter without consequences.[27] The British

[23] *Punch*, 18 January 1890, p. 30.
[24] *Fun*, 22 January 1890, p. 35.
[25] *Punch*, 25 October 1890, p. 194.
[26] Luís Filipe Moreira Alves do Carmo Reis, *Visões de Império nas vésperas do 'Ultimato': um estudo de caso sobre o imperialismo português (1889)* (Centro de Estudos Africanos da Universidade do Porto, 2008), p. 35.
[27] Valentim Alexandre, 'O Império Português (1825–1890): ideologia e economia', *Análise Social*,

encouraged such actions to pressure Portugal into ratifying a bilateral treaty. This led to the August 1890 Treaty, which aimed to define the borders of Angola and Mozambique and recognize a small land connection between them. Strong public and political opposition, along with anti-British sentiment, prevented its ratification. The dispute was finally settled in 1891, not through a better agreement, but because Portugal's internal situation had improved and the government enjoyed stronger public support.[28]

In 1891, the last year of our chronology, *Fun* published a cartoon that reinforces the sentiment of how easy would be for the British to destroy Portugal.[29] John Bull warns the 'cheeky' Portugal, here represented by Serpa Pinto, that if he doesn't immediately put a stop to his 'larks', referring to Portugal wanting land claimed by the British, he will sit on top of Portugal, a quite explicit metaphor for how simple it would be for Britain to force Portugal to accept her terms, as well the humiliation that the Portuguese would endure. In a final reference to the affair, *Punch* published an illustration relating to an incident that had happened two weeks before,[30] depicting an unplanned meeting between Cecil Rhodes, a Portuguese man, and a woman from the Mashonaland tribe.[31] Rhodes warns the Portuguese that the woman belongs to him and that the Iberian should immediately go away, adding that no one wants the Portuguese to act as a sentry to that part of Africa. This cartoon returns to the role of Cecil Rhodes on the conjuncture of the Ultimatum (he was a main opponent of Portuguese claims and stood to lose the most if Portugal succeeded), also touching on the matter of Portugal's relative international isolation during this conflict, in which the Portuguese lacked any really strong support from any other country (which explains why *Punch* drew Rhodes telling Portugal 'nobody wants you to watch or mount guard'). This international isolation was obvious, as no other nation attempted to help. It also reinforced the Portuguese view that, while the Anglo-Portuguese alliance was useful, it would be a good idea to build closer relations with other countries.[32]

Concluding this section, we can observe that the British saw themselves as superior to the Portuguese and not only from a military point of view. The British satirical press did not limit its attacks on Portugal to geopolitical issues but repeatedly looked for ways to ridicule Portugal and lower its standing in the public eye, often comparing the actions of Portugal to 'simian arts'[33] or 'monkeyish tricks',[34] or bluntly drawing Portugal as a monkey.[35] *Punch* was the

---

39.164 (2004), pp. 959–79 (p. 977), doi:10.31447/AS00032573.2004169.01.
[28]   Rui Ramos, *D. Carlos, 1863–1908* (Temas e Debates, 2020), pp. 89–94.
[29]   *Fun*, 29 April 1891, p. 177.
[30]   *Punch* cites the *Reuters Editions* from 24 May 1891 in this cartoon — 'It is stated that the Pungwé route to Mashonaland has been again closed by the Portuguese Authorities'.
[31]   *Punch*, 6 June 1891, p. 266.
[32]   Lourenço Pereira Coutinho, *Do Ultimato à República: política e diplomacia nas últimas décadas da monarquia* (Prefácio, 2004), pp. 99–101.
[33]   *Punch*, 13 July 1889, p. 18.
[34]   *Punch*, 18 January 1890, p. 30.
[35]   Reis, *Visões de Império nas vésperas do 'Ultimato'*, pp. 142–44.

satirical periodical that paid the most attention to the Ultimatum; a fact that was noted contemporaneously in Portugal, especially because of the conflict between *Punch* and Rafael Bordalo Pinheiro in the newspaper *Pontos nos ii*, in which Bordalo Pinheiro created pro-Portuguese or anti-British cartoons, sometimes referencing elements from *Punch*. For example, in one cartoon he depicts a monkey (the same one *Punch* had used to represent the Portuguese) beating John Bull with his own cane.[36] Satirical material on the theme was far more frequent in Portugal, naturally, because the Ultimatum had less impact in Great Britain. The British presented different arguments against the Pink Map, ranging from the lands claimed by Portugal already belonging to Britain to accusing the Portuguese of not doing a good job at their civilizing mission and the lingering suspicions of the Portuguese Empire still endorsing and practising slavery, likewise facilitating the slave trade.[37] In addition to this, there was the legal argument put forward by Britain that Portugal would never be able to actually occupy the territory, which would be in breach of the Berlin Conference directives. And finally, Great Britain had Scottish Anglican missionaries in Niassa, claimed by Portugal.[38]

The European Satirical Press

The British satirical press clearly supported their own government, while most European papers either supported Portugal or highlighted the imbalance between the nations, never openly defending Britain. However, the theme was even less common outside British satire. For sure, a conflict between Great Britain and a small country like Portugal about faraway lands in Africa certainly would not be one of the main interests of the target audience of this type of press.

The caricatures that were sympathetic to the Portuguese position showed their support mainly by painting the Portuguese as the victims. Such sentiments contradicted the diplomatic attitude of these countries, since none of them offered any real help to Portugal. The only possible exception was the Germans, who tried to intervene as a mediator, mostly due to their wanting to undermine the British, but also because the chaotic political situation in Portugal could have resulted in the creation of a Republic there, which could in turn have led to the destabilization of Spain and, in the worst-case scenario, the hegemony of Republicanism in the Iberian Peninsula, potentially making them more friendly towards the French.[39]

[36]   Simões, Diogo, and Urze, 'Cartoon Diplomacy', p. 9.
[37]   Maria Teresa Pinto Coelho, *Apocalipse e Regeneração*, pp. 64–68.
[38]   Maria Teresa Pinto Coelho, '"Pérfida Albion" and "Little Portugal": The Role of the Press in British and Portuguese National Perceptions of the 1890 Ultimatum', *Portuguese Studies*, 6.1 (1990), pp. 173–90 (p. 177), doi:10.2307/41104912.
[39]   Gisela Guevara, *As relações entre Portugal e a Alemanha em torno da África (finais do século XIX e inícios do século XX)* (Ministério dos Negócios Estrangeiros, 2006), pp. 110–11.

FIG. 2. 'Damit ist der portugiesisch-englische Konflikt beendigt' [This brings the Portuguese-English conflict to an end], M.H., *Nebelspalter*, 8 February 1890, p. 5. Available at <https://www.e-periodica.ch/digbib/view?pid=neb-001%3A1890%3A16%3A%3A1385>.

The imbalance between the innocence and impotence of Portugal and British aggression was the main theme in the European satirical press. Here, satirists viewed Britain as using her power in an illegitimate way to force Portugal to capitulate. The best example of this is the French caricature published by *La Chronique amusante* on the day after the Ultimatum, which compares the conjuncture to the popular Aesop fable of 'The Wolf and the Lamb', in which the wolf tries to find a myriad of excuses to devour the lamb in a legitimate way.[40] The intention of the cartoon is to transmit the idea that Britain, here drawn as

[40]   *La Chronique amusante*, 12 January 1890, p. 5.

the wolf, is using her strength to expropriate Portugal, represented by the lamb, of its rightful lands. The French satirical press commented sarcastically on the bravery of the British. For example, in the cartoon published by *Revue comique normande* on 18 January 1890, John Bull is seen threatening a man smaller than him (probably Serpa Pinto, symbolizing Portugal) with a gun and a knife at the Portuguese soldier's back.[41] This caricature not only shows a furious John Bull, reflecting the British aggressiveness and expansionism, but also the idea of Portugal being betrayed by its oldest ally, figuratively knifed in the back.

On 8 February 1890, the Swiss publication *Nebelspalter* published an illustration that shows the reader the result of the Ultimatum (see Fig. 2).[42] John Bull is seen sitting on top of a powerless Portuguese man, who is holding a document labelled 'Zambezi rights' and in his pockets there are other diplomas labelled 'Rights', possibly referring to the historical rights defended by Portuguese diplomacy. The cartoon carries a simple, but strong message. The rights invoked by Portugal had no effect on the result of the conflict and the image of John Bull sitting on an impotent Portuguese individual corresponds to the humiliation that the Portuguese endured due to this whole conjuncture. The following day, 9 February 1890, the French periodical *Le Charivari* presents the British Ultimatum as an attempt by Great Britain to help Portugal — by amputating his left leg (see Fig. 3).[43] By labelling the leg as Shiré and Zambezi, it represents them as crucial parts of Portugal that the British want to expropriate. In addition to this, the difference in size between the British surgeon and the Portuguese patient also points to the imbalance of powers in this conflict.

Another example of an Aesop fable being used to describe the Ultimatum can be seen in the cartoon published on 18 January 1890 in the Italian periodical *Pasquino*. This time it is the Roman version of the Greek fabulist that is used, and the fable used to symbolize the Anglo-Portuguese conflict is the Lion's Share.[44] Presenting Portugal as a small mouse, the periodical states that the Portuguese forgot Fedro's words *quia nominor Leo* [because I am named Lion], conveying the message that Portugal forgot that the powerful always get what they want by using their power to subjugate the weak, regardless of how legitimate or illegitimate their actions may be. In this periodical's view, just like in the fable where the lion has used his power to enforce his will upon others, Britain also imposed herself on Portugal through her strength, ignoring legitimate Portuguese claims to the territory in question. In the summer of 1890, the German *Kladderadatsch* published a small poem that contains a story about 'honest' Britain asking Portugal to help her achieve peace, but to achieve peace the British first need to take African lands claimed by the Portuguese.[45]

As we saw, the imbalance of powers was how the European (and non-British)

---

41   *Revue comique normande*, 18 January 1890, pp. 4–5.
42   *Nebelspalter*, 8 February 1890, p. 5.
43   *Le Charivari*, 9 February 1890, p. 155.
44   *Pasquino*, 18 January 1890, p. 28.
45   *Kladderadatsch*, 31 August 1890, p. 348.

FIG. 3. 'Comment ce bon John Bull cherche à panser la blessure qu'il a faite au Portugal' [How the generous John Bull seeks to bandage the wound he inflicted on Portugal], Paf, pseud. Jules Renard, *Le Charivari*, 9 February 1890, p. 155, year 59. Available at <https://doi.org/10.11588/diglit.23884#0159>.

satirical press depicted the British Ultimatum and associated Anglo-Portuguese relations. The French paper *Le Grelot* offered us its take on the situation on 26 January 1890 by painting the Scramble for Africa as a competition between mice, except that Britain is drawn as a cat.[46] The focus of the cartoon is the British cat catching the Portuguese mouse that was going to eat the cheese corresponding to Delagoa Bay and the Shiré. The caption indicates that the humorist views everyone as thieves, the only difference being that Portugal is the small thief, while Great Britain is the big one. Thus, the cartoon is not only an interesting representation of the Scramble for Africa but also highlights the imbalance

[46] *Le Grelot*, 26 January 1890, p. 1.

of power between imperialist powers. The Austrian periodical *Kikeriki* also gives its perspective on the power balance in the Anglo-Portuguese conflict, publishing an illustration on 16 January 1890 that presents Portugal as a small swordsman challenging a gigantic angry British marine, who is ready to smash the little Portuguese individual.[47]

Returning to the *Kladderadatsch*, the German periodical published a cartoon on 19 January 1890 that is divided into two images.[48] The first one displays a table full of food with a British man sleeping next to it, while a dog (corresponding to Serpa Pinto) takes advantage of the sleepy British individual to try to steal a sausage, symbolizing the Portuguese attack on the Makololo tribe. Note that the dog, which is indeed representing Portugal, appears weakened and very thin, possibly reflecting the state of the Portuguese Empire in the eyes of nearly all of Europe at the time — an irrelevant and fragile Empire that the great powers could end whenever they wanted. The second image offers the consequences of the first. As he awakes, the British kicks the dog and screams that the sausage belongs to him. The illustrations aim to represent, on one hand, how Portugal looked to take advantage of Britain's inertia in recent years and seize British territory in Africa,[49] but how the Portuguese were quickly defeated when Britain woke up, symbolizing the moment of the Ultimatum. On the other hand, the full table belonging to the British depicts British Imperialism, displaying different parts of the British Empire at the time. This periodical also published another caricature connected to this theme in the following month, which showcases the harsh reality of Portugal, a fragile man who challenges a mighty hippopotamus (labelled John Bull) in the Niassa Lake. The animal symbolizes a force that undermines Portugal's colonial policy (see Fig. 4).[50] Faced with this situation, the Portuguese only had to say 'Well, never mind', reflecting the immediate surrender to the British demands and the Portuguese government's lack of willingness to confront Great Britain. In the cartoon, the ground, which is labelled 'colonization', is in the process of being destroyed, probably transmitting the idea that this event would mark the end of Portuguese colonialism in Africa, a message that was also propagated by republicans in Portugal.

In the week following the Ultimatum, the Austrian *Figaro* published a cartoon whose caption indicates that the British and Portuguese are reconciled (see Fig. 5). However, in the illustration John Bull is shown with a very small Portuguese man in his pocket, meaning that the conflict wasn't solved in a balanced and bilateral way, but with Britain imposing herself on Portugal.[51]

---

[47] *Kikeriki*, 16 January 1890, p. 2.
[48] *Kladderadatsch*, 19 January 1890, p. 24.
[49] As we saw before, this does not paint the whole picture, since the British issued many diplomatic protests against Portuguese presence in lands that the British claimed. However, it is true that the British Ultimatum was the diplomatic action with most intensity, obviously.
[50] *Kladderadatsch*, 2 February 1890, p. 37.
[51] *Figaro*, 18 January 1890, p. 9.

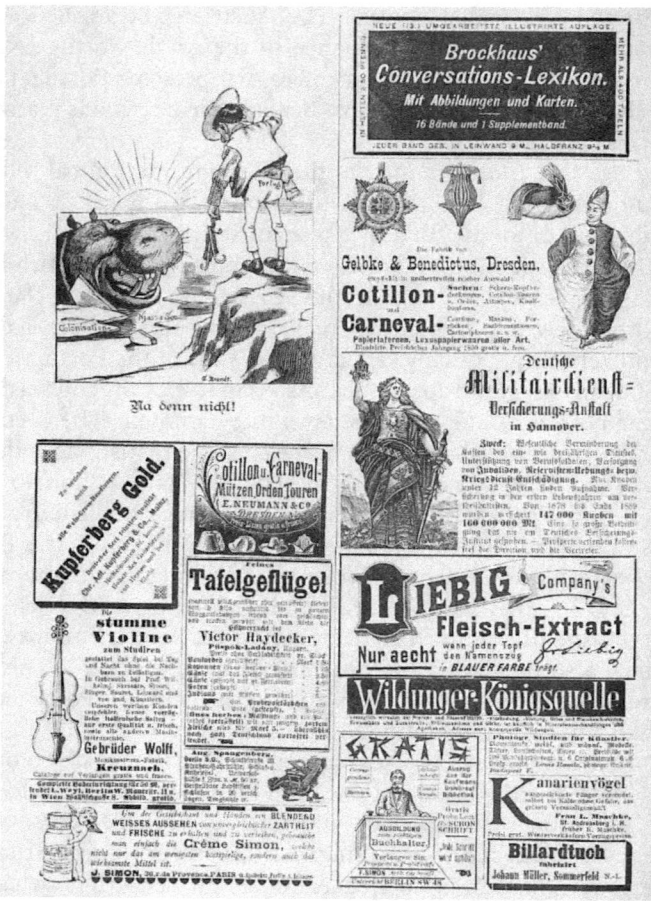

FIG. 4. 'Na denn nicht!' [Well then, never mind!], Gustav Brandt,
Kladderadatsch, 2 February 1890, p. 37. Available at
<https://doi.org/10.11588/diglit.2271#0038>.

Nevertheless, there are three other topics that do not fall within the
main two themes identified and discussed thus far, i.e. the innocence and
ineptitude of the Portuguese and the imbalance of power between Portugal
and Britain. Surprisingly, there are caricatures that expose how the Native
African serves almost as a figurant in a conflict over his own lands. Shortly
after the occupation of the Makololo tribe by Serpa Pinto,[52] the *Pasquino* on
22 December 1889 published a cartoon covering this issue, which involves
John Bull, an unidentified Portuguese man, and a Makololo in between the

---

[52] Reis, *Visões de Império nas vésperas do 'Ultimato'*, p. 27.

FIG. 5. 'Der Engländer ist mit den Portugiesen versöhnt' [The Englishman
is reconciled with the Portuguese], *Figaro*, 18 January 1890, p. 9, vol. 34.
Available at: <https://anno.onb.ac.at/cgi-content/anno?aid=fig&datum=18
900118&seite=1&zoom=22>.

Europeans.[53] In the illustration, by trying to hit each other, the British and the
Portuguese end up hitting the person in the middle, reflecting how the African
people suffer due to European tensions. In addition to this, the caption also
presents the idea that the native would not be in a good spot under either of
the parties involved. This caricature shows how the Anglo-Portuguese conflict
negatively impacted African tribes, with Europeans using them as pawns in
their plans to define and expand sphere of influences in Africa.

[53]   *Pasquino*, 22 December 1889, p. 605.

Returning to the *Nebelspalter*, this publication featured a cartoon on the day of the Ultimatum that had another anti-imperialist message.[54] With the scene set on the Zambezi, John Bull is seen equipped with a whip telling a Portuguese soldier, who is choking a native with a rope, to stop, affirming that the British are the ones that should be civilizing the African. The Portuguese, however, refuses this request, explaining that it is irrelevant for the native who civilizes him. The periodical criticizes the false morality of European colonial empires that justified colonization in this era with the idea that Europeans were in Africa to civilize the natives and modernize their civilizations, but in reality, in the name of this mission, the European people committed horrors on the African continent. This cartoon also questions if it is ethical for two European countries to be discussing who gets a certain piece of African land without the African people that live there having any kind of input.

The second matter that falls outside of the main themes is the dynamics surrounding the Anglo-Portuguese alliance. For this, we have the example of the *Pasquino*, which published an illustration on 31 May 1891 that covers the Anglo-Portuguese relations in two different settings (see Fig. 6).[55] In Europe, the British and Portuguese are seen getting ready to sing a love duet, symbolizing their proximity in European matters and how they are, supposedly, always on the same side. But in Africa, they are enemies, ready to shoot each other in order to further their colonial goals. In this cartoon, the Portuguese character is depicted with an orange in place of his head, alluding to how popular the Portuguese orange was at the time. Although it is not the case in Italy, in some countries the term for orange is very similar to the word Portugal, reflecting the connection between the Portuguese and the dissemination of the fruit.[56]

The third and final matter is the coverage of the internal situation in Portugal by the foreign satirical press, a very rare phenomenon during this period. The sole example is the caricature published by *Frankfurter Latern* in January 1890, which depicts a battle scenario with a small Portuguese swordsman standing against a giant British marine, but also against an enormous monster labelled 'Revolution', referring to the internal situation in Portugal.[57] This depiction of a revolution using a monster goes hand in hand with German reports of the attempted republican revolution of 31 January 1891, which show that the Germans were indeed very worried about the possibility of a Republic appearing from the political climate in Portugal.[58] Furthermore, as we saw before and will see later, there was a real worry that this conjuncture would lead to the end of the Monarchy in Portugal, a sentiment shared by political elites from Britain, Germany, and Spain, among others. Due to Portugal's status of a third-tier power, the internal political situation of Portugal was rarely a topic

---

[54] *Nebelspalter*, 11 January 1890, p. 8.
[55] *Pasquino*, 31 May 1891, p. 256.
[56] Anabela Ramos, *Laranjas de Portugal: séculos de cultivo e consumo* (Ficta Editora, 2022), p. 19. Maria Teresa Pinto Coelho, *Apocalipse e Regeneração*, pp. 64–68.
[57] *Frankfurter Latern*, 25 January 1890, p. 16.
[58] Guevara, *As relações entre Portugal e a Alemanha em torno da África*, pp. 110.

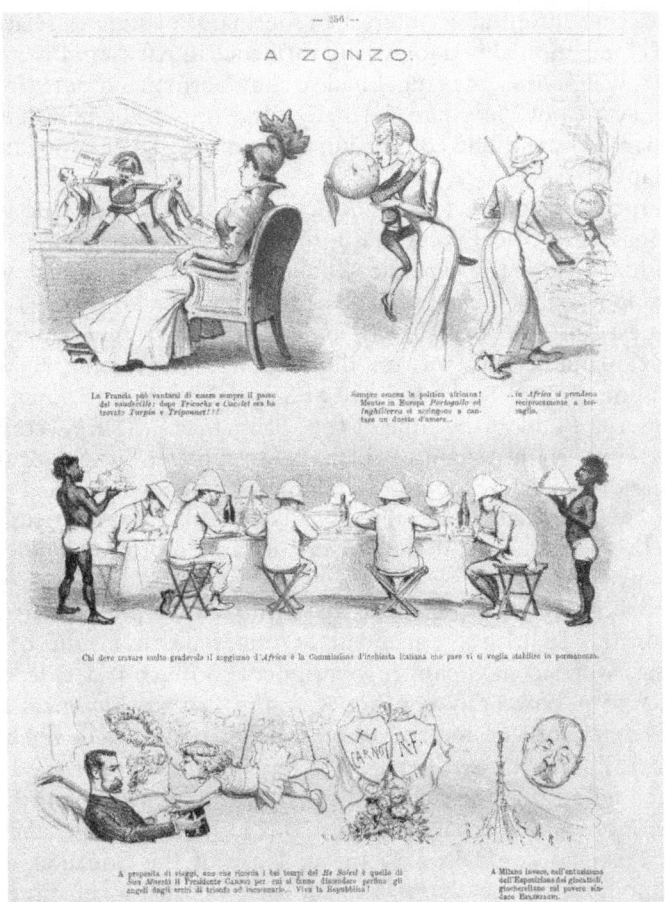

FIG. 6. 'Sempre amena la politica africana!' [African politics are always
entertaining!], *Pasquino*, 31 May 1891, p. 256, vol. XXXVI. Available at
<https://www.bdl.servizirl.it/bdl/bookreader/index.html?path=fe&cdOgge
tto=131902#page/162/mode/1up>.

for the international satirical press, which, naturally, gives this cartoon from
Frankfurter Latern an added interest.

As we have shown, we can then divide the treatment of the Ultimatum in the
satirical press (excluding Britain) into two main topics: the British aggression
and expansion conjugated with a certain Portuguese innocence and unrealism,
and the imbalance of forces between the two empires. While both topics were
dealt with in the British satirical press, in the case of France, Germany and Italy
they did not attack Portugal's claims or legitimize British actions. The satirical
press in France, Britain's traditional rival, often supported Portugal and
portrayed Britain as the aggressor. German satire ignored Germany's mediation

efforts, reflecting little public interest in German-Portuguese relations, even though such mediation aimed to expand influence in Africa in line with Kaiser Wilhelm II's *Weltpolitik*.[59] Portugal had sought German support since at least 1887, but it never came,[60] despite Germany's agreeing to the 1886 Treaty which was accompanied by the land connection between Angola and Mozambique (or the Pink Map).[61]

The Spanish case is one of the most interesting because it is possible to see in the Spanish satirical press that it more closely reflects the geo-political reality: the non-republican periodicals following a neutral policy, with timid shows of support, and the republicans producing material that was openly pro-Portuguese and anti-British. The only cartoon obtained from a Spanish non-republican publication was an illustration that presents us with three caricatures, one of Lord Salisbury, one of Serpa Pinto before going to Africa, and one of Serpa Pinto at the time of the Ultimatum.[62] There were also some satirical texts mainly criticizing British expansionism, but the examples are not as strong or as frequent as the Catalonian republican satirical press.[63] As we will see next, the Catalonian republicans were the strongest supporters of Portugal in this conjuncture, in the universities and in protests to the press and the Spanish parliament.

The Spanish republicans were also anti-British and very persistent in their demands for the Spanish government to intervene in favour of Portugal. Their protests worried the Spanish government so much it decided to repress them so as not provoke any conflict with the British. Meanwhile, Spanish monarchists opted for a more neutral route, believing this to be the best way to help Portugal. They criticized Portuguese republicans for taking advantage of the situation and putting the country's stability and monarchist institutions in danger. The monarchists from Spain recognized that the fall of the Braganza dynasty in Portugal could lead to the collapse of the Bourbon dynasty in Spain.[64] Although not directly mentioned, Iberism, the movement advocating the union of Spain and Portugal, gained a new life during this conflict, mainly in Spain. Iberists argued that only a united Iberian Peninsula could defend itself against foreign threats and avoid humiliation.[65] From this point on, all cartoons are from Catalonian republican publications.

---

[59]   Ibid., pp. 108–10.
[60]   Alexandre, 'O império português (1825–1890)', p. 976.
[61]   Coelho, '"Pérfida Albion" and "Little Portugal"', p. 177.
[62]   *Los Madriles*, 25 January 1890, p. 27.
[63]   An example would be on the edition of *Los Madriles* of 18 January 1890 — 'a pérfida Albión, imitando el ejemplo de Alemania con los españoles, ha querido apoderarse — *quia nominor leo* — de unas tierrecitas que nuestros vecinos tienen en Africa y atropellar sus derechos' [The Perfidious Albion, copying Germany's example with the Spanish, has shown interest in seizing — *quia nominor leo* — some small lands that our neighbours have in Africa and trampling their rights] (*Los Madriles*, 18 January 1890, p. 18).
[64]   Pilar Vasquez Cuesta, *A Espanha ante o 'Ultimatum'*, trans. by Maria Antonieta Soares de Azevedo (Livros Horizonte, 1975), pp. 155–56.
[65]   Ibid., p. 124.

FIG. 7. 'Inglaterra y Portugal' [England and Portugal], *La Campana de Gracia*, 1 February 1890, p. 4. Available at: <https://prensahistorica.mcu.es/satirica/es/catalogo_imagenes/grupo.do?path=3068407&presentacion=pagina&posicion=4&registrardownload=0>.

La Campana de Gracia is the periodical that paid the most attention to the British Ultimatum. In January 1890, it published an illustration with 'Albion', symbolizing Great Britain, threatening the young king, Dom Carlos, personifying Portugal, with a blunderbuss on which the word 'Colonies' is inscribed.[66] The cartoon denounces the British as universal pirates who do not respect justice, are irrational, and aim to expand as much as possible, in ways that are both legal and illegal. Note that we can also see the theme of imbalance of powers here, in this case by looking at the big British pirate

---

[66] *La Campana de Gracia*, 18 January 1890, p. 4.

(painted as the evil character and with a rather unattractive face) who wants to usurp lands owned by the small Portuguese. The illustration published by the same periodical in February 1890 depicts a more optimistic scenario and makes references to different themes, with D. Carlos provoking the British man, while holding a flag that announces a ban on British products (see Fig. 7).[67] The character representing Britain is drawn shivering with fear upon seeing his products being stuck on the beach instead of being sold to the Portuguese. This cartoon alludes to the boycott of British products in Portugal, arguing that the British had, as a result, moderated their threats. However, while the Portuguese public had boycotted British goods, the Portuguese government had not. Moreover, British exports to Portugal had already been in decline since the 1880s.[68]

Another Catalonian periodical that addressed the Ultimatum was *La Tomasa* which published an illustration that covers two scenarios connected to this conjuncture.[69] The main scenario is the conflict between the Portuguese led by Serpa Pinto against the Makololo tribe and the British, where the British are painted as commanders of the tribe, guiding them against the Portuguese. The second, in the top left corner, shows a Portuguese vandalizing a British insignia in Lisbon, sharing with the audience an example of the many anti-British protests that were going on in the capital city of Portugal. This same publication dedicated a satirical text to Lord Salisbury on the same day as the previous cartoon, accusing Britain of offences ranging from unjustified aggression against Portugal to the usurpation of Gibraltar.[70] On 28 February 1890, this periodical featured another text that supported the Portuguese cause.[71] Among other things it, like *La Campana de Gracia*, calls the British pirates and enthusiastically cheers for Portugal, the Portuguese and Serpa Pinto.

Meanwhile, *La Esquella de la torratxa* asked what would happen if the British wanted to take Barcelona in the way that they were seizing African lands from the Portuguese, answering that every Spaniard would panic.[72] However, it would be easy to defeat the British, seeing that they are addicted to drinking — the Spanish would only need to lead all the soldiers to taverns and give them a lot of wine, thus defeating the British threat without spilling a single drop of blood.

To conclude this section and going back to *La Campana de Gracia*, the illustration of this periodical in June 1890 symbolizes to perfection the sentiments that the Spanish republicans held towards Britain: it is an evil octopus that wants to control every part of the Iberian Peninsula and all of

---

[67] *La Campana de Gracia*, 1 February 1890, p. 4.
[68] Jorge Miguel Pedreira, *História económica contemporânea: Portugal, 1808–2000* (Objectiva, 2021), 117.
[69] *La Tomasa*, 24 January 1890, pp. 8–9.
[70] *La Tomasa*, 24 January 1890, p. 6.
[71] *La Tomasa*, 28 February 1890, p. 3.
[72] *La Esquella de la torratxa*, 25 January 1890, p. 50.

Spain's colonies, mostly through economic exploitation of those territories as indicated by the octopus's tentacles, where it's possible to read labels referring to economic activities such as 'mines' or 'railways'. The caption gives a warning to the Spanish that if they don't do anything against the British 'you will see how in the end we will not be able to move'. While not being directly connected to the British Ultimatum itself, it is still relevant to it, since it illustrates the extent of anti-British sentiment common to all Iberian republicans at this time, as well having a cause that is one of the main reasons that Iberism was revitalized — the fight against nations outside the Iberian Peninsula.

Conclusion

In conclusion, it is possible to extract from the analysed material three different lines of thought present in the European satirical press in relation to the question of the British Ultimatum. The first one — the British line — tries to transmit the idea that this is nothing more than a cheeky act by Portugal and that the Portuguese are wrongfully claiming the land between Angola and Mozambique for themselves; it completely disregards any kind of legitimacy that Portugal might have had to those claims. The second line corresponds to the part of the (non-British) foreign press that presents Portugal as a weak power with no chance of defeating Great Britain in this conflict and believes that the plan was a mistake by the Portuguese government. The third line, which represents the majority of the (non-British) foreign press, presents the Portuguese as victims of the British, according to which Portugal saw their rightful territories in Africa being usurped by Britain.

Another important conclusion is the clear lack of relevance that the event had outside of Portugal. If for the Portuguese at the time it was a catastrophe that made Portuguese nationalism with an imperialistic base grow exponentially,[73] abroad, including in Britain, the lack of production of satirical material confirms the lack of relevance of the event. On one hand, for the British press it was just another diplomatic incident and easily settled. On the other hand, for the rest of the foreign press it was just a moment of Portuguese ingenuousness, and the question would be quickly resolved. The Catalonian republican satirical press paid more attention to the internal situation in Portugal, mentioning the boycotts and the vandalism that targeted the British presence. The Catalonian press likely used the conflict mainly to criticize British influence on Spain and globally, with Portugal being a secondary concern. Similarly, other cartoons supporting Portugal primarily aimed to condemn Britain, portraying the dispute as another example of British wrongdoing.

Contrary to what some might anticipate, we did not find foreign satirical content mocking the Portuguese royal family (the opposite of what happened

---

[73]   Medina, 'John Bull and Zé Povinho', p. 25.

in Portugal, where the republican and the general Portuguese satirical press ferociously attacked them), and not even the Catalonian republican satirical press we analysed tried to mock the Braganza dynasty. The low quantity of material found can also be explained, partially, due to this genre of press being usually closer to less elitist social groups (what we could designate as the bulk of public opinion).[74]

Portugal had close to no diplomatic support, even after both France and Germany had shown themselves willing to back the Portuguese project for a land connection between the two biggest Portuguese colonies, something that was done mainly to undermine Britain and not out of any sympathy for Portugal.[75] The approval of Portuguese actions in the foreign satirical press, therefore, goes against the diplomatic positions of those countries, which is interesting to point out, revealing the divergences between this less elitist genre of press and the political classes of their respective countries.

As for the Ultimatum itself, Portuguese historiography has multiple conclusions and ideas about it. One key point worth noting is how Portuguese views of the event, both then and in collective memory since, do not match reality. It was and is seen as a humiliating imperial loss, even though Britain did still recognize Angola's and Mozambique's borders despite Portugal's limited control over them.

[74] Thomas Milton Kemnitz, 'The Cartoon as a Historical Source', *The Journal of Interdisciplinary History*, 4.1 (1973), pp. 81–93 (p. 86), doi:10.2307/202359.
[75] Sardica, 'Ultimato Britânico', p. 1028.

Integrating Brazilian Literature and Plurilingualism to Decolonize Latin American Studies Curricula

ANA CLÁUDIA SURIANI DA SILVA

University College London

Introduction

The online *Encyclopaedia Britannica* defines Latin American literature as 'the national literatures of the Spanish-speaking countries of the Western Hemisphere'. Although it does acknowledge that, 'historically, it also includes the literary expression of the highly developed American Indian civilizations conquered by the Spaniards' and that 'over the years, Latin American literature has developed a rich and complex diversity of themes, forms, creative idioms, and styles', only a brief nod to Brazilian literature appears as a separate entity: 'For a history of literature written in Portuguese in Brazil, see Brazilian literature'.[1] Without delving into the academic debate surrounding the origins of the concept of Latin America[2], this omission in the *Encyclopaedia Britannica* entry is inconsistent with the definition of Latin America presented elsewhere. In its 'list of Latin American countries', the region is defined as 'generally understood to consist of the entire continent of South America, in addition to Mexico, Central America, and the islands of the Caribbean whose inhabitants speak a Romance language'.[3]

The gap between how major sources like the *Encyclopaedia Britannica* define Latin America and how they portray its linguistic and literary traditions reveals an outdated perspective that lacks contemporary postcolonial and inclusive viewpoints. I do not wish to attribute this flaw to the authors of the *Britannica*

---

[1]   Roberto González Echevarría and Ruth Hill, 'Latin American Literature', *Encyclopaedia Britannica* <https://www.britannica.com/art/Latin-American-literature> [accessed 19 March 2025].
[2]   See for example, Michel Gobat, 'The Invention of Latin America: A Transnational History of Anti-Imperialism, Democracy, and Race', *The American Historical Review*, 118.5 (December 2013), pp. 1345–75, doi:10.1093/ahr/118.5.1345 [accessed 7 March 2025].
[3]   'List of Countries in Latin America', *Encyclopaedia Britannica*, <https://www.britannica.com/topic/list-of-countries-in-Latin-America-2061416> [accessed 7 March 2025]. A comprehensive literature review would be necessary to substantiate claims of the marginalization of Brazilian perspectives within Latin American Studies. Such research would analyse the underrepresentation of Brazilian topics in prominent journals (such as *Latin American Research Review* or *Journal of Latin American Cultural Studies*) and the composition of international academic bodies, such as the Latin American Studies Association (LASA).

Portuguese Studies vol. 41 no. 2 (2025), doi:10.1353/port.00047, 307–29
© Modern Humanities Research Association 2025

entry, as it reflects a broader, systemic pattern of biases rooted in historical, political, linguistic, and cultural divides; and it may also vary regionally. For instance, the US Census framework systematically distances Brazilians from the 'Latino' identification option, because it uses the term interchangeably with 'Hispanic'.[4] This systemic oversight demonstrates how even official frameworks struggle to represent Latin America's complex realities. Responsibility for this issue lies with multiple parties, including Latin Americans themselves and the ways universities in Latin America, Europe, and North America have structured, taught, and disseminated knowledge about the region. This linguistic and cultural divide in the region was observed by the Spanish writer Eva Canel during her visit to Brazil in 1900, where she gave lectures and published the article 'As brasileiras' [The Brazilian Women] in the Rio de Janeiro press. Canel noted the lack of knowledge about Brazil across the broader Americas:

> Não sei por que, sendo o Brasil uma das nações mais importantes da América, há de a América conhecer tão pouco as coisas do Brasil. Sabe-se que produz café; que há fumo na Bahia, que há açúcar; que há frutas tropicais e febre amarela e com isto julga-se estar no corrente dos pormenores e particulares deste país atraente e sedutor, porque a verdade é que ele enfeitiça uma pessoa, a ponto de não querer mais abandoná-lo.[5]

> [I do not know why, Brazil being one of the most important nations in the Americas, the Americas know so little about Brazil's affairs. It is known that Brazil produces coffee; that there is tobacco in Bahia, that there is sugar; that there are tropical fruits and yellow fever, and with this, they think they are acquainted with the details and particulars of this captivating and alluring country, because the truth is that it bewitches a person to the point where they no longer wish to leave it.]

Canel's observation underscores how Brazil, despite its economic significance, was often reduced to stereotypes, and its rich cultural and intellectual contributions were overlooked. She highlights in her article the vibrancy of Brazilian intellectual life, particularly the achievements of Brazilian women, whom she describes as 'instruidíssimas' [exceptionally knowledgeable] and deeply engaged in literature, medicine, law and other professions. She singles out Júlia Lopes de Almeida, praising her as 'a escritora de mais altos voos' [the most soaring writer] and 'reputada a melhor prosadora do país [reputed to be the finest prose writer in the country].[6] Canel's frustration with the lack of awareness about Brazilian literature in Spanish-speaking America is evident. She 'lamentava, ao começar estas linhas, que tão pouco se conhece o Brasil, principalmente no Prata, que está tão perto. Conhece-se em Buenos Aires a

[4]   U.S. Census Bureau, 'About the Hispanic Population and Its Origin' <https://www.census.gov/topics/population/hispanic-origin/about.html> [accessed 19 August 2025].
[5]   Eva Canel, 'As brasileiras', A Imprensa, 23 February 1900, p. 1, <https://memoria.bn.gov.br/DocReader/docreader.aspx?bib=245038&pesq=eva%20canel&pagfis=2079> [accessed 10 October 2023]. Translations from Portuguese are my own.
[6]   Canel, p. 1.

literatura francesa e um pouco a italiana. Por que se não há de conhecer a brasileira? Por causa do idioma?' [lamented, as I began these lines, how little Brazil is known, particularly in the River Plate region, which is so close by. In Buenos Aires, French literature is familiar, and Italian literature somewhat so. Why should Brazilian literature not be known as well? Is it because of the language?].[7] Her rhetorical question points to the linguistic barrier as a key factor in this divide, but she rejects it as an excuse, noting that Portuguese is 'uma língua doce, acariciadora e muito compreensível para quem fala castelhano' [a sweet, caressing language, perfectly intelligible to Spanish speakers].[8] Instead, she attributes the lack of engagement to negligence and a failure to foster intellectual exchange between the two cultures. As Canel argues, true friendship and understanding between nations require more than diplomatic visits or superficial exchanges; they demand a deep engagement with each other's literature, arts and ideas.

From the perspective of the history of international relations and ideas, the British historian Leslie Bethell echoes Canel's observations in his article 'Brazil and "Latin America"', while also acknowledging a reciprocal dynamic. For over a century after independence, Brazilian intellectuals and governments equally displayed minimal interest in the Spanish America beyond the Río de la Plata, focusing their attention primarily on Europe and, after 1889, the United States. Even during the Cold War, when the United States and others began to include Brazil within the framework of Latin America, Brazilian governments and intellectuals, with the exception of some on the Left, resisted this classification. It was only after the Cold War that Brazil began to actively engage with its South American neighbours, marking a significant shift in its regional orientation.[9] This mutual neglect underscores a longstanding disconnect between Brazil and Spanish-speaking America, rooted in differing cultural, political, and intellectual priorities. Bethell's analysis, like Canel's critique, reveals how this divide perpetuated a fragmented understanding of Latin America's cultural and intellectual landscape. While Mercosur has fostered economic integration since the 1990s, its cultural, political and economic impact remains limited, a gap that progressive Brazilian governments actively sought to bridge through pan-South American cooperation. Recent challenges like Trump-era tariffs have served as stark reminders of the unfinished project of meaningful South American unity.

As a Brazilian and a Brazilianist, I must take some responsibility for perpetuating some of these systemic biases. While my work has sought to address the underrepresentation of Brazilian literature within Latin American studies curricula, I recognize that my focus has been narrow. Although I

---

[7] Canel, p. 1.
[8] Canel, p. 1.
[9] Leslie Bethell, 'Brazil and "Latin America"', *Journal of Latin American Studies*, 42 (2010), pp. 457–85, doi:10.1017/S0022216X1000088X [accessed 7 March 2025].

have championed non-standard varieties of Portuguese literary expression in Brazil,[10] I have not equally advocated for the inclusion of non-Spanish and non-Portuguese literary traditions across the region. While this oversight is partly attributable to the structural limitations of academic departments, which often lack the resources to cover the full spectrum of Latin America's linguistic and cultural diversity, it remains a failure to fully challenge the frameworks that perpetuate exclusion. For this, I offer a *mea culpa*, before moving forward to propose a way to contribute to decolonizing the curriculum. My goal is to ensure that the works of Indigenous, Black Brazilian, and non-normative European language literary expressions are central to syllabi in modules with the terms 'Latin America(n studies)' in their titles. This approach aims not only to diversify the range of literary voices represented in the modules of the Department of Spanish, Portuguese, and Latin American Studies (SPLAS) at University College London (UCL), where I teach, but also to emphasize the interconnectedness of Latin American histories with colonialism, imperialism, and racial hierarchies.

This article therefore explores the integration of Brazilian literature into Latin American studies modules as a means of decolonizing the curriculum and fostering a deeper understanding of Latin American cultural and linguistic diversity. This analysis draws on a lecture delivered for the redesigned *SPAN0101: Introduction to Spanish and Latin American Studies*, a compulsory 30-credit module first offered in 2024–25 to 90 first-year students. Developed as part of the curriculum decolonization initiative, the aim of my lecture was to examine Brazil and Paraguay's cultural-linguistic diversity through literature, with explicit pedagogical aims of challenging Spanish-language-centric frameworks. While the lecture engaged with Deleuze and Guattari's concept of 'minor literature' (1975) to analyse how marginalized Brazilian voices subvert dominant languages (Portuguese/Spanish), its broader significance lies in its structural role: as the first iteration of a mandatory course, it represents an institutional commitment to reframing Latin American studies beyond colonial linguistic hierarchies and across borders. The article thus treats this case study not as an assessed pedagogical experiment but as proof-of-concept for curriculum reform, a necessary preliminary step before evaluating student outcomes.[11]

---

[10]   See for example, Ana Cláudia Suriani da Silva, Julio Ludemir, and Maria Aparecida Andrade Salgueiro, eds, *Contemporary Afro-Brazilian Short Fiction* (UCL Press, 2024).
[11]   This article was submitted for publication in January 2025 during this new module's first delivery cycle, making assessment metrics and data about student reception unavailable.

Linguistic Terms and Literary Theoretical Frameworks

A clear understanding of key linguistic and literary terms — such as accent, allochthonous and autochthonous languages, bilingualism, dialect, idiolect, monolingualism, pluricentric language, sign language, sociolect, *portunhol selvagem/portuñol salvaje*, variable mixed language, and minor literature — is crucial for understanding the complex linguistic landscape of Latin America. This is a context where the enduring tension between hegemonic (Portuguese, Spanish), other immigrant (allochthonous) and Indigenous (autochthonous) languages has fundamentally shaped the region's cultural production and the diverse literary expressions. These linguistic terms serve as foundational tools for exploring the relationship between plurilingualism and literary expressions, highlighting how language shapes identity, power dynamics, and cultural representation.

For instance, the distinction between autochthonous and allochthonous languages underscores the historical and ongoing tensions and cross-fertilizations between Indigenous languages and those introduced through colonization and immigration. Similarly, concepts like bilingualism and sociolect reveal the layered ways in which individuals and communities navigate multiple linguistic systems, often reflecting social hierarchies and marginalization.[12] By examining pluricentric languages, such as Portuguese and Spanish, we can better understand how regional variations challenge the notion of a singular, dominant linguistic standard. Meanwhile, terms like *portunhol (selvagem)* highlight the creative resistance of borderland communities, whose hybrid linguistic practices and literary works disrupt dominant narratives and assert their cultural presence.

For an increasingly multilingual cohort of students, such as ours in the School of European Languages, Culture, and Society (SELCS) at UCL, many can relate these terms to their own linguistic and cultural journeys. Whether navigating multiple languages at home, engaging with foreign languages while travelling, or encountering for the first time the rich diversity of languages and cultures in a global city like London, these linguistic terms resonate deeply with their personal narratives.

Moving into literary theory, another crucial concept to introduce to students is that of 'minor literature', as defined by Deleuze and Guattari. This framework offers a valuable starting point for understanding how marginalized groups navigate and reshape dominant linguistic systems as a form of artistic

---

[12]   While a clear grasp of these terms is essential for the arguments in this article, I cannot include their definitions here due to space constraints. These terms are standard within the fields of linguistics, and their precise definitions can be found in any major linguistic dictionary. See for example: Peter Matthews, *The Concise Oxford Dictionary of Linguistics* (Oxford University Press, 2014); Keith Brown and Jim Miller, *The Cambridge Dictionary of Linguistics* (Cambridge University Press, 2013); and International Working group on Non-dominant Varieties of Pluricentric Languages <https://pluricentriclanguages.org/pluricentricity/what-is-a-pluricentric-language/> [accessed 20 August 2025].

expression. However, its application must be critically expanded through dialogue with decolonial scholarship to avoid a Eurocentric lens, particularly when applied to Latin American contexts.

Walter Mignolo and Madina Tlostanova's concept of 'border thinking' is a form of critical knowledge produced by people who exist on the peripheries of power.[13] They use their deep understanding of the dominant system (from being 'inside' it) to critique and subvert it from their position of 'exteriority'. This concept provides a foundation for recognizing that such literary practices are not merely formal experimentation but are acts of epistemic disobedience, operating from outside the dominant system to produce subversive knowledge. This aligns with Lúcia Sá's analysis of Amazonian texts, which she frames through Fernando Ortiz's concept of 'transculturation' (a concept later revitalized by Ángel Rama and Mary Louise Pratt).[14] Sá argues against viewing these works as exotic curiosities, instead showing how they enact a dynamic, two-way process where peripheral perspectives actively determine and reshape metropolitan forms. Therefore, to truly appreciate these texts, one must see them as border thinking in practice: using the dominant language not just to critique it, but to convey alternative worldviews and produce knowledge unconstrained by the frame of Western modernity.

A student unfamiliar with Deleuze and Guattari might interpret the term 'minor literature' more literally, relying on their prior understanding of 'minor' in opposition to 'major', particularly in the context of 'major languages'. This could lead to the assumption that it refers to literature written in the languages of smaller communities, rather than widely spoken ones. In Deleuze and Guattari's framework, three defining characteristics emerge: the deterritorialization of language, the inherently political nature of all expression, and the collective value of individual narratives. The first characteristic, the deterritorialization of language, refers to the process by which minority writers articulate their cultural and political realities in a language imposed by colonizers, such as Spanish or Portuguese. For these writers, the act of writing becomes a vital tool for expressing community consciousness, rendering it both urgent and unavoidable. However, this necessity often forces them to operate within a linguistic framework that is inherently alien, a formal, distant and artificial 'paper language'[15] primarily used by the ruling class or intellectual elite. This creates a profound tension: while writing serves as a means of survival and resistance, it simultaneously alienates the artist from their native

---

[13]   Walter D. Mignolo, and Madina V. Tlostanova, 'Theorizing from the Borders: Shifting to Geo- and Body-Politics of Knowledge', *European Journal of Social Theory*, 9.2 (2006), pp. 205–21, doi:10.1177/1368431006063333 [accessed 20 August 2025].
[14]   Lúcia Sá, *Rain Forest Literatures: Amazonian Texts and Latin American Culture* (University of Minnesota Press, 2004); Ángel Rama, *Transculturación narrativa en América Latina* (Siglo Veintiuno Editores, 1983); Mary Louise Pratt, *Imperial Eyes: Travel Writing and Transculturation*, 2nd edn (Routledge, 2008).
[15]   Gilles Deleuze and Félix Guattari, *Kafka: Toward a Minor Literature*, trans. by Dana Polan, foreword by Réda Bensmaïa (University of Minnesota, 1986), p. 16.

linguistic and cultural roots. This tension is emblematic of the dual nature of deterritorialization, where the colonizer's language becomes both a medium of expression and a site of struggle. Writers are compelled to reimagine and subvert the dominant language from within, transforming it into a vehicle for articulating their unique realities.

The second characteristic, the political nature of 'minor literature', underscores the inseparability of individual narratives from broader political contexts. In 'minor literature', personal stories are always intertwined with larger social, cultural and political struggles. The third characteristic, the collective value of 'minor literature', lies in its ability to transcend individual expression and resonate with the shared struggles and aspirations of a community. In 'minor literature', what is articulated on a personal level is inherently connected to collective action, reflecting communal identities and shared experiences. This is particularly significant in countries such as Brazil, where low proficiency in reading is an indication of limited access to literary texts.[16] Artists in such contexts often serve as crucial intermediaries, amplifying the voices of marginalized groups and giving shape to collective struggles. Their works function not merely as individual stories but as 'relays for a revolutionary machine-to-come',[17] channelling the hopes and resistance of their communities. By embodying collective voices, they transform their narratives into powerful tools for social change. This collective dimension is central to the revolutionary potential of 'minor literature', as it fosters solidarity and communal identity in the face of systemic oppression.

In the context of multilingualism and translingual practices — which understand language practices as dynamic and interdependent across time and space, and which treat difference as the norm, not only in utterances marked as divergent by dominant ideologies but also to those defined as standard by conventional understandings of language, its relationships, and its users[18] — 'minor literature' offers a lens through which to examine how minority groups creatively subvert and reimagine dominant languages, such as Spanish or Portuguese, to articulate their unique cultural and political realities.

---

[16]   According to the Programme for International Student Assessment (PISA) 2022 results, half of all Brazilian 15-year-old students did not achieve the basic level of proficiency in reading, a figure that is nearly double the average rate of 26% among the Organization for Economic Co-operation and Development (OECD) member countries. PISA 2022: 'Por que o Brasil está nas últimas posições em matemática, ciências e leitura?', <https://futura.frm.org.br/conteudo/educacao-basica/noticia/pisa-2022-por-que-o-brasil-esta-nas-ultimas-posicoes-em-matematica-leitura-ciencias> [accessed 19 August 2025].
[17]   Deleuze and Guattari, p. 16.
[18]   Min-Zhan Lu and Bruce Horner, 'Translingual Literacy, Language Difference, and Matters of Agency', College English, 75.6 (2013), 582–607 <http://www.jstor.org/stable/24238127> [accessed 19 March 2025].

Multilingualism Contexts

Given the impossibility of capturing the full linguistic diversity of Latin America or comprehensively addressing how allochthonous and autochthonous languages interacted during the colonial period and in more recent times, an examination of Brazil's linguistic landscape alongside that of its border country, Paraguay, can serve as two illustrative examples. Brazil, often perceived as monolingual, is home to over 200 languages, including 202 living Indigenous languages, 20 established non-Indigenous languages, and at least twelve sign languages.[19] Paraguay's national identity is anchored in a distinctive bilingualism, with the Indigenous Guaraní holding co-official status and flourishing alongside Spanish, in addition to being home to 19 other living Indigenous languages and five living non-Indigenous languages.[20] Both nations resist linguistic homogenization, underscoring that multilingualism is a core, dynamic, and contentious component of national identity.

a) Brazil

Since the approval of Law 10,436 in 2002, Brazilian Sign Language (LIBRAS) has been officially recognized as a legal means of communication and expression.[21] This recognition makes Brazil officially bilingual, even if the idea of monolingualism is frequently proclaimed, and sometimes celebrated, as a positive characteristic of the country.[22] Furthermore, the idea that a unified, homogeneous Portuguese is spoken across a continent-sized country is what linguist Marcos Bagno identifies as the first myth of his 'Mitologia do Preconceito Linguístico' [Mythology of Linguistic Prejudice]: 'Mito #1: A língua portuguesa falada no Brasil apresenta uma unidade surpreendente' [Myth #1: The Portuguese language spoken in Brazil demonstrates a surprising uniformity]. Bagno argues that the myth of a surprising linguistic unity in Brazil is a powerful ideological construct that serves to erase the country's immense dialectal diversity and sociolinguistic reality. This official narrative of monolingualism, used for centuries to justify repression, directly fuels the second myth Bagno describes: 'Mito #2: Brasileiro não sabe português' / 'Só em Portugal se fala bem português' [Myth #2: Brazilians don't know Portuguese' / 'Only in Portugal is Portuguese spoken well], which stigmatizes the vast majority of Brazilians for not conforming to an elite standard.[23]

---

[19]   David M. Eberhard, Gary F. Simons, and Charles D. Fennig (eds), 'Brazil', *Ethnologue: Languages of the World*, 28th edn (SIL International) <https://www.ethnologue.com/browse/countries/> [acessed 19 August 2025]; Diná Souza da Silva and Ronice Muller de Quadros, 'Línguas de sinais de comunidades isoladas encontradas no Brasil', *Brazilian Journal of Development*, 5.10 (2019), pp. 22111–27, doi:10.34117/bjdv5n10-342 [accessed 19 August 2025].

[20]   Eberhard, Simons, and Fennig (eds), 'Paraguay', *Ethnologue*.

[21]   Lei nº 10.436, 24 April 2002, *Diário Oficial da União*, <https://www.planalto.gov.br/ccivil_03/leis/2002/l10436.htm> [accessed 7 March 2025].

[22]   This section is based on Gilvan Müller de Oliveira, 'Plurilingüismo no Brasil' (UNESCO Office in Brasília, Instituto de Investigação e Desenvolvimento em Política Linguística, 2008) <https://unesdoc.unesco.org/ark:/48223/pf0000161167.locale=en> [accessed 4 September 2024].

[23]   Marcos Bagno, *Preconceito Lingüístico: o que é, como se faz* (Edições Loyola, 1999).

The perception of Brazil as a monolingual nation stems from centuries of linguistic repression and policies aimed at reducing diversity. In 1500, an estimated 1,078 Indigenous languages were spoken in Brazil. However, through policies of glottocide (linguistic eradication) Portuguese was imposed as the only legitimate language. One key historical document, the Marquis of Pombal's *Diretório dos Índios* (1758), legislated Indigenous life and promoted the imposition of Portuguese as a means of 'civilizing' Indigenous peoples. It mandated that only Portuguese be used in schools.

Despite this history of repression, Indigenous and immigrant communities have resisted linguistic homogenization. Nheengatu (a language that evolved directly from Tupinambá, not, as claimed by some, a creole or missionary invention[24]) was once a vital Amazonian lingua franca. Despite its remarkable resilience through centuries of contact, it experienced a sharp decline following the Cabanagem Revolution (1835–40), which included the massacre of approximately 40,000 of its speakers, and the influx of Portuguese-speaking migrants.[25] However, it persists today in an area between Manaus and the Upper Rio Negro, covering roughly 300,000 square kilometres, and has approximately 7200 speakers.[26]

The richness of online resources allows us to give students an immediate insight into this multilingual reality. For example, the BBC's article 'Quantas são as línguas indígenas do Brasil, onde são faladas e o que as ameaça?' provides an accessible overview of Indigenous languages in Brazil, their geographical distribution, and the threats they face (Fig. 1). Students can listen to the whistled version of Ikolen (Gavião), a Tupi-Mondé language spoken in Rondônia.[27]

They can also find videos on YouTube about Talian and Pomeranian, which are neo-autochthonous languages of Italian and Germanic origin, primarily spoken in the states of Rio Grande do Sul, Santa Catarina, Paraná, Mato Grosso and Espírito Santo, and about the variety of *portunhol* spoken in Rivera, Uruguay.[28]

[24]   Aryon Dall'Igna Rodrigues and Ana Suelly Arruda Câmara Cabral, 'A Contribution to the Linguistic History of the Língua Geral Amazônica', *Alfa: Revista de Linguística*, 55.2 (2011), pp. 613–39, doi:10.1590/S1981-57942011000200012 [accessed 19 August 2025].

[25]   See Oliveira, 'Plurilingüismo no Brasil'.

[26]   Centro de Documentação Eloy Ferreira da Silva, <https://www.cedefes.org.br/quais-sao-as-linguas-indigenas-faladas-no-brasil/>. According to *Ethnologue: Languages of the World*, 'Nhengatu is an endangered Indigenous language of Brazil, Colombia, and Venezuela. It belongs to the Tupian language family. The language is used as a first language by all adults in the ethnic community, but not all young people. It is not known to be taught in schools.' Eberhard, Simons, and Fennig (eds), 'Nhengatu', *Ethnologue*.

[27]   'Quantas são as línguas indígenas do Brasil, onde são faladas e o que as ameaça?', BBC News Brasil <https://www.bbc.com/portuguese/resources/idt-2779c755-7af1-495a-a41c-d02995e459b8> [accessed 10 October 2024].

[28]   See, for example, *Documentary: Talian, the Forbidden Language of Brazil*, online video recording, YouTube, 2021 <https://www.youtube.com/watch?v=Rg_8yTRrfQw> [accessed 10 October 2024]; *Língua Pomerana no Brasil — História; Gramática da Língua Pomerana Capixaba*, online video recording, YouTube, 2021 <https://www.youtube.com/watch?v=lnAMOevOM4s> [accessed 10 October 2024]; and *Aquí se habla Portuñol*, online video recording, YouTube, 2021 <https://www.youtube.com/watch?v=dVHHmlbzXaU> [accessed 10 October 2024].

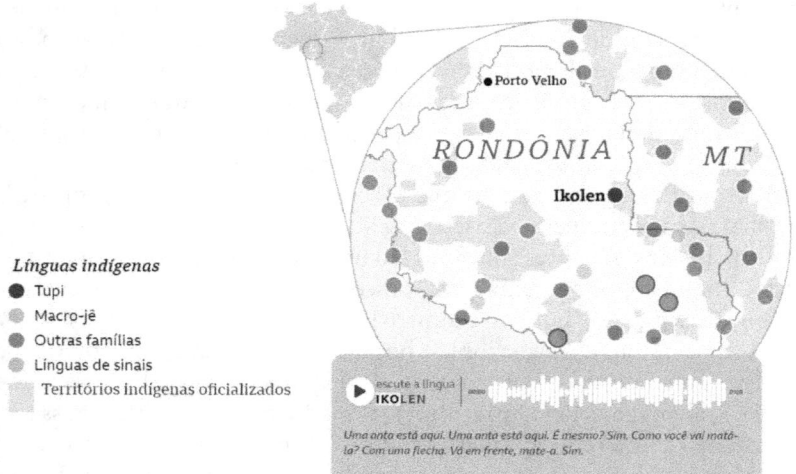

FIG. 1. The Ikolen (Gavião) language, part of the Tupi-Mondé subfamily, is spoken in the Igarapé Lourdes Indigenous Land in Rondônia. It includes a whistled version that mimics the tones of the spoken language. Source: *Quantas são as línguas indígenas do Brasil, onde são faladas e o que as ameaça?*, BBC News Brasil, <https://www.bbc.com/portuguese/resources/idt-2779c755-7af1-495a-a41c-d02995e459b8> [accessed 10 October 2024].

However, this linguistic diversity has faced significant challenges. The Estado Novo regime (1937–45) enforced policies of linguistic repression, specifically targeting German, Italian and Japanese speakers in southern Brazil. Schools and newspapers were shut down, and their use was actively persecuted, leading to a shift from written to oral usage and confining immigrant languages to rural areas (Fig. 2).

Despite these setbacks, both immigrant and Indigenous languages have demonstrated remarkable resilience. Pomeranian, for instance, maintains a deep-rooted presence and vitality, particularly among younger generations.[29] Contemporary Indigenous movements and immigrant language speakers have fought to preserve their linguistic heritage. The 1988 Brazilian Constitution marked a significant step forward by recognizing Indigenous linguistic rights, fostering a more inclusive cultural landscape. This has created opportunities for bilingualism by choice, rather than imposition, allowing communities to reclaim and celebrate their linguistic diversity.[30]

[29] Monica Maria Guimarães Savedra, 'Language Vitality and Transculturalization of European Immigrant Minorities: Pomeranian in Brazil', *Diadorim*, 22.1 (2020), doi:10.35520/diadorim.2020.v22n1a31999 [accessed 10 October 2024].
[30] For co-officialization of languages in Brazil, see Gean Damulakis, 'Cooficialização de línguas no Brasil: características, desdobramentos e desafios', *Laboratório de Estudos Fluminenses (LEF-UFRJ)*, 21 December 2017 <https://lefufrj.wordpress.com/2017/12/21/cooficializacao-de-linguas-no-brasil-uma-visao-panoramica/> [accessed 4 September 2024].

FIG. 2. General Provisions Issued by the Police Chief Prohibiting the Use of Italian, German and Japanese in Public Spaces. *A Época*, Caxias do Sul, 1 February 1942, page 8, Hemeroteca Digital da Biblioteca Nacional. Available at <https://memoria.bn.gov.br/DocReader/docreader.aspx?bib=882089&pasta=ano%20194&pesq=&pagfis=862> [accessed 7 March 2025].

b) Paraguay

Paraguay's linguistic history is unique in Latin America in that it is the only country where an Indigenous language not only survived but thrived alongside the colonial language, allowing them to coexist. Unlike many other regions in the Americas where Indigenous languages were suppressed or eradicated, Paraguay's linguistic landscape reflects a profound cultural exchange between Spanish settlers and the Guaraní people. This coexistence was shaped by historical factors such as limited migration and regional isolation. Between 1535 and 1600, only 1,000 to 1,200 Spanish settlers arrived in Paraguay, a small number compared to other colonies. This limited migration, combined with Paraguay's political and economic isolation, allowed Guaraní to maintain its dominance. The early interactions between Spanish settlers and Indigenous Guaraní people led to significant cultural and racial mixing, which further reinforced the integration of Guaraní into Paraguayan society.[31]

In Paraguay, the Indigenous language Guaraní holds official status alongside Spanish. However, the country's daily linguistic reality is defined by Jopara (also known as Yopará), a conventionalized blend of both languages that serves as 'the default variety used by the Paraguayan public'.[32] Jopara is a variable mixed language because the ratio of Spanish to Guaraní and the specific elements used can change based on the speaker and situation.

The status of Guaraní has not always been secure. In the 1920s, Guaraní was banned in schools, leading to a cultural stigma that associated the language with backwardness. This perception began to shift during the Chaco War (1932–35), a costly conflict between Bolivia and Paraguay over the Chaco Boreal region. The war marked a turning point for Guaraní, as it was designated the 'lengua oficial de la Guerra' [official language of the War] in 1933.[33] This recognition transformed Guaraní from a stigmatized language into a symbol of national identity and resistance. The war also spurred a cultural revival, with a flourishing of Guaraní literature, including poetry and plays by prominent figures like Emiliano R. Fernández and Julio Correa. These works celebrated Guaraní as a vehicle for expressing Paraguayan patriotism and resilience.

In the post-war period, Guaraní continued to gain prominence, though its status remained ambivalent. The 1940s saw a surge in patriotism that boosted the language's prestige, particularly during the presidency of Higinio Morínigo (1940–48), who actively promoted Guaraní in government and literature. This period also witnessed significant academic contributions to the study of Guaraní, including the publication of grammars and dictionaries by scholars

---

[31]   This section is based on Lenka Zajícová's 'Apuntes sobre la historia lingüística de Paraguay', *El bilingüismo paraguayo: usos y actitudes hacia el guaraní y el castellano* (Vervuert/Iberoamericana, 2009), pp. 23–48.

[32]   Elizabeth Herring Dudek and J. Clancy Clements, 'Jopara as a Case of a Variable Mixed Language', *New Perspectives on Mixed Languages: From Core to Fringe*, ed. by Maria Mazzoli and Eeva Sippola (De Gruyter/Mouton, 2021), p. 277, doi:10.1515/9781501511257-010 [accessed 19 August 2025].

[33]   Genes Hermosilla, apud Zajícová, 'Apuntes sobre la historia lingüística de Paraguay', p. 42.

like Antonio Ortiz Mayans and Juan Klug. The 1967 Constitution marked another milestone by recognizing Guaraní as a national language, further solidifying its role in Paraguay's cultural and political life. Today, Paraguay is one of the few countries in the Americas where an Indigenous language is spoken by the majority of the population. Over 90% of Paraguayans are fluent in Guaraní, while around 87% speak Spanish, making Paraguay a truly bilingual nation.

Despite this linguistic richness, Paraguay faces challenges related to language and identity. In recent years, the expansion of Portuguese, particularly in border regions, has been viewed by some Spanish speakers as a cultural threat. This mirrors historical tensions in neighbouring Uruguay, where Portuguese-speaking minorities were once stigmatized, and efforts were made to enforce the use of Spanish in education and public life. In Paraguay, however, regional integration efforts have led to increased acceptance of linguistic diversity, though stigmatization of non-standard language varieties persists in political and educational discourse.

Case Studies: Minor Literature in Brazil and Its Border Regions

Following the exploration of key linguistic terms, the theoretical framework of 'minor literature' and the historical and cultural contexts of Brazil and Paraguay, this section presents three case studies that illuminate the dynamic interplay of language, identity, resistance and artistic expression in Latin America. These case studies, Itamar Vieira Júnior's 'O espírito *aboni* das coisas', Douglas Diegues's *El astronauta paraguayo*, and Leo Castilho's 'O meu nome', exemplify how marginalized communities use literature to subvert dominant linguistic and cultural narratives.

a) 'O espírito aboni das coisas', by Itamar Vieira Júnior

In 'O espírito *aboni* das coisas', Tokowisa, an Indigenous hero of the Jarawara people from the Middle Purús River region, embarks on a spiritual and physical journey that intertwines personal struggle with broader themes of cultural preservation and environmental interconnectedness. His mission to save his pregnant wife, Yanici, from a deadly curse serves as the narrative's driving force. Tokowisa's life is deeply entwined with the natural world of the Amazonian rainforest, and this connection is central to the narrative. The concept of 'espírito *aboni*', which gives the short story its title, embodies the character's spiritual merging with the land, animals, and trees. This connection is not merely symbolic but is presented as a lived reality for Tokowisa and his community. The spiritual bond between humans and the natural world is evident in moments where Tokowisa communicates with the forest and its creatures, drawing strength and guidance from them. His journey is as much about navigating the physical challenges of the rainforest as it is about understanding and harmonizing with the spiritual forces that govern it.

The narrative also delves into the linguistic richness of the Amazon through Itamar Vieira Júnior's innovative use of language to reflect the cultural and spiritual depth of the Jarawara people. The author employs a unique syntactic construction, blending Jarawara words with Portuguese to create a layered narrative texture. For example, in the opening sentence of the short story 'O sol *bahi* cresceu no céu *neme* com muita luz' [The sun *bahi* rose in the sky *neme* with much light], Jarawara terms like *bahi* (sun) and *neme* (sky) are italicized and paired with their Portuguese equivalents.[34]

The author uses italics for the Jarawara language to highlight its cultural importance. This contrasts with *igarapé* and *mandioca*, which are not italicized because they are Tupi loanwords assimilated into Brazilian Portuguese. Their assimilated status made them more likely to be 'invisibly' translated: *igarapé* became 'upstream' and *mandioca* became 'cassava'.[35] The significance of *mandioca* is further emphasized in the original text, where it appears five times alongside its Indigenous Jarawara equivalent, *fowa*, underscoring its deep roots in native agriculture.[36]

> Source text: 'Ela tem uma matilha de cães *yome* ao seu redor e as crianças que choram querendo peixe *aba* e bolo de mandioca *fowa kabe*.' (Vieira Júnior, p. 70)
>
> Translation: 'She is surrounded by a pack of *yome* dogs and children who cry wanting *aba* fish and *fowa kabe* cassava cake.' (Vieira Júnior and Meadowcroft, p. 75)
>
> Source text: 'Plantam todas as variedades de mandioca *fowa* e as deixam guardadas debaixo da terra para, quando chegar a guerra, alimentar seu povo.' (Vieira Júnior, p. 71)
>
> Translation: 'They plant every kind of *fowa* cassava and leave it safe underground so that, when the war comes, they can feed their people.' (Vieira Júnior and Meadowcroft, p. 76)
>
> Source text: 'O cesto é para que as mulheres carreguem os frutos de suas roças. Milho *kimi*, mandioca *fowa bao*, mandioca *fowa basota*, mandioca *fowa nestona*.' (Vieira Júnior, p. 72)

---

[34] See Itamar Vieira Júnior, 'O espírito *aboni* das coisas', *Qorpus*, 11.1 (March 2021), Especial Brazilian Translation Club, p. 69 <https://qorpuspget.paginas.ufsc.br/files/2021/03/O-espirito-aboni-das-coisas_Itamar-Vieira-Junior.pdf> [accessed 7 March 2025]; and Itamar Vieira Júnior, 'The *Aboni* Spirit of Things', trans. by Victor Meadowcroft, *Qorpus*, 11.1 (March 2021), Especial Brazilian Translation Club, pp. 74 <https://qorpuspget.paginas.ufsc.br/files/2021/03/The-aboni-spirit-of-things_Itamar-Vieira-Junior-translated-by-Victor-Meadowcroft.pdf> [accessed 7 March 2025].

[35] See Ana Cláudia Suriani da Silva, 'The Aims and the Stories of the Brazilian Translation Club', *Qorpus*, 11.1 (2021), pp. 8–14 <The-aims-and-stories-of-the-BTC_Ana-Claudia-Suriani.pdf> [accessed 4 September 2024].

[36] According to Alan Vogel, *fowa* means 'manioc, cassava; bitter manioc', in Alan Vogel, *Jarawara–English Dictionary* (SIL International, 2016) <https://www.sil.org/system/files/reapdata/16/80/60/16806038828211876017589834584868119739­3/Jarawara_English_Dictionary.pdf> [accessed 7 March 2025], p. 91.

Translation: 'The basket is so the women can carry the fruits of their labour. *Kimi* maize, *fowa bao* cassava, *fowa basota* cassava, *fowa nestona* cassava.' (Vieira Júnior and Meadowcroft, p. 76)

The words *mandioca* and *igarapé*, deeply rooted in Indigenous knowledge, are woven into the narrative without special emphasis, symbolizing how Indigenous contributions to Brazilian culture are often taken for granted. This linguistic interplay serves as a subtle critique of the erasure of Indigenous heritage, reminding readers that Brazilian Portuguese is the product of a long and often violent colonial history.

The story also draws attention to the impact of colonial exploitation on Indigenous lands and cultures. Tokowisa's journey is not just a personal quest but also a reflection of the broader struggles of Indigenous communities against cultural and environmental exploitation. His growth as a character reflects not only personal transformation but also a reaffirmation of his commitment to his community and the environment. The narrative emphasizes the importance of protecting both cultural heritage and the natural world, presenting them as interdependent, a system in which all characters, both male and female, play a role. For example, Tokowisa's wife, Yanici, is described as no longer tending to the plots of cassava and maize, a detail that underscores the disruption of traditional ways of life by external threats. Tokowisa's journey tests his physical and spiritual limits through challenges like navigating dangerous rivers and confronting spiritual entities. These arduous experiences serve as a metaphor for the broader struggles Indigenous communities face in maintaining their cultural identity and connection to the land.

b) 'El astronauta paraguayo' by Douglas Diegues

El astronauta paraguayo is a groundbreaking work that embodies the spirit of *portunhol selvagem*, a linguistic and literary movement that transcends conventional boundaries of language, culture and identity. As a *cartonera* book, it reflects the movement's commitment to accessibility, creativity, and cultural resistance, using handmade, recycled materials to democratize literature, to prioritize community, inclusivity, and sustainability over profit and commercialization, making them an alternative to the traditional publishing industry. *El astronauta paraguayo* features a unique hero, who is both urban and Indigenous, embodying the fluid and hybrid identity of South America. This character embarks on a surreal, magical journey, floating ever higher 'depois de beber alguma poção mágica' [after drinking some magical potion], a narrative device that serves as a metaphor for the dissolution of rigid national and cultural borders. According to Sérgio Medeiros,

> o herói [in *El astronauta paraguayo*] está acima das nacionalidades e flutua livremente sobre o mapa lingüístico da América do Sul, expressando-se numa língua híbrida, que desconsidera divisões políticas e culturais, embaralhando fronteiras ou tornando-as incrivelmente porosas. Não existe

mais uma fronteira linear, homogênea, mas muitas fronteiras quebradas, confusas, ineficazes.[37]

[The hero transcends nationalities and floats freely over the linguistic map of South America, expressing himself in a hybrid language that disregards political and cultural divisions, blurring borders or rendering them incredibly porous. No longer does a linear, homogeneous frontier exist; instead, there are many fractured, muddled, ineffective boundaries.]

Written 'num saboroso macarrônico que mescla o espanhol com o guaraní e o português, línguas faladas na "Triplefrontera"' [in a flavoursome macaronic blend of Spanish, Guaraní, and Portuguese, languages spoken in the 'Triple Frontier'], the poem reflects the rich linguistic diversity of the region, where Brazil, Paraguay and Argentina converge.[38] This hybrid language is not merely a linguistic experiment but a profound artistic expression that challenges the dominance of colonial languages and celebrates the polyphony of South American cultures.

The poem's language 'brota como flor de la bosta de las vakas' [springs like a flower from the muck of cows],[39] a vivid metaphor that captures its raw, organic, and rebellious nature. *Portunhol selvagem* rejects conventional grammar and rules, blending Portuguese, Spanish, Guarani and other languages spoken in the border region of Ponta Porã (Brazil) and Pedro Juan Caballero (Paraguay), including Arabic, Chinese, Japanese, Korean, German, French, and American English.[40] This linguistic fluidity creates a decentralized, creative language that encourages polyphony, playfulness and the exploration of ambiguity, dissonance and multiple meanings.

The poem's linguistic experimentation is deeply intertwined with its cultural and thematic concerns. The astronaut's journey through space is symbolic of the dissolution of rigid national boundaries, as his macaronic speech allows him to float freely above the linguistic map of South America, creating a sense of interconnectedness between cultures. This journey is both a spiritual ascent and a descent into personal and social challenges. The astronaut's lucid and delirious exploration of these themes culminates in his return to the culturally complex 'Triplefrontera', symbolizing a re-grounding in reality. This duality (elevation and descent, euphoria and suffering) is central to the poem's structure and meaning, as it contrasts the astronaut's cosmic journey with the grounded realities of the borderlands.

The poem's cultural references and humour further enrich its exploration of identity and hybridity, creating a dynamic interplay between the mundane

---

[37] Sérgio Medeiros, 'Cosmonauta de coração partido', in Douglas Diegues, *El Astronauta Paraguayo* (Yiyi Jambo, 2007), p. 2.

[38] Medeiros, p. 1.

[39] Douglas Diegues, *Zunái — Revista de poesia & debates* <http://revistazunai.com/poemas/douglas_diegues.htm> [accessed 10 October 2024].

[40] See Anselmo Peres Aló, 'Portuñol Selvagem: da "língua de contato" à poética da fronteira', *Cadernos de Letras da UFF — Dossiê: América Central e Caribe: múltiplos olhares*, 45 (2013), pp. 283–304.

and the fantastical, the local and the global. On one hand, it pays homage to literary figures like Paraguayan writer Roa Bastos and Brazilian poet Manoel de Barros, whose works similarly explore the intersections of language, identity, and culture. Through intertextuality, Diegues situates *El astronauta paraguayo* within a broader tradition of Latin American literature that challenges colonial legacies and celebrates cultural hybridity. On the other, it juxtaposes the mundane with the fantastical and the local with the global and embodies the *espírito macunaímico* — a concept rooted in Mário de Andrade's *Macunaíma* (1928), which embraces fluidity, contradiction, and the blending of cultural influences — to celebrate the creativity and resilience of borderland communities, who navigate and reinterpret multiple cultural influences in their daily lives.

c) Leo Castilho's 'O meu nome'

Leo Castilho's poem 'O meu nome' is a powerful piece of slam poetry that confronts societal norms and critiques the labels imposed on the deaf and hearing-impaired community. Presented during the Covid pandemic through a pre-recorded video at Slam Cúir 2020, part of the Literary Festival of the Peripheries (Flup), the poem exemplifies how slam poetry serves as a platform for political expression and cultural resistance.[41] Delivered in a multilingual format — combining LIBRAS (Brazilian Sign Language) with corporal performance — and accompanied by subtitles in Portuguese and English, the performance amplified the voices of the deaf and hearing-impaired community while challenging dominant language hierarchies (Fig. 3). This approach transcended mere accessibility, asserting the importance of representation and the right to be seen and heard across multiple linguistic and cultural spaces.

'O meu nome'

Nasceu o Leonardo.
Mas ele é surdo, e agora?
Não entendia
as limitações que me davam.
Então me chamavam 'surdo.'
Meu nome era 'surdo'?
Muitas bocas mexendo e não entendia.
Ao usar aparelho para escutar
me diziam 'ele fala bem'
mas é surdo? 'Que bagunça!'
A sociedade dificulta
e eu não entendia
por que eles se chamam 'não-deficientes'?
Mas, o que são? São os NORMAIS?
Ué? Mas ele é surdo?

[41] Leo Castilho, 'O meu nome', Slam Cúir 2020 <https://youtu.be/CoXGqrUvi3A?feature=shared> [accessed 19 March 2025].

Surdo não é normal?
As limitações na sociedade.
Sem acesso, só, em casa.
Surdo, surdo, surdo.
Quem me deu esse nome?
Ah, os ouvintes.
Era apenas 'surdo,' sem comunicação!
É?
Sem vida. É?
Vive no silêncio. É?
Não estou entendendo.
Eu tenho minha língua materna.
Minhas expressões.
Posso transar! Somos iguais.
Afinal, sou normal também.
Sou apenas uma pessoa que se chama Leo.

['My Name'

Leonardo was born.
But he's deaf, so what now?
I didn't understand
the limits they gave me.
So they called me 'deaf'.
Was my name 'deaf'?
Mouths moving, endless, I understood nothing.
When I wore hearing aids,
they'd say, 'He speaks so well!'
But he's deaf? 'What a mess!'
Society trips me up,
and I couldn't grasp:
why do they call themselves 'non-disabled'?
What are they, then? The NORMAL ones?
Wait, but he's deaf?
Isn't deaf normal too?
The limitations of society.
No access, he has to stay home.
Deaf, deaf, deaf.
Who gave me that name?
Ah, the hearing people.
Just 'deaf,' no communication!
Really?
No life? Really?
They live in silence? Really?
I don't follow.
I have my mother tongue.
My expressions.
I can have sex! We're the same.
It turns out, I'm normal too.
I'm just a person named Leo.]

FIG. 3. Stills from Leo Castilho's performance of 'O meu nome' at Slam Cúir 2020.

Slam poetry, as an art form, emerged in the 1980s as a way to democratize poetry, making it more accessible and engaging, particularly for younger audiences. It is inherently performative, blending the oral tradition of poetry with theatrical elements to create a multisensory experience. Unlike traditional poetry, which is often confined to the page, slam poetry is dynamic and deeply interactive. The poet, the poem and the audience exist in a constant dialogue, with the audience often playing a role in judging or responding to the performance. This interactivity is central to the slam poetry experience, as it transforms the act of reading or listening into a shared, communal event.

Poetry slams are competitive events where poets perform their original work within a set time limit, typically three minutes. The rules are designed to ensure fairness and maintain the integrity of the competition while allowing poets to showcase their creativity and talent. Props and costumes are prohibited, placing the focus squarely on the poet's words and performance. Judges, often selected from the audience, evaluate the performances based on criteria such as vocal delivery, physical presence, and emotional impact. This format creates a supportive yet competitive environment that encourages poets to push the boundaries of their craft.[42]

Leo Castilho's 'O meu nome' exemplifies the political potential of slam poetry. The poem critiques societal norms and the hearing world's marginalization of the deaf community. By questioning the label 'deaf' and challenging the notion of 'normal', Leo exposes the ableist assumptions that underpin much of society's treatment of hearing-impaired individuals. The poem's refrain, 'Surdo, surdo, surdo' [Deaf, deaf, deaf], echoes the relentless categorization and othering that deaf people face, while 'Quem me deu esse nome?' [Who gave me that name?] underscores the power dynamics at play in naming and defining identities. The poem's conclusion, 'Sou apenas uma pessoa que se chama Leo' [I'm just a person named Leo], is a powerful assertion of individuality and humanity, rejecting the reductive labels imposed by society.

Minor Literature?

Deleuze and Guattari's concept of 'minor literature', as articulated through the three characteristics of deterritorialization of language, the political element, and collective value, provides an initial framework for understanding how marginalized groups navigate and transform dominant linguistic systems. Kafka's work, as analysed by Deleuze and Guattari, exemplifies this impasse, where a minority writer uses a major language in ways that both belong to and alienate them from it. This creates unique literary spaces where the writer/

---

[42] See Susan B. A. Somers-Willett, 'On Page and Stage: Slam Poetry as a Genre', in *The Cultural Politics of Slam Poetry: Race, Identity, and the Performance of Popular Verse in America* (University of Michigan Press, 2009), pp. 16–38 <http://www.jstor.org/stable/10.3998/mpub.322627.5> [accessed 19 March 2025].

artist mediates between their minority identity and the dominant culture. In that sense, 'O espírito *aboni* das coisas' exemplifies how literature can serve as a space of resistance and cultural reaffirmation, because it deterritorializes the dominant Portuguese language by infusing it with Jarawara elements. Like in Mário de Andrade's *Macunaíma* (1928) and José de Alencar's *Iracema* (1865), Portuguese is deterritorialized through its fusion with Indigenous languages and Indigenous and Afro-Brazilian cosmologies. These texts create a hybrid literary space that reflects Brazil's complex cultural identity, challenging the dominance of Portuguese while simultaneously enriching it.

The performance of 'O meu nome' at Slam Cúir 2020 also highlights the role of slam poetry as a form of 'minor literature'. Castilho's gesture-based poetry, performed in LIBRAS, creates a hybrid form of expression that deterritorializes the auditory-centric norms of traditional poetry. By privileging sign language and physical performance over the spoken word, it embodies the revolutionary potential of 'minor literature'. It offers a new mode of poetic expression that reappropriates public space and challenges the historical exclusion of the hearing impaired from audio performances. It therefore not only makes poetry accessible to the hearing-impaired community but also redefines what poetry can be and do, by expanding its sensory and linguistic boundaries.

However, the concept of 'minor literature' is not without its challenges and limitations, as demonstrated by the literary phenomenon of *portunhol selvagem*. Unlike Kafka's use of German, which operates within the framework of a major language, *portunhol selvagem* rejects linguistic borders and hierarchies altogether. It thrives in the borderlands of Brazil and Paraguay (and Argentina, Uruguay, etc.), blending autochthonous and allochthonous languages into a fluid, anarchic form of expression. This radical deterritorialization goes beyond the European Deleuzian framework, as it exists in a perpetual state of linguistic flux and disobedience. The language of *El autronauta paraguayo* thus challenges the very notion of a fixed linguistic territory, offering a form of expression that is inherently anti-systemic and resistant to codification.

In fact, *El astronauta paraguayo*, embodies a form of literary innovation that resonates with Henry Louis Gates Jr's concept of signifyin(g). The text's blending of languages creates a dynamic linguistic interplay, where meaning becomes fluid and multifaceted, echoing the subversive doubling central to Gates's framework. Just as Gates illustrates how African American vernacular disrupts the rigid equation of 'sign = signified/signifier', *El astronauta paraguayo* destabilizes conventional linguistic norms, transforming the borderlands between Brazil and Paraguay into a site of linguistic resistance and creativity.[43] The Paraguayan astronaut, reminiscent of the trickster figure in Gates's signifyin(g) tradition and embodying the *espírito macunaímico*, thrives on ambiguity and multiplicity. This figure resists fixed categorization within

[43] Henry Louis Gates Jr, *The Signifying Monkey: A Theory of African-American Literary Criticism* (Oxford University Press, 1988).

any singular national language or cultural framework, embracing instead a fluid and dynamic identity. In this way, it functions as a kind of literary astronaut, navigating the liminal space between languages, where the playful reconfiguration of words becomes both a political act and a celebration of hybridity. The text, in its irreverent manipulation of language, seems to challenge the reader, asserting that linguistic boundaries are not fixed but malleable. Through this inventive approach, *El astronauta paraguayo* not only critiques linguistic hierarchies but also invites a reimagining of meaning-making itself, demonstrating that innovation and resistance can emerge from the playful deconstruction of dominant systems.

Similarly 'O espírito *aboni* das coisas' exemplifies a form of literary signifyin(g) as theorized by Gates through its innovative blending of Jarawara and Portuguese. By italicizing Jarawara terms and seamlessly integrating Tupi-derived words such as *igarapé* and *mandioca,* Itamar Vieira Júnior creates a narrative with multiple linguistic layers. This linguistic hybridity mirrors Gates's concept of double-voiced discourse, where marginalized languages and cultures assert their presence within a dominant framework precisely because they are part of the fabric of the Brazilian Portuguese language and the lived experience of the peoples it represents.

Conclusion

The exploration of Brazilian literature through the lens of Deleuze and Guattari's concept of 'minor literature' reveals both its transformative potential and its inherent contradictions when applied to Latin American contexts. While the concept provides a valuable framework for understanding how marginalized writers subvert dominant languages, it also raises critical questions about the very notion of the 'minor'. If the majority of Latin Americans communicate in ways that diverge significantly from the 'paper language' of the colonizers, then the label 'minor' becomes problematic. Furthermore, in the context of teaching Portuguese in UK universities (where it is often institutionally marginalized and considered a 'minor' language due to lower student numbers compared to Spanish, French, and German) the tension between 'minor' and 'major' languages takes on another dimension. This is particularly striking given that Portuguese is the eighth most spoken language in the world.[44]

The texts examined in this study demonstrate that linguistic resistance operates not just against dominant languages but also through them and alongside other allochthonous, autochthonous, and sign languages. Their inclusion in Latin American studies modules aimed at students of Spanish and Portuguese underscores a profound irony: these 'minor' literatures are often taught through comparison to the colonial languages they seek to destabilize,

---

[44] The most spoken languages worldwide in 2025 <https://www.statista.com/statistics/266808/the-most-spoken-languages-worldwide/> [accessed 19 March 2025].

through their normative grammars, and through European and North American theories (including those of Deleuze and Guattari). This pedagogical reality invites reflection on how decolonizing the curriculum must go beyond mere representation and engage with the structural hierarchies that determine which languages, and whose voices, are deemed worthy of academic study as producers of knowledge. European theories can be a productive starting point, but they cannot be seen as a universal framework. Instead, they must be understood, according to Walter D. Mignolo, as localized, geo-historical products of the modern/colonial project. Therefore, it is important to confront these theories, to teach them not as natural truths but as situated knowledge, explicitly outlining their epistemic limitations in grasping realities shaped by colonialism. The goal is to move away from the assumption that European thinkers and European languages hold the only keys to valid interpretation. Pedagogically, this means shifting the role of Latin American texts from being 'objects of study' to being 'sites of knowledge' in their own right. The authors are 'producers of knowledge', whose work often performs a 'body-politics' and 'geo-politics of knowledge' that can and should generate its own analytical frameworks.[45] This involves a conscious practice of 'shifting the geography of reason', where the concepts, metaphors, and structures within the literary work itself become the primary tools for its critique, challenging students to listen for the epistemologies emerging from the literary text rather than simply applying external systems to it.

---

[45]   Walter D. Mignolo, 'Epistemic Disobedience, Independent Thought and Decolonial Freedom', *Theory, Culture & Society*, 26.7–8 (December 2009), pp. 159–81, doi:10.1177/0263276409349275 [accessed 20 August 2025].

Reviews

Daniel Mandur Thomaz, *Transatlantic Radio Dramas: Antônio Callado and the BBC Latin American Service during and after World War II* (University of Pittsburgh Press, 2023). 232 pages. HB and ebook.

Reviewed by Eva Nieto McAvoy (KCL)

Transatlantic Radio Dramas offers an important scholarly contribution to the study of the Brazilian author Antônio Callado (1917–1997), as well as to the role of radio in cultural diplomacy and propaganda during the Second World War. In this well-written study, Daniel Mandur Thomaz provides a rigorous reading and insightful analysis of Callado's hitherto unstudied early radio drama scripts. A Brazilian journalist, playwright, and novelist, and author of the modern classic *Quarup* (1967), Callado's anglophilia was well-known. It was also widely known that he had spent time in the UK during his youth, not least because towards the end of his writing career Callado wrote *Memórias de Aldenham House* (1989), an autobiographical account set in the country house of the same name from which the BBC language services broadcast during the Second World War. What was previously unknown was the nature of his work for the BBC.

Central to *Transatlantic Radio Dramas* is Thomaz's rediscovery of Callado's radio dramas, written for the BBC Latin American Service (LAS) between 1941 and 1947. A selection of the surviving scripts was made available to Lusophone readers in *Roteiros de radioteatro durante e depois da Segunda Grande* (2018).[1] In the monograph under review here, Thomaz follows his edited volume with a more in-depth critical analysis of the surviving scripts, situating Callado's work within the institutional and ideological frameworks of wartime broadcasting. Drawing on a rich array of sources — including internal BBC Latin American Service policy documents, letters, propaganda reports, and materials from Brazilian archives — Thomaz reconstructs the institutional context in which Callado wrote, as well as the political context in which his radio dramas were received in Brazil, a British ally during the war, but under the military dictatorship of Getúlio Vargas.

Thomaz argues persuasively that Callado's work at the BBC was formative in shaping the themes and stylistic approaches that would later define his acclaimed novels and plays. Already in the 1940s, his radio scripts explore concerns that would become hallmarks, including the interplay between mysticism and politics, and the relationship between aesthetic, intellectual, and political commitment. Particularly important were Callado's encounters during his time in London with the work of two Anglo-Irish modernists, James Joyce and Louis MacNeice, and the influence they had on his narrative techniques and aesthetic sensibilities. Of interest is the fact that Callado never referred to

---

[1] Antônio Callado, *Roteiros de radioteatro durante e depois da Segunda Grande Guerra*, ed. by Daniel Mandur Thomaz (Autêntica, 2018).

the existence of the scripts or the nature of his work for the BBC. The reason for this is unclear, but Thomaz speculates that Callado might have thought that his work for the BBC during the Second World War threatened his later position as an anti-imperialist left-wing intellectual — a tension felt by other writers who worked for the BBC such as Una Marson and George Orwell.[2] Thomaz carefully maps out and interrogates these tensions and contradictions in Callado's work.

Crucially, this archival recovery prompts a critical reassessment of the established chronology of Callado's literary career, which has traditionally placed his debut in the 1950s. By foregrounding these early scripts, Thomaz challenges existing narratives and repositions Callado as a politically and aesthetically engaged writer at a much earlier stage. Thomaz also traces the influence of Callado's BBC radio dramas on his later work through the evolution of the narrative voice, his engagement with Brazilian historical narratives and national identity, and his formulation of a distinctive and complex modernist aesthetic informed by a blend of mystical Catholicism, antiauthoritarianism, and literary experimentation.

Transatlantic Radio Dramas attends carefully to the tensions and negotiations embedded in transnational propaganda efforts, as well as to the cultural dynamics that shaped the 'corporate cosmopolitanism' of the BBC.[3] In doing so, the study addresses a notable gap in existing scholarship concerning the BBC Latin American Service and its role within the wider apparatus of the BBC World Service. Moreover, Thomaz constructs a rich theoretical framework to understand the transatlantic circulation of ideas, intellectual networks, and cultural exchange between Latin America and Britain during the mid-twentieth century.

The study is organized around four chapters that trace different aspects of Callado's radio dramas. Chapter 1, entitled 'Dramatizing Politics: Propaganda and Radio Entertainment in Brazil and the UK', investigates the extent to which BBC propaganda policies shaped Callado's dramatic output during the Second World War, providing a close reading of Callado's scripts against the backdrop of the wartime regulations, including the BBC's propaganda strategy for Latin America. Drawing on the minutes of the BBC Latin American Service's Propaganda Policy Committee meetings, Thomaz demonstrates how Callado navigated and occasionally tested the limits of wartime broadcasting policy, integrating his own creative and ideological sensibilities within institutional constraints, including veiled criticisms of Getúlio Vargas's military dictatorship in Brazil. In doing so, the chapter also situates these dramas within the context of Brazil's Estado Novo regime (1937–45), a period marked by authoritarian control and the strategic use of radio as a propaganda tool.

[2]   Marie Gillespie and Eva Nieto McAvoy, 'The BBC's Corporate Cosmopolitanism: The Diasporic Voice Between Empire and Cold War', in *Cosmopolitanism in Conflict: Imperial Encounters from the Seven Years' War to the Cold War*, ed. by Dina Gusejnova (Palgrave Macmillan, 2018), pp. 179–209.
[3]   Marie Gillespie and Alban Webb, 'Corporate Cosmopolitanism: Diasporas and Diplomacy at the BBC World Service, 1932–2012', in *Diasporas and Diplomacy* (Routledge, 2013), pp. 1–20.

However, as Thomaz goes on to explore, radio — and the BBC specifically — was not just a blunt tool for propaganda, but also a space for aesthetic and literary experimentation. Chapter 2, 'Leading the Story: The Narrator in Callado's Scripts', centres on the evolving role of the narrator across Callado's body of radio work. It contends that the development of his narratorial strategies parallels his growing mastery of the medium. The absence of archival recordings of the broadcasts does not prevent Thomaz from conducting an insightful chronological study that draws upon both the scripts themselves and other archival materials such as personal diaries and letters housed in Brazilian collections, mapping the progression of Callado's narrative techniques. The chapter shows how Callado's intellectual formation in Brazil — particularly his education and early literary influences — manifests in what Thomaz calls a 'historian-narrator' of his initial scripts — external, generative, authoritative, and masculine. Thomaz then traces the shift to an 'insurgent-narrator' influenced both by the aural affordances of radio — the multivocality and dialogic nature — as well as by his interactions with fellow radio dramatists at the BBC and his engagement with Anglo-Irish modernist literature. In doing so, the chapter reveals how his work with the BBC informed his script-writing style, prefiguring the narrative experimentation found in his later novels.

In Chapter 3, 'Broadcasting Brazilianness: Callado's Foundational Dramas', the focus shifts to Callado's use of radio drama to 'narrate the nation', through an analysis of a series of scripts reinterpreting Brazilian historical episodes and foundational myths — e.g. *A Eterna Descoberta do Brasil* (1943). This chapter adopts a historiographical lens, drawing on theories of nationalism and cultural identity, to argue that Callado's objective here was to 'symbolically resolve the main contradiction of Brazil's new alliance with Britain: the country was fighting for "freedom and democracy" in Europe while still under the brutal dictatorship of Getúlio Vargas' (p. 178). These scripts, the chapter suggests, were also intended to propose a reconfigured vision of postcolonial modernity, with Britain implicitly cast as a model of democratic governance (despite its own history as a colonial power) in contrast to Brazil's authoritarian past.

These apparent contradictions in Callado's work are also addressed in the final chapter. Entitled 'Mysticism, Political Commitment, and Modernist Aesthetics' it explores precisely the synthesis of spiritual and political elements in Callado's work, analysing how the author developed his distinctive literary style that merged mystical Catholic motifs with antiauthoritarianism, while also drawing upon the formal innovations of Anglo-Irish modernism. The chapter explores the particular blend of modernist influences and the tensions between these and the political and postcolonial impulses in Callado's work. While Callado is not a canonical modernist writer, Thomaz argues that this unique constellation of religious imagery, ideological engagement, and aesthetic experimentation became central to a voice that would continue to evolve in his subsequent development as a novelist.

Transatlantic Radio Dramas will be of value for Lusophone scholars, as well as for media, cultural and literary historians across borders. It offers a compelling reassessment of Antônio Callado's literary formation by placing his rediscovered radio dramas at the centre of his early career. By connecting Callado's British experiences to his subsequent literary and journalistic trajectory, the book illuminates the development of his anglophilia and his emergence as a cosmopolitan intellectual who skilfully mobilized his cultural capital in returning to Brazil to consolidate his position as a modernist writer. Conversely, *Transatlantic Radio Dramas* also reveals how Callado's participation in British wartime and post-war efforts — like that of many other diasporic intellectuals — helped shape the BBC World Service from its early days, both in its cosmopolitanism and its cultural capital. More broadly, Thomaz provides a transnational perspective on the relationships between media, culture, and politics during a critical juncture in global history. The result is a richly documented and intellectually ambitious study that sheds new light on Callado's development as a writer and contributes to broader debates on cultural production, propaganda, and intellectual exchange across the Atlantic during the mid-twentieth century.

doi:10.1353/port.00048

José Lingna Nafafé, *Lourenço da Silva Mendonça and the Black Atlantic Abolitionist Movement in the Seventeenth Century* (Cambridge University Press, 2022), 468 pages. HB, PB and ebook.

Reviewed by Selina Patel Nascimento (Lancaster University)

Basing himself on almost two decades of deep archival research across four continents, José Lingna Nafafé painstakingly reconstructs the biography of Prince Lourenço da Silva Mendonça (1620–1698), tracing his physical, social, and intellectual journeys between West Central Africa, South America, and Europe. In bringing to light this exceptional Black man's life and legacy, Nafafé also unearths an unprecedented and practically unknown Black abolitionist movement more than a century prior to organized White European agitations against slavery. Nafafé expertly crafts an impressively complex and decolonial narrative over six chapters. The first two chapters outline the violence permeating West Central Africa and the establishment of the slave trade. Chapter 1 surveys the shifting political landscape and constant conflict that gave rise to the violent enslavement, and flight, of Africans, while Chapter 2 thinks through this environment as the backdrop to Mendonça's nascent views on freedom and the integration of enslaved Africans in the Atlantic world. It is here that Nafafé explains how Portugal employed coercive means to develop a slave trade of significant volume in the region, which ultimately led to the destruction of Mendonça's native Pungo-Andongo and forced the princes and princesses of the royal family into exile in Brazil. Thus, his family's coercion into developing a slave trade with the Portuguese, the devastation of his homeland, and his exile to Brazil are framed as experiences that formed the basis of Mendonça's later court case (1684).

The following two chapters reveal how his forging of connections with New Christians, Indigenous groups, and Brazilian enslaved peoples influenced and refined his abolitionist thinking as Mendonça journeyed across the Atlantic. Chapter 3 examines his life in Brazil through a reinterpretation of the significance of Palmares, a *quilombo* (maroon settlement) that survived for almost a century. Nafafé makes a vital contribution to the Brazilian historiography that has traditionally understood Palmares as an insular settlement only for Africans, with little or no co-existence with Brazilians. This chapter emphasizes how Palmares was feared as an emerging colonial power, based on the alliances the *quilombolas* drew with Cristovao de Burgos de Contreiras (a High Court judge in Salvador) and local Brazilian Indigenous groups. Nafafé suggests that the relocation of the royal exiles from Salvador to Rio de Janeiro was a responsive effort by the authorities to weaken support for Palmares's growing influence and impede a potential alliance with the exiles, whilst also severing ties established with Angolans living in Salvador who later supported Mendonca's legal action. This period of his life, Nafafé argues, exposed Mendonça to the inhumane treatment of the enslaved and unfree, enabling him to understand slavery as a pan-Atlantic phenomenon.

Chapter 4 follows Mendonça to Portugal, where he was again exiled. It traces his education in Braga, his appointment as an attorney in the Confraternity of Our Lady Star of the Negroes in Lisbon and later Toledo, and the broader alliances he built with New Christians and Indigenous Americans residing in Europe. Nafafé posits that Mendonça's views of an *Atlantic* abolitionist movement that sought freedom and liberation for all racialized subjected groups crystallized here. Indeed, the speculation on Mendonça's motivations for his abolitionist movement over these chapters — the weight of his personal history, the horrors he witnessed, and the resulting psychological burden — makes this book methodologically current and complex, contributing to broader historiographical efforts to restore subjectivity and personhood to silenced voices of the past.

Having offered a deep and rich interpretation of Mendonça's life and influences, and the many ways in which he shaped, and was shaped by, Atlantic connections, the final two chapters explore Mendonça's journey to the Vatican, his ensuing court case, and its resulting reverberations in impressive detail. Chapter 5 forms the crux of Nafafé's key argument. He offers a compelling reading of the court case as a Black Atlantic abolitionist movement, engaging with the Atlantic as a political and legal space, and as the nexus of dialogues and interactions across different constituencies. In this sense, he moves away from Paul Gilroy's original conceptual framework of the Black Atlantic, politicizing and expanding its geographical remit to encompass the wider, non-anglophone Atlantic world. Thus, he suggests Mendonça's court case was the foundation of a Black Atlantic project of solidarity based on a common quest for liberty and freedom. Importantly, Nafafé also observes that in positioning transatlantic slavery as a crime against human, natural, divine, and civil laws, Mendonça anticipated modern semantics and grammars regarding crimes against humanity and thus pre-empted the humanitarian discourse around abolition in later centuries.

Chapter 6 examines the struggles between Mendonça, his family, and the Portuguese Overseas Council and interprets them as reflective of wider debates on the freedom of enslaved Africans and the role of Christianity. Importantly, he highlights the Vatican and the Portuguese Crown's positive responses to Mendonça's legal action and emphasizes the numerous ways in which mercantile, financial, and elite interests in Portugal sought to undermine these initial steps towards abolition. Rather than focusing on evaluating the success or failure of the Black Atlantic abolitionist movement, Nafafé invites us to interrogate *why* the Vatican and the Crown were undermined and to confront the uncomfortable evidence that this movement was buried, silenced, and almost completely erased in the name of European economic gain. While the radical abolition Mendonça and the Black confraternities sought did not materialize, Chapter 6 begs the question: who was responsible for ensuring that outcome?

Throughout this book, Nafafé's most striking and important challenges to the established narratives of transatlantic slavery are twofold. Firstly, he ruptures the historical timeline, the trajectory, and indeed the metanarrative of abolitionism. Nafafé rejects the notion that global emancipation was conceived of by eighteenth-century White Europeans as a movement that required their organized collaboration and questions the sustained focus on African involvement in the quest for freedom as sporadic, spontaneous, and highly individualized. He highlights how studies on marronage and other forms of 'resistance' amongst enslaved persons have crystallized this notion of fractured emancipatory efforts. Even works by the leading Black abolitionist figures Olaudah Equiano and Ottobah Cugoano have been interpreted as limited in scope and impact over the late eighteenth and early nineteenth centuries. Instead, Nafafé shifts the entire timeline back to the seventeenth century and reveals how abolitionism was conceived of both as a collaborative Atlantic effort between Indigenous Americans, New Christians, and Africans and their descendants *in spite of* White Europeans, and as the quest for *universal* liberty i.e. for all subject groups whose lives under European colonial rule encompassed a range of unfreedoms. The denial of religious and cultural freedom connected with the deprivation of African freedom and came to form an intrinsic component in Mendonça's philosophy of abolitionism. Thus, this book offers a deeply important redress to our understanding of the origins of abolitionism.

Secondly, Nafafé takes a strong stance against the established historiography of the early transatlantic slave trade. Through a meticulous reconstruction of the political tensions between local West Central African rulers and the Portuguese colonizing presence in the sixteenth and seventeenth centuries, Nafafé refutes the general interpretation that Europeans simply entered into, and expanded upon, an existing, well-established trade in enslaved peoples. Although the book is in danger of applying this revision to wider West Africa at certain junctures, Nafafé does pose a convincing argument for the West Central African case. He amply demonstrates how the Portuguese in Angola navigated the complex political situation to increase economic gains by leveraging the *kabakula*, a Mbundu tributary agreement developed over centuries, and reformulating it as a legally binding contractual taxation between vassal rulers and the Portuguese Crown. The now lusofonized *baculamento* became a tax that was paid not in currency or commodities, but in enslaved people — one hundred per vassal ruler per year. As slaves were not readily available through a robust market trade, Nafafé examines in minute detail how the Portuguese resorted to war, pillage, and violence to collect this tax. Therefore, he posits the *baculamento* as the mechanism to *establish* a commercially viable trade in enslaved people that necessitated violent methods of capture to maintain a supply and threatened serious consequences for non-payment. Europeans, not Africans, Nafafé emphasizes, developed the transatlantic slave trade from West Central Africa from its earliest days.

The importance of this book cannot be overstated. I believe Nafafé throws down the gauntlet, demanding that scholars reckon with the depths of European coercion and destruction in West Central Africa, a region that supplied almost half of all enslaved peoples to the Americas, and the lengths colonial powers were willing to go to obscure early organized resistance to this. Challenging decades of scholarship to revise the entire history of abolitionism and rethink the 'collaboration' of African rulers in the slave trade, Nafafé offers here a magnificent, truly decolonized Atlantic history that forces a timely re-evaluation of longstanding scholarly interpretations.

doi:10.1353/port.00049

WILFRED G. BURCHETT, *The Captains' Coup: From Dictatorship to Democracy in Portugal (1974–1976)*, ed. by Daniela Melo and Timothy Walker, afterword by Tariq Ali (Verso, 2025). 352 pages. HB and ebook.

Reviewed by JOÃO SARMENTO (University of Minho)

In 1975, Seara Nova published a book in Portuguese in its series *Coleção de leste a oeste*, based on a manuscript by the Australian journalist Wilfred Burchett (1911–1983), with the title *Portugal: depois da Revolução dos Capitães*. Luiz Sttau Monteiro had translated the original English manuscript into Portuguese, and the publication (317 pages) had a significant circulation of 20,200 copies. The book was considered the fortnightly bestseller of the *Expresso* newspaper on 2 August 1975. A year later, Burchett published a much smaller book, also with Seara Nova, translated by Ana Clara Soares, covering the events leading up to the coup of November 1975 and its aftermath. The new title was *Portugal antes e depois do 25 de Abril* (61 pages), and had a circulation of 5,200 copies. Seara Nova had already published, in Portuguese, Burchett's *Vietnam: segunda resistência* (1966, trans. by Rogério Fernandes), *Bombas sobre Hanói* (1967, trans. by Maria Helena da Costa Dias), *Novamente a Coreia?* (1969, trans. by Nuno Brederode Santos) and lastly *A segunda Guerra da Indochina* (1971, trans. by Augusto Abelaira). In Portuguese literary circles, and despite censorship, Burchett's books were well-known, as was Seara Nova, a prominent publisher. Between 1968 and 1978, it published around 200 books of a political nature.

In preparing this review, I found three copies of the original 1975 book at the library of the University of Minho, Portugal. The copy I borrowed had a stamp dated 25 July 1975, and was originally from a Braga primary school library. After fifty years, many of the pages were still uncut. After a quick search, I concluded that the book is still widely available in many public libraries throughout the country. Furthermore, the book was also cited by several academics following its publication (Medeiros Ferreira and Irene Pimentel, just to name two). An interesting fact is that the 1975 book was immediately translated into Spanish (in Mexico), Italian, Norwegian, and later into Japanese, but not into English. Of Burchett's books, these two remained the only ones from this author not published in English. In an Anglophone-centred academic world, it is not uncommon for books not published in English to pass unnoticed, even by academics who specialize in the same subjects as those books.

Wilfred Burchett visited Portugal for the first time in 1974. He was already 62 years of age and had an extraordinary journalistic track record around the world. Early in his career, in 1945, he was the first correspondent in Hiroshima, and his report 'Atomic Plague' led to his journalist credentials being withdrawn by the US authorities. He later reported on the trials in Hungary, on the Korean and Vietnam wars, and on Cambodia under the Pol Pot regime. In his own words, he spent most of his career covering 'anti-fascist wars, independence struggles and national liberation in Asia' (Melo, 2025, n.pag.). He is certainly a controversial figure in Australian history, and his legacy as a foreign correspondent and alleged traitor has been fiercely debated by journalists, politicians, the Australian government, and academics.[4]

Burchett was in Paris on 25 April 1974. In the early morning hours of that same day, the Carnation Revolution, which overthrew Portuguese fascism (1926–74) by an internal revolt, itself precipitated by a set of costly colonial wars in Africa and a deteriorating economic situation at home, was set in motion. Like many other journalists, correspondents, photographers and politicians,

---

[4] Jamie Miller, 'The Forgotten History War: Wilfred Burchett, Australia and the Cold War in the Asia Pacific', *Asia-Pacific Journal*, 6.9 (2008), e20.

Burchett took the first possible flight out of Paris to Lisbon. Coincidentally, his flight landed on 28 April, just a couple of hours after the arrival of the political exiles Mário Soares, Ramos da Costa and Tito de Morais at Lisbon's Santa Apolónia train station. Two days later, Burchett described the arrival of Álvaro Cunhal, the Portuguese Communist Party secretary general. Burchett made several further visits to Portugal during the following months, and spent quite some time interviewing members of the military, such as activists of the Armed Forces Movement, as well as people in charge of cooperatives, fishermen and farmers, among others, mostly in Lisbon, but also in various regions of mainland Portugal. He followed demonstrations and strike actions, looked at resolutions and policies, always with an eye to the larger international scene. The materials he collected were the basis for this book, which traces the captains' actions and the social, economic and cultural panorama of the country in turbulent times.

The book here under review is an edited version of Burchett's two original manuscripts, published by Verso, in 2025, with the title *The Captains' Coup: From Dictatorship to Democracy in Portugal (1974–1976)*. The editors — Daniela Melo and Timothy Walker — went on a long quest to discover if the original manuscripts still existed, and if so, to locate them. Eventually, they found the typescripts in the Papers of Wilfred Burchett in the archives of the National Library of Australia in Canberra. The period covering the various visits to Portugal consists of five boxes with approximately 1000 pages of notes, interview transcripts, dispatches and article drafts.

The book opens with a preface by Timothy Walker and an introduction by Daniela Melo. Both provide excellent context for Burchett's original words. The chapters from the 1975 and 1976 books are followed by a text by Tariq Ali, which was originally published in 1978. The book is divided into twenty chapters. The first nine chapters go over the background of the coup, the military action, the empire, and the political and economic situation of the country. The second part, from Chapters 10 to 17, reviews and returns to the economy, politics and society. Throughout the book, Burchett makes extensive use of the many and rich interviews he conducted with key people, such as Otelo Saraiva de Carvalho, Vasco Gonçalves, Melo Antunes, Álvaro Cunhal, Canais Rocha, Carlos Carvalhas, among others. Chapters 10 and 11 provide a crude and poignant analysis of the Portuguese economy, namely the functioning of economic monopolies (significantly the 'big four' companies or groups — CUF, Champalimaud, Espírito Santo Group and Banco Português do Atlântico), and the way backwardness made the country so attractive to multinationals and foreign companies such as Timex, Grundig, Applied Magnetics. In the chapter 'Decolonisation', Burchett provides a rich account of the negotiation process that led to the Alvor Agreement in 1975. At this stage, it is possible to appreciate Burchett's experience as he refers to other decolonization negotiations he covered (Vietnamese with the French and the Americans, in 1954 and 1973, respectively).

As a geographer, I find Chapters 12 and 13 on Alentejo and Trás-os-Montes, respectively, fascinating. Burchett compares Alentejo to Hungary and Trás-os-Montes to Bulgaria (suggestively, his wife, whom he travelled with, was a Bulgarian journalist and artist). As Melo argues, 'Burchett was not a scholar, but, rather, an extremely well-informed observer, with a knack for finding angles that mattered to his readers' (2025, n.pag.). Still, almost disguised as an anthropologist, Burchett reports vividly on his engagements with ordinary people, using informants and translators, and at times supporting his arguments with tables and statistics. In Chapter 14, he continues his dialogues with workers in Trás-os-Montes, where he spent ten days. Revealing his enthusiasm for the captains who led the coup, he discusses farming, forestry, the enclosure of the commons, the agro-industry, and most importantly, working conditions and people's perspectives of the country's political changes. In Chapter 15, he vividly builds the story around a conversation with fishermen in Peniche and returns to Alentejo, describing scenes of striking poverty, as well as the fights for rights and salary. Through an informant, Burchett discusses the beginning of the Land Reform, absentee landlords, and the actions of the secret police (PIDE) before 1974.

In the third part, the last three chapters refer to the 1976 book: 'Turning the Wheel Back'; 'Balance Sheet'; and 'The Future'. It provides a precise account of the episodes that led to the defeat of the revolutionary wing by social democracy in November 1975. This loss was confirmed by the elections that followed. Burchett traces the emergence of a narrative of opposing 'democracy' to 'communist dictatorship' aiming at eroding and diverting the revolutionary process, the actions of the 'Group of Nine' which aimed at a gradual and peaceful transition to a socialist society, the sixth government, the Revolutionary Council, Melo Antunes and Otelo de Carvalho divergences, and of various individual protagonists. While not himself in Portugal during the *verão quente* [hot summer] of 1975, Burchett covers, with a sense of disillusionment, the story of how, by November 1975, the revolution was over.

The publishing of the original work of Burchett is very timely, as 2025 marks the fiftieth anniversary of the April revolution. Enabling Burchett's appealing and fascinating account of the struggles and social mobilization in the streets, factories and farms in Portugal in 1974 and 1975 to reach a wider audience is an extremely valuable academic endeavour. The original 1975 and 1976 books did not include photographs. Yet *The Captains' Coup: From Dictatorship to Democracy in Portugal (1974–1976)* contains a few excellent photographs by well-known Portuguese photographers such as Alfredo Cunha and Eduardo Gageiro. Fascinatingly, during 2025 (May to August), there was a photo exhibition in Almada, by the Lisnave shipyards that Burchett talks about, showing 200 photographs by thirty foreign photographers (Alain Mingam, Augusta Conchiglia, Henri Bureau, Jean-Claude Francolon and Sebastião Salgado, to name just a few) who, like Burchett, rushed to Portugal to cover the

25 April coup. They portrayed the events in Lisbon, and in other parts of the country, just like the Australian journalist, and some even travelled to Africa, where decolonization was making its way. I felt Burchett could have written captions for most photographs, or more to the point, just quoted from this book.

doi:10.1353/port.00050

Abstracts

Translating India: Latin Accounts of Vasco da Gama's Encounter with the Zamorin

SHRUTI RAJGOPAL

ABSTRACT. Vasco da Gama's successful expedition to India in 1497–98 offered valuable information, which began to be included in various travel narratives. Descriptions in the European vernacular languages circulated widely, but how was this information relayed in Latin? European Humanists, through their knowledge of Latin, revived classical stylistic features as part of their texts, which offered a neoclassical garb to various topics, regions and cultures. My article examines how India looks in this garb through Latin translations of Gama's voyage to the Malabar region in 1498. For this, I have examined Latin works by Jeronimo Ososrio (1571), Giovanni Pietro Maffei (1588), Thomas Faria (1622) and Andreas Baianus (1625).
KEYWORDS. Portuguese voyages, humanism, Neo-Latin, Vasco da Gama, Zamorin.

RESUMO. A expedição bem-sucedida de Vasco da Gama à Índia, em 1497–98, trouxe informações valiosas, que começaram a ser incluídas em diversas narrativas de viagem. As descrições em línguas vernáculas europeias circularam amplamente, mas como é que estas informações foram transmitidas em latim? Os humanistas europeios, através do seu conhecimento do latim, resgataram características estilísticas clássicas nos seus textos, o que ofereceu uma roupagem neoclássica a diversos tópicos, regiões e culturas. O meu artigo examina a forma como a Índia se apresenta sob esta roupagem através de traduções latinas da viagem de Vasco da Gama à região do Malabar em 1498. Para isso, examinei obras latinas de Jeronimo Osorio (1571), Giovanni Pietro Maffei (1588), Thomas Faria (1622) e Andreas Baianus (1625).
PALAVRAS-CHAVE. Viagens portuguesas, humanismo, neolatim, Vasco da Gama, Zamorin.

War and the Walls Within: An Analysis of *A General Theory of Oblivion* by José Eduardo Agualusa

ALEXANDRA LOURENÇO DIAS

ABSTRACT. This article examines how José Eduardo Agualusa's *A General Theory of Oblivion* (2012) redefines the war genre within Angolan literature by turning from collective struggle to an intimate portrait of isolation and memory. Centring on Ludovica Fernandes Mano — a Portuguese expatriate who walls herself into her apartment for nearly three decades — the novel critiques colonial violence, the aftermath of independence, and the internalization

Portuguese Studies vol. 41 no. 2 (2025), doi:10.1353/port.00051, 341–48
© Modern Humanities Research Association 2025

of trauma. Through a digital-semiotic approach combining lexicometric tools such as InfraNodus and Sketch Engine with literary theory (Genette's paratexts, Bakhtin's chronotope, and Ricoeur's memory studies), the article traces recurrent thematic clusters and examines how memory, forgetting and isolation articulate Angola's transition from colonial rule to civil war. This interdisciplinary reading shows how Agualusa complicates conventional war narratives by foregrounding psychological scars over battlefield heroics, personal oblivion over national myth, and fragmented perception over linear history, offering a more nuanced understanding of Angolan identity and the legacies of conflict.

KEYWORDS. Postcolonialism, Lusophone African literature, Angolan fiction, memory, war narratives.

RESUMO. Este artigo analisa de que modo *Teoria Geral do Esquecimento* (2012), de José Eduardo Agualusa, reconfigura o romance de guerra no contexto da literatura angolana, ao deslocar o foco da luta coletiva para um retrato íntimo de isolamento e memória. Centrada em Ludovica Fernandes Mano — uma portuguesa expatriada que se barrica no seu apartamento durante quase três décadas — a narrativa constitui uma crítica à violência colonial, às consequências da independência e à interiorização do trauma. Através de uma abordagem digital-semiótica que combina ferramentas lexicométricas como o InfraNodus e o Sketch Engine com teorias literárias (o paratexto de Genette, o cronotopo de Bakhtin e os estudos da memória de Ricoeur), este artigo identifica recorrências temáticas e examina de que forma memória, esquecimento e isolamento articulam a transição de Angola do regime colonial para a guerra civil. Esta leitura interdisciplinar demonstra como Agualusa subverte as narrativas convencionais da guerra ao privilegiar as cicatrizes psicológicas em detrimento da heroicidade bélica, o esquecimento pessoal sobre o mito nacional e a perceção fragmentada sobre a linearidade histórica — oferecendo uma compreensão mais subtil e complexa da identidade angolana e dos legados do conflito.

PALAVRAS-CHAVE. Pós-colonialismo, literatura Africana lusófona, ficção angolana, memória, narrativas de guerra.

Representations of Austerity Urbanism in Contemporary Portuguese Film: The Case of *São Jorge*

MARIA INÊS CASTRO E SILVA

ABSTRACT. Precarity has emerged as a key conceptual shift in discussions surrounding social exclusion, particularly in contexts marked by economic crisis. In this sense, it serves as a timely and pertinent concept for understanding the lived conditions produced by neoliberal restructuring. In Portugal, the financial crisis of 2008–14 significantly reshaped the urban landscape, giving rise to what may be described as Portuguese geographies of precarity. This article examines precarity as a socio-political consequence of the austerity measures implemented during the Portuguese financial crisis, through an analysis of the film *São Jorge* [*Saint George*] (2016), directed by Marco Martins. The study explores how austerity policies are represented and made tangible through cinematic space, highlighting how austerity urbanism structures the spatialization of precarious lives. The analysis offers a critical lens into the proliferation of precarious urban spaces, where marginalized communities are disproportionately affected by intersecting forms of exclusion, including racism and sexism. Furthermore, the analysis considers the impact of the crisis on both the workplace and the domestic sphere, revealing the multifaceted nature of precarity as it unfolds across everyday urban life.

KEYWORDS. Austerity, precarity, Portuguese film, urban space.

RESUMO. A precariedade tem emergido como uma mudança conceptual significativa nas discussões em torno da exclusão social, sobretudo em contextos marcados por crises económicas. Neste sentido, constitui um conceito oportuno e pertinente para compreender as condições de vida geradas pela reestruturação neoliberal. Em Portugal, a crise financeira de 2008–14 transformou de forma significativa a paisagem urbana, dando origem ao que se pode designar geografias portuguesas da precariedade.

Este artigo examina a precariedade como uma consequência sociopolítica das medidas de austeridade implementadas durante a crise financeira portuguesa, através da análise do filme *São Jorge* (2016), realizado por Marco Martins. O estudo explora como as políticas de austeridade são representadas no espaço cinematográfico, mostrando como o *urbanismo da austeridade* estrutura a espacialização das vidas precárias. A análise oferece uma leitura crítica da proliferação de espaços urbanos precários, onde comunidades marginalizadas são desproporcionalmente afetadas por formas interseccionais de exclusão, incluindo o racismo e o sexismo. Considera-se ainda o impacto da crise tanto no espaço laboral como na esfera doméstica, revelando a natureza multifacetada da precariedade tal como se manifesta no quotidiano urbano.

PALAVRAS-CHAVE. Austeridade, precariedade, cinema português, espaço urbano.

Geospatial Analysis of *O Quinze* by Rachel de Queiroz: Mapping Literary Spaces with ArcGIS Pro
MARIA VITÓRIA DE REZENDE GRISI

ABSTRACT. This article examines how digital mapping can function as a form of literary analysis, moving beyond illustration to serve as a critical reading exercise. Although a central challenge of literary maps is that fictional spaces are by definition different from the real world — requiring a negotiation between representation and reality — this study demonstrates how such negotiation can itself produce valuable insights. To illustrate this, the study analyses the Brazilian novel *O Quinze* (1930) by Rachel de Queiroz, set during the 1915 drought in Ceará. Using ArcGIS Pro to georeference locations of the narrative and map the journeys of the characters, the study highlights the pattern of those displaced by the drought: the wealthy escaped by train with ease, while poor migrants walked nearly the same distance on foot, facing hunger and death. The final maps exposed the unbalanced parallel of social inequality and demonstrated how GIS tools can contribute to literary analysis. KEYWORDS. GIS, literary geography, *retirantes*, drought narratives, digital humanities.

RESUMO. Este artigo examina como o mapeamento digital pode funcionar como forma de análise literária, indo além da ilustração para servir como exercício crítico de leitura. Embora um desafio central dos mapas literários seja o fato de que os espaços ficcionais são, por definição, diferentes do mundo real — exigindo uma negociação entre representação e realidade — este estudo demonstra como essa negociação pode gerar leituras valiosas. Para ilustrá-la, o estudo analisa o romance *O Quinze* (1930), de Rachel de Queiroz, que se passa durante a seca de 1915, no Ceará. Utilizando ArcGIS Pro para georreferenciar os locais citados na narrativa e mapear as jornadas dos personagens, o estudo evidencia o padrão daqueles deslocados pela seca: os mais ricos escaparam facilmente de trem, enquanto os *retirantes* percorreram quase a mesma distância a pé, enfrentando a fome e a morte. Os mapas finais expuseram o paralelo desigual da injustiça social e mostraram como ferramentas de GIS podem contribuir para a análise literária.
PALAVRAS-CHAVE. GIS, geografia literária, retirantes, narrativas da seca, humanidades digitais.

'Orphans of water. Orphans of land': Capitalism's Life of Violence in *Maria Altamira* and *The Need for Roots*
PEDRO DAHER

ABSTRACT. Maria José Silveira's *Maria Altamira* (2020), a novel which centralizes the multiple instantiations of violence caused by the Belo Monte hydropower dam in Pará, Brazil, brings to the reader the utmost representation of Simone Weil's description, in *The Need for Roots* (1987), of capitalism's intrinsic, all-encompassing structure: uprootedness. By spotlighting Belo Monte, one of the world's largest hydroelectric plants, Silveira's writing allows for a reading of capital, colonial, and racial violence as the manifestations of a life-system structured around uprootedness as its only possible horizon of being. Separated by time and continents, Simone Weil and Maria José Silveira might seem disparate thinkers. However, because the former attempts to locate the non-material articulations of modern capitalist violence in order to understand its manifestations while the latter provides a material historical account of the deployment of said articulations, taken together they elucidate the simultaneous violences of capitalism — its cosmo-philosophical underlying order and its never-ending assaults on humans, nonhumans, and nature — thus creating a more comprehensive framework to critique the capitalist mode of devastation.

KEYWORDS. Belo Monte, uprootedness, capitalism, violence, colonial.

RESUMO. O romance *Maria Altamira* (2020), de Maria José Silveira, centraliza as múltiplas violências causadas pela usina hidrelétrica de Belo Monte, no Pará, Brasil, e assim traz ao leitor a representação máxima da descrição de *O Enraizamento* (1987), de Simone Weil, sobre a estrutura intrínseca e abrangente do capitalismo: o desenraizamento. Ao destacar Belo Monte, uma das maiores hidrelétricas do mundo, a escrita de Silveira permite uma leitura da violência capital, colonial e racial como manifestações de um sistema de vida estruturado em torno do desenraizamento como seu único horizonte possível de existência. Separadas pelo tempo e por continentes, Simone Weil e Maria José Silveira podem parecer pensadoras díspares. No entanto, porque a primeira busca localizar as articulações não materiais da violência do capitalismo moderno para compreender suas manifestações, enquanto a última fornece um relato histórico material da implantação dessas articulações, quando tomadas em conjunto, elas elucidam as violências simultâneas do capitalismo — sua ordem subjacente cosmo-filosófica e seus assaltos intermináveis a seres humanos, não humanos e à natureza — criando, assim, uma estrutura mais abrangente para criticar o modo capitalista de devastação.

PALAVRAS-CHAVE. Belo Monte, desenraizamento, capitalismo, violência, colonial.

The 1890 British Ultimatum in the International Satirical Press
MÁRIO SEQUEIRA

ABSTRACT. In recent decades, the satirical press has received increasing interest as a valuable source for the analysis of different noteworthy events, contributing to our understanding of how the press and public opinion perceived certain issues or entities. This article investigates the 1890 British Ultimatum through that non-traditional lens: we analyse cartoons from the satirical press of different European countries, in search of a new or renewed interpretation of an event that generated significant turmoil in Portugal and for the Portuguese Monarchy. Using cartoons from Austria, France, Germany, Great Britain, Spain, and Switzerland, we aim to establish comparisons and illustrate how cartoonists from these countries represented not only the Ultimatum, but also Anglo-Portuguese relations and Portugal itself.

KEYWORDS. Anglo-Portuguese relations, cartoons, colonialism, imperialism, satirical press.

RESUMO. Nas últimas décadas, a imprensa satírica tem suscitado um crescente interesse como uma fonte relevante para a análise de diferentes acontecimentos

relevantes, contribuindo para a nossa compreensão de como a imprensa e a opinião pública percecionavam determinados temas ou entidades. Este artigo investiga o Ultimato Britânico de 1890 a partir dessa perspetiva menos tradicional: vamos explorar caricaturas da imprensa satírica de vários países europeus, procurando uma interpretação nova ou renovada de um episódio que originou imensa instabilidade em Portugal e na Monarquia portuguesa. Utilizando caricaturas da Áustria, Alemanha, Espanha, França, Grã-Bretanha, e Suíça, temos o objetivo de estabelecer comparações e ilustrar como os caricaturistas destes países representaram não apenas o Ultimato, mas também as relações luso-britânicas e Portugal em si.
PALAVRAS-CHAVE. Caricaturas, colonialismo, imperialismo, imprensa satírica, relações luso-britânicas.

Integrating Brazilian Literature and Plurilingualism to Decolonize Latin American Studies Curricula
ANA CLÁUDIA SURIANI DA SILVA

ABSTRACT. This article details a UCL research-led teaching initiative for first-year undergraduate students, designed to decolonize the Latin American Studies curriculum. Moving beyond a Hispanic focus, the module integrates Brazilian literature to stimulate interest in the Portuguese language and, crucially, to illuminate the profound linguistic diversity of the region. It explores historical and contemporary multilingualism, examining not only dominant languages but also hybrid forms like *Portunhol Selvagem*, immigrant languages such as Talian and Pomeranian, and the significant presence of sign languages in Brazil. Using Deleuze and Guattari's concept of 'minor literature' (1975) as a methodology, the study analyses how diverse literary expressions subvert dominant tongues. This approach demonstrates how writers deterritorialize Portuguese and Spanish to articulate unique political and cultural experiences, providing students with a critical framework to understand language as a site of decolonial struggle and creative resistance.
KEYWORDS. Decolonization, Latin America, linguistic diversity, multilingualism, minor literature, deterritorialization.

RESUMO. Este artigo relata uma prática docente embasada em pesquisa desenvolvida na UCL para alunos do primeiro ano de graduação, com o objetivo de descolonizar o currículo de Estudos Latino-Americanos. A proposta pedagógica integra a literatura brasileira não apenas para despertar o interesse pela língua portuguesa, mas sobretudo para evidenciar a notável diversidade linguística da região. O percurso analisa o multilinguismo histórico e contemporâneo, considerando desde línguas hegemônicas até variedades híbridas como o *portunhol selvagem*, idiomas de imigração — como o talian e o pomerano — e as línguas de sinais no Brasil. Apoiando-se no conceito de 'literatura menor' de Deleuze e Guattari (1975), a abordagem demonstra como expressões literárias diversas subvertem línguas majoritárias. Através da desterritorialização do português e do espanhol, tais narrativas articulam experiências culturais e políticas singulares, oferecendo aos estudantes um quadro teórico crítico para compreender a língua como espaço de embates descolonizadores e de resistência criativa.

PALAVRAS-CHAVE. Descolonização, América Latina, diversidade linguística, multilinguismo, literatura menor, desterritorialização.